OUTLAW CHICS

PART·THREE

ISBN: 9781735086637

Thank yous go out to all who ever supported a Clever Black Novel. Each and every time I write one of those, I can't help but to feel as if someone's being left out. Those who rock me strong know who they are, and I know who you are you as well. With that said, if you've ever rocked with me, from the bottom of my heart I thank you. This has become a story all unto itself; one I never envisioned grasping so many people's attention. I'm humbled by the process of it all and it's readers like yourselves that motivate me to write the very best story I can each time out and keep it in accordance with what has already been written. If anyone is offended by the content within this story, I apologize as I'm not out to offend, but to entertain. It is my intent that you all take something away from this story. Your belief is your own, however, as well as your viewpoint and I take no offense, but only give respect. Again, thank you all for supporting what I do, and may you enjoy my latest work.

Sincerely,

Clever Black

CHAPTER ONE

THE CONFESSION

June 1, 1976

Fifty-six year-old Mabel Sougherbraun-Mobley was over to her one hundred acre ranch moving about inside the spacious kitchen of her luxurious one story ranch house. The ambitious congresswoman was ever proud of her sixteen year-old daughter on this windy, sunny late spring day. Mary Beth would be moving ahead to the eleventh grade after the summer. The scholarly teenager had straight A's on her report card and the highest G.P.A. in the entire school. She had been President of her sophomore class and she was already in the process of running for junior class President this last day of school.

Mabel was planning on taking her daughter on her first trip to Washington D.C. over the summer. Her second election for congresswoman for her Iowa district was to occur in November, which was only five months away. Mabel's district was highly conservative. She was in a close race to keep her seat, but she believed she would be reelected based on the promise she'd kept to her constituents throughout her first term.

The freshman congresswoman had run on providing government subsidies for farmers in her district who qualified for the government grants. A year earlier, Mabel had brought half of a billion dollars home to her district and had quickly set up a co-op in her hometown of Patterson to allow farmers to apply for subsidies. The money was still being disbursed, but Mabel had stacks and stacks of letters from people all across the district thanking her for bringing aide as the nation slipped into an energy and economic crisis.

Mabel was running her second campaign on the promise of improving the waterworks system in the rural areas to allow for better crop irrigation. She'd released a commercial on Sunday's Meet the Press revealing her campaign slogan, *Making Government Work for Us*. She recalled the day she first used the phrase, which wasn't prepared and had actually come from the heart, and decided to make it her campaign slogan. Raising taxes during an economic downturn was a risky move, a possible career ender for a conservative such as Mabel. Her republican colleagues watched bedazzled as she took her message back to her constituents. Her brown eyes were in a dreamlike state and she had a proud smile on her face over her first big political accomplishment and the way her second campaign was unfolding.

Mabel's republican opponent had accused her of buying votes in her first term during a debate the previous week. She'd countered with the fact that she couldn't possibly be buying votes if she was proposing a tax increase. She then went further, citing the fact that the people in southern Iowa needed the money she'd given them to stimulate the local economy, in which she did based on government data. Now that the counties she represented had been restored financially, Mabel reasoned that the monies raised through a local tax increase could pay for new roads. She then went on and told her challenger that she'd loss many republican allies over getting the subsidy bill passed and for her it wasn't about politics, it was about helping the people in southern Iowa reestablish their family-run businesses and improve upon their living conditions.

"I'm not giving handouts to anybody, sir," Mabel defended inside a crowded hall meeting in downtown Patterson just the week before. "I'm improving the quality of people's lives here in southern Iowa. If you can't see that the people agree with me to the proposal to raise taxes to pay for new roads, something they've ask me to help them do, then you shouldn't be running for congress. We're using the government correctly," she said sternly while eyeing her opponent. "We're making it work for us. And for us, the show must go on. We're changing our lives for the better and we're doing it in a short period of time through good government."

Mabel's retort to her opponent's allegation sent the crowd into a thunderous uproar of approval. Mabel had the people's backing through action. She was a politically tough woman that understood how D.C. operated.

On top of that, Mabel had good business sense. She was not only promising to upgrade her district's infrastructure, she'd made a deal with several manufacturers to use the improved roads to open up the transport of corn and dairy products. The new equipment and improved county roads would allow farmers in the most rural parts of the state to reach the main highways quicker and increase their shipment of goods further north, and south into the states of Missouri and Kansas. The increased revenue would expand paychecks, bringing more money into the local economy, which would help offset the proposed tax increase.

Mabel had a lot riding on the next five months, and her image was now everything, as it was the only thing her opponent had left to attack her on; if she won, she would have four more years to do good by the people, and to also be able to steer Mary Beth into a political career.

Mary Beth used to query Mabel for hours on in whenever she was home during congressional recesses. The two would often go out and meet with the people, something outgoing teen-aged Mary Beth had enjoyed in the beginning. She would talk about political issues right alongside her mother and had often made suggestions. In Mabel's eyes, she and Mary Beth were not only mother and daughter, they were best friends in life.

Mabel had noticed about a month earlier, however, that Mary Beth had become less talkative and seemed frustrated most days. When she'd asked her daughter what was troubling her, Mary Beth told her that she was stressed over exams and having to write a speech that she was going to give on the last day of school to announce her campaign to run for Junior Class President.

To cheer Mary Beth up, Mabel had decided to take her on a trip to D.C. and show her around after she'd help her write her speech. She was going to have her staff set up a special luncheon with a couple of Supreme Court judges inside the congressional chambers for Mary Beth, being she knew her daughter had a keen interest in the judicial branch of the government.

The proud mother actually saw her daughter becoming a U.S. Attorney someday. Thoughts of Mary Beth attending Georgetown University right there in D.C. and the two of them being able to still spend time together filled her mind as she went into the refrigerator and pulled out a silver tray of sliced deli sandwiches and set it on the counter. She was thinking of giving Mary Beth her first internship over the summer by working within her campaign.

Mabel had also ordered a special ring for Mary Beth. She'd been repeatedly calling Sophia, the town jeweler, but was getting no reply over the phone. She had in mind for her and Mary

Beth to ride into town in order to check on Sophia and see if the ring she'd ordered had been delivered. She went about setting up lunch with that thought in mind as an engine's hum caught her ear.

With a smile on her face, Mabel walked over to the vista window inside her spacious kitchen and pierced out of the silk curtains, believing that it was Mary Beth's school bus riding across the land. Her entire demeanor changed, however, when she saw her oldest son's black Dodge Charger speeding up the dirt road and leaving a trail of dust in its wake.

The two-door, sleek black hot rod with chrome wheels skidded to a halt and Mabel watched through worried eyes as Jeremy Mobley, her eighteen year-old stringy-haired, slender son, and the oldest of her three, stepped out of his muscle car and stood amongst the blowing dust kicked up from his car. He turned around and looked over the hood of his ride in a suspicious manner, seemingly expecting to be trailed by someone, although no one was in sight.

Mabel had a sickening feeling land in the pit of her stomach as she eyed the black steel revolver poking out from the back waistband of Jeremy's jeans. Sophia hadn't answered her phone nor returned her call, and Jeremy was acting mighty suspicious. She stood in place while peeking out the curtains, witnessing Jeremy pulling the black t-shirt he was wearing down over his back as he leaned down into the car. Several seconds later, he emerged with a white pillowcase in his hand and slammed the car's door shut.

The pillowcase Jeremy toted was a bad omen for Mabel. It gave her a premonition, one that she hoped wasn't true. She wanted to believe, deep down inside, that her son wasn't the reason as to why Sophia wasn't answering her phone so late in the day, but her mind's eye would not allow that thought to take hold.

Reason being was because Jeremy had left earlier in the day and had returned home speeding onto the property. He looked as guilty as the day is long to Mabel as he walked with the lumpy pillowcase draped over his shoulder, his dark, sullen eyes constantly scanning the entrance to the property.

Mabel eased the door open and eyed her son. "Where were you, Jeremy? What did you do now?" she asked in an exasperated manner.

Jeremy brushed his mother aside as he cavalierly walked into the house. "It's none of your business where I was and what I did," he said nonchalantly with his back turned.

"Did you go into town? Did you see Sophia?" Mabel questioned as the screen door slammed shut.

"I not only saw Sophia," Jeremy said in a casual tone of voice as he turned and faced Mabel with a condescending look displayed upon his face. "I took everything she had that was of value inside that jewelry store," he stated matter-of-factly as a slick smile appeared. "I got you something," he then enthusiastically added as he opened the pillowcase. "These fancy-looking watches called Rolex. It's got diamonds in it around the edges."

"You'll have the police all over this place, Jeremy! I'm in the middle of a campaign!" Mabel scoffed under her breath.

"What are the police gonna do?" Jeremy asked while staring his mother down. "My father is sheriff of this town, and he runs the investigations here. I can do whatever the hell I want and I'll get away with it every time."

Mabel had no reply as she stared at her son in frustration for the simple fact that she knew he was right. She would shamelessly uphold him if only to protect her image and political career. The budding criminal was a disappointment for Mabel. She once had plans on seeing her oldest son attend the University of Iowa, which was her Alma Mata, and join her in her political endeavors upon graduation. She envisioned Jeremy running for mayor of Patterson by his mid-twenties or so after coming up under her guidance. It didn't take Jeremy reaching high school, however, before Mabel realized her oldest son had not the moral compass, nor the ambition it took to enter into the realm of politics as he was a rebellious, callous child with no dreams or goals set for the future except to chase women, get drunk and break the law. Most likely, he would end up becoming a Deputy alongside her Sheriff husband, something she wasn't in agreement with given her son's reckless behavior.

Amid the tense silence, Mabel watched as Jeremy proudly rummaged through his stolen merchandise just as another rumbling sound caught her attention. She looked over her shoulder through the tinted screen door and saw the school bus toting her daughter and youngest son cruising over the land.

"There's dad," Jeremy nonchalantly remarked as he knelt down and grabbed a couple of watches from the pillowcase. He rose to his feet and stared Mabel in the eyes. "Don't worry," he stated through a callous attempt at comfort. "I won't ruin your 'political career', since that's the only thing that matters to you anymore," he mocked, imitating quotation marks with his fingers as he pushed the screen door open and scornfully walked out of the house.

Mabel eyed the pillowcase resting on the floor beside her; she could see an entanglement of watches and gold chains protruding along with a couple of diamond rings that had rolled out onto the wooden floor. She knelt down and picked up one of the rings and eyed its precise princess cut and its gold setting. It was the very ring that she'd purchased for Mary Beth as she'd recognized the design. The jewelry store back in town hadn't had this caliber of jewelry on its shelf in quite some years. The plan to improve the economy was working. Even the thieves were benefitting from her bill; too bad one of them resided in her own home and she was not a woman willing to put up a protest concerning his actions.

While looking around, as if someone was actually watching, Mabel slid the rings back into the sack and carried it to her bedroom where she would hide the items in her safe, but not before placing the ring she'd ordered for Mary Beth inside her apron.

Meanwhile, back outside, sixteen year-old Mary Beth Mobley had just stepped off the school bus after running past her father, who was sitting in the driver's seat. Her younger brother, fourteen year-old Wendell Mobley, was attempting to follow her off the bus, but before he did, his father held him back.

"How was it?" Sheriff Corey Mobley asked through a chuckle.

"Tastes funny. Not bad but..." Wendell's voice trailed off.

"All you have to do is ask to sleep in her bed if you wanna go further, son."

"That's all I have to do?" Wendell asked in an unsure tone of voice as he pulled up on his baggy denim jeans.

"She'll know what you mean when you do. It's a way of being respectful."

"Okay, dad," Wendell smiled. "I'm gonna go ask her right now," he said as he ran his hands through his curly black hair.

Corey pulled his son back at that moment and dropped his smile. "Look now, you can't say nothing to your mother," he warned sternly while pointing to his son. "Both of you is still young and Mabel may not approve. She can't ever find out what you and Mary Beth are doing."

"Why can't momma know? I love Mary Beth." Wendell asked curiously. The fourteen year-old actually had no clue that what he was doing was a mortal sin.

"It's because of your age," Corey reasoned, downplaying the immoral act. "Trust me, it's better this way. Keeps down the confusion," he explained.

"Okay, dad," Wendell responded before running off the bus and calling aloud for Mary Beth.

Mary Beth brushed a wave of brown hair from her face against the blowing wind and kept walking at a frantic pace as her brother Wendell ran up behind her. The sixteen year-old was sick to her stomach over what had transpired on the school bus and hell bent on alerting her mother to her plight as she was going out of her mind having to deal with the madness.

"Can I sleep with you in your bed tonight, Mary Beth?" Wendell asked just as casually as he would ask his mother for a scoop of ice cream.

"No! I'm putting an end to this!" Mary Beth scoffed as she picked up the pace, eager to get before her mother.

"Come on, Mary Beth," Wendell reasoned as he ran up behind his sister and grabbed her arm. "Just one time and I want ask ever again," he pleaded.

17

Mary Beth snatched her arm away from Wendell, turned around and stomped her foot to the ground. "What dad and Jeremy are doing to me isn't right. What daddy told you to do to me on the bus was not right, Wendell!" she declared through a heartbroken whisper.

"Dad says it's okay and it's normal between a girl and a boy."

"This isn't normal behavior. There is nothing normal about what's going on between us all, Wendell, because we're related! You can't possibly be that dumb!" Mary Beth countered as she raised her hands even with her shoulders.

"But dad says it's all right," Wendell reiterated as just as Jeremy walked up on the two.

"What's going on with you two?" Jeremy asked casually while running a comb through his hair.

Wendell and Mary Beth both remained silent and looked off into space. Jeremy stopped combing his hair at that moment and smiled over to Wendell. Right away, he knew what was going down. "You can't ask like that," he stated as he wrapped an arm around his younger brother and walked off with him while whispering in his ear.

"How should I ask? Because she's mad at me, Jeremy." Mary Beth heard her brother ask while walking off. "Wendell?" she called out anxiously.

"I'm trying to learn how to be respectful, Mary Beth. If I asked wrong I'm sorry. But will you? Please?"

"You're just like them!" Mary Beth fretted as Jeremy stepped closer to her and grabbed her arm and began squeezing it. "Ouch! Jeremy, stop!" she hissed while pulling away.

"Listen to me," Jeremy stated through gritted teeth as he grabbed hold of Mary Beth a second time. The two tussled for several seconds until Jeremy caught a grip of Mary Beth's upper arm. "Listen to me, bitch!" he scowled, squeezing Mary Beth's arm so hard her bones began to ache. "Now listen to me," he gritted once Mary Beth had calmed down. "You say a word to anybody about what's going on inside that house I'll kill you. You're going to shut up, and you're going to take it because you're nothing but a nasty lesbian whore."

"I'm not a whore," Mary Beth defended lowly while wincing in pain.

"You won't deny being a lesbian, though," Jeremy chuckled as he shoved Mary Beth away.

"It's better than being what I am now—you and daddy's come dump," Mary Beth seethed.

Jeremy pulled Mary Beth back to him and went into his back waistband and placed the barrel of the gun he was toting to her stomach. "If you even think about telling what goes on here you'll regret it."

"I've already come to regret it," Mary Beth scoffed as she eyed her father, the main source of her distress, walking off the school bus. At that moment, tears flooded her eyes as the day of her father's betrayal rushed her mind.

Mary Beth was only twelve years-old when her father began molesting her. She first thought he was sincerely interested in helping her study after school while her mother was away in D.C. The subtle pats on her thighs at times was endearing in the beginning as the two sat side by side at the desk in her bedroom.

Corey soon began ending their studies with a tender kiss on the lips, however; and a month into it, the kissing was accompanied by the groping of Mary Beth's breasts and center. Corey would warn his daughter each day before Mabel was scheduled to return home to not say a word and then threaten to kill Mary Beth's mother if she ever told.

Out of fear of losing Mabel, Mary Beth remained silent and let her father do as he pleased with her body. Day after day she was violated by her father. It was when she was in her most weakened state, a year into the abuse, that her brother Jeremy entered the room. Mary Beth was prepared to tell her brother of her sexual abuse, but to her horror, Jeremy began repeating the very same acts that his father was engaging in.

With memories of how her life had spun out of control, Mary Beth backed away from Jeremy. "You would really kill me!" she realized in frightened disbelief as she turned and ran towards the house where she climbed the stairs with wet eyes and was met by her mother, who'd just returned to the porch after hiding Jeremy's stolen jewelry.

"Welcome home, Mary Beth!" Mabel spoke softly as she hugged her daughter briefly. "How was your last day of school?"

"Momma," Mary Beth stammered in a desperate manner while clutching her mother's arms, "daddy's been forcing me to have—"

"How'd the speech that you and I wrote pertaining to you running for Junior Class President go?" Mabel interjected as she turned and walked into the living room. "Did you give it in the garden like I suggested?" her voice rang out as she grabbed her car keys off an end table. "I have sandwiches made and wonderful news to share with you about the things I have planned for you and I over the summer months, but we're going to go and check on Sophia back in town first. I've been calling her all morning and she hasn't picked up."

"How can you not know what's been going in this house? In this town?" Mary vehemently screamed as she took off running through the living room towards her bedroom where she slammed the door so hard it vibrated the wooden floors.

Mabel's jaw had dropped as she watched her daughter run through the living room with her hands over her face crying a fit of tears. "I take it the speech didn't go well!" she sighed loudly as she threw her hands up and looked out the screen door where she saw her husband and two sons walking back towards the house.

Corey, Jeremy and Wendell traveled over to the side of the home and stood just out in front of the kitchen door. The three looked as if they were attempting to hide something given the way Corey kept peeking back out at the road. Curious over the males in her family's activities, she walked over and eased the side door to the home open, slightly cracking it in order to eavesdrop on their conversation while peeking out at their actions.

"What's your plan on covering up the jewelry store heist downtown, dad?" Mabel heard Jeremy ask while witnessing him hand a Rolex to Corey and Wendell.

"Bandits was robbed last night by a female biker gang who call themselves The Urbandale Gals," Corey responded as he inspected the $11,000 dollar price tag on the watch. "I was on their tail for a spell last night coming out of Bevington but they left my ass in the dust on those Harleys they were riding. I knew right away who they were, though."

"What does a female biker gang have to do with me robbing Sophia's joint?" Jeremy asked.

"I rode up to Des Moines and got up with Izzy and the Oslavskys last night and the four of us took ourselves a drive over to Urbandale early this morning and raided the bar the Gals hole themselves up inside and caught three of the six."

"What'd y'all find?" Jeremy asked as he placed the watch on his wrist and held it up eye level.

"A stack of rolled up bills along with the cash register receipts from inside Bandits was what we first discovered. Claire got to searching the place further and found about four barrels of moonshine in a hidden cellar," Corey let it be known. "Haul was worth thousands of dollars, son. We killed the women and took the cash and the moonshine. I reckon we got until this evening before the band that supposed to play up there tonight show up for rehearsal and find those corpses," he ended as he pulled down on his ten gallon hat, subtly dropping a hint.

"I know what you gettin' at, dad," Jeremy remarked, picking up on his father's implication. "Wendell? You and I got a job. We're gonna have to take these two watches back to that club in Urbandale and place 'em alongside the bodies."

"What's the reason for doing that?" Wendell asked.

"It has the name of the jewelry store Sophia owned back in town here. The law will find the watches with the tags and all, and trace them back to the jewelry store here in Patterson and we'll be able to pin Sophia's murder on the motorcycle gang up in Urbandale and keep me in the clear." Jeremy answered.

Corey looked over to Jeremy and smiled. "You'll make a good deputy soon enough, son," he stated proudly. "Now, while you're doing that, I'll try and get to the bottom of just who it was that robbed and killed our beloved town jeweler."

Corey, Jeremy and Wendell laughed amongst themselves for a moment as Jeremy began walking to his car. "Where're you going, Jeremy?" Mabel then heard Corey ask. "Me and your mother be leaving soon to head over to Bevington for a spell inside Bandits. You'll have the house to yourself, you, Wendell and Mary Beth. Ain't ya' up for a spell? You still have time before you head up to Urbandale."

"Got my fill this morning," Jeremy smiled. "It's Wendell's turn," he said as he patted his brother's shoulder before turning and walking over to his car.

"Is that Mister Patterson coming this way, dad?" Wendell then asked as he eyed a blue tow truck cruising up the dirt road.

"Sure as hell is. Wonder what he wants." Corey complained as the tow truck rolled up to the home.

Back inside the Mobley home, Mabel was stood in shock. Jeremy had basically admitted to killing the town jeweler. She couldn't believe it. And she feared what Corey would do to her if she ever told. As tough a woman as Mabel was in the political arena, she had not the intestinal fortitude whatsoever when it came to her husband at this point in time. The things he was involved in was beyond her wildest imagination and too horrible to phantom. Yet, in spite of her abhorrence, she was still choosing remain silent on the robbery and murder to keep her campaign for congress on an even keel, not mention she'd helped herself to a piece of the jewelry her son had stolen.

Turning her attention back towards Mary Beth, the emotion-ally-weary woman began pondering over Jeremy's remark in reference to him 'getting his fill' and it being 'Wendell's turn' as she eased the kitchen door shut and walked over to Mary Beth's room where she tapped the door. A few seconds later, the door was pulled open and Mary Beth poked her head through the opening.

"What?" Mary Beth asked dryly as her lips curled on one side of her mouth.

"What did you mean exactly when you said your father is troubling you, Mary Beth?" Mabel asked, hoping that what she believed in her heart wasn't true.

"Dad's been, he's been having sex with me, momma," Mary Beth confessed meekly as she stared into her mother's eyes.

"Are you hungry?" Mabel asked through a smile as she turned and walked up the hall.

"Momma? Did you hear me? I said dad's been—"

"I said are you hungry?" Mabel asked again, this time with more fervor and the raising of her voice as she turned and faced her daughter.

"You don't believe me," Mary Beth solemnly realized as she eyed her mother. "How could you not believe me, momma? Why would I make something like this up?" she pleaded with her hands out in front of her body.

"I don't have the faintest as to why you would make something like that up, Mary Beth! Don't you know I'm in the end game of a campaign election? Your actions could ruin everything for me!"

"My actions?" Mary Beth defended as she patted her chest. "This is not my fault! I'm telling you what's been going on under this roof with dad and my brothers so you can help me and all you care about is your stupid campaign?"

"Remember the day I caught you and the girl from the gas station kissing out behind the horse stables? I knew then that you were a sexual deviant." Mabel stated as she pointed a finger at Mary Beth.

"I'm not a sexual deviant. We were thirteen and playing around at the time. The psychiatrist you took me to see in Kansas City even said it was a normal curiosity for girls my age, but that wasn't the case. She didn't know what she was talking about! I was just looking for someone to understand me!" Mary Beth defended.

"I had to pay off that girl's mother to keep quiet on your illicit affair," Mabel countered. "Your actions nearly cost me my first election, but I was willing to overlook it. Now this?" the angered congresswoman scowled as she pointed to the floor beneath her feet. "This has the potential to derail my campaign and march our family off the cliff into shame and infamy for generations to come! I can't believe you would do this to me, Mary Beth!"

"Can't believe me? It's dad you shouldn't believe!" Mary Beth angrily bit back. "You're so worried about your campaign! What about everything else going on around here?"

"We'll talk about this…after the election." Mabel responded in a near whisper that did nothing to hide her shame and angst.

"You wanna know why dad drove the school bus home today?" Mary Beth asked matter-of-factly as she stepped into the hall and placed her hands on her hips and sauntered over to her mother.

"I don't want to hear any more of this nonsense! Silence it!" Mabel scoffed as she backed away from her daughter. The thought of such an abhorrent act unfolding inside her home was pushing the woman into the realm of deniability.

"You will hear it!" Mary Beth seethed as she ignored her mother's plea of silence. "Because there's way more to the story, momma, and you need to hear—"

"I will hear nothing of the sort!" Mabel screamed as she covered her ears.

"You will hear it!" Mary Beth scoffed as she slapped her mother's hands from her ears. "Daddy made Wendell put his mouth on my lips on that bus after he dropped everybody else off. And I'm not talking about the ones on my face."

Mabel tried to grab Mary Beth, but she backed away with a mocking smile on her face while swatting her mother's hands away. "That's right," she smiled teasingly as she eyed her stunned mother. "And the moaning you heard this morning when you tapped on my door? It wasn't a stomach ache like I told you, momma. It was Jeremy making me moan. Jeremy— while he was inside of me, momma."

Mabel reached out and slapped Mary Beth across the face. "Blasphemy!" she yelled towards her stunned daughter. "This is insane, Mary Beth! Insane! I will not have you spread your lies all over the place and ruin my career! From this point on I will hear no more!"

Mary Beth leaned up the wall inside the hallway stunned as tears fell from her eyes. She realized there was no convincing her mother that she was being sexually abused by the male members inside her family. The one person she felt she could count on was instead blaming her for the abuse and she was left feeling helpless. She'd tried everything she could think of to get her mother to believe her, up to and including revealing the sordid details of how she was being molested, her last revelation meant to hurt her mother just as much as she'd been hurt over her refusing to believe her while calling out for help. Dejected over the fact that nothing she could ever say would ever earn her mother's belief and compassion, Mary Beth walked into her bedroom, closed and locked the door.

As thoughts on what to do concerning Mary Beth's confession filled her mind, Mabel was interrupted when her son Wendell walked into the home and entered the kitchen. "Hey, momma," he spoke softly. "Mister Patterson's outside and he wants to know if he could ask you a question about some bill you passed last year?"

Mabel looked over to her son with trepidation. "Did, did you and Mary Beth get involved in something on the school bus, son?" she asked while staring into Wendell's eyes.

Wendell dropped his gaze and put on an exaggerated smile in order to remain true to what his father had told him about not speaking on what he and Mary Beth were actually up to. "No," he falsely declared through a nervous laugh. "Just the usual talk about the things we see on the way home and what happened at school. Can I have a sandwich?" he asked with his head in an easily discernable bow that derived from a place of shame.

Mabel stared at the top of Jeremy's head for several seconds. She could easily detect when her youngest son was lying to her and this was one of those moments. Mary Beth, it appears, was telling the truth. But for Mable, her daughter's confession was not a strong enough force to push her to action, neither was her oldest son's murdering of the town jeweler. "Wash your hands first," she remarked, while walking off.

Mabel walked out of the home's front door stupefied. She couldn't believe, nor was she ready to accept what she knew to be true: that her husband and oldest son had killed the town jeweler along with three more people, and were sexually molesting Mary Beth. She descended the home's stairs and walked under the blazing Iowa sun headed towards fifty-one year-old Franklin Patterson, a friend of hers for decades who resided on the north side of town. She was hit with an immediate reminiscent feeling upon nearing a friend of hers going back three plus decades.

For years now, Mabel had been carrying with her the belief that she'd become a part of the wrong family. Her life was supposed to be with Paul Patterson, Franklin's older brother; but tragically, Paul, who'd joined the Army Airforce, had been killed when his B-17 bomber plane exploded shortly after landing on an airstrip in Bassingbourn, England in September of 1944.

"Franklin?" Mary Beth asked through a warm smile as thoughts of what could've been with the Patterson family danced through her mind. "Wendell says you have a question concerning the subsidy bill?"

"Yeah," Franklin responded kindly as he removed his fedora. "Now, with a portion of my subsidy, I was able to buy a new tractor, but I have somewhere around two hundred dollars left over. I was wondering if I should return the unused portion back to the county, or could I use it for other things? Say, a new hydraulic pump for the lift in my garage?"

"You rode all the way over here to ask that, Franklin?" Corey chided, having eavesdropped on the conversation. "No one cares what you do with that money, son."

"Well," Franklin replied while dipping a finger into the corner of his eye. "I just wanna make sure I'm doing the right thing by using the money for what it was meant to be used for that's all, Corey. You understand, don't ya'?"

"I understand what a fool you are," Corey laughed. "You think people 'round these parts is buying tractors and hydraulic pumps, Franklin? No, sir! They're buying copper tubing, plastic barrels and generators for condensation on the wheat. Moonshine is the economy that drives these parts of Iowa."

"Not for everybody," Franklin remarked in a serious tone. "Some of us is actually trying to earn a decent living, Corey."

"Losers," Corey mumbled as he headed towards his home while fanning Franklin off. "Come on, Mabel. Tell Franklin he can do whatever he wants with his money and see 'bout making my lunch before I go back on duty."

Mabel sighed as her husband walked past her. She then smiled over to Franklin and said, "Pay him no mind. You do what you see fit with the money, sweetheart. I know you, like so many others I in represent, will do right by the bill that was passed."

"We sure will," Franklin assured as he nodded politely. "Everything okay with Mary Beth and all?"

"You know too?" Mabel bequeathed.

"Know what, Mabel?"

"Nothing. It's nothing, Franklin."

"Okay. Well, the reason I asked is because, because Paul always wanted a daughter. I sometimes wonder what things would be like had he survived the war. Mary Beth being around just touches my heart and makes me feel sorry you and Paul never got to finish what the two of you started." Franklin admitted.

"Mabel, get in here and leave that square dance to go on home to his pathetic existence!" Corey yelled from the front porch.

Mabel stared at Franklin somberly while ignoring her husband. How she wished she was on the other side of town where Paul once lived. "You should have nieces and nephews bearing the Patterson name, Franklin," she spoke softly.

"If only Paul had not died."

"Why didn't you take my hand in marriage after he passed?" Mabel asked, almost pleading as her eyes watered.

"It wouldn't have been right by Paul, and it wasn't my life to live," Franklin confessed as he choked back tears.

"Paul wouldn't have minded," Mabel whispered. "Neither would have I, Franklin. You would've made a far better husband and father than Corey," she ended as she reached out and touched the man's heart briefly before turning and walking away.

After parting ways with Franklin, Mabel reentered her home where she eyed her husband sitting at the dining room table going over Mary Beth's report card. "She's gotten straight A's once again," he stated proudly.

"Yeah," Mabel responded faintly as she made her way into the dining room. "Corey," she spoke as she went and stood across the table opposite her husband. "Mary Beth said something to me that kinda got me in a mental pickle."

Corey looked up at his wife somewhat unnerved. "Something like what?" he asked apprehensively.

"She told me that Jeremy and Wendell have been taking advantage of her sexually. She even said you know what's been going on, Corey."

"And you believe her?" Corey asked dryly. "The one you call a sexual deviant?"

Mabel, at that very moment, had the chance to stand up to her husband and get to the bottom of things concerning the allegations brought forth by her daughter. She'd had more than enough evidence having overheard conversations held between Corey and Jeremy. Rather than stand up for Mary Beth, however, Mabel capitulated and took on the stance of a woman unbelieving of her own child in order to continue her political endeavors. "I didn't say I believe her, Corey," she declared. "I just wonder why she would even make such an accusation knowing what's at stake for me."

"She's trying to ruin your campaign is what she's trying to do, Mabel," Corey remarked upon realizing that his wife was going to side with him in spite of the obvious. "Ever since you found her with that girl from town and took her to a psyche doctor she's been nothing but a thorn in your side."

"I had plans for us," Mabel stated in a mocked manner of dejection, trying to convince herself that Corey was telling the truth. "I'm confused as to what to do because she can't continue to spread these lies around."

"Well," Corey remarked as he sat back and crossed his legs. "There is something we can do—to qualm this here rumor Mary Beth is spreading, I mean."

"Something like what?" Mable asked. "Because, because if this was to go public?"

"No more government job for you," Corey chimed in, knowing the very thing his wife cherished most, that of her political career, was the main factor behind her willingness to turn a blind eye to what was transpiring under her own roof and within her family. "Look, Mabel. I know how much your political career means to ya'. I have a way to settle this matter."

"What's that, Corey?"

"The store we own back in Bevington. We'll send Mary Beth over to Bevington and let her work the store for the summer. Maybe her being away from the family for a spell will serve her mind right. Let her know what she's throwing away by...by spreading this malicious lie about the family," he spoke nonchalantly.

Just then, Mary Beth walked into the kitchen. Midway to the refrigerator, she caught sight of her mother and father talking in the dining room. "Hey," she said in a near whisper while coyly removing hair from her face.

"Mary Beth, what's this I hear about you spreading lies about you and your brothers?" Corey asked from his seated position.

"They aren't lies and you know it, daddy," Mary Beth replied nonchalantly as she pulled the refrigerator door open. "And you're the reason behind it all."

Corey jumped up from his chair, stormed past Mabel and hurried into the kitchen. Mary Beth was holding onto a picture of lemonade when her father neared her and knocked the jar from her hands. A second hand from her father was quickly placed to her neck and she was pinned against the opened refrigerator door as the picture of lemonade shattered onto the floor.

Mabel rushed into the kitchen and covered her lower face. "Corey, no!" she screamed.

Wendell entered the kitchen at that moment. "Dad, what's going on?" he asked puzzled.

"Ole Mary Beth here done got it in her mind to try and ruin the family name by telling her mother that the two of us, along with Jeremy, is engaging in sexual activity inside these walls with her sinful ass. Now, that couldn't possibly be true could it, Wendell?" Corey asked as he tightened the grip on Mary Beth's neck and stared back at his youngest son.

"Never, dad!" Wendell bellowed. "Mary Beth, why are you lying?"

"Momma," Mary Beth called out in fright as her eyes locked with her mother's.

"You're wrong, Mary Beth. Just say you're wrong!" Mabel screamed.

"I'm not wrong!" Mary Beth squirmed through tears. "You have to believe me, momma! Believe me, please!"

"There's no place left here for you inside this home, Mary Beth," Mabel professed. "You've ruined everything! You live a lie here and for that you must go!"

"Damn right!" Corey followed angrily as he pulled Mary Beth forward and shoved her towards the dining room. "You're outta here!" he vehemently screamed.

"Fine! I hate it here anyway!" Mary Beth screamed as she ran through the living room, headed towards her bedroom where she hurriedly began packing her clothes.

****

The memory of the day she'd allowed her husband to remove her daughter from the family home was as fresh in Mabel's mind as the fallen snow on the ground as she sat behind the wheel of her SUV on this cold December night in 1983. How she'd succumb to the deception perpetrated by her husband and two sons seven years prior was a question she knew the answer to and had known for some time: her own political ambitions.

For Mabel Sougherbraun-Mobley, her position of power inside Washington D.C. had superseded the welfare of her own daughter. Deep down inside, she knew Mary Beth was telling the truth the entire time; but the allure of power and prestige had placed a veil over her eyes, one she'd willingly accepted, if only to be able to deny what'd become obvious.

Mary Beth's plight was an issue Mabel could no longer ignore. She knew she'd conceded to her daughter being sent to a place befitting of hell and she now had to face the harsh reality that years of denial, and willful ignorance, had allowed things within her family to descend into a form of depraved perversion whose end result had led up to her own daughter bearing two children by her blood brother and biological father.

Corey, Jeremy, and Wendell had been using Mary Beth for their own personal pleasure, and Mabel not only knew it, but had granted the men in the family the right to do so when she'd backed her husband's plan to ship Mary Beth thirty miles east to the town of Bevington to work the family's store. A place where she knew the abuse would only continue on unfettered.

Mabel's political career was soon-to-be over in her eyes. She was prepared to let the family secret be made known and fade away into oblivion with her daughter and the two children she'd borne, if only to make amends with Mary Beth. A divorce was in order for her husband at the very least, and the family land would be sold off was what she'd seen on the horizon. From there, she and Mary Beth would relocate to a place unbeknownst to the world and reestablish the love that'd been lost, if it was at all possible. With tears forming in her eyes over how weak she'd been over the years, Mabel climbed from her SUV and made her way through the frigid cold air and entered the family's small grocery store.

Inside the store, Mary Beth had seen her mother pull up minutes earlier. She continued pacing up and down the middle aisle with her sleeping daughter in her arms as the chimes on the door clinked against one another. Memories of the day her mother had forsaken her ran through her mind as she sensed her growing nearer. "Merry Christmas, momma," she managed to say with her back turned and her heart racing.

"Mary Beth, I'm sorry. I apologize for choosing not to believe you. Everything you've gone through is my fault—entirely my fault. I was a moral coward and a selfish bitch. You have every God-loving right to hate me the rest of your life if you want to. I'd understand."

Mary Beth turned slowly and eyed her mother with tears streaming down her face. "Say it again," she spoke softly.

"What? That I'd understand if you were to hate me for the rest—"

"No!" Mary Beth panted.

Mabel closed her eyes briefly as she, too, let tears flow, all-the while knowing exactly what it was that Mary Beth wanted to hear. "I'm sorry," she spoke humbly as she neared Mary Beth. "I was a moral coward and selfish—"

"Bitch!" Mary Beth interrupted through a scream as she spat at her mother's feet. "You were a selfish bitch, momma! Bitch! You fuckin' bitch!" she cried aloud while staring Mabel in the eyes.

"Yes. A selfish bitch is what I was," Mabel admitted. "I'm scum, but I want to make things right for all of us."

Mary Beth laughed mockingly. "So I guess we can live happily ever after now, right?" she facetiously asked through her tears. "It's not going to be that easy, momma. You owe me!" she then screamed. "I have to live with these bastard kids and the memory of what dad and my brothers did to me! It's hard to look at you right now! I thought you of all people would believe me! I was confused as to why you didn't. Now I know you did believe me, but you put politics first! You owe me!" Mary Beth forcefully reiterated.

"Whatever it is that you want to do, Mary Beth, I'll do it." Mabel stated as she stepped close to her daughter and sheepishly reached out a hand and touched her elbow.

A chill shot through Mary Beth upon her mother's touch. All the good memories the two had shared came rushing back to her mind. Despite her mother's betrayal and denial, the twenty-three year-old brown-haired, brown-eyed petite woman still had a spot in her heart for the woman whom she once viewed as her best friend ever. She may have stood by and ignored the obvious, but she wasn't the one forcing her to do ungodly acts under threat of bodily harm in Mary Beth's eyes, and this was one person whose affection she wanted deeply. Timidly, she leaned into her mother and mumbled, "I'll go home with you."

Mabel quickly grabbed her daughter and held on for dear life. "Forgive me, Mary Beth," she begged through her tears. "Forgive me for ruining your life!"

"It's not your fault, momma." Mary Beth whispered humbly. "I can forgive you," she stated. "But not daddy, and not my brothers. I can't forgive them ever."

"Where's the boy?" Mabel asked tenderly.

"He's in the back room sleep."

"I'll get him together and we'll close this store. Let's go home. I have to talk to your father."

An inward smile shot through Mary Beth at that moment. She couldn't wait to get home. If Faye was indeed telling truth, she would get to see her mother squirm. The look on Mabel's face upon discovering her dead father would not only be priceless to Mary Beth, it would also be the best present she could ever hope to receive and would, in her eyes, even the score with her mother.

CHAPTER TWO

MERRY CHRISTMAS

The drive over to Patterson was a silent ride for Mabel and Mary Beth. Mother and daughter were alone in their thoughts as the SUV glided over the snow-plowed road leading to town. Mary Beth sat in the passenger seat thinking about her and kids' futures. Her son, five year-old Dillon Mobley, was borderline retarded, a side effect of her incestuous relationship with her brother Wendell.

Early on, Mary Beth had been proud of her son, but over time, the child's ailment had augmented and it now brought about shame for her, and pity towards the child. Dillon was a lethargic, stringy-black-haired child with grey eyes that cried constantly. He was fragmented in his speech, and far behind in vocabulary for a child age five. Evil thoughts filled Mary Beth's mind concerning Dillon as she rode beside her mother in deep thought with her eyes closed and tears falling ever so slightly as she contemplated on what exactly she was going to do with the child.

41

Mary Beth's daughter, two year-old Delilah Mobley, on the other hand, was her pride and joy. She was a brown-eyed, curly-brown-haired, pale-skinned little girl who was always alert when she was awake. Her constant warbles and involuntary laughter warmed Mary Beth's heart each and every day. She was the one bright spot in the emotionally-wounded young woman's life at this point and time.

After a ride back to Patterson that seemed to last longer than normal, mother and daughter had made it home. Mabel pulled up to the front of the house under the dark night sky and falling snow and placed the SUV in park as Benny Mardones' song *Into the Night* played over the radio. She looked over to her daughter with apologetic eyes and said over the music, "Whatever happens when I confront your father tonight, I want you to know that I stand with you, Mary Beth. I'm going to go in there," she said through trembling lips as she stared at the home's front door, "I'm going to go in there and tell Corey that you and I are leaving. And I hope to high heaven that that son-of-bitch tries to stop us. If he does I'll kill 'em," Mabel confessed as she leaned over and pulled the glove compartment open and pulled out a nickel-plated .357 magnum.

Mary Beth eyed the gun for several, tense and silent seconds in the darkness before looking up into her mother's eyes. This was a move unexpected by the twenty-three year-old, but highly welcomed at the same time. For the first time in a long time, the woman Mary Beth knew to be her mother was showing some spine. She leaned over and turned the volume down on the radio and asked her mother, "Would you really kill dad?"

"I have every right as a mother to go in there and blow Corey away for what he's done to you, Mary Beth," Mabel responded while staring at the front of the house. "But I might as well put the gun to my own head right after because I'm just as guilty," she ended as she turned and faced her daughter.

"I don't want you to kill yourself, momma," Mary Beth stated tenderly. "You're the one person I can forgive and couldn't live without."

Mabel leaned back in the seat with the gun resting in her lap as she stared out the windshield. She exhaled as she closed her eyes and clutched Mary Beth's hand. "Look what I've done to us," she cried. "I live this life before the American people as this God-fearing conservative, but the reality is that we're an incestuous family comprised of murderers and thieves."

Mary Beth climbed into the seat on her knees at that moment while holding onto her daughter. "I'm no murderer or thief, momma. Neither are you. Neither one of us asked for this!" she heaved through her tears as she pressed her face into her mother's shoulder. "This is all daddy's fault!" she accused as she tightened her grip. "Daddy's fault!"

Mabel had no natural understanding as to why Mary Beth was so on her side, nor could she understand the reasons why she was forgiven; but her daughter's mercy meant the world.

Mary Beth had the right to kill the entire family given their transgressions against her if that is what she wanted to do; but yet, she was willing to forgive Mabel for knowingly concealing deep, dark family secrets that had shattered her life. "Forgive me for what I'm about to do, God," the contrite woman remarked as she pushed her door open and meshed her knee-length ostrich skin boots into the fallen snow while cocking her pistol.

Mary Beth eased the door open on the SUV and stepped out into the falling snow with Delilah wrapped up in a thick blanket and trailed her mother towards the home. "He won't admit to anything, momma," she declared.

"He doesn't have to, Mary Beth. I know the truth—been knowing it," Mabel painfully admitted as she began to ascend the stairs with her nickel-plated .357 magnum draping the side of her $20,000 dollar rhinoceros skin trench coat and matching brim.

Mary Beth ran and stood at the bottom of the stairs with a look of exhilaration displayed across her face while rocking her daughter. There wasn't a doubt in her mind that Faye Bender hadn't actually killed her father and shocking revelations lay ahead. Mary Beth knew it. She hoped for it. She needed it to be true. More than eager to see the look on her mother's face when she found her husband dead, she ran up the stairs and waited, peeking over her mother's shoulder with a smile uncontainable while watching her fumble with the keys.

The moment Mabel placed the key to the hole, the door eased open and Bing Crosby's song *White Christmas* was heard playing low on the radio. "Why's the door unlocked, Corey?" she asked aloud as she entered the home. "Corey, where are you?" she called out over the music.

It was only after Mabel had moved toward the bookshelf in the living room to turn the radio down that she noticed its dire condition. The room seemed to have been disturbed, as if a struggle had taken place given the knocked over coffee table and the recliner where her husband often sat. She looked around and caught sight of numerous bullet holes lining the wall just outside the foyer.

"Corey!" Mabel called out once more while raising the gun. "Wait here, Mary Beth," she added as she walked over and peeked down the hall where she saw a light emanating from what was once her son's Jeremy's room at the end of the passage to her left.

Mary Beth watched her mother cross the living room with the gun in her hand and she grew ever excited. She knew. She just knew her father was dead somewhere inside the home and her mother would be the one to find his body. "Did you find anything, mother?" she called out happily.

"Stay where you are!" Mabel yelled back as she crept down the hall with her gun out before her while checking her kids' bedrooms. Mary Beth's bedroom hadn't been touched since the day she left and it wasn't disturbed. Corey would often go into his sons' bedrooms and change the furniture around from time to time, but nothing was out of place. The last bedroom was hers and Corey's. Just outside the bedroom she shared with her husband, Mabel paused as a bloody hand came into view. "Corey," she whispered.

Getting no reply, Mabel crept along the wall. "Corey," she called out again as she stepped into the bedroom where she let out an immediate gasp over the carnage that lay before her eyes.

An unknown muscular bald-headed man lay dead at Mabel's feet as she walked around the body dumbfounded. A bullet was lodged into his head and a gun lay loosely in his hand.

On the other side of the room, the shocked woman could see blood splattered up against the lower half of the wall beside the bed. "Oh my God," she mumbled as she crept to the foot of the bed, knowing what she was about to encounter.

When the sight of her dead husband came into view, Mabel had no solid reaction. She merely stared at her husband's life-less, bullet-riddled corpse as he lay in his pajamas surrounded by a sea of frozen blood.

Even though he lay in an undignified state, Mabel couldn't cry for Corey. Her only regret was that she didn't get to confront him and take a stand for Mary Beth and clear her own conscious of the regret she'd been carrying for some years now. As far as she was concerned, her husband had gotten his just due. With a wry smile appearing on her face, she patted the gun on her side several times before tucking her hands inside her trench coat. She was turning to walk out of the room and alert the authorities when Mary Beth walked into the threshold holding onto her daughter.

Mary Beth eyed the unknown dead man for several seconds as she walked into the room, showing no emotion. She could see the legs of her father's pajamas extending out from the other side of the bed, but she just had to make sure that what she felt in her heart was true. Her pearly whites began to show, and the smile she'd donned only increased as more and more of her father's lifeless body came into view.

By the time she reached her murdered father, Mary Beth was in an boisterous state. "This is the best gift I could've ever received," she exclaimed while smiling from ear to ear. "Merry Christmas, daddy," she ended through animated laughter as tears of joy filled her eyes. "Merry fucking Christmas."

CHAPTER THREE

SPEAK NO EVIL

The sounds of flashing cameras and the cackling of walkie talkie radios filled the Mobley home as a half dozen Iowa patrolmen and a trio of crime scene technicians processed the crime scene. The bodies of Corey Mobley, and a man preliminarily identified as one Webster Holden through an identification card found on his person, were in the process of being tagged and bagged for transport to the Medical Examiner's office in Des Moines.

In the eyes of the law, the crime scene before them told a story that involved Corey Mobley, and that of at least two intruders. Given the glass of egg nog and brandy resting on the night stand, coupled with the damage done to the front door, it appeared as if someone had kicked in the front door and caught the sheriff by surprise.

Bullets lodged into the wall further led the authorities to believe that Sheriff Mobley had fired on the intruders before running to the back of the home. The family dog had tried to his best to ward off the invaders before he was shot to death, and the intruders then made their way down the hall, trailing Corey to the back bedroom. In an attempt to deceive his aggressors and have them believe he'd escaped, Corey raised the bedroom window, hid beside the bed and opened fire, striking the guy Web when he ran into the room.

The wounds to Corey's legs led authorities to believe that a second intruder had shot and wounded the sheriff before entering the room and taking his life completely. And initial ballistics tests were showing that Webster Holden had possibly taken his own life with an Uzi that lay clutched in his hands. Whoever'd aided Webster Holden was now long gone, and his abettor had left behind nothing more than a slew of unresolved questions that warranted answering.

"What a way to spend Christmas, Captain Olsen," one of the troopers remarked as he zipped up the black leather bag containing the corpse of Webster Holden.

"I wouldn't have it any other way," Captain Rance Olsen remarked seriously as he stepped aside to let four of his comrades carry Corey Mobley's body out to a waiting van.

Fifty-nine year-old Captain Rance Olsen was a longtime acquaintance of Corey Mobley. The two men had a rapport in the realm of the law, and Rance carried about a sense of gratitude towards Corey over an incident that had transpired five years earlier. He was a friend of the Sheriff, but didn't always agree with the man's methods. Corey was a known outlaw in rural

Iowa, a man that made his own rules and had more power in the town of Patterson than the town's elderly, old-fashioned mayor, who was just a local farmer popular with the town folk.

In Rance's mind, what'd happened to Corey had to be over some criminal deed him and his sons were known to engage in. Maybe that of selling moonshine, or shaking down one of the biker gangs known throughout the area, only he wasn't sure. Either way, a man of the law had been murdered and Rance Olsen was aiming to get to the bottom of things.

While in the opening phases of mentally deciphering the case he now found himself working, Rance trailed his four subordinates out of the room and up the hall towards the living room where he laid eyes on Mabel and Mary Beth.

Mabel was stirring a cup of coffee while sitting comfortably in the recliner that was once knocked onto its side as Mary Beth sat on the sofa opposite her mother spoon feeding her daughter as her baby boy slept soundly beside her. There wasn't a tear in nary an eye of either woman and both appeared to be calm given the circumstances in his eyes.

With a suspicious gaze, having had a portion of his crime scene disturbed, Rance walked into the kitchen and pulled a chair back into the living room and took a seat before Mabel and Mary Beth while pulling out a notepad. "Now," the frost-white-haired, slender state trooper began as he sat before the two, "neither of you women know the gentleman that was killed alongside Corey is what you both are telling me?" he asked as he eyed the two women.

Mary Beth eyed her mother nervously as she held Delilah in her arms inside the cozy living room while rocking the baby to keep her quiet during her feeding. Mabel had rehearsed with her some of the questions that may be asked so she was well-informed and knew what to expect. "I don't know the man Webster Holden, Mister Olsen," she spoke lowly, which was the truth.

Rance leaned forward and made an attempt to rest his right arm on his knee, but an immediate sting shot up through his right arm and forced him to cringe.

"Is your arm okay, Rance?" Mabel inquired.

"The bone aches from time to time, Mabel," Rance grimaced while shaking his arm, flexing his elbow in the process.

Rance had gotten his right arm run over while investigating a couple of rum runners on I-35 back in August of 1978. Corey Mobley had helped capture one of the assailants in Bonita Bender, a woman who Rance knew had been sent up state for twenty years shortly after being apprehended outside of CM's Grocery Store on that very night.

That aiding of a fellow lawman, had endeared Rance to Corey, but the more he got to know the man, the more he came to despise him. Corey favored rum runners, even sold the product, and upheld his sons, who were suspected of numerous burglaries in the surrounding counties; but when it got down to it, Rance Olsen was nothing more than a good officer looking to solve Corey and Webster Holden's murders, nothing more, as he sort of had a disdain for Corey after coming to know the man's lifestyle inside the law.

"Okay," Rance grimaced as he reached into his top pocket and pulled out a bottle of pain pills and popped two into his mouth, swallowing them without the aid of liquid. "Where were you throughout the day, Mary Beth?"

"I was back in Bevington at our family store." Mary Beth answered.

"You can confirm my daughter's whereabouts via store receipts and a few witnesses, Mister Olsen," Mabel chimed in as she crossed her legs. "She's the only employee over there. I picked her up about two hours ago and we made our way home to enjoy the Christmas holiday. When we arrived, the front door was unlocked. I pushed it open and called out for Corey but—"

"Got no answer, went and investigated and found the bodies on the floor inside the bedroom. I got it!" Rance remarked in frustration as he removed his trooper's hat and set it on the floor in between his boots.

"You seem disgruntled." Mabel stated unnerved, determined not to reveal much to the officer.

"I am disgruntled, Mabel," Rance remarked in a suspicious tone. "This here is a crime unprecedented and we have nothing to go on."

"I wish we could help you more, but the Patterson Massacre is also a crime unprecedented and it too hasn't been solved," Mabel remarked casually before she took a sip of her coffee.

"I'm working the Patterson case," Rance stated in a self-protective manner. "Those are citizens, but we're talking about the murder of a town sheriff here. You sure you haven't any more information for me to go on? Because we have a lot of unanswered questions here—one in particular being the whereabouts of your sons Jeremy and Wendell."

"You think they have something to do with this and are on the run?" Mabel asked in mocked wonderment.

"You know good and well that is not my thinking, Senator," Rance stated in a condescending tone of voice as he stood up from the chair and eyed Mabel and Mary Beth with contempt.

"Well, what is your thinking, Mister Olsen?" Mabel asked in pretention as she stood up from the recliner.

"Wendell and Jeremy haven't been heard from in over five years. Now, I'm not your sons' keeper, but with all that's going on? You didn't feel the need to contact Corey's boys to inform them of their father's demise? Wherever they are?"

"Can't reach them," Mable remarked in a wry tone as she stared Trooper Olsen in the eyes and sipped her coffee.

"Mary Beth?" Trooper Olsen questioned as he turned his attention to Mabel's daughter. "Do you know anything? Anything concerning your brothers' whereabouts?"

"Sorry, Mister Olsen," Mary Beth responded as she dropped her gaze and looked into her daughter's grey eyes. "I don't know where my brothers are right now."

Rance eyed the Mobley women with contempt. There was something strange going on with the two, with the entire family actually, only he couldn't place his finger on it. One thing was certain: Mabel and Mary Beth seemed too calm for a family that'd discovered their patriarch and an unknown man laying dead inside their home on Christmas Eve.

"If you haven't any more questions, Mister Olsen," Mabel remarked, shaking Rance from his thoughts, "if you haven't any more questions? Me and Mary Beth would like to see to the securing of our home. We have a lot to worry about here with the man of the house being deceased."

Rance, being the polite man he was, even in his suspicious frame of mind, couldn't help but to ask, "Do you need me to stay and help, Mabel?"

Mabel picked up her .357 magnum and patted her side with it. The gun looked like a sledgehammer in the woman's tiny hands, but the freshman Senator was one tough woman. She'd been handling guns for over decades and knew her way around a weapon. She was unafraid in her home as she knew the truth behind her sons' absence and the reasons why her husband was killed. They'd all gotten what they deserved in her eyes and she feared no retribution. "We'll manage, Mister Olsen. How's your arm holding up by the way?" she asked as she made her way to the front door.

Rance looked down at his right arm and rubbed it gently. "On cold days like this it reminds me of that night," he replied. "Wish Corey could've got 'em both. Maybe none of this would be," he added as he looked over to Mabel suspiciously.

The Senator nodded her head in seemingly approval, but inside, she was thankful Faye Bender had gotten away. Mabel had a certain amount of gratitude in her heart for what the young woman had unwittingly done five years ago to Jeremy and Wendell, and just a few hours earlier by killing Corey. She had done what Mabel herself had wanted to do all along, which was to free her daughter from the pain and strife she had to endure at the hands of her father and brothers while she so selfishly pursued her political ambitions.

Mabel knew firsthand that she would have to weather a tumultuous storm that was ripping through her family like a plague of locust—a storm consisting of a cover-up. She was on the road to repairing the damage she'd done to Mary Beth, but yet and still, she knew that much more had to be done in order to cover-up incest and murder. As Junior Senator for the state of Iowa, however, she knew she would be afforded some resources that would enable her to conceal the family's secrets.

****

Back outside of the Mobley home, Trooper Olsen sat in his car staring at the ranch home's front porch while pondering the mystery that had landed in his lap before he placed the car in reverse, turned it around and left the home. Traveling back to Des Moines, the officer went inside his troop's headquarters and sat at his desk. He opened the filed report on Webster Holden and just stared at the man's crime scene photos. The address on his wallet had him living in the city of Pittsburgh. "What's a guy from Pittsburgh doing way out here in Iowa?" he asked himself lowly as he picked up the phone and dialed the Pittsburgh Police Department.

After a few rings, the line picked up. "City of Pittsburgh Police Department. You've reached the records division how may we assist you today?" a man asked politely.

Trooper Olsen held onto Web's folder, patting it in his hand. "Yes," he replied as he eyed the dead man's photograph. "This is Iowa State Trooper Captain Rance Olsen speaking. I have a murder victim in the city of Des Moines, Iowa's Coroner's Office by the name of Webster Holden and I was calling to ask if you could give me any background information on the fella?"

"Give me a minute. I'll put you on hold and see if we have a file on the guy," the man responded as he placed Trooper Olsen on hold. Several minutes later, the policeman returned and gave the police background on Webster Holden. It was information that would place Rance on the road to possibly solving the case of a lifetime.

CHAPTER FOUR

RIGHT BACK TO IT

It was two days after the discovery of Corey and Web's bodies, Christmas Day across the world. Twenty-five year-old Faye Bender had just completed the thousand mile drive down New Orleans using Web's Suburban. She'd stopped over to a payphone and called Tanya Weinberger just outside of the city to have her next move confirmed. "You remember how to get back to the Saint Bernard?" Tanya asked her.

"Yeah, I remember." Faye responded as she stretched.

"Cool. Head over to The Night Owl. We have to get rid of that jeep. I got everything set up for you."

Faye climbed back into the SUV and made her way into the Seventh Ward over to The Night Owl Lounge. The place was packed Christmas night of 1983. Parking was hard to find, so she parked in a driveway just up the street from the club and made her way inside.

The Night Owl Lounge was filled to capacity and there was standing room only. Cigarette and marijuana smoke was heavy in the air and partyers were out on the dance floor. The pool tables to the back of the club were surrounded by gambling hustlers dressed to the hilt in colorful silk suits and gator shoes that toked joints while exchanging money and shucking with one another.

Faye looked through the crowd and spotted Willameena Slack behind the bar counter. She was bobbing her head to the music as she held onto a fifth of vodka while using a tin scoop to spread ice cubes into clear plastic cups that lined the bar.

"I ain't setting up these drinks for nothing, now!" Willie yelled towards the crowd that was three rows deep before the bar. "I need to see some green, people! The hell y'all standin' around with y'all thumbs up ya' asses for? If ya' ain't ordering nothin' ya' need to get the hell up outta here!"

"Seven and seven!" "Rum and Coke!" "Rum on the rocks and a vodka and orange juice!" patrons began to call out.

Faye smiled and scratched the side of her nose as she casually began making her way through the crowded lounge. She brushed off a couple of flirtations from various men as she neared the bar counter.

Through the crowd, Willie spotted Faye approaching the bar counter. Her eyes grew wide and a pleasant smile crept across her face as she turned the bar over to her mother and stepped from behind the counter, welcoming Faye with open arms.

"We was worried about you, girl!" she laughed happily as she held onto Faye for several seconds before leaning back and smiling at her. "How'd it go in Iowa?" she then whispered.

"It went well. I did what I set out to do," Faye stated matter-of-factly.

"Okay. You did the gangster shit up there," Willie nodded. "Tanya told us you was coming here tonight. Brenda and the King Sisters waiting on you upstairs. Let me get you straight right quick."

Willie went and mixed Faye a drink and let her up the staircase behind the bar. She made her way up to the loft over the lounge and rounded the wall where she saw eighteen year-olds Zelda and Vivian King sitting at a small, round, wooden table before three plates full of brown-looking powder she knew to be heroin.

Twenty year-old Brenda Marshall was standing beside the counter polishing a black steel Uzi with a pile of banded money resting on the counter. "Look what the wind done blew in," she stated as she eyed Faye and continued polishing the gun in her hand. "Make yourself at home, chick."

"Where you parked that jeep at?" Zelda quickly followed as she sprinkled lactose on top of the heroin and began mixing it with a wooden spoon.

Faye was expecting a bigger welcoming. She quickly realized, however, that she was no one special and was only a small cog in a big wheel she had no control over at the present time. She went with the nonchalant flow of things by stating, "It's in the driveway over there. The one down from the tree across the street."

"Good. That's our driveway," Vivian replied. "We'll move it after we repackage this boy. Give us about an hour. In the meantime, go on down to the club and enjoy yourself," she ended through a smile.

"I'd rather remain behind the scenes. You two need help with that?" Faye countered.

Zelda and Vivian eyed one another with apprehension. "What you know about this here boy?" Zelda asked as she stared Faye up and down.

Faye had spent some time with the King Sisters back in June and had attained a measure of respect for them, as well as Brenda, through conversations she'd had with the women over to Tanya's loft in days following the Patterson Massacre. She understood fully that this faction of the crew was all about business, but so was she for that matter.

Faye didn't take kindly to being taken as a lightweight, but by right, she was now a part of someone else's crew. She was welcomed in on the strength of Tanya, and Brenda had gone above and beyond by agreeing to look after Maggie the time she was away committing murder. Always being one to play the angles, Faye's instincts were telling her that she shouldn't try and assert herself, but rather win these ladies over through action to avoid conflict while earning their complete trust. "I dealt heroin in Cincinnati," she told the King Sisters.

"Yeah?" Zelda asked seriously. "Well, pull up a chair. Show us something," she beckoned as she leaned back in her seat.

Faye pulled a chair over to the table and poured a shot of vodka from the fifth the fraternal twins had sitting on the table and went to work mixing the heroin. She was a wizard with her hands, blending fourteen grams of lactose and fourteen grams of black tar together and bagging up an ounce within minutes to produce a freshly wrapped bundle.

Zelda and Vivian bumped elbows, the fraternal twins smiling at Faye as they sat side by side opposite the table. "Okay," they spoke in unison while nodding their heads.

"So what happened up in Iowa?" Vivian asked the as the three started packaging the remaining product.

Faye went on to explain everything that had gone down and what had led up to her returning to Iowa. Brenda was still breaking down the Uzi, but she was listening in on the conversation. "You sayin' this sheriff in Iowa was fuckin' his own daughter and she had his child and another child for her own brother? And even though he killed your family you got charged with it?" she asked Faye in wonderment.

"It's fucked up all the way around," Faye replied matter-of-factly as she wiped her hands with a damp rag and eased up from the table. "Thing is, is how will I clear my name of the capital murder charges I'm facing? The law in Iowa believes I killed my own family. I can't let that stick. In order for me to fight it, I need money."

"How much money you talking about?" Vivian chimed in.

"Enough for a lawyer to clear my name. I'm guessing a hundred thousand dollars minimum. I mean, I got some things working, but I can't cover the full cost."

"I can help you out, but I'm gone need a favor in return." Brenda remarked.

"What kind of a favor," Faye asked as she began pacing the floor with her hands on her hips.

"It's an Asian crew settin' up a heroin network in Cincinnati," Brenda let it be known as she walked back over to the kitchen counter and eyed three black steel Uzis. "They stepping our toes up in Ohio. That's our turf. They need to be removed from the scene ASAP." Brenda stated as she set the polished gun down on the counter.

"What you need me to do?" Faye asked as she walked over to the counter and stood beside Brenda.

"You say you sold heroin up in Cincinnati so I'm assuming you know your way around the city," Brenda remarked. "Zel and Viv in the middle of moving weight right now as you can see. With them two overseeing the product? Me and my old man been looking for another gunner to join us on this Cincinnati job. You down for that?"

"How much money we talkin'?" Faye asked as she picked up the polished Uzi and began breaking it down.

"You join the hit you get twenty-five grand. Help move the heroin we got when we get back and you'll have the rest of the money you need in no time," Brenda stated.

Faye was feeling as if her back was against the wall. All she had at this point in time was the clothes on her back. She'd made plenty of money on the streets, but she now found herself looking up at the sky from the bottom of a barrel. Her mind was in a thousand places, and the recent past, the murder of her family and the crimes she'd committed herself, gnawed at her soul.

The Cincinnati job just may do her some good was Faye's thinking. At least she'd be able to keep moving and avoid the distraction of grieving over the loss of her family. And at the same time, she could begin to formulate a plan to counteract the capital murder charges she was up against back in Iowa. She would still be facing an attempted murder charge, she knew, but she viewed that as a lesser problem. It had been over five years since the incident. The guy she'd run over had probably retired for all she knew; either way, she believed that the passing of time would lessen the blow on that particular charge, but a woman wanted for killing her own family was not going to go away no time soon, if ever at all.

Faye knew it was only a matter of time before the walls closed in on her. To ward off apprehension, she knew she had to keep moving, and in order to do that, she needed money. Brenda and the King Sisters were going to give her a start, but the run she had in mind far exceeded any goal she foresaw the three women sharing the loft with her accomplishing. All she had was her name, Bender, and she'd be damned if she was destined to be a woman convicted of killing her own family, whom she loved more than life itself.

"Count me in," Faye remarked coolly as she began planning her next move after she'd completed the Cincinnati job.

"Tanya was right, yeh? Zel and Viv? This arrangement gone work out damn good," Brenda chuckled over to her girls. "Let us finish bagging this heroin and I'm a take you over to the French Quarters by Tanya so you can see her and Maggie," she ended.

CHAPTER FIVE

BORN KILLERS

Twenty-year-old Tanya Weinberger was on the second floor of her three-story, three bedroom four bath loft sitting at a large, lacquered cherry wood table. Hers was a pristine nineteenth century style wood and stone domicile located on Saint Louis Street, just a half block away from Bourbon Street in the heart of the French Quarters. Tanya was an eccentric woman of German-Jewish descent, and her taste in home décor lended her to that fact.

Upon entering the first floor of the three-story home, one was greeted with dark-grey wooden floors and a black marble fireplace on the left in the center of an olive green wall. The celling was painted white and there was a crystal chandelier hanging down in the center of the room. A tan leather chair and a dark green love seat were situated on either side of the fireplace and deer antlers hung over its mantle. A large glass supported by a stuffed giant sea turtle set in between the chair and the love seat and Tanya had spread out numerous Dr. Suess books along with a crushed diamond and glass vase with a single black rose rising from it to use as centerpieces.

Tanya's man, Alfredo Lowes, was just as eccentric as she. A fan of rock and classical music, the thirty-three year-old man of Jewish descent, who resembled John Lennon with two pigtails and black hair, added his own touch by placing a signed Jimi Hendrix electric guitar. An eighteen century bass violin once handled by Wolfgang Amadeus Mozart, rested on fourteen karat gold stands on the right side of the room.

The black-painted wall was adorned with oil paintings of naked angles, both male and female, their private parts on full display. Alfredo had also placed hand-carved marble busts of the Greek mythological gods and goddesses Mars, Aphrodite, Eros and Venus along the wall behind his instruments that were valued at over two hundred thousand dollars.

A threshold at the opposite end of the room separated the living room from the modernized kitchen of the era. A microwave, four toaster and in-wall stove along with a double door refrigerator were the most up-to-date appliances of the eighties. Marble counter tops and floors with a garden-style bathroom accented the spacious area that led out to the back patio.

Stairs off to the right at the far end of the kitchen curved around and led to the second floor, which was a plush-carpeted open area with a club-style theme that had one bedroom to the far right if you were facing the front of the home.

The King Sisters, Sally Irving, Willie and Brenda had all camped out in the spare bedroom countless times after parties that had lasted well past sunrise winded down. There was a pool table, twenty-five inch floor model TV and a Fischer component set with four fifteen inch house speakers in each of the corners.

A dark green velvet couch faced the french doors that led to an open balcony that overlooked the block where one could get a clear view of the activities unfolding on Bourbon Street off to their right. Here in the living room, Willie's son, one year-old Popeye, and Brenda's son, nine month old RJ, along with three year-old Maggie McPherson, were all sitting in front of the console TV watching Frosty the Snowman and playing with their Christmas gifts.

To the back of the room was a library area that overlooked the back patio and back alley behind the home. There in the library seated at the cherry-lacquered table was Tanya Weinberger, who was eight months pregnant, along with her man, Alfredo Lowes. The two were in the process of finishing up their phase of crew's plan on the upcoming job, which was to supply two cars, and the money needed for the trip. Situated on the table was an Olympic Camera, two sets of car keys, hair dye, and twenty-five thousand dollars, which was Faye's payoff for a job Tanya just knew Bonita's sister would sign up for upon learning the payout.

"The cars Yabba Dabba supplied us with been checked out thoroughly, baby—one's a Lincoln Town Car and the other's a Ninety-eight four door Oldsmobile. And I have your flight set up to Venezuela." Tanya stated as she went over the route her people would take up to Cincinnati with the aide of a road Atlas.

"I hope your chosen one doesn't bungle the job in Ohio," Alfredo replied as he looked over documents that secured his owning of a newly-purchased club on Mulberry Street up in Cincinnati.

"I know you been operating up there in Cincinnati for some time, but Faye ran heroin out the same city around the same time you got started. She can be an asset to Brenda and Mouse."

"Faye is somebody I'm not in agreement with at the present time." Alfredo remarked as he shook his head somberly and threw the documents aside.

"What's wrong with Faye going up to Cincy with Mouse and Brenda, Al?" Tanya asked while rolling her eyes. "Trust me okay? It's gonna work."

"Faye has some heat on her from the deal in Iowa. Her name is known, even her alias name Audrey Greenburg is known to the law. Not to mention she may get fingered on picture alone."

"Well, if they finger her, it's nothing we can do," Tanya admitted. "But Audrey Greenburg will not come into play," she added as she threw down a driver's license that was missing its picture. Alfredo eyed Tanya, who was smiling back at him. "Trust me now on this?" she chuckled. "We'll use the hair dye to change her hair color and I'll take a picture, develop the film and scale it down to make another fake identification card for Faye."

"I'm still not convinced." Alfredo complained. "We barely know this broad. And this is a big move we're making with the Darvish men over to Venezuela."

"What is it that's got you bothered about the woman exactly? You think she'll roll over on us if she gets caught?" Tanya asked while staring her man in the eyes.

"That's not it." Alfredo responded as he eased up from his chair and ran his hands over his thick, black beard.

"Then what?"

"It's another woman. An attractive woman. If you know Mouse and Brenda, they swing, the same as we do. Faye might get turned off if they were to...to come on to her?"

"Who gives a fuck about that?" Tanya chuckled. "If Faye wanna suck and fuck some black dick while she on the clock fine let her have at it. I just want the job done. I don't care who busts a nut in the process."

Just then the door bell rung.

"Mutter!" (Mother) three-year-old Maggie McPherson yelled out in fluent German upon hearing the buzzing sound. The red-headed, chubby little girl got up from her seated position in front of the television and ran through the club area towards the stairs yelling, *"Dass meine Mutter! Meine Mutter kommt zurück"* (That my mother! My mother come back!)

Alfredo knelt down and grabbed Maggie by her waist to prevent her from running down the stairs. "I can't ever understand this little girl's dialogue. What is she saying? Is she okay, Tanya?" he asked concerned.

Alfredo's tenderness with children was a quality Tanya loved about her man. She couldn't move around too well in her pregnant state, but Alfredo always made sure the kids were never neglected when they were inside the home. And Tanya, although being German herself, didn't speak the language from birth, but she'd been studying the verbiage to better communicate with Maggie. "She thinks it's her mother at the door. Poor baby," she remarked while eyeing Maggie sadly.

"Can't help but to feel for her," Alfredo remarked as he stood to his feet. "I'll be right back."

"Mutter!" Maggie exclaimed happily as she jumped up and down in one place.

Alfredo descended the stairs and entered the foyer where he spotted Brenda and Faye standing on the sidewalk through the creases in the stained-glass window. He opened one of the doors to welcome them inside. "Look who's here," he stated through a smile as he held the door open.

The time Faye stepped into the home, she could hear Maggie's voice calling for her mother. She hugged Alfredo briefly and thanked him for looking after her best friend's daughter. "Has she been any problems?" she asked Alfredo.

"No way," Alfredo soothed as he rubbed Faye's back. "She had several gifts to open this morning, has been eating like a Billy goat the whole time she's been here and has made two friends with RJ and Popeye. She's fine," the man let it be known as he reached out and hugged Brenda.

After securing the home, the three made their way back upstairs. Faye's heart was pounding with anticipation and anxiety as she climbed the wooden staircase. She could hear Maggie repeatedly calling for her 'mother'. How she was going to deal with this toddler, take care of her and give her the love and nurturing she deserved while fulfilling a murder contract was questions she had no answers to at the time. The best she could do for three year-old Maggie McPherson at this moment was to just be there for this mother and fatherless child who hadn't the ability to comprehend the tragedy her family had befallen.

When Faye reached the top of the stairs, Maggie was there to greet her. She watched as the child's smile dropped. Maggie looked beyond Faye and saw another person approaching, someone she knew not to be her mother. The disheartened toddler leaned into Faye's legs, heaved and asked, *"Wo meine Mutter?"* (Where my mother?)

Faye knelt down, reached out and ran her hands through Maggie's thick head of red hair. *"Sie ist hier richtig,"* (She's right here.) she told the toddler, she herself having studied the language with Gayle when the two were on the farm back in Patterson, Iowa.

Maggie grew confused. She recognized the person standing before her, but she didn't look like the person she knew to be her mother. The little girl stared at Faye through her hazel eyes, kissed her on the cheek, and quietly walked back into the living room and sat before the TV to continue waiting for her mother to return.

Faye stood up and ran her hands through her short, black--dyed hair. "I don't know how to tell her what happened to Gayle," she admitted.

Tanya eased up from her seat and wobbled around the table and stood beside Faye. "She's too young to understand, Faye. Don't trouble yourself with that right now."

"I know that's real. Maggie will be all right," Brenda re-marked as she went and poured herself a glass of vodka. "Al-fredo, meet me and Mouse's accomplice on the Cincinnati job —again," she added as she nodded over to Faye.

"I'm aware. You sure you're up to this job, Faye?" Alfredo asked as he eyed the woman carefully. "I know what you set out to do in Iowa. I take it you got the job done. But, are you in the right frame of mind given your losses?"

Faye nodded to say yes. "I have to keep moving," she remarked. "If I sit still I'll go out of my mind."

There was a brief moment of silence before Tanya spoke. She was actually waiting on Alfredo to ask about Lisa Vanguard, but he never bothered so she kept the conversation moving. "Okay," she sighed as she went and sat back down in her seat. "Faye, we were just going over the plans for the hit. You wanna pull up a chair?"

"If you don't mind," Faye countered, "I'd like to bathe first? But I haven't any clothes."

"Sure. Follow me," Tanya replied as she eased up from her seat once more.

"Umm, baby?" Alfredo interjected.

Tanya turned and gripped her back, her pregnant belly poking out through her silk maternity dress. She widened her eyes and stared at Alfredo in wonderment.

"The third floor?" the man smirked.

"Oh. Right," Tanya chuckled.

Brenda shook her head. Reason being was because no one had ever been up to Tanya's third floor the year or so she and Alfredo had been living in the loft and there was much left to the imagination. If Brenda and the King Sisters had to tell it, there was a sex chamber on the third floor. No one was certain, but it was a given that Alfredo and Tanya were varied in their intimacy. The numerous oil paintings of naked gods and goddesses on the first floor and pornographic movies consisting of bondage that they sometimes left laying around had their friends in wonderment over just what was going on upstairs on the third floor. More than once the friends had tried to sneak upstairs to see what it looked like, but Tanya always kept the door locked to what she and Alfredo often referred to as 'The Jungle'.

"If Faye go up there, I'm going up there!" Brenda playfully chided as she walked over to the foot of the stairs.

Tanya laughed as she let Faye up and blocked Brenda's path by placing her right arm across the threshold. "There's nothing to see here, Brenda," she stated as she turned and eased up the stairs. "We be back down shortly."

Once up the stairs, the door was locked by Tanya after Faye stepped up onto the loft. It was pitch dark inside until a small candle was lit. Amid the yellow hue, Faye caught sight of chains hanging from the ceiling, only she couldn't make out what they were used for exactly.

"This way," Tanya said as she held the candle close to her face.

Faye was now curious to know what was so secretive about this third floor. She kept trying to get a full glimpse, but she couldn't make out what was behind her given the lack of light. The two reached the end of the hall where Tanya clicked on the bathroom light. Faye turned around to try and see the bedroom, but again, her line of sight blocked. "Towels are fresh, and there's body soap on side of the tub. Make yourself comfortable and I'll get you some clothes to wear."

Faye settled into the bathroom, sitting down on the toilet to relieve herself before standing up to remove her clothes. She waited a few seconds and saw a red light come on through the door's cracks. She moved to open the door, ready to view what lie out in the master suite, but the door had been locked from the outside. She fumbled the door knob a few times and then beat on the door. "Tanya, what the hell is this?"

"I knew you were going to open that door!" Tanya yelled back. "You can't see it unless you become a part of it!"

"Part of what?"

There was brief moment of silence before the door was unlocked. Tanya eased it open holding onto a pair of freshly laundered sweat pants, a pair of socks and a t-shirt with a pair of slippers. With the light bulb coating the room in a deep, soft shade of red, she stepped aside to give Faye a glimpse of her sleeping quarters.

Faye could only stare in amazement over what she was witnessing. "I see why you and Alfredo call it the jungle," she remarked nonchalantly as she grabbed the clothes from Tanya and stared at herself in the mirror, removing strands of black hair from her face.

"You can't say that shit out there doesn't look like a world of fun," Tanya smiled as she rested her back against the threshold.

"It does," Faye smirked while staring at Tanya's reflection in the mirror.

Tanya dropped her smile at that moment and eyed Faye seriously. "Alfredo ain't too comfortable with you going to Ohio with Brenda and Mouse." she told her.

"Is he not now?" Faye asked casually as she went and turned on the water inside the tub. "What does he think I'm going to do?"

Tanya leaned back on the threshold and said, "It's not what *you* would do, it's what Brenda and Mouse may do. They umm, they have a set up like this at their house."

Faye looked over her shoulder towards Tanya with a serious look on her face. She wrung her hands and stood naked facing her friend. "Is that so?" she asked curiously, lost for words.

"Let me tell ya'. Whatever happens, leave it all behind."

"I understand what's on the line, Tanya. Brenda and Mouse will just have to trust that I won't let my desires cloud my judgement."

"I trust you won't, but I wouldn't blame you if something were to happen. Just don't disappoint me on the contract," Tanya declared before she handed Faye a bottle of dye. "You're going blonde for the trip to Cincy. I was going to use black, but you make a better blonde. When you're done coloring your hair I'll need to take a photo and finish your new ID card. Your new name is Valerie Smith, by the way," she ended before closing the door.

Faye exhaled as she climbed into the tub. The steam from the running water was rinsing the black dye from hair and droplets began falling onto her shoulders and coloring the hot liquid as she tilted her head back on tub's edge and stared up at the ceiling with a heavy heart. The last six months had been the most trying time of her life.

In that span of time, she'd lost her best friend, her son and her husband, a friend in Webster 'Web' Holden, and had murdered a town Sheriff in Corey Mobley. The weight of it all hit her full force as she sat inside the tub. In silence, she kept her green eyes on the ceiling as tears began to leak from their corners. Her lips trembled as she leaned forward suddenly and clutched her body tightly. "You should've taken me, God!" she cried. "Where's the justice in the killing of my son? He was, he was the best thing that ever happened to me," she professed as she raised her head and stared wide-eyed in utter disbelief.

The image of her son laying dead stayed with Faye every waking moment and it was a vision that she felt would never be erased from her memory. To be strong was Faye Bender, however; even when up against a form adversity that would drive most people insane, she was one able to remain firmly grounded and continue moving forward.

Times like these, times when she was alone, was where she would release her grief, if only to not burden those around her with the mental anguish she was suffering through. There was much more work needed to be done and if ever she wanted to clear her name, she knew she had to stay focused. She was lucky to have linked up with Tanya Weinberger and her crew. Without them, there wouldn't be much she could do on her own and she knew it all-too-well. She was grateful for friends who carried the same mentality as she when it came to the occupation they were all involved in as they were rare gems in a world littered with fugazzis from all walks of life.

New Orleans was where Faye Bender was planning to regroup. She still had boundless fight within her and an upcoming job in Cincinnati, a job that would put her right back in the game if she were to succeed. Lisa Vanguard would get hers soon enough, but now was not the time, was her thinking as she began to plot her future moves should the job go unhinged as thoughts of her sister Bonita filled her mind.

CHAPTER SIX

HIT AND MISS

"Tumble out of bed and I stumble to the kitchen...pour my-self a cup of ambition and yawning, stretching...tryna come to life...jumpin' in the shower and the blood start pumpin'...out on the streets the traffic starts jumpin'...with folks like me on the job from nine to five..."

Dolly Parton's 1980 country hit song *9 to 5* rung out over thirty-four year-old Isabella 'Izzy' Lockhart's radio alarm clock inside her darkened bedroom. She extended her pale, white hand from under her thick cotton comforter as she lay on her stomach and knocked the alarm clock off the night stand. She rubbed her dark-brown eyes to awaken herself as she rolled over onto her back where she sighed while staring up at the ceiling. The covers beside her shifted as a thick-framed, black-haired Caucasian woman pushed the covers up off her body and eased her back up against the king-sized bed's leather headrest.

"Thought you left with your husband last night, Claire," Izzy mumbled as she reached over and clicked on the lamp beside her bed.

"Donovan went home to get the next package ready, remember?" Claire responded through a yawn. "Besides," she added in a sexy voice as she nudged up against Izzy and began running her hands across her stomach, "he got his fill of us both and was only getting in our way is what you said before he left the room last night."

Izzy laughed lightly as she spread her legs, allowing Claire to diddle her clitoris as the two briefly flicked the tips of their tongues together. "I remember now," she smiled as she pulled back from Claire and put her feet to the floor. "I don't know what I was thinking agreeing to work the morning shift the day after Christmas, girl, knowing how you, me and your husband behave now whenever we get together."

"God, I know," Claire sighed as she slammed her head against the headboard of Izzy's luxurious bed while running her hands through her long, shiny, black hair. "I was wanting to taste you again, baby," the forty-four year-old buxom housewife stated through a pretentious pout.

"And I would love for those sexy ass lips to suck it dry again," Izzy chuckled as she climbed from the bed naked and flung her short, auburn hair back into style.

Donovan and Claire Oslavsky were Izzy's street connect. The three had been friends for nearly five years. The married couple had become Bonita and Izzy's moonshine connect shortly after Bonita's arrival back in 1978 and now were supplying Izzy and Bonita with several pounds of potent marijuana.

Donovan and Claire was a dangerous couple. Drug dealing and contract killings was their livelihood. Together with Corey Mobley, the two often went on raids in times past, pretending to be cops alongside the Sheriff. Their biggest score occurred seven years earlier when the two, along with Corey, raided a bar over in the suburb of Urbandale and killed three female biker gang members and made off with thousands of dollars' worth of moonshine. That sting had propelled the married couple to the forefront of the criminal underworld in Des Moines and they were now making several thousand dollars a day.

"What a moment in time," Claire moaned in appreciation as she exhaled and replayed the things she, Izzy and Donovan had done the night before. "Now it's back to work. Got a few deals to make this morning outside of our deal," she sighed. "Donovan should have everything ready to go for you right about now. You need me to ride up to the prison with ya'?"

"I can handle it. Same price for five pounds. That's ten grand," Izzy responded as she picked up an envelope from her nightstand and threw it in Claire's lap. "Just hand the package to me in the backyard once we leave the house like we always do on shipment day."

"You ever told Bonita about us?" Claire asked as she pulled the money from the envelope and quickly counted out one hundred, hundred dollar bills.

"I did," Izzy stated. "She didn't take it all too well, but she appreciated my honesty. We both have the understanding that the love we share when we're able to is meant to be monogamous. So long as she's on that tier in Camp A? I belong to her and her alone. She wanted to know everything we did, and that was the way I wanted it," she adamantly confessed through a proud smile.

"You told her all the dirty details while she was in the hole didn't you?" Claire asked through naughty laughter.

"It got her off, honey. She loved that dirty talk," Izzy chuckled. "I'll be glad to be able to make love to her once she settles back onto the tier. It's been six months for her so I know she's hot and bothered."

Claire eased out of the bed and stood in her nudity. "Nothing's wrong with that, Isabella," she stated in a matter-of-fact tone while holding up a bent wrist. "Hell, you ain't givin' up Bonita and I sure as hell ain't givin' up my Donovan. That's my bread and butter, sugar. And if he don't mind me swinging the other way from time to time while we're married then he's a keeper by all measure." her voice trailed off as she picked up her .38 revolver, bra and panties and headed for the bath inside the bedroom.

"I feel the same about my Bonita," Izzy responded as she turned and checked her well-toned, pale-skinned physique inside a full-length mirror. *My ghost white self need a tan* she thought silently as the smell of fresh-brewed coffee encompassed her exquisite bedroom inside her pristine one story four bedroom home as she prepared herself for work the day after Christmas in 1983.

Thirty minutes later, Izzy and Claire were fully dressed and finishing off mugs of coffee and preparing to leave Izzy's home in order to make an exchange. Claire was headed for the patio door inside the kitchen where she would normally exit and walk alongside the wooden fence that led back to her own patio door on the house situated directly behind Izzy's home where she would hand her the marijuana.

"Dammit! Trash goes out today," Izzy remembered as she donned a thick, black wool parka that matched her dark brown correctional officer's uniform after stuffing a blue steel .357 magnum revolver into her back waistband.

"I'll give you a hand before I go and get the stuff," Claire remarked as she stepped out into the cold air and swift-blowing snow while tightening a green and red scarf around her neck and buttoning up her white cashmere coat.

Together, the two women began pulling two large plastic green garbage cans from the side of the home past Izzy's 1984 Ford Bronco and down the driveway towards the edge of the curb. After setting the garbage cans out, Izzy walked over to her mailbox at the foot of the driveway being she hadn't checked the mail in nearly a week. She'd just pulled the mailbox door open when she was suddenly blinded by a set of fog lights resting atop a pickup truck that was speeding her way. "Claire, get down it's a hit!" she yelled aloud as she ran past the woman while pulling out her .357 magnum. Bullets began flying into the early morning air as she took off running towards her Bronco to shield herself from the hot lead whizzing by.

Claire was surprised, but it didn't prevent her from turning around in haste and pulling her own gun to defend herself as what sounded like firecrackers began erupting into the air. Bullets penetrated Claire's chest and exited the back of her cashmere coat just as she'd raised her weapon to return fire. She screamed out in agony as she stretched her arms to the dark sky and fell face up into the snow with blood spurting from her mouth and nostrils.

Izzy had run and hid behind the engine block of her Bronco. She was able to peek out from the front side of her ride where she caught sight of the pickup speeding by with two occupants that were firing off revolvers from the bed of the truck. Shielded by the Bronco's engine, Izzy rose up and let off four rounds from eight shot her .357 magnum. "Claire?" she called out to her fallen comrade. "Claire?"

Over screeching tires, and realizing that Claire was down, Izzy ran back down the side of her home while reaching into her parka for more bullets. "Finish Claire! I'm gone make the block!" "I going after Izzy!" she heard two female voices randomly yell aloud as she ran through the fence leading to her backyard.

When Izzy reached the edge of her home, she pointed the gun to her left and hunched over as she emerged from the side of the one story brick domicile. She knew she was being hunted and was expecting a shooter to greet her the time she stepped out into the open and she was right. More gunfire erupted as she and one of the attackers fired upon one another under the darkness of night from opposite sides of the backyard under the falling snow. Splinters on the wooden fence shattered as Izzy disappeared from sight on the opposite side of her yard, lucky to not have been hit amid the rapid exchange of bullets. She ran in between the two houses where she leaned up against Claire and Donovan's patio door in order to reload her revolver as the footsteps of her potential killer was heard nearing the fence just to her right.

To Izzy's left, she could see the fog lights on the truck that had rounded the block approaching from the front side of Claire and Donovan's home. Gunshots off in the distance let it be known that Claire had just been dealt the death blow. "Where she at?" she heard a female ask aloud.

"We got her pinned in behind her house!" Izzy heard the second attacker yell as she grew closer to the fence's edge.

Izzy was so nervous she'd dropped the last of her slugs into the snow and was unable to reload the gun. Knowing she was about to be wedged in inside the alleyway, the panic-stricken woman took the gun in her hand, leaned outwards and slammed the butt of her .357 magnum down into the large patio window, shattering it in its entirety.

Donovan was in the home's den packaging the last pound of marijuana while listening to Steppenwolf's song *Born to be Wild.* The music was up extra loud, preventing him from hearing the gunshots. The man did, however, hear a faint sound coming from the front of his home. He set the joint he was toking on down into an ashtray and replaced it with a loaded twelve gauge shotgun and got up and turned the stereo down before easing the door open. "Claire, that you?" he asked while easing into the hallway with the gun pointed outwards.

Izzy had just entered the hall at that moment. "We being hit!" she blurted out as she ran past Donovan.

"Where's Claire?"

"She's down and I'm out of bullets! It's at least three of 'em!" Izzy answered hysterically.

"Hit the trunk in the room!" Donovan snapped as he racked the twelve and moved towards the kitchen. He eased up the hall and peeked out into the open area just as two silhouettes decked out in black trench coats and welding chrome pistols entered through the shattered patio glass.

Without hesitation, Donovan opened fire and an intense gun battle exploded out into the home's kitchen, shattering the cabinets and refrigerator. One of the shooters dropped to the floor on her stomach and didn't make a sound as the second gunner stepped back out into the patio and shielded herself; she extended her arm and fired off random shots from behind a brick partition, aiming nowhere in particular.

Donovan's twelve gauge was thundering aloud as bullets ripped through his silk shirt. He fell up against the kitchen counter and re-racked the shotgun with blood running down his legs and squeezed the trigger one last time while falling to the marble floor.

Izzy, meanwhile, had run to Claire and Donovan's bedroom where she knew the two had a trunk full of guns. Over the sounds of crushing glass and footsteps that alerted her to the fact that the killers were now entering the home in order to finish the job, she removed five pounds of marijuana from the trunk's top, opened it, and pulled out a Browning .410 rifle, a four shot rifle that was powerful enough to take down a polar bear with a single shot.

Donovan was heard pleading as Izzy racked the rifle and emerged from the bedroom. A gunshot went off in the kitchen and Izzy quickly followed with a thundering shot of her own. A quarter of the threshold leading into the kitchen was shredded by the buckshot and she quickly discerned that she'd garnered her attackers' undivided attention. She continued to fire, repeatedly racking the weapon and squeezing the trigger. Several seconds later, the screeching sounds of tires where heard.

Izzy ducked back into the bedroom to grab more shells and saw a light grey pickup truck speeding off the block through the bedroom's vista view window as she began reloading the rifle. She turned and crept back through the home where she saw Donovan laying in the kitchen on his stomach with blood surrounding his body. Laying just inside the patio entrance on her side was that of a Caucasian brunette in her early twenties. With glove-clad hands, Izzy turned the dead woman's head and stared into her face. Right away she recognized the woman as that of a prisoner who'd been paroled by the warden along with two other females not even a month earlier.

The women were all part of a biker gang who called themselves The Urbandale Gals. They were known to be working for the warden inside the prison and it seems as if their being paroled was meant to do nothing more than further the warden's criminal intent. While steadily putting the pieces of the hit together in her mind, Izzy ran out the patio to check on Claire. It was obvious the woman was dead when she reached her and checked for a pulse. Blood had pooled into the crevice of Claire's neck, and the front of her pristine, white cashmere coat was covered in blood as she lay on her back with her mouth and eyes wide open and a shocked expression frozen onto her lifeless face.

Izzy went into Claire's coat and retrieved the envelope of cash she'd given her and made a beeline for her Bronco. She was out of the neighborhood before police had ever arrived on the scene. She intentionally left the drugs behind in Claire and Donovan's home to throw off the police as best she could. Given all that she believed was going down on this early morning, just a day after Christmas, she knew she had to get to Mitchellville lest her worst fears come to fruition. Knowing she would not make it to the prison in time and was possibly already too late, she pulled into a gas station and used a payphone to call the only person she trusted behind the walls outside of Bonita and Cikala.

"I'm am heading that way right now, Isabella," the person on the other end stated pedantically before hanging up the phone and heading down to solitary confinement where Bonita Bender was holed up.

******

"Today is your lucky day, sweetheart!" a correctional officer snapped as she pulled the small window open on twenty-one year-old Bonita Bender's cell down in solitary confinement.

Right away, Bonita grew suspicious. Izzy was supposed to walk her back on the tier this morning. Instead, she heard the voice of an officer she knew to be friendly with the warden, Evelyn Pulaski, calling for her out on the floor. "I'd rather wait on Izzy," she told the woman as she stood up and bumped her fists together while staring at the door's small opening.

"You ain't got a choice," the Caucasian woman retorted as she pulled the door open and eased into the cell with two more guards following close behind. "Are you resisting?" she asked mockingly as she pulled out a wooden club and looked back at her duo. "I think she's resisting, girls. Let's make quick work of Miss Bender—give her a late Christmas gift she'll never forget."

The third guard was pulled back out of the cell and flung up against the opposite wall at that moment. When she moved to pull herself off the wall, she was punched in the stomach and immediately went down to her knees gagging for air. The lead guard turned around and recognized the officer standing before her and her remaining cohort and she grew anxious over the woman's commanding six-foot-one stature. "I thought I told you to man the halls outside the cafeteria," the lead guard growled.

"I'll be escorting Bonita Bender back to Camp A," the tall, burly woman stated, ignoring the lead guard's protest as she walked into the cell and stared down the lead guard while beckoning Bonita forward.

Bonita knew the woman who'd rescued her from a brutal beating by face only, but she'd rather take her chances with this stranger than face Evelyn's crew as she knew that outcome more than she'd cared to express. She walked out of the cell without giving it a second thought. The denim jeans she'd been wearing for the past six months, ever since the day she'd attacked a fellow inmate by pouring a mixture of her own feces, urine, hot grease and metal tacks into her face, hung off her waist and were rolled up over her black jack boots. She carried the matching denim jacket in her right hand as she walked with her head down in deep thought, wondering just who this woman was that had cared enough to put her out of harm's way. Her brown hair hung wildly over her shoulders and her eyes were darkened around the edges as she'd found it hard to sleep on the concrete floor inside the cell. She wiped sweat from her face, using her dingy long-sleeved shirt as a towel as she walked up the long hall leading out of solitary confinement as the heat was blazing down in the dungeons.

While walking up the corridor in silence for several lingering seconds, Bonita couldn't help but to ask, "Who are you?" as she tailed the blonde-haired woman.

"I am your guardian angel," the guard responded with her back to Bonita as the two walked up the dimly-lit, isolated corridor.

"What if I told you I don't believe in a god or its angels?" Bonita asked while eyeing the officer's backside through suspicious eyes.

The correctional officer turned around, stared down at Bonita and sternly stated in her deep-pitched, raspy voice, "What if I were to walk you back down the channel we've just traveled and place you back inside your cell with Evelyn's crew? I am willing to gamble my own soul that when Evelyn's girls lay their hands upon you, you will cry out for a god in utter agony—some god—if only to save your own skin—just as I have done on this morning. That is what I know to be true knowing what you are up against inside these stinky prison walls. Be grateful for me, Bonita Bender, because I am the only object standing in between you and the God that you believe does not exist."

The woman standing before Bonita was named Sascha (pronounced Sasha) Merkendorf. She was a thirty year-old six-foot-one tall blonde-haired woman of German descent that was thick in all the right places. Her arms were sleeved in tattoos consisting of red roses with black stems that dripped blood from their pointed thorns over shattered black Swastikas that contrasted perfectly against her pale, white skin. She was Izzy's unspoken co-conspirator on the force inside the prison. With Bonita and Cikala moving five pounds a month inside Mitchellville, Izzy knew full well that around-the-clock protection was a must for her girls. It had taken some time, but Izzy had reached across the Atlantic Ocean and had tapped a trusted source from her hometown of London.

Sascha Merkendorf had been Izzy's silent partner for seven months now; having made it over to the United States a month before Bonita was sent to the hole. She'd come from a bloodline of Nazi war criminals. Her parents worked for Adolf Hitler inside the Dachau concentration camps exterminating Jews during the Holocaust.

At war's end, Sascha's parents were brought up on multiple murder charges and executed for their crimes shortly after Sascha was born in August of 1953. The surname Merkendorf was nearly as infamous as the last name Hitler in Germany, and Sascha had paid a heavy price in her youthful years for the sins of her parents. She was moved to a hostel in London where she met Izzy while riding the subway home from school. The two became good friends and had kept in touch over the years. Sascha had always dreamed of living in America, and through Izzy, her dream had come to pass. She was ever grateful for Izzy, and to show her gratitude, she chose to be a woman loyal to her friend's Cause come hell or high water.

"Hell has been my life for as long as I can remember." Bonita remarked while staring up into Sascha's eyes. "Whether god exists or not, and should I call upon that person in my most weakest moment, should I ever become weak, I don't expect to receive help. I put no faith in a person I can't see."

"You are contradicting yourself right now, Bonita." Sascha remarked.

Bonita looked up at Sascha befuddled. "What makes you say that?" she asked.

"The whole time you were in that hole you believed in Izzy. She came to see you, shared her sexiest secrets while you played with your pussy inside that cage and then fed her your come-soaked fingers through that little window."

"I don't follow you, umm?"

"Sascha is my name. You wait for Izzy every day in faith that she will show. And she always does. On the days you know that she will not be around, you wait with the anticipation that she will return. Even though you cannot see what it is that she is doing outside, you wait—faithfully. You are a woman of faith whether you chose to believe it or not." Sascha remarked through her naturally sleepy eyes while staring down at Bonita.

"Izzy is different. She's here near me. I can see her, get my point?"

"Having one near isn't a guarantee that they will always be around, Bonita Bender."

Bonita paused at that moment and had a moment of clarity. Worried, she asked Sascha, "Did something happen to Izzy? Is this why you are here and not her?"

"Your attack on that spy six months ago silenced things with the crew from East Iowa, but a new problem has emerged. They hit Izzy this morning, but they missed."

"They had to have had helped on the outside. Who's pullin' the strings?" Bonita asked as her mind began to work.

"It is the warden that is calling the shots," Sascha told Bonita as she extended her hand, welcoming her back onto the prison tiers. "This morning she's taken a stance against us. I've pulled you out of harm's way," she remarked lowly as she handed Bonita a pointed piece of metal with a duct tape handle.

"You'll need this going back to Camp A. I'll take you to your friend Cikala," she ended as she guided Bonita up the corridor.

The two reached the tomb-like tier of Camp A and the steel door thundered loudly against the silence. Only three lights in the corridor were illuminating the long hall and the faint sounds of a prisoner's radio at the far end of the tier could be heard. Seven or eight cells in between each hanging lamp was darkened, leaving one to wonder who exactly resided behind the steel bars as their faces were unseen. Bonita remembered walking up and down this corridor on many a night going to meet Izzy or returning from some solo mission. Being gone for six months, she knew it was a possibility that the living arrangements had changed so she had to be brought up to date. She hadn't had the time to ask Sascha, but she knew who to ask on the tier in order to get the low down.

While walking past one of the darkened cells, an inmate called out to Sascha, "What your Barry White sounding ass doing down here? You know you trespassing, right, bitch?"

Sascha paused and took several steps back. She reached for her flashlight, clicked it on and shined it down towards the floor so as not to blind the inmate. "I know who you are," she spoke calmly as she stared into the inmate's eyes. "Do I really sound like the Barry White singer? Or are you just being factious with me?"

The inmate spat in Sascha's face. "Fuck you, Barry White!" she scoffed.

Bonita was expecting Sascha to open the cell and deal with the inmate, but she remained ever calm as she removed the spittle from her face with the fingertips of her black leather gloves and wiped them on her black leather trench coat. "I was willing to share a laugh with you because you are a woman of heart. But because you spit in my face? Your fate has now been sealed," she professed before walking off.

Bonita eased past the cell and stared at the inmate. "You spit in my face you'll be dead at breakfast. Heart or no heart," she snarled.

"Fuck you, too, Bonita! Fuck you and ya' crew!"

"Her time will come." Sascha told Bonita, stating it loud enough for other prisoners to hear. "A new day is upon us!" she then stated loudly as she walked with her hands behind her back and a black Captain's cap pulled down low over her eyes. Her deep voice echoed throughout the chamber as she continued in her speech, "I know it is the warden some of you are loyal to," she added as she turned around and walked backwards while eyeing the cells to her left. "But I will have a say in matters! And my say, will be the final say! My measures will not be crippled by any bureaucracy because here I don't have to worry about justice! My mission is only to destroy and to exterminate those in opposition to—the family! Nothing more, ladies! So fear *me*! And stay out of *our* way!"

Sascha Merkendorf was indirectly quoting Herman Goering, founder of the German Gestapo, at this very moment. "*My *measures will not be crippled by any bureaucracy. Here I don't have to worry about Justice; my mission is only to destroy and to exterminate; nothing more,"* was Goering's original quote from a speech in Frankfurt in 1933, but Sascha had made it her own. Although never sympathizing with the Nazis, Sascha, who knew her family's history well given all the ridicule she'd faced back in her home town of Dachau, could appreciate a lot of the tough talk the Nazis engaged in during their height of power. She imitated their tactics and speech, but not their racism.

For Sascha, an enemy was an enemy, no matter the race. She could be just as loyal to people from a different nation just as much as she was loyal to her own kind. Bonita didn't know it, but she was trailing the woman who would become one of the most important people inside an organization whose wings were about to spread wide open and soar like that of a condor —the world's largest bird that survived off the dead, as such would be the case with this budding organization over the years to come.

CHAPTER SEVEN

RUNNING THE SHOW

"...for forty days and for forty nights...the law was on her side...but who can stand when she's in demand...her scheming plans..."

Michael Jackson's thumping bassline and intense vocals to his hit song *Billie Jean* lit up the second to last cell inside of Camp A the closer and closer Bonita and Sascha neared the cage. Inside the cell, twenty year-old Cikala Dunbar was sitting up on her bottom bunk zoned out with her head tilted back and eyes closed when she heard the steel door leading to the tier buzzing. She jumped up and grabbed the two knives Sascha had given her and shut off the radio and was standing in the center of the cell with her hands behind her back when Bonita appeared and stood outside in her denim jeans, white shirt and black boots with their hair pulled back in a single ponytail.

"Oh shit," Cikala stated through laughter when she saw Bonita standing outside the cell. "B, it's crazy 'round here, chick!"

"I heard," Bonita spoke lowly as Sascha unlocked the cell.

"I'll leave you two alone and will stand on the other side of the channel so you can talk," Sascha remarked.

When Sascha cleared out, Bonita turned to Cikala. "Thanks for takin' care of things while I was way. Now, who this chick on our tier?" she asked after embracing her friend briefly.

"It's three of 'em from Urbandale around our age." Cikala remarked as she reached under her bunk and handed Bonita a rolled up joint. "Merry Christmas. I bought you some new jeans and a hooded sweatshirt knowing you was gettin' out the hole today, but they in Izzy locker."

Bonita chuckled as she dapped her round that was holding it down. "I appreciate that gesture. I got you back once I get settled in. But first we got business. I wasn't talkin' about those lames on the tier, though. I'm talkin' 'bout the Nazi imitator on the other side the wall."

Cikala laughed and said, "Sascha hardly used to come down here until about a week ago, but she be on the yard hard. She had my back when Izzy was out and while you was in the hole. She solid. I mean, she be quoting crazy Nazis and shit, but that bitch there? You don't wanna get on her bad side."

"I'm gone take your word on Sascha. Now, who these chicks on my tier?"

102

"Like I say, they from Urbandale. They part of some biker gang calling themselves The Urbandale Gals." Cikala remarked as she handed Bonita a lighter.

"Urbandale, huh," Bonita casually remarked as she lit the joint. "What all you know about 'em?"

"They in tight with the warden. Three of 'em got paroled about a month ago and went right back to selling marijuana. They leader named Dorothy Unger."

"Grace's older sister," Bonita remarked as she choked on the weed.

"Yeah, that bitch there," Cikala scowled. "She couldn't get paroled with the rest of 'em last month. Dorothy 'nem working the outside now. The warden been tryna get they product inside the prison, but Izzy been blocking that shit."

"That explains why they went after Izzy this morning," Bonita remarked as she passed the joint to Izzy.

"Say what?" Cikala asked before taking a toke.

"Somebody killed Claire and Donovan and tried to get Izzy this morning. I'm willing to bet it was them bitches the warden paroled." Bonita remarked as she paced the cell.

"They killed the connect?" Cikala asked surprised. "Fuck we're gonna do now?" she complained as she paced the cell's floor.

"I think I know how to get to at the warden, but I need to talk to Izzy first. In the meantime, we keep our eyes on those three biker chicks at the front of the tier." Bonita answered.

"They not hard to get at. You get one, the other two gone bow down. That way we won't rack up too many bodies." Cikala replied.

"We gone take care of one Unger sister in Dorothy. No need to let Grace carry on by herself. That's our mark." Bonita remarked seriously. She then turned to Sascha and asked, "You on duty until Izzy get here, right?"

"Until breakfast when Izzy takes over." Sascha replied as she walked over and closed the cell door.

"Tell her to—"

"She knows to come see you when she arrives," Sascha interjected. "In the meantime, I have to go to the other end of the channel and talk with this woman who believes me to sound like the Barry White singer," she stated before abruptly walking off.

Bonita and Cikala laughed to themselves as Sascha walked off and resumed smoking their weed. Things were back to normal for Bonita, whatever that could possibly be inside a place like Mitchellville.

Sascha, meanwhile, walked back down the corridor casually with her hands behind her back and went and stood before the prisoner's cell who'd violated her just minutes before. The inmate was sitting on her bunk talking to her cellmate when she felt eyes upon her.

"The fuck you want now?" Grace Unger, the petite, short in stature blonde scoffed at Sascha.

"You have a serviceable neck, Miss Unger," Sascha remarked as she stepped closer to the cell and tilted her head to the side. She then pointed her finger and said, "I know what I am going to do with it when your day comes. Breakfast is soon," she ended before walking off.

Grace stood up from her bunk and ran to the cell bars where she placed her thin head in between the steel rods to get a better look. "You don't scare me you—"

Just then, an open palm from Sascha's glove-clad hand struck Grace in face. She stepped back and ran her hand over mouth and nose and saw that she was bleeding lightly from both orifices. "Crazy bitch!" she screamed at Sascha through her bloody lips and nostrils.

"Crazy? No!" Sascha exclaimed as she took a military stance. "Spiteful is what I am. Call me petty even—but you have awakened a thirsty desire inside of me that only you not being here anymore will quench. Like a frog in a pot of water you now simmer on my stove—until I decide to turn up the heat. Wait for your season." Sascha ended as she walked away from the cell and went and sat in a stool near the entrance to Camp A.

Grace was left dumbfounded over Sascha's remarks. This new officer always talked in riddles, but it was easily discerned by all in which she conversed with that she dished out nothing but threats time and time again.

"The warden will hear about this! I'll have your ass fired!" Grace yelled.

"You and the warden's ships sail the same waters. And neither of you have a rudder to steer your direction," Sascha smirked as she leaned back and crossed her legs and opened the pages of Mein Kampf, which was Adolf Hitler's manifesto and future plans for Germany, while imaging in her mind not only what she was going to do to Grace, but where inside the prison she would carry out her deed at the appointed time.

****

Meanwhile, out in the prison's parking lot, Izzy had just pulled up the facility in her Bronco. At any given moment, she was expecting to be confronted by officers investigating the murders that had unfolded outside her home. She'd regretted leaving the scene, but she was so worried about Bonita that she was compelled to rush to the prison and check on her friend and lover. After climbing out the SUV, she walked briskly to the prison's entrance and checked in. She didn't even bother garnering her prison-issued firearm as she traversed the hall, anxiously making her way to Camp A where she ran into Sascha just inside the entrance to the tier.

"Is she okay?" Izzy asked in reference to Bonita as she scanned the tier.

"Your lady is doing fine with her friend Cikala down there in the same cell. I'll take you to see her."

"No," Izzy replied as she checked her watch. "We'll have our moment. Breakfast is a little under an hour. Continue watching her for now."

"What are you about to do?"

"Pay Evelyn a visit," Izzy answered as her attention now shifted over to the warden upon learning Bonita was in safe hands with Sascha on the tier. Boiling over in anger, Izzy left Camp A and headed for the officer's locker room where she retrieved her service revolver and headed towards the warden office.

****

Fifty year-old Evelyn Pulaski was pacing her floor in frustration with a glass of moonshine in her hand when she heard a hard knock on the double wooden doors leading to her office. Right away she knew who it was. One of the members of the biker gang she'd sent to kill Izzy had phoned her and informed her of the fact that the hit had failed. Izzy had loss her connect, but she was still alive. On top of that, one of the members of The Urbandale Gals had been killed and she knew it wouldn't be long before Izzy found out who the woman was, if she didn't already know.

Evelyn knew all-too-well that that Izzy surviving of the hit and Bonita's release from solitary confinement now posed a threat to her operation inside the prison, but she was aiming to stall until the remaining members of The Urbandale Gals could regroup and plot another hit. She downed the four ounces of liquor she was nursing, straightened her business skirt outfit, and went and pulled the door open. "Izzy," she smiled pretentiously as she went and stood behind her desk. "What brings you here at this early hour? Shouldn't you be on the tier?"

Izzy smiled and politely closed the door inside the lavish quarters that was laced in cherry oak without turning her back on Evelyn. "I'll get to my duties soon enough," she stated matter-of-factly. "What I wanna know is how you get the nerve to attack me in my own home?"

"Attack you in your own home?" Evelyn laughed lightheartedly. "Whatever makes you think that I—"

"Don't lie to me!" Izzy hissed under her breath. "If you're wanting to kill me the least you can do is look me in the eyes and have the heart to admit it!"

Evelyn eyed Izzy without blinking. The game of deception she was aiming to use had just been shunned aside. "I have way too many allies for you to handle," she declared. "You have Bender and Cikala and that crazy ass German, Merkendorf, but your crew's power extends no further than the gates bordering these prison walls. This is the only place you can fight me, Isabella. And it will be a difficult task. If I were you I would consider negotiating before things get real ugly in Mitchellville."

"There will be no negotiating," Izzy told Evelyn. "I've managed to survive all this time. I have no doubt that I will continue on."

"Things happen inside of prisons, Isabella," Evelyn remarked as she grabbed a stack of files for new arrivals and eased from behind her desk. "If I were you, I'd watch my back at all times in this place."

Izzy didn't bother responding to Evelyn. The warden had unwittingly playing right into her hands. Whatever she had formulating in her mind, Izzy would be prepared, especially since she'd dodged the bullet so-to-speak, back in her neighborhood. She'd given up some information concerning her activities, but it was only to decipher Evelyn's next move. And in that process, she'd quickly uncovered the warden's vulnerability. "I have a shift to cover, Evelyn," she said as she reached and opened the door.

Izzy left the warden's office, turning her back on Evelyn, a silent, defiant action that the woman hadn't picked up on as she was too high-strung on the crew she was running inside the prison and drunk off power. Little did she know, her days would soon be numbered.

****

Several hours later, Bonita was buttoning her prison jumper having just been orally serviced by Izzy. The two of them were hidden in one of the aisles of the prison library as Sascha stood guard at the entrance. A Christmas play was being put on by the prison's drama club inside the prison's cafeteria during lunch and inmates who weren't in attendance were either locked up in their cells or enjoying visits with their family so the two had free reign of the area.

"Was she better than me?" Bonita asked in reference to Claire as she ran her fingers over Izzy's moist lips.

"No, baby," Izzy moaned through closed eyes as she licked Bonita's fingers.

"Then why did you do it? Why did you let her do it, you fuckin' slut?" Bonita asked mockingly as she pushed Izzy back against the bookshelf and knelt before her.

"I thought of you the whole time," Izzy groaned. "It was a fantasy! Just a fantasy, baby!" she panted aloud as Bonita's lips made contact with her clitoris. Several minutes in, she shuddered, her legs trembling and nearly giving out as she slumped up against the bookshelf.

"Don't you ever give my pussy away again," Bonita commanded as she kissed her way up Izzy's body where the two locked lips.

"You got off on my stories with Claire," Izzy laughed as she pressed her head to Bonita's forehead.

"Yeah. The shit was hot," Bonita confessed. "I loved hearing about it. I fingered myself a lot of nights wishing I was there," she added while gently stroking Izzy's hair with a loving gaze in her eyes.

When it got down to it, Bonita cared deeply for Izzy. She'd actually had no intentions on developing feelings for the woman in the beginning. For her, it was just a way to pass time. But the more they got to know one another, a bond of trust had developed. They were criminals first, but the two also had a sordid relationship behind the prison walls. One filled with illicit sex and swirling around violence and neither cared. They had a deep passion for one another and could be honest about any and everything that went on in their lives.

Izzy felt the same way about Bonita. She hid nothing from this incarcerated woman ten years her junior, and would do anything within reason to make her happy. She'd originally felt guilty about partying with Claire and Donovan and had to confess it.

Truth be told, Bonita really didn't care. She knew she was powerless to stop Izzy from being intimate with other people, but she appreciated the woman's openness. Locked up in solitary confinement, Izzy's sexual exploits gave her an attachment to the outside. Business was good, and all she was doing was biding time until her six months in solitary confinement were up.

Now that she was back in the midst of things, and having had her sexual desires quenched, Bonita was ready to get back to business. She was given the full scoop on Sascha Merkendorf, members of The Urbandale Gals, and the murders of Claire and Donovan. "The warden is in our way," she told Izzy as the two began straightening their clothes inside the last aisle of the library.

"That's a given," Izzy remarked while buttoning her shirt. "Question is what are we gonna do? Because she can't continue on as warden. Before long, she'll overtake us here inside the prison."

"Urbandale is her muscle and her connect," Bonita pondered out loud as she and Izzy emerged from the aisle. "If we get rid of Evelyn and her girls on the outside we'll corner the market here inside the prison."

"I would love to kill Evelyn. She hangs in this bar called TUG's over in Urbandale. Those biker chicks are always around her. I would recommend Sascha for the job, but Evelyn would see her coming because she knows she's aligned herself with you and me. And given the conversation we had before I left her office, she'll be on guard for a hit."

"TUG's is a lesbian joint. They have free sex in that place inside this bathroom stall near the back. There's an emergency exit door just outside. That place would be perfect for a hit. We just need someone bold enough to slip inside this place to get next to 'em," Bonita said aloud as she looked to the floor in deep thought.

"You talking about striking Evelyn on her own turf?" Izzy asked in a surprised manner.

"That's exactly what we're gonna do," Bonita replied matter-of-factly. "Keep an eye on the warden, but do nothing. I want you and Sascha out of this deal," she ordered. "You two just hold down Camp A and prevent any drugs from being sold until we get our own product in."

"What are we gonna do about the warden and Urbandale?" Izzy asked.

"Leave them to me," Bonita replied casually. "Take me back to my cell now. I have to write a letter. I'll see you soon, baby. Love you," she ended as she tenderly ran her hand over Izzy's breasts and kissed her goodbye before being escorted back to her cell by Sascha.

CHAPTER EIGHT

THE PACT

"Her name is Evelyn Pulaski," Tanya told Faye as the two sat out under the canopy of Café Du Monde, the city's famed coffee shop located in New Orleans' French Market that dated back to 1862. "Her muscle on the streets is this motorcycle gang by the name of The Urbandale Gals. They hole up inside this bar or whatever called TUG's. Bonita wants us to take them out. We do that, we get control of the drug trade throughout northern Iowa, including the prison."

It was a week after Bonita was released from solitary confinement. New Year's Eve down in New Orleans and across the world. The Saint Louis Cathedral, which lay just to the north, was filled with Catholics looking to receive communion from the bishops on hand. Horse and carriages lumbered up and down busy Decatur Street toting tourists through Jackson Square on this unusually warm December afternoon while mimes with painted bodies stood frozen on milk crates like statues for all to admire under the bright winter's sun. Horns from the famed Steamboat Natchez could be heard woofing to the south, where the Mississippi River lay, as the smell of coffee and chicory and fresh beignets encompassed the entire area surrounding Café Du Monde.

Faye and Tanya sat talking about the letter Tanya had received the day before from Bonita stressing the importance of a job that needed doing back in Des Moines as quickly as possible while three year-old Maggie sat beside Faye savoring the gooey, sugary dough of a fresh beignet. The toddler had four missing teeth and was only able to gum the doughnut, but she was relentless in her endeavors. Tanya and Faye couldn't help but to chuckle over the child's attempt to bite into the beignet as they sat smiling, enjoying a moment of innocence inside their world of violence.

"Sie'll get it, Maggie. Macht weiter so, meine Liebe." (You'll get it, Maggie. Keep trying, my love.) Faye spoke lovingly as she sat beside Maggie stroking the child's thick head of red hair.

Maggie leaned over and extended her hands, presenting Faye with the beignet that was now covered in her saliva. *"Ich kann't Biss! Biss für mich!"* (I can't bite! Bite for me!) she complained.

"Wie das." (Like this.) Faye remarked as she leaned into Maggie, bit into the doughnut with her front teeth, pulled back and began chewing.

Maggie took the sweet dough and held it before her mouth while staring at it; she'd been trying to bite into the sugary treat for minutes on in, but every time she did so, it would just slide over her gums and out of her mouth. Ever determined, the toddler placed the dough back into her mouth and bit down, only to have the beignet slide across her gums and through her lips once more. *"Ich kann't bit!"* (I can't bit it!) she screamed in frustration. She then ripped the beignet apart, shoved a clump of powdered dough into her mouth, and began chewing with her bottom teeth. The three year-old sat chewing like a spring gazelle munching on a bunch of twigs. Her hazel eyes hung low and only the lower portion of her jaw was moving, but she seemed content, finally able to crack open the full flavor of the sweet pastry treat whose complete flavor she'd been trying to decipher for what seemed like an eternity as she wobbled her big head in delight.

Faye and Tanya were reared back in their seats laughing at the toddler. "I can't wait until Helen arrives," Tanya remarked through laughter as she rubbed her swollen belly. "I hope she's as animated as Maggie."

"She's her mother's daughter," Faye declared. "Gayle had an unwitting sense of humor. She was funny even when she wasn't trying to be," she ended somberly.

"You miss Gayle don't you?" Tanya modestly asked.

"I do," Faye admitted as she picked up her ceramic coffee mug and took a sip. "With all that's about to go down? If Gayle were with me? I'd be unstoppable."

"You got us now, Faye." Tanya stated seriously as she rested her elbows on the table and stared her friend in the eyes. "You're still unstoppable, sister. Brenda? Willie? The king Sisters? We're all unstoppable."

"Bonita ist gefragt, haben ein Aufseher getötet." (Bonita is asking to have a warden killed.) Faye remarked lowly. "No one here knows Iowa like I do. We have the names and the locations—it's just a matter of getting there and knowing what we're doing to pull the job off."

"We still have time before the Cincinnati job," Tanya remarked. "That's a month away. By then? Helen will be here and a month or so later, I'll be ready. I'll handle Evelyn. You just focus on the job you and Alfredo have to do up in Cincy."

"We talking at least six weeks," Faye countered. "I don't know if Bonita has that much time on her hands."

"It's gonna be a gamble," Tanya admitted as she broke off a piece of her beignet and dipped it into her coffee. "They gone have to hold on for now. They're tough enough."

"The quicker we get this Cincinnati job done, the quicker we'll be able to set matters straight in Iowa." Faye stated.

"You focus on the task at hand, Faye. When the time is right? We'll deal with the Iowa situation. I'm on it." Tanya let it be known as she slid the coffee soaked beignet into her mouth.

Faye leaned back in her chair and pointed at Tanya while crossing her legs. "A lot is being asked of me on this Cincinnati deal. I'm putting my neck on the line for you, Tanya. Are you willing to do the same for the sake of my sister?"

Tanya thumbed her nose and leaned back in her own chair and crossed her legs while staring into Faye's eyes. "Bonita was my sister long before I ever knew who you were, Faye," she countered. "Her survival means just as much to me as it does to you. We may have different methods of achieving our goals, but the end result is the same, and that's all that matters. I'm trusting that you will go to Ohio and do what needs to be done there. In return, I'm asking that you trust that I will take care of what needs to be done in Iowa on behalf of Bonita."

Faye remained silent as she analyzed the situation before her. Through Tanya, she was able to hide in plain sight. She'd dyed her hair blonde, had gotten a couple of painted on tattoos and had changed her apparel, going from that of an outlaw laced in the latest fashion, to that of a tourist who wore denim, and long sleeve sweaters with Mardi Gras logos on the front. The entire week she'd been in the city, she and Tanya had been perusing the French Quarters with Maggie, often times walking right pass uniformed officers who only smiled and welcomed them to the city.

Potential lay within this young, budding organization in Faye's eyes. If she were to succeed in her latest campaign of violence, the rewards would be boundless. Political power lay in their grasp given all that was at stake, but those were prospects that Faye felt not compelled to share with Tanya, just yet. A run unprecedented lay in the grasp, but it all depended on how things would unfold in Cincinnati, and the outcome concerning Evelyn Pulaski and her cohorts. With those thoughts in mind, Faye reached out and shook Tanya's hand, thereby sealing the deal on what would become the pact of a lifetime.

CHAPTER NINE

THE ASIANS

A week after her discussion with Tanya outside of Café` Du Monde, found Faye Bender cruising through Cincinnati in an area called Over the Rhine with Mouse and Brenda as the sun set over the city. The sleek, black four door '98 olds with tinted windows the two were riding in glided to a halt on the corners of Mulberry and Lang streets. This particular area of west Cincinnati sat tucked in between I-75 to the west, and I-71 to the east. To the south was a heavily-populated area dominated by stories tall brownstones and spacious offices and ware-houses. Mulberry and Lang was to the north of the neighbor-hood nestled amongst a few brownstones with an open field behind the building that gave a clear view of the brownstones on the next block.

Faye eyed the club, which was actually owned by Alfredo, and its surroundings. The building was in a good locale. One would have to travel deep into the Rhine neighborhood to make contact and it was no easy way out if soldiers were set up correctly. They exited the vehicle and walked under the night sky and falling snow. One lone Heineken beer sign dangled from the club's corner and numerous parked cars lined all four blocks at least halfway down the blocks. The light green, two-story building seemed decades old and it had more of an Irish pub appeal rather than being a German-themed bar in Faye's eyes.

"The guys should be here pretty soon," Mouse remarked as he pulled out a set of keys and unlocked the door.

An immediate smell of musk and mildew filled the trio's nostrils upon entering the club. Brenda and Faye followed Mouse inside after he'd unlocked the door. They walked through the circular foyer underneath the low ceiling where Mouse flipped a switch. Low-hanging lights illuminated the club's main floor as covered tables and upturned chairs out in floor area came into view. A long bar counter with a set of double doors resting behind the center of the counter was off to the right, and that was where Mouse headed. He walked behind the bar and got on a phone. "Alfredo got the line up," he re-marked. "I gotta call the Italians and let 'em know I'm ready. You girls take a look around."

"What do you think of this place, Faye?" Brenda asked as the two walked around the open area.

"It's nostalgic. This area is a lot like the French Quarters with the architecture. What's it called?"

"Thirty-Six Hundred Mulberry will be its name," Brenda answered as she walked over to a set of stairs.

"It's an innocuous title," Faye responded as she followed Brenda up the narrow staircase and stepped onto a wooden dance floor bordered by wooden rails with floor to ceiling mirrors all the way around. The heels of her leather boots left subtle echoes inside the large room as she walked around, admiring herself in the numerous mirrors. "It's beautiful," she spoke aloud.

"Yeah. Ya' boy Alfredo want this place to be Helen's when she's old enough. He wanna get her involved in dance or some shit like that in the meantime."

"Is that so?" Faye smiled. "My husband was a good dancer."

"Was he now?" Brenda asked as she walked around the room, checking to make sure the sure the windows were secure. "Do you miss him?"

"Of course I do. I miss all of my family. Not a moment goes by that I don't think about them, Brenda."

"Well, you just might need something to take your mind off the matter for a while," Brenda remarked as she strolled past Faye.

"Like what?"

"Let me show you something in the downtown area. Follow me, chick."

The two headed back downstairs and met up with Mouse. "You gone be okay here, baby? Everything is locked up back upstairs."

"Yeah, I'll be fine," Mouse remarked coolly.

"Cool. Me and Faye headed over to the hotel to kick back."

"I be there after I secure the guns from the LaRoccas," Mouse stated as he kissed Brenda's lips.

****

Brenda and Faye rode into downtown Cincinnati towards the Hilton Cincinnati Netherland Plaza where they rode up to the top floor and entered a suite at the end of the hall. The pad was laid out with a living room and floor model television along with a mini bar and a fascinating view of the Cincinnati skyline. A king-sized bed lay inside a set of french doors and plush carpet ran throughout.

Brenda removed her leather trench coat and clicked on the heat inside the suite before pulling open the mini bar. "Girl, you better make yourself at home," she told Faye after noticing her take a seat at a small desk inside the living room.

Faye had been reserved in her mood the entire trip. She had a lot on her mind and was actually rethinking the move. She'd just come off a murder where she'd killed a sheriff. Bonita was heavy on her mind also. By keeping on the move, she thought she would be able to cope with the stress she was under, but the drive to Cincinnati had given her nothing but time to think about the loss of her husband, son and best friend. "It's hard to make yourself at home when your heart is hurting," she told Brenda.

Brenda walked over to Faye with two drinks in her hand. She set one down before her friend and went over to her leather coat and pulled out a plastic bag of rolled up joints. "What you need is Calgon, girl," she told Faye while smiling down at her. "Come on, let me show you the bathroom. This shit is laid the fuck out!"

"You been here before?" Faye asked as she grabbed her glass and followed Brenda into the master suite.

"Nah. Tanya showed me some pictures and shit. She and Alfredo stayed here a few times when they was buying Thirty-Six Hundred."

The women walked through the large suite and Brenda stepped off into a white, marble-floored room that had a large Jacuzzi situated on the back wall. "Ain't this nice? I need a bath after that long drive, yeh, girl?" Brenda yelled out to Faye as she sat on the edge of the bath and turned on the hot water. After allowing the water warm, she walked out of the bathroom where Faye was sitting on the bed removing her boots. She went and turned on the stereo inside the master suite and began to undress while vibing to Debarge's song *All This Love*.

Faye blushed as she got up from the bed and left the room. Brenda eyed her backside with a sly smile on her face as she continued to disrobe. She lit up one of the joints she'd smuggled on the trip, grabbed her .357 magnum and sashayed over to the bathroom with the gun, drink and an ashtray. The water soothed her brown skin the moment she climbed inside the spa as she removed her paisley rag from beneath her thick afro. "Faye, you wanna order room service? Some steaks and shrimp and shit! And a large ass cake for dessert!" she blurted out after taking a toke off the joint. There was no answer. "Faye!" Brenda called out. The young gangster had grown a little suspect at that moment, so she picked up her pistol, just in case Faye had ulterior motives.

Several seconds later, Faye appeared in the bathroom's threshold. She was laughing to herself as she held onto a menu.

"What's funny?" Brenda asked as she set the joint down and reached over and flipped a switch that fired up the jet streams.

"This reminds me of the time me and Gayle killed this guy named Bunny back in Kansas City the night everything went down with me and Bonita."

"Yeah? I never heard that story. See? I'm bringing back some good memories." Brenda remarked, all-the-while gripping her pistol.

"I don't know about the memories being good," Faye chuckled as she went into the story briefly, giving some of the details that led up to the shooting.

Brenda listened to Faye as she poured Calgon into the bubbling water. Before long, she was covered up to her breasts in a soothing bubble bath. Along the way, she'd come to the realization that she'd misjudged Faye. She'd let her guard down briefly, and for a split second, the rules of the street, which was to trust no one, had kicked in. She continued listening to Faye as she sunk further into the tub.

Faye hadn't missed Brenda's move. The woman didn't have it on her heart or mind to do what she knew a person she viewed as friend was suspecting of her, but she couldn't let what she'd witnessed slide without acknowledging it. She came from behind her back with a .357 magnum of her own and held it at her side. "If this is what I was aiming to do, it would've been done a long time ago, Brenda," she stated matter-of-factly.

"Oh, you saw that," Brenda stated seriously. "Well, you just can't be too sure in this business, Faye. You only get one life to live, and to lose it on some humbug shit would be a waste."

"I have no intentions on going against this outfit. I need you all just as much as you need me and I don't think neither of us is expendable. We all need each other."

"But if ever we didn't need each other?"

"We would part as friends. At least that's how I feel about it." Faye replied as she held onto her pistol.

"No offense." Brenda remarked while clutching her .357.

"None taken. I'll order some food," Faye told Brenda as she opened the menu and walked back into the bedroom to use the phone.

"Get something for Ricky, too! And two bottles of champagne! The good shit! They ain't got none in that bar out there!" Brenda requested loudly.

After ordering the food, Faye disrobed and joined Brenda in the Jacuzzi, sitting opposite her as she set her pistol on the tub's ledge. "They say an hour on the meals," she told Brenda.

"Cool," Brenda responded as she lit up a second joint and tilted her head back. She swallowed a great portion of the smoke and let a thin mist escape her nostrils as she set her .357 magnum on the spa's ledge. "So what else happened the night you and Gayle took a bath together in Saint Louis? Y'all fucked?" she asked Faye.

"We didn't fuck at all ever. Me and Gayle was close, but we were never lesbians. Not that anything is wrong with that, but, it wasn't our thing. What about you?"

"What? Have I ever been with another woman?"

"Yeah," Faye answered as she poured herself another glass of vodka.

"I ain't never lick no pussy and ain't no broad ever licked my crack. Now, me and Mouse get into some freaky shit, but I ain't never been with another woman."

"Makes two of us, sister. Tanya said you and Mouse got the same set up in y'all bedroom. That true?"

"I knew that bitch had a swing set up there!" Brenda laughed as she rose up and kicked her legs inside the tub. She leaned back and raised her hands and said, "But, see? Her and Alfredo be sleeping with them crazy mutherfuckas in the French Quarters! They take people back to they house and fuck 'em to death! Men and women!"

Faye laughed over Brenda's confession as she sipped her vodka. The tension had subsided quickly and the two talked until they heard the door to the suite being opened. Both females grabbed their guns and crept to the edge of the bathroom dripping wet and naked. Brenda peeked out and saw two men walking into the room pushing a silver cart. Mouse was behind them holding onto a leather satchel. "I got it, baby. Y'all ready to eat?" he asked Brenda once he saw his woman's head poking out from the bathroom.

"Nah, we in the tub. Just set up everything." Brenda responded as she eyed Mouse's slender, dark-skinned frame draped in silk and leather.

"Set that over by the desk," Mouse told the men as he set the satchel down beside the sofa in the living room.

"Lucky man," one of the men complimented as he wheeled the cart deeper into the room.

Brenda waited until the men left and she and Faye returned to the Jacuzzi where she relit her joint, and Faye topped her vodka. The two were talking amongst themselves when Mouse appeared in the threshold. Faye had to do a double take when her green eyes fell upon the tall and slender, yet muscular specimen of a man standing before in the complete nude.

Mouse had a head full of braided hair and sported a mouth full of gold teeth at the top and bottom and sported a thin-trimmed beard. His smooth, dark skin had not a flaw and his abs was ripped. Faye eyed the man's package and instantly thought of Bunny and the long rod he sported, according to Bonita. She'd never seen such a large pole in her life.

"Like what you see?" Brenda asked, shaking Faye from her thoughts.

"It, he's nice," Faye replied a little rattled as she poured a shot of vodka and downed it.

"Make some room for me, baby," Mouse requested as he walked into the bathroom while holding onto a corkscrew and two bottles of champagne.

Faye was the one who slid over first inside the Jacuzzi. She may have picked up on Brenda's play with the gun earlier, but the subconscious move she'd just made was all Brenda and Mouse needed to know. In their eyes, she was susceptible.

Mouse said nothing as he eased into the tub and sat beside Faye. "Hold this, baby," he said as he handed her a bottle of champagne. He picked up her empty glass and without being told, Faye topped it off with Dom Perignon and did the same for Brenda before pouring Mouse a glass. Another joint was lit as Stevie Wonder's song *Ribbon In The Sky* came across the stereo.

"So, Faye, how you liking the trip so far?" Mouse asked as he sunk into the tub as the crew entered into light conversation.

****

About an hour later, Mouse eased out of the tub and followed the women into the bedroom. Faye had gotten worked up over the conversations with Mouse and Brenda about their sexual escapades and she was now willing to explore.

Brenda stood beside the bed and nodded to Faye. "Climb in," she spoke softly.

Faye eased into the bed a nervous wreck. She didn't know what had overcome her, but she was too far gone to turn back, even if she wanted to. She lay on her back watching as Mouse lay down beside her on his back. She raised her head slightly to allow his arm under her neck and Brenda slid into the bed and lay opposite her man. The three laid together in silence, enjoying the music through closed eyes as their skin touched one another in intimate manner.

Faye could feel the heat from Mouse's groin area and sense Brenda's hand stroking his pole given the movements of his pelvis. She wanted to, only she wasn't sure of her position.

Smacking sounds told her Brenda and Mouse were kissing. She wanted to join in, but didn't know how, or when it was appropriate for her to do so. When Mouse removed his arm from beneath her neck and turned his back on her, she felt left out completely. She lay on the bed on her back, peeking out the corner of her eye as Mouse climbed atop Brenda. Immediately her brown-skinned legs went into the air. Seconds later, she moaned out, "Ricky, baby," as the two entered into a hard fuck.

Faye was about to climb from the bed until Ricky placed a hand on her right breast and began tweaking her nipple. That simple touch ignited a fire. She grabbed Ricky's hand and began nudging it down to her center; her head tilted back and her mouth dropped open the time Ricky began circling her moist opening with the tip of his finger. Having not engaged in sexual activity for over six months, Faye had to reach down and spread herself to allow Ricky's finger to penetrate her insides. She let out a pleasurable shriek as his extremity pierced her vagina. Ricky's finger went on for what seemed like an eternity.

Faye creamed right away and had no choice but to raise her hips off the bed and began a slow rotation on Ricky's long finger. She raised her hands and ran them over his braids, trying to press her face against his as she imagined herself being fucked by this man who'd mastered the art of seduction. Ricky leaned over and sought out Faye's lips. Needing no instruction, she raised her head and stuck her tongue out. She met Ricky face first where the two engaged in a passionate kiss that sent tremors coursing through her body as she rocked back and forth on his finger that was now so deep in her pussy she could feel the palm of his hand slapping against her clitoris.

Ricky's hand was covering Faye's vagina completely. He was palming her pussy as she held her legs wide, she and Brenda's knees touching on occasion as Ricky long-dicked Brenda while finger-fucking her to orgasm. No longer able to resist, Faye blurted out, "Ricky, make love to me! Make love to me, please!"

"You gone have to ask my ole lady if I can do that," Ricky teased as he slowed his motions inside Brenda and paused his finger strokes inside of Faye while palming her pussy.

"Make love to me, Ricky. Please."

"You heard what he said?" Brenda asked as she lay beneath Ricky. "Ask me can you fuck my man."

Ricky had a grip on Faye's pussy with his finger planted deep inside. It was an erotic torture that left her helpless. And if she had to ask to be made love to, if she needed permission to receive this man's rod, then ask she would. "Can he make love to me?" she asked aloud while gripping Ricky's hand and pressing it deeper into her widespread legs.

"Can he fuck me what? What's my fuckin' name, bitch?" Brenda asked. She grunted when Ricky slammed into her. "Baby!" she hissed.

"Show respect," Ricky told Brenda as he resumed a slow rotation.

"Brenda, I wanna be made love to! I wanna make love!" Faye panted as her paces picked up on Ricky's finger.

"Do it, Ricky!" Brenda groaned as she climaxed beneath her man. She actually got off on Ricky fucking another woman before her eyes.

Ricky was tuned into Faye's request. This woman was asking for more than a fun-filled fuck, which was the reason why he'd told his woman to be respectful. He climbed off of Brenda and nudged Faye's legs. She got the point and rolled over onto her stomach and lay face down on the mattress. She was surprised when Ricky spread her cheeks and planted his tongue on her pussy from behind. "God," she moaned, letting out a deep, guttural sigh as she spread her knees wider and hiked her ass up higher in order to savor the warmth of a man's tongue for the first time in a long time.

Over Faye's pleasure, thoughts of Franklin ran through her mind at that moment, forcing her to place her head into her arms and hide her face in shame as she realized she was now moving on with her sexuality. As much as she loved Franklin, she was a woman in need of affection. She would always love Franklin Patterson, and as odd as it was, for Faye, this was therapy. She hadn't been touched by another in quite some time. Letting go wasn't easy, but it was necessary. "I'm sorry, Franklin," she cried with tears in her eyes as she slammed back against Ricky's probing tongue.

"It's okay," Brenda comforted as she rubbed Faye's back. She, too, now realizing that she and Ricky was dealing with a woman hurt over her past experiences and still in mourning.

Faye rose up at that moment, knocking Brenda's hand free. She had no intentions on engaging in lesbian sex.

Brenda picked up on the vibe right away. "Enjoy yourself," she stated in a caring manner as she leaned over and away from Faye and reached for a half-smoked joint and a lighter.

Ricky sucked and licked and Faye's pussy for what seemed like an eternity as marijuana smoke from Brenda's joint filled the room. She could no longer moan nor groan as she rested on her elbows. All she could do was lay face down and enjoy the tongue flicking over her opening and the occasional suck of her clitoris as sweat beaded up on her white skin as she became a slave to lust. Tired of the tongue, Faye pulled away from Ricky and rolled over onto her back and spread her legs wide.

The look in this woman's eyes told a story for Ricky. She was emotionally pained, but also in need of sexual fulfillment. She was offering herself to him in any way he wanted, so long as she was made whole, if only for a fleeting moment in time. The finger and tongue was nice, but this woman needed to be taken, he understood. With tender care, he leaned into Faye and eased the head of his shaft into her opening.

"Franklin," Faye called out as she raised her hips and implanted herself on Ricky's pole. Her arms instinctively went around his back and she kissed him deeply. "Baby," she moaned in between the tongue lashings.

Whatever Faye was imagining, it set right with Ricky. He knew he was taking Faye to wherever it was she wanted to go with his skills. Love was what the two made, per Faye's request. The kisses were tender and the strokes were gentle. There was a lot of facing rubbing and hands running over flesh as the two meshed their bodies together.

"No babies," Faye moaned as she tilted her head upwards and kissed Ricky deeply. "No babies. I'm about to come! Ricky!" she screamed aloud in sheer ecstacy. "Ricky, I'm coming!" she declared as her body stiffened and sunk deeper into the mattress. "Jesus!"

Ricky was on the verge of exploding inside of Faye, but he, too, knew better. He gripped her tightly and drove deep inside and rotated his hips inside her gaped legs as her pussy quivered on his rock hard dick. She'd given herself completely.

"You're coming?" Faye asked in a raspy voice. "I want you to come on me, baby!"

Those words drove Ricky over the edge. He picked up his pace and gripped Faye's hips tighter. When his balls tightened, he pulled out, his pole covered in Faye's cream. It took one touch from Faye for Ricky to erupt. She rose to her knees and kissed him deeply as his semen shot up on her stomach and over her stroking hands. Spent, Faye fell back onto the bed gasping for air. "Thank you, you two," she panted. "That was, that was incredible."

"Don't say I ain't never do something for your ass," Brenda quipped as she passed the joint to Ricky.

Faye could only laugh as she lay on her back naked. The three were splayed out over the large mattress, body parts intertwined and what not as they relished in the afterglow. "And something you did," Faye remarked while still breathing heavy. "I really need that. But that was pleasure, now it's time for business. What's the deal on our marks?" she asked the two.

"We still got dinner in there, yeh?" Brenda remarked. "We can talk about that while we eat after we wash up."

The trio went on take another bath and enjoyed steak dinners with grilled shrimp while discussing the upcoming job. Afterwards, they convened to the bedroom where another round of sex had taken place, this time, both women taking turns riding Mouse to satisfaction. Shortly thereafter, they'd all drifted off into a deep slumber with thoughts of their upcoming job now one their minds.

CHAPTER TEN

INTERNATIONAL SMUGGLERS

Two days after Faye and company's arrival to Cincinnati found Alfredo Lowes fresh off a flight from Israel that had landed in Venezuela. He made his way through the crowded Caracas Airport, located in the state of Miranda in the country of Venezuela.

Caracas is the capital city of Venezuela located near the Caribbean Sea. With a population of well over two million, it is one of the largest cities in the country with an economy thriving off of tourism and shipping. The Port of Caracas was a massive container terminal, a hub for ships coming in from the Middle East and bound for ports in America, including the Port of New Orleans.

Alfredo hopped a taxi over to a local Hilton Hotel amid a bustling tourist section in downtown Caracas and entered the building. He rode up to the fifteenth floor and eyed three men of obvious Jewish descent with their black beards and kippas. The men were all decked out in black suits and dark shades standing in front of a door to his right. They waved him over and patted him down before allowing him to enter the room before closing the door and returning to their proper stance.

Several seconds later, a man emerged from a side door inside the extravagant suite. "Alfredo Lowes," he remarked in a heavy Middle Eastern accent. "Glad you could make it on such short notice, my friend. My father and I have been expecting you," he remarked as he stepped aside to let Alfredo further into the suite.

The man standing before Alfredo in his $2,200 dollar, charcoal-colored silk suit and white ostrich skin shoes was named Sanjar Darvish Junior, better known as Sanjar. He was a clean-shaven bronze-skinned man of thirty-three. He had a head of thick, black hair, and he often sported a pair of clear, studious-looking eyeglasses like the ones he wore on this night.

"Where's your father, Sanjar?"

"Ahh, yes!" Sanjar stated as his mood shifted to that of business. "Father? Our guest has arrived!" he called out.

A minute or so later, Sanjar's father, fifty-eight year-old Sanjar Darvish Senior, walked out into the open area of the suite. Sanjar Senior, who was better known as 'Old Man', was a slender, pepper-haired man with a close-shaven grey beard. He was a man of distinction and prominent on the D.C political scene.

Operating alongside his son, Old Man imported heroin grown in Afghanistan that was smuggled into the United Sates through Venezuela on leased Israeli freighters. The Darvish men, at their core, were internationally-connected political figures whose tentacles touched several continents, including South America, Europe and Asia.

Fluent in Arabic, Spanish, German and Chinese, these two men were responsible for a third of the heroin entering into the United States through the ports of New York. They'd both been educated in America, earning degrees in Political Science from Harvard and the University of Cincinnati respectively. They were worth millions of dollars in the upper eight figure range. They'd used their ill-gotten wealth to prop up several Senators and President Reagan himself during the 1980 election campaign. For their endeavors, Sanjar Senior was given a position inside the White House by being appointed ambassador to Venezuela.

In American government eyes, the Ambassador to Venezuela was a meaningless position as the country's biggest political gripe was high tariffs on agricultural exports, but for Sanjar Senior, it was the perfect job and front. He and his son could travel back and forth to Venezuela under the guise of conducting diplomatic affairs, but in all actuality, the two men oversaw one of the largest heroin rings in the United States and had direct ties to Pablo Escobar himself.

"Sorry to keep you all waiting," Sanjar Senior remarked as he entered the room with a manila folder tucked under his arm. "Come. Sit," he motioned towards the sofas inside the suite that overlooked downtown Caracas.

After everyone had settled in, Old Man opened the folder and pulled out several sheets of paper. "How are things going with the Asians in Ohio, Alfredo?"

"Family's still on it, but it won't be long. A couple of weeks at the latest."

"Good. They were bringing their heroin in through New York, you know? But given the indictment of the bosses of the five families in New York by Rudy Giuliani and the moratorium the underbosses of the five families has instituted on all illegal drug shipments? It is urgent that we find a new port of entry."

"I can help you out with that, Old Man," Alfredo remarked as Sanjar Junior set a twelve ounce bottle of beer before him. "Have you gone over my proposal for the new shipping lane?"

"I have," Sanjar Senior remarked as he leaned forward and handed Alfredo the folder he carried into the room.

Alfredo opened the folder and quickly read over the numbers. He looked at the Darvish men with a cold stare. "Are you guys serious?" he asked disdainfully. "I give you guys a route that leads directly to the heart of heroin country and you go up on the prices per kilogram?"

"It is a much shorter distance to New Orleans than it is New York," Old Man replied casually.

"But the product is now going to my home city. The container will bear my name on the manifest because we have no other businesses set up. Until we do, my ass is on the line." Alfredo retorted as he twisted the top off the beverage.

"I told you a long time ago to set up more than just night clubs so you can create a manifest to said businesses. You ignored me and told me it wasn't necessary. Now it is necessary and you have no business."

"No one could've foreseen a federal investigation of this magnitude, Sanjar. I'm keeping your name out of the entire deal, my family is overseeing a hit on major players in the business and we get rewarded by being taxed on the product? If you don't go down on the price, your ship won't dock—not in New Orleans at least."

"If the ship doesn't dock, the Medellin cartel will want answers. You can't hold up an entire freighter over one container. It will lead to a war here in Venezuela. Our lives will be at risk."

"You should've thought of that before you tried to strong arm cash from my family's coffers," Alfredo remarked before taking a swig of the beer. "Now," he added as he handed the folder back to Sanjar Senior. "Let's talk real numbers."

Sanjar Senior scooted to the edge of the couch and stared Alfredo in the eyes. "Without me and my son it would be impossible for you to expand outwards in the opium business, Mister Lowes," he declared. "And it would not be wise to protest my objections given my position."

"You're objections are unsubstantiated, man." Alfredo remarked casually. "And your position is meaningless to me unless you yourself decide to pick up a gun and get your hands bloody or deliver a package on the streets. If you're not going to reconsider your asking price, then we can end the deal here and now. I'll call my people and pull them out of Cincinnati."

"Wait a minute," Sanjar Junior protested. "Dad? Calm down. You two debate, but Alfredo is making the most sense. There's no need to get greedy. And pissing off the Medellin cartel is not what we want."

Alfredo leaned back in his chair and crossed his legs while smiling at Sanjar Senior. The man was a master negotiator and fearless in his speech. He knew the moment Sanjar Senior went up on the price, that if he were to refuse shipment, both men would have to answer to Pablo Escaobar something neither wanted given the man's violent reputation. "Listen to your son," he told Sanjar Senior.

Sanjar Senior had never figured Alfredo to be so astute in his dealings. He'd viewed him as that of a pusher and nothing more. Alfredo, however, understood the chain of command. The Darvish men had power in Venezuela and Israel primarily, but their influence had little impact on the decisions made by the Medellin cartel, which owned the freighters they were using to ship drugs and merchandise. They'd gotten into bed with the wrong organization and Alfredo knew it all-too-well, he now realized. "Excuse us," he told Alfredo as he beckoned his son towards one of the bedrooms inside the suite.

Alfredo remained out in the open area. He stood up and walked around the room while running his hands over his head before resting them on a stand as he stared at his image reflecting back in a mirror. The John Lennon look-alike stared at himself, wondering if he was going to make it out this meeting alive as he knew he'd practically told the Darvish men that he cared less if they were to fall out of favor with Pablo. Three men he knew to be armed were outside the room and there was no telling if Sanjar Junior and Old Man had guns themselves.

Despite the anxiety, Alfredo couldn't walk out of the room. The deal he needed to make would be a windfall for the crew. Their biggest deal to date. And they would be the ones in control of distribution. The price Old Man was asking was beyond reason, but given Sanjar Junior's protest, he was somewhat certain a deal could be worked out. After a lengthy wait, Sanjar Junior walked out of the room and pulled the door shut.

"Once you get the marks removed, the cost per kilogram will go down twenty percent I can assure you. The wholesale cost will be thirty-two thousand versus the forty my father was asking, and the Rhine area in Cincinnati will be yours to do with as you please." Sanjar Junior remarked as he extended his hand towards Alfredo.

"Sounds fair," Alfredo remarked while shaking Sanjar Junior's hand.

"It wasn't easy convincing my father, but he wants no problems with the Medellin cartel. Good angle," Sanjar complimented.

"Thank you, sir. Now, if you don't mind? I will excuse myself and get to work on the docks back home."

"Notify me when the job is done and you're all set up," Sanjar Junior stated as he extended his hands towards the door, allowing Alfredo to exit.

CHAPTER ELEVEN

LOW HANGING FRUIT

Forty-nine-year-old Kazuki Moto was fresh off a flight from Tokyo, Japan, three days after the Venezuela meeting. The 5'5" one hundred and forty pound Japanese man walked into customs inside Cincinnati/Northern Kentucky International Airport and threw the black satchel he'd toted off the 747 onto a table and removed a wallet from his silk trousers before spreading his arms in preparation to be searched.

"No need for a pat down or baggage search," a security guard stated as he slid Kazuki's satchel over to his side of the table.

"I requested a limousine upon my flight's arrival. Has it arrived?" Kazuki asked in a casual manner while combing out his silky black head of hair.

"It has, sir. And your wife is waiting as well," a second security guard answered while handing Kazuki back his wallet.

"Efficiency is the hallmark of good business." Kazuki smiled as he handed each of the guards $1,000 dollars in cash, scooped up his satchel and walked out of customs.

Meanwhile, outside the airport's main entrance, forty-eight year-old Cho Moto sat in the back seat of a stretched Cadillac limousine awaiting her husband's arrival while reading a letter from her daughter, who was away at a private academy. *"I was so glad you and father visited for the Christmas and New Year holiday, mommy,"* the letter read. *"I have a debate scheduled for later this month and the administrators have allowed me a furlough for next week! I'll need you and father's help with this task. If I win, I will be in the running for student of the year! I'll call with the details once I know the exact time of my train's departure."*

Cho folded the letter, ever-so-proud of her fifteen year-old daughter, just as her husband tapped on the tinted window of the limousine.

The chauffer unlocked the door and Kazuki climbed into the backseat beside his wife and kissed her lips. "How'd everything go?" Cho asked while raising the partition.

"As expected. The guys were cool and calm back in customs," Kazuki stated. "Being an international businessman has its privileges," he added as he unzipped the satchel and pulled out a kilogram of heroin. "The authorities wouldn't dare suspect the owner of a string of camera shops to be transporting drugs into the country."

"So, you're saying—"

"That our temporary pipeline has been established for the foreseeable future." Kazuki stated, finishing his wife's remarks.

"Our daughter has written a letter," Cho stated as the limousine left the airport terminal. "She's wanting to visit next week."

"Now isn't a good time. Can you delay it?" Kazuki asked as he crossed his legs and looked over to Cho.

"We've been here in Cincinnati since last summer establishing business and she hasn't come. A weekend wouldn't be detrimental to our affairs. She's dying to see the bedroom I keep writing her about, plus she's seen the pictures, love. And I miss her," Cho pouted as she rubbed her husband's thigh.

Kazuki smiled and removed his wife's hand from his thigh. "I miss her, too. Any other time I would welcome your touch and accept your proposal, Cho—but it is a dangerous time now and I don't think the move would be a good one."

Cho's slender eyes grew downtrodden as she gazed out into the evening night as a light snow fell. "It was just a simple weekend, Kazuki. Can we set business aside for forty-eight hours for our daughter's sake?" she complained.

"I've just flown into this country with five kilograms of heroin, Cho. My family back home has expectations that they want met in a timely fashion, and you pick now to invite our child home for a weekend visit?"

"I didn't pick the time, Kazuki. She chose it." Cho retorted. "The princess has requested to see her king and queen. Are you going to deny her presence?"

Kazuki's resolve melted away within seconds. His firstborn was his very existence—the first to make her way to America and benefit from the country's educational system. Power and prestige could best describe Kazuki and Cho Moto. The family's position inside of Washington gave them a measure of security, but their confidence was unwittingly placing them on dangerous ground, ground that would unwittingly sink beneath their feet in the blink of an eye.

****

"Y'all saw that, huh?" Mouse asked as he, Brenda and Faye rode inside their Ninety-eight Oldsmobile trailing Kazuki and Cho with Brenda behind the wheel.

"Alfredo and Tanya were on point with their information. How you wanna take 'em down?" Faye asked from the back seat.

"Let's follow 'em and see where they go from here." Brenda remarked as she steered the car.

The Moto family traveled over into a part of Cincinnati called Indian Hill. Faye recognized the area right away as she'd dealt with a couple of heroin dealers back when she and

Gayle were moving weight down from Pittsburgh. "This here is a million dollar neighborhood," she told Brenda and Mouse. "These people working with serious money to be living out this way."

"That I know," Mouse remarked as Brenda continued up the street and rode by the block where the Moto family resided. "I bet they have an alarm system. We gone have ta' crack the code."

"You disable the alarm it may go off anyway if you cut the wire."

"You know a better way, Faye?" Brenda asked.

"Fancy me this, y'all two." Faye answered as she looked over the back seat and eyed the home fading off into the distance.

"I'm fancying," Brenda chuckled as she wheeled the car out of the neighborhood.

Faye shared her thoughts on the job with Brenda and Mouse and the two couldn't help but to look over in her direction. "Well," Brenda remarked while nodding her head in approval. "Let's take a trip downtown."

"Just to let you know? I would've come up with that same plan eventually." Mouse chimed in.

"Bullshit!" Faye and Brenda remarked in unison as they laughed lightly.

****

"Everything is going fine here in Ohio," Kazuki Moto stated over the phone as he sat inside his office on the second floor of his luxurious two story condo, two days after his return to Cincinnati. "We have the Kodak shop opening up next week and the product is moving efficiently."

"What about things here in Pennsylvania," the voice on the other end of the phone asked with a hint of reservation.

"The heat coming down on the five families from Rudy Giuliani is making things in Philadelphia a little uneasy as you know," Kazuki responded. "For now, it is safer to move inland for the time being. My contacts in Philadelphia are telling me that the Philly mob is in an upheaval over the events in New York and are the verge of a war."

"Which would be beneficial for us if we were to continue operating here on the east coast," the person on the opposite end of the phone call interjected. "I have people on the streets here in Philadelphia that are tellin' me there's a drought setting in. We'd be foolish not to intervene."

"I understand your ambitions," Kazuki reasoned. "But trust me, my contacts in Philadelphia know far better than your 'street contacts' in Philadelphia. Any ship, train and truck entering the city of Brotherly Love will be subject to search without warrant at any given port of entry for the foreseeable future. Informants are everywhere. It is a risk you and I could neither afford."

"Fear has no place inside this business, Mister Moto."

"Neither does imprudent behavior." Kazuki countered.

"I know nothing about the city you're setting up in, Mister Moto. I have no contacts or resources there. Until I can establish a ground crew, I advise against this move in Ohio."

"We've already established a pipeline here in the city," Kazuki declared. "The mandate stands for now," he ended before hanging up the phone on his associate and returning the reading of his blueprints on his upcoming Kodak store in downtown Cincinnati.

Meanwhile, on the first floor of the pristine condo, Cho Moto sat inside the living room filling out the final papers needed to have her two sons, elven year-old Arata Moto and his younger brother, Raiden, brought to the U.S. on visas to enroll them into Thorton Academy, a boarding school located on the coast of Maine.

From their inception, the Moto Family was survivors of the aftermath of World War II. Their hometown of Hiroshima had been all but destroyed when an atom bomb was dropped onto their city by the United States in August of 1945. Eighty-thousand people in the city of three hundred and forty thousand people were killed instantly, and the total by year's end due to radiation was an estimated one hundred and sixty-six thousand, nearly half the city's population.

Kazuki and Cho were only two years old at the time of the destruction. Miraculously, they, along with their respective parents had survived the horror. The two met in their third year of elementary school in the city of Yokohama. Being from the same home city, and having parents both working for Kodak Films, Kazuki and Cho became best friends and lovers moving into their teenage years. Kazuki was the first to make the trip abroad. His parents had sent him to America upon his graduation from high school after he'd been accepted into Stanford University.

Cho soon followed after her application to Pepperdine University was accepted and she'd been given a full scholarship. Whereas the Moto family had power and prestige back in Yokohama, Cho's family wasn't as fortunate. Everything Cho had obtained in life, she'd had to earn. Hers was a struggle down in Malibu, California where her institute of higher learning was located. She worked as a stagehand by day and cleaned high rises in Los Angeles at night. She had a hard time learning the English language and had no friends in this foreign land. The college's setting beside the Pacific Ocean and the spectacular weather did nothing to enhance her drab psyche and she missed, Kazuki, her one true love, who was attending college just over four hundred miles to the north in the city of Stanford, California.

When Kazuki learned of Cho's plight, he persuaded his mother and father to pay the remaining tuition needed in order to have her join him up at Stanford. Cho was beyond excited to be reunited with her lover, but it didn't take long for her to realize that the Moto family wasn't the upstanding family they portrayed themselves to be back in Yokohama.

Kazuki and his techy colleagues did more than just come up with new and innovative ways to process film; they often sat around smoking marijuana and snorting fine white powder. Cho had also witnessed what she knew to be drug transactions unfolding inside Kazuki's dorm room on several occasions. When she'd confronted her lover and expressed her concern, Kazuki assured Cho that what was going on was 'the American way of doing things'. It was how one propelled themselves to wealth in the United States was what she was told.

Cho hinged her life on Kazuki's words, and all seemed to be going along well the two years the two had spent up to Stanford University. Upon graduating with a degree in Film and Media Studies and Architectural Design respectively in the year of 1967, Kazuki and Cho sought to build their own wealth. They moved to Rochester, New York shortly after graduating from Stanford University after Kazuki had obtained a job inside the engineering department of Kodak Film. Two years later, in the year of 1969, Kazuki and Cho gave birth to a daughter. In the year of 1972, Cho gave birth to a son whom she and Kazuki had named Arata, and in 1974, Cho gave birth to a son named Raiden, which was the last of their three off-spring.

With their family intact, and having amassed a certain amount of wealth that afforded them trips abroad and a mansion back in Yokohama for their family, Kazuki and Cho had made an investment into Kodak that had made them rich beyond compare. Kodak's decision to open numerous film development stores throughout the United States had proved to be a shrewd business investment for the Moto family. They'd opened several stores in New York and Philadelphia and now had one on the horizon in Cincinnati. Kodak was importing material from their native Japan and it didn't take long for Kazuki to reconnect with his old contacts from Stanford University. Under the guise of importing materials needed to sustain his Kodak franchise, Kazuki soon began funneling heroin inside his container shipments. Several years later, he'd become one of the most powerful heroin dealers on the east coast.

Cho knew all that her husband was involved in; she sincerely believed that what she and Kazuki were doing was no different from any other American family of wealth and prestige. Having kids that were attending the best of schools in America and maintaining million dollar homes in several cities around the world was a way of life in her eyes, but little did she know, she and her beloved husband were involved in a business that would inevitably cost them their lives.

While filling out papers to have her sons join her and Kazuki in America, Cho heard the chiming of the condo's doorbell. She got up and walked through the pristine home and answered only to see a Caucasian woman dressed in a light blue denim uniform with a white mid-length wool coat and a light blue skull cap. A black man was standing beside her dressed in the same fashion wearing a pair of dark sunshades.

"Good afternoon, ma'am," the woman spoke as she looked down at a clipboard she was carrying and made a few scribbles. "We're from Cox Cable and we're walking the neighborhood today offering free one year subscriptions to HBO and Cinemax with free installation. We also have an ongoing offer for—"

"I'm not interested." Cho interjected as she moved to close the door.

"I think you are," Faye quickly retorted as she placed the toe of her boot inside the threshold.

Cho was caught off guard by the woman's actions, and she never noticed the man pulling a revolver from his jacket. Only when the gun's muzzle was placed to her temple did she realize that these were no cable specialists. She was forced back into the home by the male gunman, unable to scream as she was frozen with fear.

"Take care of her," Mouse whispered as he eased through the foyer and stepped out into the vast living room to begin searching for Kazuki.

Faye forced Cho into a closet inside the foyer while aiming a gun at her stomach. The woman screamed and threw several fur coats into her face, catching her off guard. She then lunged out at her attacker, clawing at her face and neck.

"Everything okay down there, Cho?" Kazuki asked aloud from his office upon hearing his wife scream briefly.

Mouse, meanwhile, was creeping through the home's extravagant first floor when he heard Kazuki's voice call out from upstairs. He was unaware of Faye's conundrum as he made his way over to the home's staircase and crept along the wall while easing up the white marble stairs with his muzzled gun aimed forward.

At the same time, Kazuki had jumped up from his desk and started for his office door. "Cho?" he called out as he knelt down briefly and reached under his desk.

The time Mouse reached the top of the stairs, he'd heard Kazuki's voice once more coming from a room down the hall to his left. He stepped back behind the wooden partition and crouched low just before the door on his right opened. From his position, he was able to see the wing-tipped shoes of his mark as he stepped out into the hallway.

Kazuki started to call out for Cho again, but the dead silence in the home unnerved him all-of-a-sudden. He looked down the hall at the staircase and aimed the .38 revolver he was clutching towards the corner near the staircase. "Cho?" he called out in a near whisper as he crept out into the hallway.

Sweat began forming on Mouse's temple at that moment. He could sense Kazuki nearing. Any sudden movement would alert the man to his presence if he were to retreat. With snake-like precision, he crept out from behind the corner of the staircase and squeezed the trigger on his muzzled Uzi.

Kazuki was ready. He opened fire on his attacker the time he emerged from behind the wall. His aim was off, however; bullets from his gun crashed into the wall above his attacker's back as the two exchanged gunfire. Over the rapid fire of the semiautomatic firing at him, Kazuki eased into a partition out in the hall as bullets ricocheted off the marble pillar he was now hiding behind as he reloaded.

Mouse had fired off numerous rounds, all of the bullets missing his target. He was preparing to reload the Uzi, but a quick burst of bullets froze him in his tracks.

"Who sent you?" Kazuki asked as he neared the unknown assailant.

Meanwhile, back downstairs, Faye and Cho were battling inside the walk-in closet.

Cho had her hands on her attacker's wrists and the gun was aimed to the floor. Faye was trying to prevent the woman from firing the weapon by covering the hammer, but the gun went off anyway.

"Oh my God!" Faye shrieked through a deep, guttural groan as she collapsed to the floor. The closet walls began spinning as she lay on her back looking up at Cho. She could feel her blood streaming down her leg as she looked up at the nose of the gun now aimed at her face.

Hot lead has a way of making even those who ride bareback atop the horse of death alongside the devil himself call out to the Almighty when struck, and Faye Bender had become living testimony. She shielded her face, preparing to check out of the game over a job foiled as a thundering gunshot vibrated the walls of the closet. Still alive, Faye looked up only to see Cho staring at her through wide eyes as she held onto the gun. The left side of her face was torn and her left eye was left dangling as she fell over to the wall with blood matting her long, black hair.

Back on the second floor of the mansion, Mouse was on bended knee looking up at Kazuki as he stood over him with the gun aimed at his face. "I asked who sent you." Kazuki stated once more as stood over his home's invader.

"The U.S. government," Mouse laughed as he looked up into Kazuki's eyes.

Kazuki frowned and squeezed the trigger. When the gun didn't fire, he pulled it back and looked at its chamber perplexed. Mouse wasted no time. He let go of his gun and lunged out Kazuki's legs, tackling the man as the two entered into an all-out fist fight of survival. Blows from the gun Kazuki was holding landed upon Mouse's skull, but he was able to sustain the pain as he clawed his way up the man's legs and began landing punches of his own before he knocked Kazuki down.

The men rolled around on the floor for several seconds trying to gain the advantage. Kazuki went for another swing with his jammed pistol, but Mouse had blocked it with his forearm. He snatched the smaller Japanese up from the floor and flung him up against the wall and began landing punches to his stomach and face. When Kazuki leaned forward, he was met with a knee to the chin. His tongue had been captured in between his teeth and a small bit of flesh was spat from his mouth as he shrieked out in agony. Mouse then shoved Kazuki back towards the staircase at that moment. He watched as the Asian flailed about and fell onto his back landing just before the staircase.

"Get your bitch ass the fuck up!" Mouse scoffed as he walked over and kicked Kazuki in the groin.

Kazuki clutched his privates and rolled over onto his side. "We have money!" he pleaded.

"We ain't here for no money, brer," Mouse retorted before kicking Kazuki hard in the face with his steel toe boots, thereby loosening his mark's teeth and splitting his lips in several places. He then pounced on the lighter man and pulled him back up to his feet and turned him around to face the railing on the second floor balcony.

Back downstairs inside the walk-in closet, Brenda was now standing over a wounded Cho. Although taking a shot to the head from a .357 magnum, the woman was still struggling to live. "You good?" Brenda asked Faye as she reached out a helping hand.

"Yeah. She got me in the knee," Faye grimaced as she rose up on her feet, careful not to place pressure on her wounded right leg.

Brenda looked down at Cho, who was choking on her own blood as she lay against the wall. She fired two rounds into woman's face before wrapping Faye's arm around her neck and escorting her out of the closet. The two stepped out into the home's open area in time to see a man in a white suit falling through the air, his arms and legs flapping wildly as he slammed down onto the marble floor from the second level of the home. Both women made eye contact with Mouse just as he appeared on the balcony. "Faye, you been hit?" he asked casually while peering over the balcony.

"It went through and through. I'll be all right so long as I keep pressure off it." Faye spoke through her pain.

"Clean yourself up. Take the towels with you and wipe down everything you touch with bleach. I'll do a quick search," Mouse stated through heavy gasps before straightening his sunshades and disappearing back into the interior of the home's second floor.

Satisfied that the home was void of any other living occupants, Mouse went and turned the AC unit on and turned the thermostat down as far as it could go. He headed down to the first floor and entered the living room where he doused the log fire Cho had going and turned on the first floor AC unit. Once Faye had cleaned herself and Brenda had cleaned up the evidence, the three left the Moto home and climbed back into the Oldsmobile and left Indian Hills and quickly vacated the city of Cincinnati like that of ghosts who'd blown in with the wind and had vanished into thin air.

CHAPTER TWELVE

THE STUDENT

Fifteen year-old Tammy Moto had been calling her parents the whole train ride home from Linden Hall, her boarding school in Lititz, Pennsylvania that was costing her parents $49,500 dollars a year. Each town the train had stopped in, she was on the payphone dialing her parents' number, but to no avail. Her last call was from Columbus, Ohio. She boarded the train wondering where her parents were while sipping a final of round of tea.

When the train arrived into Cincinnati, Tammy grabbed the handbag she'd brought with her and exited. She walked through the station searching for her parents, believing they'd gotten the letter she'd written three days earlier announcing her arrival and they were merely waiting her return. Tammy walked the entire Amtrak station in search of her parents. *"Maybe they had a meeting,"* she thought to herself as she made her way to the taxi stand and gave the address to Indian Hill.

Tammy paid the fare and climbed from the car. As the cab pulled off from the home, she noticed her parents' cars in the driveway. Both cars were completely covered in snow and the driveway hadn't been shoveled. The sidewalk leading up to the home hadn't been cleared either, she noticed. Puzzled, the short and petite black-haired Japanese teen slushed her way through the snow covering the sidewalk leading up to the home and unlocked the door using a key Cho had mailed her when the family first brought the home.

It was all of twenty-six degrees this early morning down in Cincinnati, but the moment the door opened, Tammy was hit with a wave of cold air rushing out from the home. "Mother? Father?" she called out as she walked into the home and closed the door behind her. "Mother! Father!" she called out again as she set her bag down. "The least you could've done was meet me at the train station this morning! And why is it so cold here when it's freezing outside!"

Getting no response, Tammy sulked and stomped into the home, walking past the walk-in closet's slightly ajar door and emerging out into the living room. "Does either of you two even care that your daughter whom you haven't seen in over seven months has returned and is..."

Tammy's rant was silenced when she spotted her father laying on the mansion's marble floor in the center of the living room just below the second floor balcony. The fifteen year-old's lower jaw dropped and her knees nearly gave out when she saw her father laying face up with his eyes and mouth wide open with his body bent in ways that defied human capability. Kazuki's left arm was behind his head and his left leg was bent like that of a contortionist, the heel of his foot resting underneath his left shoulder blade. Tammy looked up towards the second floor balcony and her slender, brown eyes slowly followed the path she believed her father had traveled to his obvious death.

Frightened, the fifteen year-old screamed aloud and ran back towards the home front door while calling for her mother. Only then did she see the pair of legs poking out from the walk-in closet inside the foyer. Tammy recognized her mother's diamond-studded heels right away and immediately collapsed to the ground. "Who's here?" she whispered as her eyes scanned the first floor. "Momma?" she called out as she crawled over to the closet door and nudged it open with the heel of her orange leather boot while resting back on her matching gloved hands.

The door opened with the gentleness of a butterfly landing on a rose petal, only to reveal what would become the most horrifying image a child could ever encounter. Tammy's mother lay on her side. Her eyes were bulging from her head, and blood that had turned into icicles streamed down from their corners; frozen foams of blood was lodged in Cho's mouth and a yellow and white substance coated her top lips.

Frightened out of her mind, Tammy scurried over to an antique phone situated on an ivory nightstand. She'd pulled the table down while grabbing the phone before dialing the first number that'd come to mind, a number her parents had always instilled in her to call if ever trouble arrived.

****

"Mister Moto," the voice on the other end of the phone responded coolly upon answering the call. "I hope this call is in reference to your reconsidering the market you're establishing in Cincinnati?"

"My mother and father are dead!" Tammy cried. "You have to help me!"

"Tammy?" the voice on the other end of the phone questioned.

"This is Tammy Moto. My, my parents always said to talk to you if ever they got in trouble. I was away and came home and...they've been killed!"

"Are you alone? Are you in any danger?"

"I screamed—I don't think nobody is here. It's cold. This didn't just happen," Tammy cried lowly as her eyes continued scanning the first floor. "I haven't been upstairs."

"If anybody else was in the house, you'd be dead already. Did you call the police yet?" the voice on the other end of the phone quickly answered.

"No," Tammy spoke through tears as she eyed her mother's lifeless legs.

"Well, don't you dare. I'm eight hours away. I want you to find a safe place to hide and wait until I get there. Fill a jug with water and grab whatever you can to put in your stomach and hide until I get there and utter the words Linden Hall after ringing the doorbell. Do it now!"

"Okay," Tammy replied through streaming tears before hanging up the phone.

CHAPTER THIRTEEN

THE TEACHER

"Sometimes I wonder will I figure something out...will I find a reason good enough to live...'cause, Lord if it don't dawn on me pretty soon...I think something's gonna give...yeah, and it might be me...yeah it just me be me, yeah..."

The bluesy sounds of Lynrd Skyrd's song *One In the Sun* jumped from the interior of an immaculate 1964 red Mustang as it cruised into the east side of Cincinnati and took the exit off of I-70 that led to Indian Hills. The person Tammy had talked to just over eight hours earlier arrived at the address Kazuki had given her and climbed from her father's Mustang and eyed the scene. The snow-covered driveway and cars told a story, one that led her to surmise that Kazuki and Cho hadn't left the home in days. A single trail of footprints in the snow leading up to the home revealed the path Tammy had taken that led to discovery of her deceased counterparts. After a quick assessment of the scene outside of the home, Tammy's tutor walked up the sidewalk and rung the doorbell.

Tammy had never moved from her spot in the foyer. She'd never bother gathering water or food as she was too terrified to move. The doorbell's chime shook her from her morbid trance and she scooted across the floor inside the foyer. "Yes?" she asked meekly.

"Linden Hall," the voice outside the door called out while tightening the belt on her cashmere trench coat.

Tammy crawled and opened the door and fell back, her legs tucked beneath her body as she pointed to her murdered mother. "Who would want to kill my parents, Lisa?" she cried aloud.

Lisa Vanguard walked over and pulled the closet door open and eyed a dead Cho Moto. She remained silent as her eyes peered out into the open area of the living room. From her position, she could see the top portion of Kazuki's twisted body laying on the floor. Her head tilted upwards towards the balcony and she'd quickly surmised that the man had been thrown to his death from the second floor of the home.

"I have an idea who's behind this, Tammy," Lisa remarked casually as she walked out into the living room area and placed her hands on her hips. "Have you been upstairs?" she asked while looking back at Tammy.

The teen shook her head to say no and that prompted Lisa to begin doing a search of her own. She walked over to a desk that had a chair removed from its center and eyed the paperwork. She saw Cho's signature on a couple of the papers and the names Arata and Raiden. Lisa knew from past conversations with Cho that the woman was planning on having her two sons sent over to America. It was going to be a surprise for the brothers and Tammy as well. The siblings hadn't seen one another in nearly three years and it was to be a summer surprise. With Cho and Kazuki dead, Lisa knew Tammy would be sent back to Japan and placed in the care of her uncle. That was something she couldn't let happen. The federal agent had plans for Tammy Moto, and if she had any say so in the matter, her goddaughter would remain on American soil and be of use to her in the upcoming years.

Knowing Tammy and her uncle had no idea concerning Cho's plans, Lisa scooped up the documents Cho had been filling out and tucked them inside her trench coat. "Tammy," she spoke softly as she extended her hand and beckoned her over. When the teen reached Lisa, she placed an arm around the youngster. "We're going to search the home, and then we'll have you call the police and report your discovery once I leave."

"Why can't you stay here?" Tammy cried as she and Lisa began walking through the home.

"Listen to me," Lisa whispered while climbing the stairs. "If we don't handle this right, you'll be sent back to Japan. Here in America is where you belong. Everything, this house, your parents' bank accounts, their cars, all of this belongs to you now, Tammy. Your parents wanted the best for you, and so do I. As your godmother, it is now my responsibility to make sure you are taken care of in the same manner in which your parents wanted. I know it hurts, but you have to be strong. It's up to you to carry on your family's name. Don't let them die in vain. Honor them by continuing your education."

"Will the people responsible be brought to justice?" Tammy asked as she and Lisa reached the top of the stairs.

"They most certainly will," Lisa answered while peering into one of the home's bedrooms. An orange, white and black color scheme came into view as Lisa's eyes scanned the area. The stucco walls where painted snow white and trimmed in black in the corners and along the baseboard. Lacquered orange wooden floors supported a white armoire, white dresser and a white four post king-sized bed with a comforter made of authentic Bengal tiger fur complete with matching fur pillows. "I take it you're a Cincinnati Bengals fan," Lisa stated as she stepped aside.

Tammy eased past Lisa and walked into the bedroom and stared wide-eyed. Her hands covered the lower portion of her face as she eyed her mother's creation. She was a Bengals fan through and through; although she'd never seen a single game in person, she followed them faithfully on radio and television. The pictures Cho sent her daughter did nothing to show the time taken to design and decorate her sleeping quarters. Tammy broke down in tears in the center of the room, dropping to her knees and reverting back to her native tongue. "She loved me," she spoke out in Japanese. "This room is beautiful just like her!"

Lisa said nothing in response. She felt pity for Tammy, and she was angry at Kazuki for being so callous. He'd grown too comfortable in his surroundings in her eyes and that was the thing that'd led to his and Cho's downfall. Tammy's sobs echoed throughout the second floor as Lisa walked the halls, peeking into room after room until she came up on Kazuki's home office. She'd seen the Uzi laying out in the hall and could tell a fight had unfolded on the second floor. Whoever killed Kazuki had overpowered the man and threw him to his death. The attacker wasn't alone given preliminary investigations, but Cho and Kazuki's death was not her main concern as she felt little compassion for such a careless duo. A quick search of the office uncovered a satchel behind Kazuki's marble desk that contained five kilograms of heroin. "He never even moved an ounce," Lisa whispered to herself as she donned a pair of black gloves.

The agent stood motionless for several seconds before she began pulling the drawers open on Kazuki's desk and dumping the contents onto the floor. She went over to his library shelf and knocked all of the man's books onto the floor. Lamps were knocked over and pictures were snatched off the walls.

Tammy heard the commotion and ran to her father's office. "What are you doing?" she asked Lisa perplexed.

"Just help me!" Lisa huffed as she pulled a chair resting in the corner of the office over onto its side.

"I don't understand!" Tammy cried.

Lisa stepped over the fallen chair and went and stood before Tammy. "Your parents were killed by at least two assassins," she declared while staring into her eyes. "You may not know all that they were involved in, but this is beyond Kodak. What I'm doing is keeping the authorities from looking into your parents' background. Now, help me wreck this place before I leave. When we're done, and I'm gone, you will wait ten minutes and call the police. They will ask if you have any surviving family or guardian you can call while processing the crime scene. That is when you call me. I'll come back tomorrow and pick you up from the police station and take you back to Baltimore."

"You're asking me to destroy my family's home? Lisa, I can't do—"

"Fine! Step aside!" Lisa snapped as she resumed wrecking Kazuki's office. "Go to your room and cry if you want!"

Tammy left the room and Lisa resumed her task. When she was done with Kazuki's office, she went into the couples' bedroom and tore clothes from both of their closets. She then confiscated jewelry consisting of expensive watches, rings and bracelets before leaving items on the dresser open and empty.

Satisfied she'd staged the scene, Lisa went back to Kazuki's office and picked up the bag of heroin. She headed back to Tammy's room and said aloud, "I'm going to leave now. You have to come back downstairs to call. It would look suspicious for you to be upstairs when your parents are on the first floor dead. I was never here—and you know nothing about what has happened up here."

Tammy rose up from her bed crying and shook her head to say yes.

Lisa could tell the teen was more than troubled over the death of her parents. Feigning ignorance would not be hard for her to do. "Straighten the covers back on your bed," she told Tammy. "Remember, you haven't been upstairs yet."

Tammy did as instructed, when she turned around, Lisa was standing before her. "I didn't mean to go off on you a minute ago," she comforted. "What I'm trying to do is keep you here in America and protect your family's honor. If the authorities learn your parents were executed, they will look into their background. That's not what we need to happen."

"I understand." Tammy replied while wiping tears.

"Good!" Lisa quipped. "Now, my little helper, I need you to go downstairs, wait ten minutes after I leave and make your call. In the morning, you'll be with me in Baltimore and we can set about going after the people who've killed Kazuki and Cho. Are you up to it?"

"Yes," Tammy spoke humbly. "Please, come back for me."

"I wouldn't leave you behind for the world, Tammy. I need you more than you could ever know," Lisa ended as she placed an arm around the youngster's neck and walked her down-stairs.

CHAPTER FOURTEEN

MURDER PRELUDE

"Okay. Helen has fresh formula in the refrigerator, a month's supply of diapers, new onesies and the number to her pediatrician is on the shelf out in the library," Tanya stated to Faye as she stood before a full-length mirror and clamped a diamond bracelet onto her wrist. She then ran her hands through her blonde hair and said, "The big guns are in the closet over there as you know, and of course, the swing hanging from the ceiling is off limits the entire time I'm gone."

Faye smirked as she sat with her back to Tanya looking out towards Bourbon Street at all the late night revelers out celebrating carnival season. The swing dangling from the ceiling and the other sexual devices laying around the room was arousing, to say the least. Her imagination wandered briefly, wondering what it would be like to sit inside and be serviced, but she was able to contain herself and remain focused on what lay ahead. "Me and the kids will be fine here. I just wish I was able to go with you and Brenda," she declared in a serious tone.

"You have enough to deal with after the Moto job. You have to get that bullet wound healed." Tanya replied as she backed away from the mirror and walked over to her dresser.

Faye looked down at the bandages covering her leg. Brenda and Mouse had wanted to take her to a hospital, but she refused as she knew all gunshot wounds would be reported to the authorities. Although she had an alias name, she didn't want to give officers investigating the Moto job a single lead. She suffered the pain with the aid of Tylenol and had wrapped the wound in towels soaked in alcohol. The wound was still fresh, but it was healing without infection setting in, and that's the only thing that mattered to Faye. "You could've dropped me off in Patterson," she told Tanya.

Tanya turned and stared at Faye. "You must be overdosing on those pain pills. Going back to Iowa where you're wanted on a capital murder charge is way too risky so that's a no go and you know it. I'll check on things in Patterson for you while I'm up there," she stated in a cool demeanor she tucked a chrome .44 magnum into the back waistband of her leather pants, donned a leather three-quarter-length hooded London Fog jacket and headed for the stairs leading to the second floor of her loft with Faye limping behind on crutches.

It was two months after the Moto hit, March of 1984, a week before Mardi Gras down in New Orleans. The murder of a prominent Japanese businessman and his wife had made headlines across the country, appearing on the evening news for several days in a row until it was replaced by the nation's presidential campaign race.

Whereas Brenda and Mouse where unconcerned, Faye and Tanya had been paying especially close attention to the investigation as certain details surrounding the hit didn't fit into the equation of how things went down in Cincinnati.

Kazuki and Cho were said to have been victims of a home robbery. Their home had been ransacked and valuables had been stolen. Faye knew neither she nor Mouse and Brenda had ransacked the home, however; they'd each had faced some rebuttal with their marks before killing them, but they'd never bothered with looting the Moto home. The only thing had been done was for Mouse to turn down the AC units to keep the bodies from decomposing and creating a foul odor.

In Faye and Tanya's eyes, someone had come behind them and staged the crime scene—only they didn't know who, nor the reasons as to why. News reports had also mentioned that it was the Moto's' young daughter who'd discovered their bodies after returning home from boarding school. She was now under federal protection and allowed to remain in the United States to finish her education.

The connection between fifteen year-old Tammy Moto and twenty-five year-old Lisa Vanguard had gone undetected by Faye, Tanya and all involved for the simple fact that Lisa had never given a formal statement, nor was she involved in the ongoing investigation in Cincinnati.

Under the belief that Tammy Moto posed no threat in her youth nor the years to come, Tanya Weinberger was now moving forward with her plan for the events unfolding in her home state of Iowa between Bonita Bender, Isabella Lockhart, Sascha Merkendorf and Mitchellville's warden, Evelyn Pulaski. This was to be the death stroke for the Germans. The removal of Evelyn Pulaski and her cronies would usher in a new era for the family—one that would place them at the helm of the heroin drug trade in the Midwest.

Tanya and Faye descended the stairs and met up with Brenda Marshall, Willameena Slack, and the King sisters, all four of whom were milling about tending the kids. Maggie, RJ and Popeye were situated in front of the console TV playing with the King Sisters while Brenda and Willie sat in the library entertaining Tanya's daughter, who lay in a bassinette. It seemed as if the baby had sensed her mother's presence the time she'd entered the room given the way she'd tilted her head and stretched her arms while crying aloud.

"Aww. She wants her mommy," Tanya cooed as she walked over and scooped Helen into her arms.

"You have work to do," Faye chimed in. "Let me hold her," she added softly as she took a seat inside the library.

"I know you'll take good care of her no matter what happens out there," Tanya said in a confident tone as she passed Helen to Faye. "Now back to business," she stated as she eyed two twelve gauge shotguns resting on the table. "These chicks we going after hang out at a lounge in Urbandale, Iowa. Me and Brenda may be gone for a while trying to track these women down and I don't want any shenanigans while I'm away," she added as she stared directly at Willie.

"The fuck you eyeing me like that there for?" Willie asked through laughter as she sat at the table inside the library room polishing her fingernails.

"Because I know your ass," Tanya snapped. "My bedroom is off limits. Faye is allowed up there only because it's where Helen's nursery is located—the rest of y'all stay y'all asses on the first and second floors."

"How come only white folks is allowed upstairs?" Willie quipped as she shook her crossed legs and blew her nails while smirking. "We gone have ta' boycott some shit around here I see."

"Don't you make this a race issue, bitch." Tanya laughed. "Like I say. I know your *ass*," she emphasized. "Don't think that you and the King sisters over there is gone run down on Bourbon Street to Big Daddy's and hook a trick and take him back here for a trip around the world while I'm gone. The Jungle is off limits to you chicks."

"Told y'all she had a sex chamber up there," Brenda said through nonchalant laughter as she stood up from the table and picked up the second twelve gauge.

Tanya had given birth to a daughter she'd named Helen Weinberger during the time Alfredo and Faye were completing the Moto contract. Helen was a long, pale-skinned, brown-eyed baby. She had a head full of course, tan hair in only her first couple of months and her long, slender arms constantly flailed about as if she were warding off unwelcomed guests. Everybody thought Tanya and Alfredo's child was simply beautiful and they all looked forward to seeing how she would progress as Tanya and Alfredo both had let it be known that Helen Weinberger would be reared to live the life her mother and father were leading, an attribute none seem to have a problem with as those who had children were doing the same thing in some shape, form or fashion.

Faye ran her hands through her silky brown hair and sighed as she cradled Helen. "They won't see you coming," she re-remarked. "Should be an easy job."

"Let's hope," Tanya replied as she scooped up a duffle bag of money and shotgun shells. While heading for the door, she called out to Zelda and Vivian. "Yo," she yelled aloud. "Alfredo and Mouse be back from Venezuela next week with a new shipment. Y'all got the buyers on call, right?"

"We got it!" Zelda snapped as she fanned Tanya off while dancing with Maggie.

Tanya eyed the King Sisters for several seconds before descending the stairs. She'd much rather take Faye with her and leave Brenda behind if only to make sure that the ten kilograms

184

of heroin the crew was bringing in was moved in a timely fashion. True enough, Alfredo and Mouse were on hand, but it was the women in the crew who were actually moving the weight down in New Orleans. Mouse was a gun dealer. He knew people who used the drug, but he wasn't a dealer. Alfredo hadn't the contacts in the city that Tanya knew. His main market was in the city of Cincinnati; and until the heat died down from the Moto job, the women in New Orleans had the responsibility of moving nearly a million dollar's worth of heroin on the city streets.

Tanya Weinberger was intricate to the family. She was a mastermind extraordinaire and had a deep understanding as to what all she and her girls were involved in. Brenda and the King Sisters were more muscle in her eyes. And even though it was Brenda who'd welcomed her into the crew early on, Tanya saw a bigger vision, one that spanned beyond pushing heroin on the streets of New Orleans. She saw political power, an avenue that would make the crew hard to topple. She and Faye often talked about propping up Willie, who was majoring in political science and had an ear to the streets and the problems ailing the people in her community.

That vision was years off, however, as Willie was more satisfied with being a prostitute instead of a politician. Much work needed to be done to solidify the crew in Tanya's eyes, but if she could execute their plan fully, she would have an ally in Faye that shared the same vision as herself; and it was for this reason, that Tanya had taken it upon herself to make sure that the Iowa job got done correctly, not only to help Faye, but to clear the path for an ally she knew would be around for years to come. With those thoughts in mind, Tanya stepped out into the brisk night air with Brenda following and climbed into her brown station wagon to begin the thousand mile trek north towards Iowa.

\

CHAPTER FIFTEEN

THE MISSION TO IOWA

"Some of them want to use you...some of them want to get used by you...some of them want to abuse you...some of them want to be abused..."

Eurythmics' song *Sweet Dreams (Are Made of This)* was playing loud on a jukebox inside T.U.G.'s, the lounge run by The Urbandale Gals. T.U.G.'s was nothing more than a large wooden shack located on the northwest side of the city of Urbandale, which was just to the northwest of Des Moines. The dingy, rundown hovel was packed with females from all over the greater Des Moines area. The dancefloor was overflowing with women in tight leather outfits, jackets and knee-length leather boots while others, dressed less dominant in denim and/or cotton pant suits. There was a series of red lights spanning the low ceiling of the lounge from front to back and the bar and the drinks behind it were barely visible. Only the silhouette of the bartender could be made out as women meshed together waving money in the air and calling out for beers and mixed drinks.

In the back of the club inside a single booth sat five women in a circle. One woman inside the booth, the one sitting in the center, had her arm stretched out and the sleeve of her black t-shirt rolled up over her shoulder as she sat on the edge of the circular red leather couch. "Put some 'shine on it to numb it up! Numb it with some hooch, bitches!" she yelled with a stogie hanging out the corner of her mouth.

"You need it numb, Dorothy? I thought you was a hard stud," one of the women chided.

"Evelyn? Bitch, you know you I have a tolerance for pain!" Dorothy retorted over the music. "She been working on Grace's tattoo for damn near three hours now! Hey, you know what? Fuck it! My arm going numb anyway! Go on with it, mutherfucka!" she added as she stiffened her arm and took to one knee while toking on the joint she was smoking.

"The green light is on, honey! You wanna get a stall in the ladies room?" a tall, slender Caucasian female asked aloud while dancing with the female everybody knew to be 'the new woman in town'.

Brenda looked over towards the hall leading towards the bathroom inside the club while dancing with her partner. The woman dancing with her was one of the first women to befriend her over a week ago when she'd first entered the lounge looking for a good time. They'd been flirting off and on the entire time, and the woman had been trying to seduce her latest conquest since the day she'd bought Brenda a drink.

"I don't know if that's a good idea. I mean, I want to, but can we really go in there and have sex?" Brenda asked, feigning naivety.

"It's how things are done in here, sugar," the woman replied as she pulled her leather vest open and revealed her bare breasts inside the smoke-filled, dimly-lit lounge. Women near Brenda and her partner yelled aloud in appreciation when the woman revealed her pert breasts. "You coming or not?" she asked while dancing before Brenda.

Brenda took a quick glance over to where Evelyn and Dorothy were hanging out and could see that neither was close to leaving the booth. "Let's get a drink!" she leaned over and yelled into her partner's ear.

The woman dancing with Brenda rolled her eyes in disgust. "Come on," she sighed loudly while yanking her by the hand. "I don't know why you're denying me the privilege, baby! I wanna be the first to taste this rare treat!"

"When you're done let me have a spell! I'd pay for a chance to suck that sweet black pussy!" a female yelled aloud.

Brenda's nose flared and her body stiffened as she balled her fists. She was about to swing on the overweight white woman that'd eavesdropped on the conversation until Tanya poked her spine with a knuckle of her finger. "Ignore it," she counseled while shoving Brenda through the crowd.

Brenda Marshall was the star of TUG's. Black women were a rarity inside the lesbian lounge, but they were highly sought after for their exotic beauty. They were so revered inside of TUG's that some had their pictures on the wall behind the booth where Evelyn and Dorothy sat. Brenda had had every opportunity to sit on the 'The Throne', which was nothing more than the toilet at the back of the lounge, and have white woman after white woman kneel before her and lick her pussy until she was satisfied while she sat astride the porcelain throne.

This was sexual deviance in its highest form if Brenda had to tell it. For the past week she'd been warding off women of different sizes and walks of life in order to build up anticipation. One of the women in the lounge was 'going to get her' was what she told several females, only she didn't know who as it was her first time being with the opposite, was the story she was selling.

The day before, Tanya, who'd been on the scene for two weeks prior to Brenda's arrival, had pretended to take an interest. It was easy for Tanya to blend in being she was from Iowa. She talked about her hometown of Cedar Rapids, although she was actually from Davenport, and she also spoke the lingo of those running the streets in Iowa. No one paid any attention to her arrival, nor were they suspicious of her presence given her race.

Brenda's arrival on the scene had actually livened things up. Everyone was vying for her attention, Evelyn and Dorothy included. Tanya and Brenda had tried tailing the women to their respective homes, but where they stayed left no doubt as to the fact that they were being followed. The tail would be picked up easily. The only way to catch the women was inside of T.U.G.'s, but it was the things the women had to experience, namely that of Brenda, that'd made the job difficult up until this point.

"You white mutherfuckas is beyond crazy," Brenda whispered into Tanya's ear as the two stood before the bar.

"It's no different than what Willie do over to Big Daddy's," Tanya countered.

"It ain't a hard dick in this joint." Brenda retorted in disgust. "You know they wanna take turns licking my pussy, right?"

"I would fuckin' love that!" Tanya laughed.

"You not actin' are you?" Brenda realized. "How many women you done been with since you been in here?"

"Enough to get the job done," Tanya answered seriously as she eyed Evelyn and Dorothy's booth. "She's done with that tattoo," she whispered. "Let's go, honey!" she then stated loud enough for others to hear as she jumped back into her role.

Brenda followed by leaning into Tanya and nuzzling her neck with the tip of her nose. To outsiders, it appeared as if she was licking Tanya's earlobe. A few women grew jealous while watching the short, voluptuous black woman with a thick afro following her white companion towards the bathroom stall.

Back inside the booth, Evelyn had spotted the two women headed towards the stall. She watched as the white woman clicked on the red light before disappearing into the hall. She patted Dorothy's leg and nodded towards the hall. "What you say we go in there and spy after while," she smiled.

Dorothy crossed her thick leather-clad thighs and took a sip of her moonshine. "I'm not sure about those two just yet," she said in a suspicious tone. She looked over to two of her cronies and nodded back over to the hall. "Wait five minutes and go down there and see just what it is those two are up to," she ordered.

Both women nodded while looking over towards the hall that was now illuminated with a red light, signifying that at least two women were in action. Eurthymics' song started over again and the two females eased up from their seats and made their way over to the bathroom stall. The emergency exit door at the end of the hall was checked by one of the females to make sure it was still locked before she and her counterpart went and stood before the bathroom door and eased it open.

"Yeah, lick that mutherfuckin' sweet black pussy," a woman was heard moaning from inside the bathroom stall.

"You like that shit?" another woman was heard asking aloud in a desperate manner.

One of the women pulled out a .38 revolver and stepped closer to the stall and pulled it open. Her eyes instantly fell upon the slender white woman resting on her knees before the 'new girl in town'. The sexy, dark-skinned woman was laying back on the toilet with her legs planted on either side of the handrails. The woman's jeans were laying on the floor and she held her panties in one hand while palming the back of the woman's head that was planted in between her thick thighs with the other. She wore a maroon leather trench coat that was covering her lover's head, but there was no doubt as to what was going down.

Brenda looked up at the women standing before her as she palmed the back of Tanya's head through her trench coat. "You want a taste?" she asked seductively as she eased a hand inside her coat.

"You'll never get the privilege of having me bow before you, nigger bitch," the woman holding onto the revolver snapped in disdain.

"Then you're in the minority, sweetheart," Brenda smiled as she spread her legs wider and tilted her head while eyeing the two women. "Tell anybody that now's their chance. I'm open," she moaned as she gripped Tanya's head tighter and rotated her hips as she sat atop the toilet.

"I'll do it," the second female responded through awestruck eyes that were fixated on the black woman's creamy thighs.

"Are you serious?" the woman holding the gun guffawed.

"I've always fantasized about going down on a black woman," the second female responded enthusiastically.

Tanya rose up at that moment and licked her lips. "You're gonna have to wait your turn," she declared.

"I want to do it now," the second woman commanded as she, too, pulled out a revolver and changed up her demeanor.

Brenda and Tanya quickly discerned that they'd been put to the test. Tanya slid her head from underneath Brenda's coat and pulled it open to reveal her lover's slickened bush.

"Was the wait worth it?" the first woman asked while smirking while lowering her gun.

"Damn right," Tanya smirked as she planted her face back into Brenda's pussy.

Brenda's eyes widened and she eased up on the toilet. "Mutherfucka!" she gasped.

The women standing out before the stall smiled at one another before leaving. When they were gone, Brenda pushed Tanya's head away from naked pussy. "What the fuck are you doing?" she asked surprised.

"I did it to save face. If I didn't put my mouth down there they woulda killed both our asses," Tanya retorted. "And trust me—your shit ain't all that sweet, honey," she smirked.

"That's what your mouth say," Brenda responded as she bit her bottom lip. She then thought back to the day Tanya first entered the Saint Bernard projects and the night the King Sisters had tried to get Tanya to go down on the both of them inside their apartment the night they'd killed Penelope. Brenda wanted to know what it was that was exciting the King Sisters so much about letting a white woman lick their pussies. It was as if they couldn't get enough of the act as they constantly sought it out whenever they traveled into the French Quarters with Willie.

Tanya was a bad chick in her own right in her eyes. Brenda didn't really swing that way, but she was like, 'what the hell'. It would be her and Tanya's secret after all; and being around scores of attractive white women who adored had become arousing all-of-a-sudden for Brenda. "Do it for real," she requested as she placed the heels of her boots back atop the rails bordering the stall.

Tanya was making the sure the twelve gauge she'd smuggled into the lounge was still secured behind the toilet when she heard Brenda's command. "Say what now?" she asked on bended knee while looking up at Brenda.

"You already put your mouth on it," Brenda said in a sexy voice. "Do it for real this time."

Tanya had always been a sexually experimental woman. The things she and Alfredo engaged in up in their loft were to never be shared with her friends for fear of judgement. The day she'd been tested by Zelda and Vivian rushed back into her mind as she stared at Brenda's slickened vagina with its pink, glistening lips protruding from a matted bed of silky, black hair. Truth was, Tanya would have gone down on the King Sisters just for the fuck of it, but she knew if she'd given in so soon, the crew would've never respected her; she'd opted to participate in a murder rather than be sexed into the crew, and for that, she was respected and now had a commanding position inside the family, one that she felt gave leeway to her satisfying a curiosity without facing any repercussions.

"And you won't hold this against me?" Tanya asked as she smiled up at Brenda while rubbing her soft, thick thighs.

"It'll be our secret," Brenda assured as she sunk down on the toilet seat.

A glare filled Tanya's brown eyes as she rested on her heels and began rubbing the inside of Brenda's thighs. Then she did it. She dove face first into Brenda's pussy and planted her mouth over her friend's opening and sucked for all she was worth.

"Ssssss," Brenda gasped over the sensation. "I see why Zel and Viv into this shit. Do it, Tanya! Do it!" she groaned as she palmed the back of her friend's head with her freehand.

Back on the main floor, Dorothy and Evelyn had been filled in on what was going down inside the bathroom stall. "The chick from Cedar Rapids was going to town," one of the women said in reference to Tanya. "That nigger said she takin' on all comers."

"Ole gal from Cedar Rapids might have the snack, but we're going in for the main course! Let's get a line started on that nigger bitch!" Dorothy remarked over the loud music.

Evelyn laughed aloud and swatted Dorothy's arm, hitting her tattoo and forcing her to grimace. "Owww!" Dorothy pouted. "Kiss my tattoo and make it all better!"

"I'm bouta touch a sweet honey pot, baby. These lips are reserved!" Evelyn sassed as she stood up and removed her leather vest. "Of all the women in Mitchellville I've never had a black woman and I be damned if I miss this moment!"

"You not by yourself!" Dorothy laughed as she and Evelyn began making their way towards the stall.

Dorothy and Evelyn danced up the narrow hall leading towards the bathroom while holding on their drinks. *Sweet Dreams* had been played for a third time in a row and the two were singing along with the song while gyrating up the corridor under the red lights illuminating the way.

"*Keep your head up…keep your head up…*" Dorothy sang as she led the way.

"*Moving on…*" Evelyn quickly followed while sashaying up the hall with her eyes closed.

"*Hold your head up…*" Dorothy sang.

"*Moving on...*" Evelyn followed as the two approached the bathroom door.

Evelyn shushed Dorothy by placing a finger over her lips. She reached down and checked the door knob. The handle turned fully and she eased the door open while looking over to Evelyn with wide, jubilant eyes as the sounds of sex eased into her ears over the music.

The kicking up of the volume from the music alerted Brenda and Tanya to the fact that the door to the bathroom had been opened. "Aww suck my pussy you white bitch," she moaned as she rolled her eyes. She had her eyes focused on the stall as she kept one hand to the back of Tanya's head with the other tucked inside her trench coat.

When the stall opened, Evelyn's pearly white teeth came into view. She was all smiles as she stepped inside the stall. "I'm here for sloppy seconds, baby," she remarked in a seductive manner as she hovered over Tanya.

"Let's get it on," Brenda remarked, letting Tanya know that their marks had arrived.

"Let me see it! I wanna see how she look down there sucking that black pussy!" Dorothy exclaimed while peering over Evelyn's shoulder while aiming a Polaroid camera to capture the moment.

The camera had flashed milliseconds before Brenda squeezed the trigger on the muzzled Uzi she had tucked inside her trench coat. With her legs gapped and Tanya's face planted in her pussy, she opened fire on Evelyn and Dorothy, spraying both women with a volley of bullets that ripped through their bodies like holes through Swiss cheese.

While Dorothy's body had fallen back out of the stall onto its side, Evelyn had fallen onto Tanya's back, pressing her breasts to the edge of the toilet seat momentarily. She groaned in agony briefly before shoving the corpse off her body and reaching behind the toilet.

Brenda and Tanya then scurried about the stall, Brenda going for her panties and jeans while Tanya confiscated the camera.

"Where's the picture?" Tanya asked hysterically as she looked down at the bloodied vinyl tile floor. She spread Evelyn's blood around with her freehand while gripping the twelve gauge, desperately searching for the picture she knew the woman had taken.

Brenda, meanwhile, had slid a fresh magazine into her Uzi and pulled Dorothy's body back into the bathroom as part of the woman's arm had left the door ajar. She peeked out into the hall and saw two women, the same women who'd approach them earlier, approaching the bathroom. "We gotta get the fuck outta here! Two more coming!"

Tanya grunted as she shoved Evelyn's body over and uncovered the bloody Polaroid. She stuffed the picture into her jacket and racked the twelve gauge.

Brenda, at the same time, pushed the door open as Eurthyth-mics' song coated her ears once more. "...*Sweet dreams are made of this...who am I to disagree...I traveled the world and seven seas...everybody's looking for something...*" Amid the thundering house track, she opened fire on the two women approaching, dropping them where they stood as things played out in seemingly slow motion under the red light in the hallway.

The music was just that loud, and no one had a clue that a quadruple murder was unfolding inside of TUG's. Tanya soon emerged from the bathroom and made a beeline for the exit. The door was barricaded from the inside, but the locks didn't stand a chance as she let off a shotgun blast, shattering the top lock. Screams were heard the time she squeezed the trigger, but she followed it up with another blast that shattered the bottom lock. She then leapt into the air and kicked the door open with her boot-clad foot. She and Brenda ran through the gravel parking lot towards a Fifth Avenue supplied by Sascha Merkendorf and hastily climbed inside. They were speeding off just as a couple of females emerged from the club, stunned over what'd gone down.

Brenda began putting her panties and jeans back on as Tanya drove. "That shit was crazy!" she snapped while removing her boots.

"We got four of 'em." Tanya said unnerved as she merged onto I-80. "That should be the hand Bonita and Izzy fan with back inside Mitchellville."

"Not that," Brenda laughed. "You ate my pussy, girl!"

"Hey! I only did that to play shit off in there!" Tanya defended as she drove at a calm pace so as not to draw heat.

"The first time," Brenda stated, tickled beyond belief as she slid her panties over her thighs. "But the second time? You did that shit just because I asked you to."

"Nahh, it was to keep the...hey, you what? Yeah I ate the mutherfucka, but you wanted me to do it just as bad!" she snapped as she went into her jacket pocket and pulled out the bloody picture Dorothy had snapped just before Brenda had shot her to death. "And here's the evidence. You with your legs wide open! All they can see is the back of a bitch's head, but that's your face! They won't know it's me!"

"Let me see that." Brenda requested.

"Hell no!" Tanya snapped as she stuffed the picture back into her pocket. "This is insurance. Tell the crew if you want, but they gone look at you funny before they do me. They already think I'm a freak because of what's on the third floor."

"You won't say nothing would you?" Brenda asked seriously.

"Did you like it?" Tanya asked, cutting her eyes over to Brenda.

"Eh, none of that matter. This shit just don't need to get out in—"

"Did you like it?" Tanya asked again, cutting Brenda short.

Brenda exhaled. "It, it felt good," she admitted coyly while sliding her jeans back up over her thighs. "But that there is our secret."

"And I have insurance," Tanya smiled as she patted her jacket pocket. "Don't worry, I won't share this with nobody— not even Alfredo will know that you let me eat that sweet pussy of yours," she laughed.

"Fuck you," Brenda scoffed as she lay her head back in the seat.

Tanya laughed to herself as she continued driving. Truth was, the picture Dorothy had snapped was an image of Brenda sitting with her legs gapped open holding onto her Uzi. Dorothy had snapped the camera at the exact time Brenda had fired off a shot. The woman had photographed her own death. TUG's was written on the wall behind the toilet along with several visible names and phone numbers. It was enough to send Brenda away, but Tanya wouldn't dare betray her friend. It was a classic photo, however, one she would tuck away for safe keeping and pull out from time to time and solitarily reflect on one of the most cunning hits the crew had pulled to date.

With all jokes aside, Tanya drove the Fifth Avenue to a deserted grain silo facility where she and Brenda transferred back over into her station wagon after setting the car ablaze. Before jumping back onto the interstate and heading towards the town of Patterson to the south, Tanya pulled over and called Izzy, who in turn notified Sascha. Time was now of the essence. It wouldn't be long before Mitchellville got word that their warden had been killed so they had to act fast and precisely.

Tanya had one more job to complete. She hadn't the time upon entering the state of Iowa, but she had to keep her promise to Faye. She and Brenda would spend the night in Bevington, where Tanya would continue on with the last phase of the mission to Iowa before heading back to New Orleans. The woman had no idea, however, what a world she would soon uncover.

CHAPTER SIXTEEN

GO HOME

"Please! Let me down, please!" Grace Unger pleaded as she hung from a metal pipe inside the storage room in the prison's laundry by her wrists.

Sascha Merkendorf was pacing the floor before Grace inside the hot, damp and cramped room while casually licking an ice cream cone. It was two hours after Tanya and Brenda had killed Evelyn. Word hadn't spread about the warden as of yet, but Sascha knew the full scoop.

"Several weeks ago," Sascha stated before licking her vanilla cone once more. "Several weeks ago you insulted me by spitting into my face. And I know that you and the warden have been trying to smuggle drugs into Izzy's facility. You have been a thorn in our sides for quite some time now, you bad little girl."

"I repent. I'm sorry," Grace cried aloud as she hung naked with her wrists above her head.

Sascha smiled an evil grin. "Now you have found religion," she mocked. "Was god there the day you spit in my face?" Did he tell you to do that to me? Or did you leave his side and take it upon yourself to berate me?"

"Come on, Sascha." Grace whined while shaking her head. "This isn't right. I was just—"

"Answer my question!" Sascha hissed. "Did God tell you to spit into my face?" she asked coldly while staring up into Grace's eyes.

"It wasn't God! It was me!" Grace cried out.

"I don't believe you," Sascha remarked casually as she resumed eating her ice cream cone. "I have a friend who says God doesn't exist. Do you believe in God, Grace Unger?"

"Yes."

"Do you want to live?"

"Yes."

"Okay," Sascha remarked calmly as she finished the remainder of her ice cream cone and dusted her hands. "Ask God, right now, to walk through that door at the end of the chamber on your behalf. If your god comes inside of five minutes, I will take you back to your cell. If not, I will kill you as promised before."

Grace began to cry heavily at that moment. She knew what Sascha was asking her to do was impossible. God was not going to walk through the steel door at the end of the hall and save her. During her entire ordeal, she'd been wishing she'd never volunteered to work the prison laundry. She was operating on orders from Evelyn Pulaski, however; the warden was in the beginning phases of reestablishing her drug pipeline into Mitchellville. The prison laundromat was closing for the night when Sascha nonchalantly asked Grace to make sure that the bleach tanks were refilled before she signed off for the night. She went and checked the large plastic bins, and while she had her back turned, Sascha crept into the storage room and choked her from behind until she passed out. When Grace had awakened, she found herself naked and shackled to a pipe above her head.

Sascha knew was that Grace and the warden were getting close to funneling drugs into the prison; and that was something neither she nor Izzy could allow to happen. Having been giving the order by Izzy herself, Sascha held Grace hostage the duration of the night shift inside the laundry room. When everybody cleared out, she did a count, signing off for Grace before she and several other guards escorted the women back to their cells.

The plan to exterminate Izzy's most outspoken, and last rival inside the prison had been in motion since the day Tanya and Brenda had touched down in Iowa. The week before she was accosted, Grace's cellmate was conveniently moved to another tier and she now had a single person cell. Sascha was in charge of the nighttime count so it was easy to for her to mark Grace off as being in her cell during headcount.

Sascha knew all-too-well that she would be under suspicion after this night, but her future was secure. Her task inside of Mitchellville would be fulfilled on this night and she was scheduled to move on to another assignment courtesy of Bonita Bender. In the meantime, however, a job needed doing on this night in order to assure that Isabella 'Izzy' Lockhart would become warden of Mitchellville Women's Correctional Facility.

"You have two minutes for your god to show," Sascha said to Grace. "Look where your faith has gotten you!"

"You shouldn't put God to the test. You're not supposed to test God."

"The book of Matthew. Chapter four verse seven," Sascha remarked calmly as she walked over and stood before the plastic bin propping up Grace's feet. "And Jesus said unto him, 'you must not put your god to test'," she quoted from the scriptures. "Ninety seconds!"

"Sascha, no!" Grace begged. "I won't say anything about what's going on in here!"

"Sixty seconds!" Sascha scowled as she placed her boot to the plastic bin beneath Grace's feet. "How does it feel to know death is forthcoming, Grace Unger? Are you afraid to die?"

The mental torture being placed upon Grace Unger was indescribable. At times she felt she would live; at other times she was certain she would die at the hands of Sascha Merkendorf. This game had been played repeatedly for several hours, but this time around, Grace knew for certain that she was about to check out, still, she tried to plea for her existence. "I'll do anything you want! I'll side with you, Bonita and Izzy! Sascha, please! God, please!"

"Yes!" Sascha exclaimed as she dropped her boot from the plastic bin. "Who are you calling out to now? You're calling out to *me*! You're calling me a god! Am I your god, Grace?"

The look in Sascha's eyes told Grace that she'd best not say no—even if she believed what she was being asked wasn't true. "You're my god," she whispered through her physical and mental anguish.

"Say it again," Sascha sadistically requested. "Let me hear it!" she panted happily.

"You're, you're my god." Grace replied defeated.

Sascha eyed Grace with sudden disdain while climbing onto a ladder and placing a chain around the woman's neck. She then released the handcuffs that held her secure to the pipes and placed them back onto her wrists behind her spine.

Sascha had been experimenting with Grace the whole time by using a twisted German tactic, one that pitted a person against God and/or family before imminent death to the utter amusement of those loyal to the Nazi Cause. Her torturous psychological experimentation was based on the things Bonita had told her about not believing in a God. She wanted to know firsthand that if a person was confronted with the mere threat of death, would they call out to a higher source, and if death was imminent, how far would an individual go just to live just a few seconds longer. Although Bonita and Grace weren't the same person, they were both mentally tough in her eyes. Sascha was aiming to break Grace Unger for the sake of proving a point to herself; and she'd just done so to her complete satisfaction.

"Being that I've just been declared your god," Sascha stated jubilantly as she walked around in a circle before Grace with her hands on her hips. "As your god, it is I who has the final say so over your life."

"Sascha, please! I can't take—"

"Your god is speaking!" Sascha interrupted as she faced Grace with her hands on her wide hips. "Do you dare interrupt your god?"

"I'm sorry," Grace cried aloud as sweat poured from her body.

"Sorry you are!" Sascha admonished. "You have angered your god! For every sentence that you have uttered since you've been shackled has done nothing but displease me! And when a god is angry at her servant? She has to render punishment!"

"God, kill me now!" Grace screamed aloud. "Kill me, mutherfucka!"

"As you wish," Sascha spoke calmly as she placed her boot back onto the plastic bin and tilted it slightly. "But before you go, you must know that your sister Dorothy Unger and the warden Evelyn Pulaski will meet the same fate. Maybe you three will all see one another again in the place where people like us *all* go when we die. Ten seconds!" she announced.

The look upon Grace's face was priceless for Sascha. She knew Dorothy and Evelyn was Grace's only hope for retaliation, but her dreams had been crushed. All the broken woman could do was cry pitifully as the last seconds of her life ticked by. "You're the devil!" she screamed aloud at Sascha. "Lucifer himself!"

"And in this world, Lucifer is a god." Sascha retorted. "Time's up, Grace Unger! I'll see you in hell!" she stated coldly as she pushed the plastic over onto its side. Grace's feet stretched down to the floor as the chain around her neck tightened. Her body twitched violently as she released her bowels, her tongue hung out the corner of her mouth like a panting dog as her eyes bulged and began hemorrhaging.

Grace's body was still trembling when Sascha went and removed the handcuffs from her wrists. She placed a gentle hand to the woman's heart and whispered, *"Nach Hause gehen, die Liebe. Nach Hause gehen."* (Go home, love. Go home.) until the woman stopped moving.

CHAPTER SEVENTEEN

SAINTS AND SINNERS

The day following the hit inside TUG's found Tanya Weinberger cruising onto the Patterson farm on a cloudless, but cold Sunday morning. She had traveled into Patterson the night before after she and Brenda had checked into the Bevington Inn, but the Patterson Farm was too eerie a place for her to travel onto under the darkness; but even during the day, the place had a sinister appearance. The land was barren and the home itself was a drab shade of white that made it look saddened over the tragedy that unfolded underneath its roof some months ago.

Tanya pulled her station wagon up to the front of the home and climbed from behind the wheel clutching her twelve gauge. She walked towards the front porch while reaching into her trench coat for the keys Faye had given her. As she climbed the stairs, Tanya swore she saw someone peeking at her through the home's front window on her left. She'd been uneasy approaching the creepy-looking structure the entire time so she brushed it off as her mind playing tricks on her.

She unlocked the door and pushed it open, cautiously remaining on the porch as her eyes scanned the interior of the home. The floor in between the foyer and the threshold leading into the home, where Franklin had supposedly been killed, had been cleaned she noticed.

"The police cared enough to clean up the blood," Tanya thought to herself as she racked the twelve gauge and eased into the home.

Right away, a smell filled Tanya's nostrils. Not a stench, but a sweet smelling aroma that seemed to linger. It wasn't the smell of the home, but one that emanated from a bottle, a perfume bottle filled with lavender or some other incandescent fragrance. It was a recent smell, one that forced her to raise her twelve gauge and place her back against the wall as she crept towards the opening. A rattling glass, one coming from a room to her right caught her attention.

Tanya looked around with wide eyes and a rapidly-palpating heartbeat. There were stairs straight ahead. She leaned down to make sure no one had the advantage on her before she quickly rounded the wall separating the living room from the foyer. She waved her twelve gauge around the room, ready to fire, all-the-while sensing another person's presence. She hadn't paid any attention at first as she was preoccupied with laying eyes upon an intruder like herself, but the television was running. The volume was turned down, but she could see the image of the singer Beverly Battle playing over the screen as she stood beside Mavis Staple. She remembered this particular performance. It was a concert held over in London, England that was attended by Ronald Reagan. His face, along with that of Queen Elizabeth, Prince Charles and Princess Diana appeared briefly before Beverly's face came back on the screen.

"I was watching it while cleaning the place," a soft voice was heard echoing through the home as a petite female appeared on the opposite side of the hall with her hands raised above her shoulders.

Tanya aimed her racked twelve gauge at the woman. "Who the fuck are you?" she asked lowly.

"My name is Mary Beth," the woman replied just as a car was heard pulling up to the front of the home.

"Get over here!" Tanya commanded as she peered out at the middle-aged woman exiting a black Lincoln Towncar.

"It's just my mother," Mary Beth whimpered while walking over to Tanya with her hands still raised. "She's a Senator and she won't hurt you. Neither of us is going to hurt you."

"I know that's real. I'm the one with the gun," Tanya quipped as she attempted to place Mary Beth down onto her knees.

"No!" Mary Beth protested. "Mother says I don't have to take shit from no one! I said we mean you no harm and we don't! Who do you think has been caring for this home ever since Faye left?"

Just then the front door to the home opened. "What's going on here? Who are you?" Senator Mabel Mobley-Sougherbraun asked cautiously with a black .44 magnum draping her side as she eyed a slender blonde woman in an extravagant leather trench coat and heeled knee-length boots welding a twelve gauge on her daughter.

Mary Beth's words had eased Tanya a bit. She knew of her and Mabel courtesy of Faye Bender. Amid the awkward encounter, she lowered her twelve gauge and said, "I'm a friend of Faye Bender."

"There's that name again," Mabel chuckled as she released the hammer on her jammer. "Okay," she sighed. "Now is where we began to establish grounds."

"Meaning?" Tanya asked curiously as she unracked her weapon.

"Thank you." Mabel replied through an appreciative smile. "If and when you see Faye Bender again? Tell her Senator Mabel Sougherbraun says thank you for freeing my daughter and giving me the strength to face my demons. Tell her just like that and don't you forget it."

Tanya nodded with understanding. "I most certainly will," she assured. "And I'm sure she'll be grateful for you two taking care of the home. I was, I was actually expecting something macabre giving the outside, but the inside is, it has life."

"We can do so much more, but the weather, my campaign, not to mention what all Mary Beth has been through. It'll take some time, but the home is in good hands." Mabel stated proudly.

"Well, I'll be going," Tanya remarked as she started for the door.

Mabel blocked her exit. "Oh no," she chuckled. "You have to stay and learn what it is that Faye has done for me and my daughter."

Tanya was only on the Patterson Farm to check on the house and give an update to Faye. She was taking great risk remaining in Iowa after she and Brenda had murdered four women inside a lesbian bar, but she was willing to face the risks on behalf of Faye, if only to find out what remained of the Patterson Farm. "Faye will know of you two's gratitude," she told Mabel and Mary Beth, "but I really have to get going."

"What's the rush?" Mabel asked as she walked into the home. "No one would ever suspect that the murderer of a warden and three other lesbians would be in the presence of a U.S. Senator."

Tanya coughed at that moment, wondering how Mabel knew what'd happened the night before.

"I'm a former judge," Mabel spoke, shaking Tanya from her thoughts. "I swore a woman by the name of Isabella Lockhart in as interim warden over Mitchellville Women's Correctional

Facility not even an hour ago. Now," she continued as she tucked her hands into her rhinoceros-skinned trench coat, "I'm not saying Faye was directly involved in what happened in Urbandale, but the pedigree matches. Something's astir here, and there isn't a doubt in my mind that it all stems from what happened in my hometown five years prior."

"I don't know about five years prior," Tanya retorted. "Matter of fact, I don't know nothing about Urbandale, a pedigree, or this Izzy woman you're talking about."

"How do you know she's called Izzy?" Mabel asked seriously, leaving Tanya searching for an explanation. "Look," the woman followed. "If you want to play games with your friend's freedom then have at it—but I'm willing to help Faye get over being accused of murdering her own family inside this very home."

"What's your stake?"

"The resurrection of my daughter's future," Mabel responded in a caring tone as she went and stood beside Mary Beth.

"I'm not understanding," Tanya said as she stared at the odd duo perplexed.

"Let me show you what we've done to the home, and then? I want to show you what your friend has done for me and my daughter. This Sunday was truly meant to be. Come on," Mabel stated tenderly as she beckoned Tanya forth and began telling her and Mary Beth's story.

Tanya left the Patterson home a little paler than she was before entering the place. Her brown eyes were watery and her heart simply went out to Faye as drove of the property tailing Mabel with thoughts of what'd gone down ran through her mind. For whatever reason, Mary Beth wanted to tide with her. She sat beside Tanya with her head bowed. "I really like that house," she spoke lowly.

"You like that scary home? Why?" Tanya asked befuddled.

"It wasn't scary before the murders. It's actually quite peaceful. I spend nights there alone sometimes."

"And you aren't afraid?"

"After all I've been through? Nothing scares me anymore—not even people who kill people for a living," Mary Beth said while smiling over to Tanya.

Tanya cut her eyes at Mary Beth. "Hey, I know what you're implying here, but I don't kill people for a living."

Mary Beth clapped her hands and laughed aloud with her head tilted back. "Doesn't it feel wonderful to be able to just, just outright lie despite the obvious? And before you ask how do I know you're lying? You're a friend of Faye Bender. Me and mother know all about her, honey," she blurted out with a raised hand. "And the way you carry that twelve gauge? Please," Mary Beth sighed as she fanned Tanya off. "If you don't kill for money, those around you do and you reap the benefits."

Tanya remained silent as she drove off the property. She didn't confirm nor deny Mary Beth's beliefs, nor did she have to. Mable had disclosed a lot of information during the tour of the home and she had plenty of dirt on the family. The right one had been pegged to travel to Patterson as Tanya had been the recipient of some of the vilest acts she'd ever heard in her life. When asked why she was being told such things, Mabel replied by telling Tanya that she was forging an alliance. Right away Tanya understood the implications. Both parties had dirt on one another, Tanya more than Mabel, but the Senator was willing to concede an advantage, if only to have an ace-in-the-hole in the future as she was now playing a game of dirty politics in order to maintain her seat in Congress.

With those thoughts in mind, Tanya tailed Mabel onto the Mobley ranch. It was a short drive to the other side of town, but a lot had been digested during the ride. This was a surreal experience she was willingly partaking in, if only to have access to a Senator. Willie was soon to enter politics, and it was plain to see that Mabel Sougherbraun-Mobley would be more than an asset to the crew. "Who's this guy?" Tanya asked as she eyed a decrepit, long-limbed man sitting on the porch with a young boy beside him and a stroller at his feet.

"That's my pastor," Mary Beth stated proudly. "I'm getting baptized today, Tanya."

"Those are your kids you told me about I assume?"

"Yes! Dillon and my little Delilah," Mary Beth stated as she hopped out the car and ran towards the porch.

Tanya remained in the car for a moment while staring at the front of the home. Mabel had been very forthcoming with her, and Faye herself had told her what'd gone down the night she killed Sheriff Mobley, including the fact that Mary Beth had borne children by her brother and father respectively. A feeling of pity encompassed her as she watched Mary Beth pick up her daughter and hold her close.

Mabel soon stepped onto the porch and she and the man began talking. From time to time, the old man would look over to Tanya's direction. She remained seated with her twelve gauge in her lap while scanning her surroundings. After a few minutes, the old man walked down the stairs and approached the station wagon. He leaned down as Tanya rolled her window down and said in a throaty voice, "I reckon you'll be attending church with us this morning?"

"I know nothing about going to church. I'm actually headed back to Bevington."

"Bevington is where we *all* are going this morning, lady," the man responded with a smirk on his face. "Name's Reece Duggan, but everybody for miles and miles around calls me Scorpion. Got a knack for spotting talent," he added as he tapped his glass eye.

"I've heard of you. My name is Tanya," Tanya replied kindly as she rolled the window down completely.

"I haven't heard of you until this morning, Tanya, but Mabel tells me that you're a friend of Faye Bender?"

"That I am."

"What an exceptional woman she is," Scorpion stated seriously as he stared into Tanya's eyes. "She did a good thing for ole Mary Beth last year. Family's grateful."

Tanya didn't respond to Scorpion's remarks. She was wondering what it was that was holding her captive to these people she'd never met a day in her life. The entire situation seemed odd in her eyes, but yet, she couldn't pull herself away.

"Not going to keep you waiting much longer," Scorpion remarked, shaking Tanya from her thoughts. He then stood up and called out, "Mabel, let's get the show on the road! Our guest has to be going shortly—given all she's done in Iowa," he stated through a chuckle.

"Give us a minute, Reece! I have to gather up some signs!" Mabel yelled back as she left the porch and walked over to a small shed sitting beside the home and pulled the doors open.

"Why does everyone make implications here?" Tanya sighed as she watched Mary Beth carry her daughter over to Mabel's Lincoln.

"I make no implications, lady," Scorpion stated while staring down at Tanya. "I know your kind and I welcome it," he said as he opened Tanya's door and extended his hand. "You have a goldmine in your midst, but I don't think you have a clue as to what power lays within your grasp."

"I understand fully," Tanya retorted as she eased from the car.

"Do you really?"

"The Senator is willing to keep quiet on my friend murdering her sons and husband. And for that? I'll keep quiet on her family secret so she can hold onto her seat. She knew with me being friends of Faye that I knew everything that went down here the past five years or so."

"Ohh," Scorpion growled. "You think ole Mabel came clean so you can keep quiet on the incest between Mary Beth and the men in her family. Well, you're only partly right."

"What am I missing, Scorpion?"

"I don't know what all it is that Faye's into at this moment, but knowing the woman? She isn't, shall I say, a law-abiding citizen? Don't know if Mabel told you, but she sits on the Foreign Relations Subcommittee."

"Meaning?" Tanya asked curiously.

"The FRS deals with all matters dealing with the United States in the western hemisphere. Canada? Mexico? Central and South America? The Caribbean and even Cuba," Scorpion disclosed. "Mabel, Mabel can get you and Faye passports and visas into any of those countries in a matter of days."

"Shut the front door." Tanya stated in disbelief as she set her twelve gauge on the front seat and closed the door to her station wagon.

"Mabel's not one to get her hands dirty, Tanya. Doesn't mean she's not willing to say, pay to see problems go away if you know what I mean."

"Who she have in mind?"

"Your services aren't needed as of now as far as I know," Scorpion answered. "Mabel is holding onto her seat over her accomplishments, but there's another who has an idea what may have happened to Corey, Wendell and Jeremy—a state trooper by the name of Rance Olsen."

"How much does he know?"

"Enough to arouse suspicion over Faye Bender and Mabel both. He needs more pieces to make his case, though. Guy may be a problem later on for Faye and the Senator. Don't know about Faye, but for Mabel it'll be devastating. The guy may have to, have to meet an untimely death, if you get my drift. And of course, the job would pay above street market."

Tanya began to think deeply. Passports and visas were crucial to what the crew had going on over in South America. Whenever Alfredo had to meet the Darvish men, he would have to travel to Israel and catch a flight to Argentina and then fly into Venezuela. It took weeks to prepare for a flight and gain clearance. And Brenda's old man, Mouse, couldn't even get into Argentina. He had to fly over to London and book a flight to Venezuela in order to join Alfredo. Having Mabel in her pocket would make things just that much easier for the family.

"Here's the kicker," Scorpion spoke, removing Tanya from her thoughts. "The Foreign Relations Committee also oversees international crime and illicit drugs. Mabel knows of on-going investigations before the public ever catches wind."

Tanya could only smile and lick her lips over what she'd stumbled upon. She was somewhat apprehensive about the entire deal with Mabel, but Scorpion had shed a whole lot of light on just what it was she'd signed up for with the Senator. "How much will this cost us?" she asked Scorpion.

"I'm Mabel's go-between," Scorpion replied. "All monies transferred will go through me and be funneled into Mabel's coffers. Nothing goes until you get the word from Mabel herself. All she will say is, 'do it', that's you cue to get in touch with ole Scorpion."

"How will I contact you?"

"Ahhh," Scorpion said through raised eyebrows. "You know where to find Mabel and Mary Beth—now, you must become familiar with Scorpion and how he operates in order for this network to get up and running."

Just then, Mabel emerged from the side of her home holding onto a bunch of square, white signs stapled to wooden sticks. "Can someone please give me a hand?" she asked aloud.

After helping load the signs into the back of Scorpion's pick-up truck, Tanya tailed the group back towards the main road where they headed east, back towards the town of Bevington. Mabel led the way in her black, four door Lincoln with dark-tinted windows. Her grandchildren sat in the backseat and Mary Beth was at her side as the gangster whip cruised up the highway. While wheeling the car up the two-lane road bordered by withered cornstalks, Mabel picked up a mobile phone and pressed a red button.

"Reagan."

"Hey, Ronald!" Mabel exclaimed happily.

"Senator Sougherbraun," President Ronald Reagan said as he leaned back in his oval office chair and placed his feet atop the oval office desk. "How's the campaign going in Iowa?"

"Better than expected, Mister President."

"Well, that's what I was hoping to hear, Mabel. It's pertinent that we, that the republicans hold on to as many seats as possible in order to get this tax increase passed in the next congressional session in order to further arm ourselves against the Russians. As good a benefit as we did last year with the queen of England, it did little to reduce arms reductions. We're the only ones at the table and we shall not eat alone."

"Our Russian counterparts will just have to be force fed, Mister President. I'm with you on this nuclear proliferation deal."

"Good! And you have my full support in return, Mabel. If I'm reelected, Mister Gorbachev will indeed, tear down those walls. I just need the support of my republican Senators."

"After I'm sworn in once again, I'll bring a bottle of champagne by the east wing to celebrate your second term," Mabel spoke confidently before she and the President ended the call.

Mary Beth looked over to her mother at that moment. "You're in good with the President, momma. I hope I can do my part as mayor of Patterson—if I were to win."

"It's our name that will assure your victory, Mary Beth," Mabel reassured. "You're where I had plans for each and every one of my children," the Senator confessed. "Jeremy and Wendell weren't worthy, nor were they built for this life, Mary Beth. The things you've been through makes you who you are today."

"In spite of its abomination," Mary Beth replied.

"In spite of," Mabel agreed as she hugged her daughter's neck. "The counseling's working, and, and we're making amends. I don't like bringing up the past, but I want you to know how sorry I am. I am forever indebted to you."

"Your sins have been forgiven," Mary Beth spoke calmly as she leaned into Mabel and pressed her face to her mother's right arm. "I'm just grateful that you finally believed me over daddy and my brothers."

"That was a terrible time never to be repeated, Mary Beth. You know all that's all going on now. Just follow my lead, sweetie, and once it's all said and done? You'll never have to worry about you and my grandchildren's future. Now, let's go and win our respective elections," she stated proudly as she meshed the gas pedal.

Tanya hadn't a clue as the caliber of woman she was dealing with in regards to Mabel Sougherbruan-Mobley. This Senator had descended into depths unimaginable for a woman of her social status and hid her transgressions well. It was a way of life for Mabel, one she was hoping her daughter Mary Beth would soon adapt to as she knew she hadn't much time life, two decades maybe, but it was more than enough time to tutor Mary Beth, school her and have her become as shrewd a politician as she herself had become.

The caravan cruised into Bevington's town limits, approaching I-35 from the west. Tanya's brown eyes focused in on CM's Grocery Store, the place where Faye had encountered Mary Beth and had uncovered the Sougherbraun's family secret. She turned her head away from the closed gas station and trailed Mabel and Scorpion in seemingly slow motion as the group made their way in to the town of Bevington. Knowing she was in it for the long haul, Tanya looked over to her right as she rode past the Bevington Inn where she knew Brenda was holed up.

It was never Tanya's plan to stay away for so long. She could only imagine what Brenda was enduring. The only thing she had in her pocket was the fact that Brenda had no one else to turn to under the circumstances. Greyhound buses ran infrequently, and a taxi cab was out of the question. "*Bear with me, sister,*" Tanya said to herself as she cruised past the Bevington Inn. She trailed Mabel and Scorpion over to a club called Bandits. The parking lot outside the large wooden structure was overflowing with cars and people on this cold, sunny Sunday morning. A stage was off to the right of the entrance and a band was set up. A woman was on the platform rallying the people as she held onto an electric guitar that was draped across her shoulder like a soldier welding a machine gun.

"We have to remember what all it is that our good Senator has done for our beloved state of Iowa!" Tanya heard the woman yell into her microphone as she exited her car. "Now, I'm from Ames! And I see the improvements to my hometown. It's been some time since I've been to southern Iowa, but this place looks nothing like it was when I first began my singing career right inside the club behind me! And that's a good thing!" the woman admitted as the crowd united behind her with loud cheers.

"Bev—erly! Bev—erly! Bev—erly!" the crowd began yelling and clapping.

"No, no, no! No, now, come on! It ain't about Beverly Battle! It's about Senator Sougherbraun-Mobley, you guys!" the famed country and blues singer corrected. "And here's our beloved Senator now!" she stated as she extended her hand towards Mabel, who was being helped from her car by Scorpion. "Let's play! Box Top Frogs!" Beverly quickly followed, cueing the band up just as Mabel and Mary Beth began making their way through the crowd.

Signs that read, 'Where I Started From' were passed out from the back of Scorpion's pickup truck and supporters quickly fell in line behind Mabel and Mary Beth as they made their way to Bandits' entrance as a few campaign aides followed with Mary Beth's children in tow.

"*A-haa...*" Beverly began to hum as she pulled her guitar down from her shoulder and began strumming her guitar. "*A-haaa...*" she sang softly. "*A-haaa...*"

Together, the entire began to hum as Beverly began to strum her guitar and fall off into a song titled *Where I Started From*, which was Mabel and Mary Beth's campaign slogan.

Campaign workers fired off blow guns filled with confetti, and Mabel as Mary Beth walked in between the crowd hugging one another with wide smiles on their faces as Beverly's voice coated their ears. "*My wheels are burning...to get away...I can't stand the city...for another day...I'm gonna go back... where I started from...*"

Tanya watched from a distance in awe as Mabel and Mary Beth, who had true rock star appeal, shook hands with their constituents over the loud music while walking through the crowd in seemingly slow motion as confetti rained down onto their heads.

This was Iowa politics the way she'd remembered it having grown up in the state. Whenever a candidate was in a heated campaign, they would always return to their roots, where they were strongest and had the most loyal support. Mabel and Mary Beth seemed to have the people's complete backing in her eyes. Should they succeed, Tanya knew what valuable allies the crew would have in their midst. She continued watching as Mabel and Mary Beth entered the building as everyone followed suit.

Just as quickly as the parking lot had filled with people, so was its emptying out; many of the people where now inside Bandits. Several dozen remained outside as the place had become filled to capacity was Tanya's best guest. Scorpion had given her all of the necessary information she needed on how to contact him and Mabel. She'd just placed her station wagon in drive and was preparing to head back over to the Bevington Inn to pick up Brenda and vacate the area when Scorpion walked up and tapped on her window.

"Yeah," Tanya asked after rolling the driver's side window down. She eyed the man strangely as his attire had been changed. Instead of the denim outfit and wool trench coat he wore, he now had on a black robe and was holding onto a bible.

"Mabel's a looking for ya'. She's requested that you stay and see what Faye has done for her daughter so you can report back, and it's a person you do good in meeting today."

Again, Tanya was held captive by her own curiosity. Anybody in their right mind would've been long gone after committing a quadruple homicide the previous night, but Tanya was bold enough to stay behind, if only to leave Iowa with a complete understanding and the sure backing of Mabel Sougherbraun-Mobley. She exited the car and followed Scorpion down the right side of the club and entered through a side door.

Immediately, a smell of marijuana filled Tanya's nostrils. Some of the band she saw on stage outside was resting their backs up against the walls in the hallway. A half dozen men with long, stringy hair and thick beards wearing long sleeved colorful silk shirts and leather pants with matching boots lined the wall on either side as they toked joints and went over key points on their upcoming performance.

Just then, Beverly Battle herself stepped out into the corridor and immediately eyed her band members in dismay. "This is a place of worship this morning!" the singer gasped in an all-out stunned manner as she stormed down the hall and began slapping the joints form her bandmates' hands. "You are all being very disrespectful to Mabel and Mary Beth and this is not how the Battle Band conducts business and you guys know it! There's a place and time for everything and this isn't the time nor the place!" the petite brunette admonished further while standing amongst her band and stomping out the joints.

"Marijuana is god's door to the other side without one having to die," Scorpion chimed in as he walked in between the band and stood before Beverly. "It allows one to see him or herself without the veil of deception we all put forth just to gain the world's approval."

"It doesn't make it right, Pastor Duggan. And anybody affiliated with me will not shame a place of worship."

"Pastor Duggan? Place of worship?" Scorpion chuckled as he smiled down at Beverly, his lanky, slender frame swaying back and forth as he held into his bible. "You and I both know the real deal here, Miss Battle. I gave you your start inside these very walls...and we had no church during your ascension to fame and fortune now did we?"

"No we didn't. But we're having church today, Scorpion," Beverly retorted. "The least you can do is not allow these guys to taint the building with the devil's mist!"

"Alright, alright!" Scorpion relented. "Guys? Smoke session's over. Cool your lighters until you get back to the bus. Now, Beverly? It's someone I want you to meet," he added as he looked back at Tanya.

Beverly eyed the slender, blonde, brown-eyed woman standing at the back of the hall. The lavish London Fog leather trench coat and the expensive, knee-length leather boots that adorned her feet superseded much of the attire many around these parts of Iowa could afford, let alone even knew existed when it came to fashion.

In Beverly's eyes, the woman wasn't from no parts of Iowa. "You done snuck a reporter in, Scorpion?" she asked dismayed. "I'm not going on record as to why I'm supporting Mabel and Mary Beth. I did not agree to this event in order to gain recognition, man, come on! You know me far better than that and I would never—"

Scorpion leaned down and whispered into Beverly's ear. "She's a friend of Faye Bender."

Beverly went silent at that moment as she leaned back and stared at Scorpion while clutching his forearms. She looked over in the blonde woman's direction and wobbled her head a bit as she approached. "I'm Beverly Battle!"

"You need no introduction. I'm Tanya," Tanya responded as she shook the woman's hand.

"I'm humble with mines, Tanya girl!" Beverly quipped. "So you're friends with Franklin Patterson's wife?" she asked while smiling proudly.

"Yeah, we umm, we—"

"Not here, honey!" Beverly interjected. "Come into this office they set up for me so we can discuss some things!"

Tanya followed Beverly into her makeshift office and the two sat and talked. "I want you to tell Faye that she needs to keep herself out of trouble until I can get my lawyers established here in Iowa. They have to pass the bar before they can practice law here in the state," she remarked as she sat before Tanya and picked up a pack of Camel cigarettes and removed the plastic.

"How long?"

"My guys aren't the brightest bunch, okay? For them I know it's a tall order, but the stipulations for passing the bar here in Iowa is difficult, you know? My guys have to go back and take a few more courses in criminal law at one of the universities before they're even able to go before the bar," Beverly answered as she slammed the pack of cigarettes against the back of her wrist and pulled one from the pack.

"That is a tall order," Tanya responded somewhat dejected.

"But one that's worth it to keep our friend off death row don't ya' thank, honey?" Beverly asked as she leaned back puffed on her fag.

"I'll let Faye know what the deal is here in Iowa. I just hope she can continue to lay low until your lawyers come through," Tanya stated as she leaned forward in the wooden chair and looked to the floor in deep thought.

"You do that," Beverly responded as she blew smoke from her lungs. She then eyed Tanya with a certain understanding of the life she presumed the younger woman before her was living, a life that paralleled that of her friend Faye Bender. "You outlaws have a way about yourselves, as do I being a world famous musician."

"What's that supposed to mean?"

"I look at you and I imagine you have a child or children," Beverly remarked. "You want the best for them in life, even if the best comes from the life you yourself now live. You need a blessing today, honey! When was the last time you attended a revival?"

"Never," Tanya smirked. "I'm not big on religion."

"What was your parents' religion?"

"They were Catholics."

"At least you can claim a faith," Beverly remarked as she dabbed her cigarette out into a crystal dish. She then stood up and said, "I have no religious affiliation, but it doesn't mean I do not believe in a higher source. Before you leave? Stick around for another ten minutes or so, you might find yourself uplifted."

"I was asked by Mabel to stay. I don't even know what's about to happen."

Beverly picked up her guitar and smiled down at Tanya, "A friend of mine, the guy Scorpion? He told me the first day I performed inside this club that I was to receive a baptism by fire. It was my first gig ever. I wouldn't say I bombed? But I was disappointed over the attendance that night—seven people. Three days later? This place was packed wall-to-wall. I was revered that night and never looked back. When I heard what had happened to Mary Beth and the reasons why Faye killed that sheriff? I told myself that I would never turn my back on these people. All they need is a little help—just a little!" Beverly emphasized as she leaned into Tanya.

Just then, there was a tap on the door. Scorpion eased it open and peeked inside, "I'm going on stage to do the introduction. Are you two okay? You ready, Beverly?"

"We're fine and I'm ready," Beverly responded. Once Scorpion pulled the door shut, Beverly turned back to Tanya. "I know it would mean a lot to Mabel and Mary Beth if they were to see your face here today during Mary Beth's baptism. Give them that much, then you can leave the way you came."

Tanya couldn't leave Bandits even if she wanted to. She'd gone from the Patterson farm, to the Mobley ranch and now found herself smack dab in the middle of a political campaign whose crescendo was the baptism of a woman who'd borne children by her own father and brother.

"This may all be a sham," Beverly said as she tightened the guitar around her waist. "But the people Mabel and Mary Beth represent believe in them. It's my job to make sure they continue on in their belief because these people mean good."

Without another word spoken, Beverly exited the office and walked amongst her band members with Scorpion leading the way. Tanya followed the group and stood offstage and watched as Scorpion went and stood before the rambunctious crowd and tapped the microphone in order to garner their attention.

Once they'd quieted down he looked over the crowd with his jagged face and scraggly beard on full display. Amid the silence, he leaned down and placed a hand to his face. When he arose, he was holding onto his glass eye. "Through me, the lord is watching all of you," he laughed slyly as he held his glass eye above his head. "That's right," he snarled. "He works in mysterious ways is the saying, and one could never look at a man and say, 'he's not of the lord'. Christ's message is delivered through all avenues, and he is speaking to us all on this beautiful morning and I am the vessel!" he yelled aloud as he stretched his arms wide, still holding onto his glass eye.

"Yes you are, Pastor Duggan!" "Bless us, holy man!" "Redeem our sins!" patrons in the crowd yelled aloud and at random.

"Yes, I am your pastor! And this holy man will bless you all today! I will wash your sins free in the blood of our lord and savior!" Scorpion professed. "Is Jesus all right?" he then asked as he removed the microphone from the stand and ran to the left side of the stage.

"Yes he is, Pastor Duggan!" parishioners yelled aloud while clapping their hands.

"Is Mabel all right?" he asked while extending his hand out to members closest to the stage.

"She sits beside my lord!" "God lives in her!" "Our faith is in Senator Sougherbraun!" people yelled enthusiastically while jumping up and down in place.

"What about Mary Beth?" Scorpion asked.

Many people went silent upon hearing Scorpion's question. "As expected," he said as he walked back to the center of the stage. "But Mary Beth isn't, isn't she all right? Is not Mabel's daughter all right?"

"She's all right!" "Iowa loves Mary Beth!"

"Not good enough," Scorpion growled. "It's gone take more than just little ole me to get you people in the spirit," he said as tambourines and drums were heard playing. The curtain was pulled back and Beverly Battle and her band came into view.

"Jesus is just alright with me...Jesus is just alright oh yeah...Jesus is just alright with me...Jesus is just alright..." they all sung in unison, bringing the Doobie Brothers' song *Jesus Is Just Alright* to life over the roaring crowd, who all rose to their feet in one fail swoop and began clapping loudly as Beverly and her band played on.

Scorpion leapt from the four foot high stage into the crowd and began dancing at the foot of the middle aisle. For an older man he knew how to move, stepping wildly with his arms spread as if he were in a trance while waving a tambourine. He stiffened his body as shuffled his feet down the aisle towards Mary Beth, who was singing and clapping loudly herself. "Your moment has arrived, young sister!" he yelled aloud as he danced before Mary Beth.

Mary Beth looked around at all the people supporting her and was overcome with gratefulness. She'd indeed come a long way, and today was the day her past would be forgiven in the eyes of the lord. "I repent, father god!" she yelled aloud over the music with a raised hand. She then tilted her head back and stepped into the aisle and began dancing as if she'd caught the Holy Ghost. Her eyes were closed and she gyrated wildly in the middle aisle.

Meanwhile, on stage, Beverly Battle and her band was working the crowd up into a frenzy with their upbeat version of the Doobie Brothers' song. The entire building was rocking as the musicians played the perfect song leading up to Mary Beth's crowning moment. Drums pounded, tambourines were being slapped and worshipers were jumping up and down in place to the funky tune. Beverly and her band sung on as over two hundred people inside the makeshift house of worship became filled with the spirit.

Mary Beth had danced her way to the front of the aisle. She removed her leather trench coat and the crowd grew louder when they saw the white silk dress she was wearing. A bathtub was carried to the center of the stage. Water sloshed out from its sides as the three men toting it set it in its proper place. Suddenly, the band went from playing that of a jubilant song and the lights were dimmed. Beverly and her band entered and entered into a bluesy, gospel tune as she strummed her electric guitar.

"Jesusssss...he's my friend..." Beverly sung with pure unadulterated soul as she played her guitar through closed eyes...*"Jesussssss..."* she screamed aloud in her raspy voice... *"he's my friend...he took me by the hand...led me farrrr from this land...Jesusssss...he's my friend..."* the talented singer stepped back from the microphone at that moment and entered into one of her famous guitar solos.

While Beverly played on with her band, Scorpion went and stood before Mary Beth as she stood with her back to the tub. He cradled her forehead in the palm of his right hand and placed his left hand behind her waist. "In the name of the father and the holy spirit, I profess you free of your past sins!" he yelled over the band's gospel melody. "Today is the beginning of the rest of your life, Mary Beth!"

"Free me, pastor! Lord, make me whole again!" Mary Beth cried aloud as she spread her arms wide. Her body grew limp and Scorpion had to hold her up as Beverly continued to sing.

As she was being dipped into the baptismal waters, Mary Beth's life flashed before her eyes. The day her father raped her, the day Jeremy raped her when she believed he would be the one to help her overcome. Wendell and his abuse on the school bus entered her mind along with her mother's denial, and finally, the birth of her children. She held her eyes open, watching Scorpion's face blur and hearing the cheers and the music muffle as the man covered her nose and mouth and held her beneath the water's surface for what seemed like an eternity. She was on the verge of slapping Scorpion's arms for having run out of breath when she was suddenly jerked from beneath the water and returned to her feet.

Beverly and her band returned to their festive, orchestrated tune at that moment and the tambourines were once again ringing aloud as the congregation began dancing up and down the aisles once more, celebrating Mary Beth's redemption. "Another child of Christ has returned home, everybody! Mary Beth Mobley! Dance, Mary Beth! Show the Lord you appreciate his sacrifice!" Scorpion coaxed as he danced beside an overjoyed Mary Beth.

"Jesus is just alright with me...Jesus is just alright oh yeah..." Beverly and her band began to sing once more....

Mary Beth looked over to her mother and children, smiled and began dancing on stage beside Scorpion. Finally, she was able to begin to live with the demons she'd been carrying for most of her life. Hers had been a long journey, and no one was more deserving of having her sins forgiven than Mary Beth, an innocent in a world of chaos and betrayal perpetrated against her by those who were put on Earth to protect her and watch out for her welfare.

Mabel was so overcome with emotion she had to excuse herself. She shuffled through the crowd and made her way out the front door. She leaned against the wooden doors of the club and covered her face and shed tears. Her daughter was a beautiful soul. Doing the best she could to simply survive and eek out an existence. Hers was a heavy burden to bear, and Mabel knew all-too-well that she was partly responsible.

Tanya, meanwhile, was still offstage watching. She had never seen such a riveting moment unfold inside of a church. She knew all that Mary Beth had been through and was happy for the woman. Deciding it was time to leave, she exited the side door of the club and made her way back towards her station wagon. She rounded the front of the building and saw Mabel resting on her heels in front of the doors leading into the club. "Are you okay, Senator?" she asked.

Mabel quickly right herself, stood to her feet and said, "Yeah, yes, Tanya. That was, that was quite a, quite performance."

"You're not talking about Beverly, are you?"

"Of course not," Mabel admitted through a sigh as she pulled out a silk scarf and dabbed her tears. "It just really hit home for me."

"As it should," Tanya admonished. "You two still have a lot of work to do."

"Yes," Mabel responded softly while nodding her head in agreement. "I know you have to be going," she added as she pulled out an eye liner and reached for Tanya's hand. "This is the number to my car, and my number in DC. You already have my home number. I know of Beverly's intentions to help Faye, but that's a long shot at best. If there's anything I can do for you, please, don't hesitate to call."

Tanya held up the hand with Mabel's number on it and waved at the woman with it as she walked off. She'd had an unbelievable experience from the time she'd ridden up onto the Patterson farm up until her departure from Bandits and she would not only never forget the things she'd seen and learned, but she was indeed going to hold both the Senator and Beverly to their words as they now mattered in the big scheme of things. She left Bandits with more knowledge about the people that knew of Faye's on goings. The reward had indeed been worth the risk. She couldn't wait to tell Brenda what all she'd learned as she made her way back to the Bevington Inn. Before she could knock on the door after exiting the car, however, Brenda was there to pull it open.

"Where the fuck you been for the past four hours and shit, bitch? You done left me in this country, backwoods, redneck ass town not knowing if the police done caught up with your ass or not! We need to get the fuck outta here not now but right now!"

Tanya shoved Brenda into the room, slammed the door, locked it, and ran over to the curtains where she anxiously peered out into the parking lot. "You hollering at me and shit when I'm tryna get away!" she scoffed lowly as her head bobbed to and fro while peeking out the curtains.

"Get away?" Brenda asked shocked. "You got somebody on your ass and you brought 'em here where the fuck I was hidin'?" she asked hysterically as she jumped up and down in place.

"It was the only place I knew, alright!" Tanya said in a panicked manner. "Oooohhh! They fuckin' comin', too!" she snapped as she closed the curtains. "They coming!"

"We got guns and shit! Let me flush this weed!" Brenda declared as she ran and scooped up a bag of marijuana off one of the nightstands and ran towards the bathroom.

"Wait a minute!" Tanya retorted. "I was just fuc—"

"Fuck that! I ain't going to jail in this hick town!"

Tanya heard the toilet's swoosh just before Brenda reappeared dusting her hands. "Okay, the weed gone. We got registered guns with no bodies so we good. Where they at?"

"Ain't no law, man!" Tanya complained with her hands on her hips. "I was fucking kidding! I was fuckin' kidding and you go and flush all the weed! Now we gotta ride home sober and shit!"

Brenda laughed and pulled out the bag of marijuana. "Nahhh, bitch. You riding sober." The look on Tanya's face was priceless for Brenda. "That's right," she laughed. "I know your ass. If the law was on you, you wouldna ran here and blocked yourself in. Let's go. You drive while I get high. Sober ass!"

"Fuck you," Tanya sighed through a chuckle as she began gathering her belongings.

CHAPTER EIGHTEEN

THE HOMEFRONT

"First shipment's done made its way into Mitchellville." Tanya stated to Faye as she walked into her library.

"That's my cue to get the show on the road in a few days," Faye remarked as she continued writing a letter to Bonita.

It was a year after the Iowa job, March of 1985. The heroin pipeline coming in from Venezuela was now up and running. Product was being sold on the streets of New Orleans and Cincinnati, and two kilograms a month were being pumped into Mitchellville. Izzy was now interim warden pending approval by a board of members headed by Senator Mabel Sougherbraun-Mobley; she was the go-between. Alfredo would visit and make a simple drop off to her and she would float the drugs into the facility for Bonita and Cikala to off.

All was well with the crew. The murders of the warden and three members from the biker gang sparked a major investigation, but nothing was ever traced back to Mitchellville. The warden's involvement with The Urbandale Gals sent authorities in a totally different direction. Grace Unger's death was ruled a suicide and Izzy had only been questioned once regarding the deaths of Donovan and Claire. Everybody had lain low for the past twelve months to let the investigations blow over, and after getting away with outright murder, it was business as usual once again.

"You gone be okay out there by yourself?" Tanya asked as she sat across from Faye.

"I'll be fine in Kansas," Faye responded, looking up from the table top. "I just plan on laying low until I figure a way to beat these charges. If I'm caught beforehand, I'll deal with it. I'm just tired of running and want to go home."

"Hiding in plain sight isn't a bad idea. You know where we at. Now, I'm going make myself a daiquiri and get lit this Mardi Gras day," Tanya replied as she checked the time on watch and left the library.

While Faye sat at the table mapping her strategy, Brenda was out on the second floor balcony with Mouse and Alfredo. The three were drinking and overlooking the revelry unfolding in the French Quarters while they took turns working the grill that was going. One year-old Helen lay asleep in the spare bedroom and Maggie, RJ, and Popeye were playing quietly on the carpeted floor while watching cartoons.

"Anybody heard from Willie?" Tanya asked as she stepped out on the balcony with her drink.

"You know what she doing," Mouse replied as he closed the lid on the smoking grill after flipping the chicken. "She back over to The Night Owl handlin' her business."

"She 'bout her money," Tanya replied as she sipped her drink.

"That shit ain't end gone good with Willie, I'm telling y'all." Brenda remarked.

Brenda was worried about Willie. The reason was because she had witnessed Willie and Sally's mother in the Jummonville Driveway passing words a couple of weeks earlier about Sally hanging with Willie. Willie told the lady that her daughter was old enough to make her own decisions and she needed to mind her business. Brenda knew what Willie was doing this day; she only hoped she didn't have Sally with her at the time as she just knew Ms. Betty was sure to cause problems and possibly wreck Willie's hustle if she ever caught her daughter engaging in prostitution with Willie again.

****

"...I just love that smiling face...in the early sun...if I can't have you to myself...then life's no fun...I'd rather be with you hoo(yeah)...yeah I'd rather be with you hoo..."

While most of crew parlayed over to Tanya and Alfredo's home, Willie, meanwhile, was inside The Night Owl with Sally, Vivian and Zelda hosting a special party. Hers was a private affair. She and her girls had only three attendees this day:

Yabba Dabba and two of his comrades from the precinct. The young women were all either partially, or totally naked, serving drinks, and dancing for and with the three officers. The loft on the second floor was frequented on occasion for sex. The music was loud and raunchy, and cigarette and marijuana smoke lingered heavy in the air behind the barricaded doors.

Yabba Dabba loved to party. And he loved to party with young, black women. Willie provided the man with what he craved and he was willing to pay out the ass for what he wanted. Much of the money Yabba Dabba spent was money he received from payoffs from the crew and other dealers in other parts of the Seventh Ward. It was also fair to say that Yabba Dabba and his buddies were Willie's biggest clients, and Sally was her biggest draw.

The Sergeant was out on the dance floor wearing only a wife beater, boxer shorts, his silk socks and shoes. He was gyrating to Bootsy Collins' song *I'd Rather Be With You* as he ground against Vivian's naked backside.

Zelda, who was wearing Yabba Dabba's police shirt and Sergeant's cap and nothing else, was bumping up against his rear end and toking on a joint as the man rocked to and fro while yelling aloud incoherently, trying his best to sing along with the artist's vocals in his drunken state. Together, the three rocked in unison, clapping their hands and rocking side to side while laughing loudly.

Sally, meanwhile, was upstairs with Yabba Dabba's two comrades. The two white officers, both in their mid-forties and slightly overweight, were taking turns eating her out from behind as she stood on the mattress with her hands planted against the wall. Sally had on a short, plaid Catholic school girl uniform with no panties underneath and her hair in two pigtails. Clients loved the under-aged looking eighteen year-old—especially when she wore the school uniform. Willie had turned Sally out completely. She had become a bona fide freak under her tutelage and she was loving every minute of her young life.

When the night was done, the girls cleaned the lounge and tidied themselves up in the bathroom in the loft. Willie, having showered and dressed, now sat at the bar counting the girls' money as Sally, Vivian and Zelda sat at a booth enjoying Marvin Gaye's song *Got to Give it Up*. They talked about going shopping as Willie counted the earnings. She and her girls had made three thousand dollars for five hours of smoke, drink, dance and sex. She gave each of her girls five hundred dollars and kept fifteen hundred for herself. They then all exited the bar and headed for the Jummonville driveway.

Willie's girls were dressed like she, wearing high, tight-fitting mini-skirts, low cut tops and knee length boots. Wherever they went, Willie and her crew drew attention. One could tell right away that they were hookers. When not servicing Yabba Dabba, the girls could often be seen leaning into the driver's side of a car or talking to a group of men trying to work out a price for their time. They were known throughout the St. Bernard and highly sought after for their willingness to engage in sex for money. Many a married man and common-law men paid the young women for sex.

Willie and her girls walked casually up the Jummonville driveway. They were slowly approaching Brenda's old apartment, which set downstairs on their left, as they discussed future moves. "I want y'all girls to take a couple of days off," Willie remarked. "Take some of that money and get y'all hair and nails done. Do some shopping and we gone meet up again Saturday night. The players gone be out looking for a good time and I want y'all girls to be looking and feeling fresh," she stated calmly as she eyed Ms. Betty emerging from the back door of her home.

Ms. Betty, a mid-forties, tan-skinned heavy-set woman with curly black hair and dark eyes, stepped out onto her porch with a scowl on her face. "Sally, what I told you about hangin' with that fuckin' hoe?" she yelled aloud to her daughter in reference to Willie.

"What the fuck I told *you*, old lady? You need to mind your fuckin' business!" Willie snapped back as she stood in the middle of the driveway.

"Sally is my business, bitch! You stay away from my daughter before I kick your li'l nasty ass!"

"If you was a real mother—she wouldn't be with my *li'l nasty ass!*" Willie countered sarcastically as Sally broke and ran towards her back porch.

Willie had lot of nerve to be challenging Ms. Betty at this moment. She had a mouth on her that would sometimes land her in trouble, but she was not one to back down from a confrontation. This day was no different. She stood in the driveway with her hands on her hips calling for Sally to come back outside as Ms. Betty walked down her stairs. The woman crossed the driveway and approached Willie, but Vivian and Zelda stepped in the way, impeding her progress.

The fraternal twins eyed Ms. Betty; brown-skinned Vivian standing in her black silk outfit with her neatly-styled permed hair and matching knee-length boots, and tan-skinned Zelda, dressed the same in evergreen with her tapered Afro standing beside her, both twins sizing Ms. Betty Irving up as she walked up the driveway.

The angered mother quickly took note of the twins. "I ain't scared of you two big bitches!" she screamed.

"You should be!" Zelda barked. "Step your ass over here and get ya' some!"

Ms. Betty stared the twins down as she remained in place. The woman was a fighter, but she wasn't foolish enough to take on both Zelda and Vivian. One twin was rough enough; with the two of them together she stood no chance. "Willie! This shit here ain't over between me and you! You got it comin', mutherfucka! You wrong! You dead wrong!" she yelled in near tears.

Willie stood behind the King Sisters in her orange outfit and matching boots dancing in place. "That's right," she laughed as she shuffled her feet and snapped her fingers. "Your fat ass know how far to go. Now go and get your daughter so she can sell some more of that good pussy she got for me."

Ms. Betty was angered to tears. Her face displayed a look of sheer rage as she turned and walked quickly back towards her apartment. Her face was wet with tears as she entered her apartment. The time she slammed her door, Willie, Vivian and Zelda could hear the woman screaming at Sally. Their smiles dropped when they heard Sally yell, "Momma, why you hit me?"

"You want me and Viv to go over there and handle that, Willie?" Zelda asked seriously as she looked back and pulled a .38 snub nose from her back waistband.

Willie knew the King Sisters would willingly go over and knock on Ms. Betty's door, but she wasn't going to send the twins over to the woman's home to shoot her. "Nahh, I'm gone deal with Betty myself when the time comes. Let's go," she ended somberly as she and the twins walked towards Foy court to buy another bag of weed.

Later that night, Brenda, Tanya and Faye were sharing a bottle of Amaretto and sitting in the living room inside Tanya's home talking amongst themselves over the on-going revelry in the French Quarters when Willie let herself in with the spare key. She was heard mumbling to herself as she climbed the stairs. Upon reaching the library, she threw her purse aside and her three friends watched as she pranced over to the bar, steadily mumbling and cussing as she went about fixing herself a drink.

Brenda and Tanya eyed one another. They knew right away that Willie had gotten into it with Ms. Betty again. "What happened this time, Willie?" Brenda asked as she sat upright on the couch.

Faye and Tanya both eyed Willie, who was obviously under intense pressure. "You okay, girl?" Tanya asked concerned.

Willie stomped into the room with a glass of vodka on the rocks and explained to her girls what transpired between she and Betty and she was sure they were going to side with her.

"Betty did right, Willie," Brenda objected.

"You keep fuckin' with that lady and she gone put something on your ass," Tanya warned.

Willie then looked over to Faye, who was sitting with her legs crossed. She felt Willie's eyes on her and turned to face her. "What? You want my opinion?" she inquired with a slight smirk.

"Might as well," Willie said as she threw up her freehand. "Everybody else think I'm dead ass wrong."

"You are," Faye admitted. "I knew the time I saw Sally and learned what you had going on it wasn't good—but I can't judge. That's your way of making money and the woman is impeding business."

"You would be the one to encourage her," Brenda quipped as she side-eyed Faye while shaking her head.

"I'm not encouraging her. I'm just stating the facts," Faye smirked.

"See? That's why I like that woman!" Willie laughed as she pranced over and high-fived Faye.

"While you high-fiving your buddy, just know she would kill your ass if it was Maggie you was fuckin' with," Tanya chimed in as she sipped her vodka. "I would too if you was fuckin' around my daughter like that."

"Well, it's not your daughter and it's not your problem!" Willie sassed. "Sally of age and she can make her own decisions."

"Not as long as she's under her mother's roof," Tanya countered. "You should respect that."

"I say fuck that! This my hustle to run!"

"Willie," Brenda spoke as she sat upright on the couch and opened a bag of weed Willie had thrown down onto the table. She grabbed a sheet of Zig Zag rolling paper in order to roll a joint. "That's Betty's *daughter*," she explained. "Sister, you making good money out there with your game. I know Sally your biggest draw, but when a mother steps in, you have to respect that. Betty can handle her business. Just because she in her forties and a little overweight don't mean she can't get down. Remember, she was out there long before we came on the scene." Brenda ended as she poured marijuana into the sheet of cigarette paper and began to roll it up tightly.

"Yea, but she gotta lotta nerve to try and, to try and, and tell Sally not to do shit when Sally get everything she learned from that fat bitch!" Willie snapped back as she handed Brenda a lighter.

"No, Willie," Tanya chimed in calmly. "Sally gets everything she learned from *you*. Ms. Betty may man hop—but you do too. You do it to get paid—but Ms. Betty do it only to keep company. And Betty never encouraged Sally to do what she doing now—let alone accept money for it. *You* did all that to Sally. As hard as it is, you wrong on this one. You turned that woman's daughter out and now she's pissed off with you. Maybe you should just lay off on Sally until later on down the road." Tanya reasoned as Brenda nodded in agreement while taking tokes off the joint she'd lit.

Willie wasn't hearing Tanya's rationale. Sally had come to her after all. And now that money was being made, she wasn't about to let her go. "Fuck that shit! Sally workin' for me regardless of what her momma say! That's my top earner and she gone stay in that position until I say otherwise. Fuck Betty!" she ended as she walked out onto the balcony.

Brenda, Tanya, and Faye knew Willie would have to learn a hard lesson. That lesson being: you don't fuck with a woman's daughter when she is involved in her child's life. Sally had a mother who really cared; her working double shifts at a downtown hotel left her alone most times and she was unable to control her daughter's actions. Willie was taking advantage of a hard working woman and using said woman's child for her own personal gain. She may have been getting away with it for the moment, but what would come of the situation would be a lesson learned and something never to be repeated.

CHAPTER NINETEEN

COCK-BLOCKING

It was the following Saturday after the dispute with Ms. Betty. Willie was in the loft of The Night Owl with Vivian and Zelda. It was approaching midnight and the club was filled to capacity as usual. The players were out and the women were hot and ready. Drinks were flowing, the conversation was cheery and the music was on point.

Tanya was working the bar with Wanda Slack, Willie's mother, at her side. Working the bar kept Tanya close to the action. It was also the perfect front for the crew to supply some of the well-known dealers around town with the potent black tar the crew was selling. The women were raking in thousands of dollars a night and sitting on top of the heroin industry in the city, and they weren't taking any shorts. They ran the streets with tenacity and refused to let other dealers set up shop. The seventh ward, fourth ward, fifteenth ward and the French Quarters was their domain and everybody knew who controlled those territories.

While Tanya worked the bar and made sales, Mouse and Al-fredo sat inside a booth at the back of the club, each armed with an Uzi, watching the customers Tanya served heroin to in order to make sure a jack play didn't go down or was not in the process of being put together.

Brenda, meanwhile, was lurking in the back alleyway, which was where Willie's tricks entered the club via the stair-case to engage in sexual activities. The operation the crew had going was a smooth set up. Everybody was making descent money, including Willie; but Willie was irate on this night.

The reason being was because Ms. Betty, if Willie had to tell it, was obstructing her cash flow. She had been calling Sal-ly's house for the last two hours unable to reach her top earner. It was now well past midnight and she had already missed out on nine hundred dollars on Sally. She had her young trick's brand new black and red school girl uniform laid out and ready to go, but Sally had never showed at the appointed time.

Willie knew Sally was being kept against her wishes be-cause every time she called, Ms. Betty would answer the phone. The woman was always out in the streets on Saturday nights, but she was home on this evening. Willie sat at the kitchen counter inside the loft fuming over Ms. Betty's inter-ference in her and Sally's affairs—ever mind the fact she was exploiting the woman's daughter for her own personal gain— in Willie's eyes, Sally had made the decision all on her own. And even if she did, in a round-about-way, encourage Sally to sell herself, Willie felt that Ms. Betty had no right to interfere because Sally was eighteen-years-old.

Willie then thought about the fucked up way in which Ms. Betty was thwarting her profits when she heard a loud, rhythmic knock on the emergency door. She got up and the twins and their clients all paused on the bed. "That's Brenda. It's smooth, brothers. Y'all go on." she stated to the customers as the four returned to their previous duties.

Willie cracked the door and saw Brenda standing on the stairs with her Uzi, "This dude say he know you, but I ain't never seen him before." she stated as he stepped back.

Willie peeked out the door and down the stairs and saw a man she recognized. He was a Times Picayune newspaper editor she had met at Al Scramuzza's Seafood Market. "She ain't here." Willie whispered to the man as she made a slicing motion across her neck with her right hand.

"Can you call her?" the man asked politely as he ascended the stairs in his navy blue silk suit and black wing tips. "We set this up a few days ago, remember?"

Brenda cocked her Uzi. "You heard what she said. The bitch ain't here!" she scowled.

"Chill out, B. He cool," Willie stated as she quickly thought back and remembered the day she introduced Zelda and Vivian to the man several months back. She had shown the man a picture of Sally the week before in the seafood market's parking lot. The picture displayed Sally in her school girl uniform with no panties on, her ass and pussy on clear display. The man offered Willie six hundred dollars to take Sally anally and they had agreed to meet the following Saturday, which was this day. Willie had just loss a total of fifteen hundred dollars over what she deemed as Ms. Betty's 'cock-blocking'. In an attempt to still make a few hundred, she offered Vivian to the man. The man had been with Vivian and Zelda both two times before, but he wanted what he saw in the picture—he wanted Sally.

Willie decided to try and contact Sally again. She had the man wait with Brenda outside as she tried repeatedly to call Sally, only Ms. Betty kept answering the phone. Willie would hang up and call right back, only to get a dead tone. She did that repeatedly for almost five minutes until the man had finally left and Brenda informed her that he was gone.

Willie dialed Ms. Betty's number again, this time to cuss her out, but Ms. Betty beat her to the draw. "Bitch, if you call here one more time for my daughter, the next time I see your ass I'm gone drag it up and down the sidewalk!" Ms. Betty snapped as she slammed the phone down in Willie's ear.

That was it for Willie. Those were fighting words. Ms. Betty had just given her a reason to whip her ass. She dialed the number one more time. Ms. Betty didn't answer her phone, but she got the message: Willie had just called her on her bluff. Only Ms. Betty wasn't bluffing. Neither was Willie. These two females were now on a collision course.

Willie was deciding on how to approach Ms. Betty when Tanya ascended the stairs from inside the club that led to the loft and she tapped on the door lightly. She pulled the door open and Tanya entered the room and stared at the scene.

The room was lit with a red light bulb. The music from the club was playing low on the speakers beside the bed which had mirrors on the ceiling. It was a sexy set up no doubt. Tanya briefly eyed Zelda, who was sitting on the edge of the bed giving slow head to a client that stood before her; only her thick afro could be seen as her head move back and forth over the man's rigid pole.

Vivian lay on her back beside her sister with her legs spread eagle; a muscular black man driving in and out of her at a fast and furious pace as she moaned aloud like a woman possessed.

Tanya had to admit that Willie had the skills to get females to do her bidding, but she knew Willie was pissed about Sally not being on hand this night because every time Tanya entered the loft to re-up on her heroin, Willie would state her anguish concerning Ms. Betty.

"That bitch over there got Sally hemmed up! I'm missing mutherfuckin' money fuckin' with Betty." Willie whispered angrily to Tanya.

"How you making out tonight without her, though?" Tanya asked Willie lowly as the two walked towards the kitchen.

"I got like four more people lined up for those two. But Yabba Dabba came through with his two friends. They left when they learned Sally wasn't on hand. This other man just left 'cause she wasn't here. I swear on my fuckin' son—I'm gone slay that hoe for fuckin' up my money tonight!" Willie replied through gritted teeth.

"What? You gone kill Ms. Betty?" Tanya asked, somewhat dismayed by Willie's remark.

"No! But I'm gone catch that bitch going to church tomorrow morning and wear her ass out!" Willie stated angrily as she poured herself a shot of Taaka Vodka.

"You sure that's smart? I mean, Ms. Betty—"

"Yea, yea, yea! I know—she was a gangster back in the fuckin' sixties. This the eighties! The bitch past her prime!"

"Alright! Alright! I'm just saying—don't judge a book by its cover. You want me to go with you when you do that?" Tanya asked as she grabbed her .9mm from her left hip and checked to see if it was still on safety before placing it back into its holster.

Willie thought for a minute. She felt she didn't need back up for Ms. Betty; but she wanted a witness on hand to watch her knock the old woman out before she went to church. "Yeah! Meet me here at eight-thirty tomorrow mornin'! I'm gone catch her ass at the bus stop and give her what the fuck she been askin' for!" Willie replied matter-of-factly.

"I hear ya', girl. See you in the morning after I send Faye off," Tanya said as she grabbed her next package of heroin and left the loft.

****

The following morning, Tanya was up bright and early. It was a cloudy, cool Sunday in March of 1985. She and Faye were milling about the kitchen feeding Helen and Maggie breakfast. This was Faye's last morning in New Orleans for a while. She and Maggie were on their way to Cherryvale, Kansas. She'd made nearly a half million dollars the year or so she spent in New Orleans by distributing heroin, and she was now aiming to clear her name in Iowa and see what could be done about the seven year-old attempted murder charge she was still facing while rejuvenating the land back in Kansas.

A newly-purchased 1984 white Porsche 911 with black trimming and dark grey and black, mag wheels in Tanya's name was her ride of choice. She had an undetectable speed indicator in the dash and leather seats. She and Maggie would ride into America's heartland in style.

With her alias name and dyed hair and makeup, Faye wasn't the least worried about being captured on her journey. She knew how to drive the highways. On top of that, she had her faithful friend Maggie tagging along. If she were to get pulled over, a woman with a toddler in tow would arouse the least suspicion. And she wasn't too worried about the townsfolk in Cherryvale finding out about her warrants as the town did little investigations into outside criminal activities and weren't patched in to the national database.

An hour later, the friends were set to part ways. Tanya was waiting for Faye on the first floor of her loft when she came down the stairs holding Maggie's hand and a satchel in the other. "I'm taking a hundred thousand with me," she told Tanya. "You know where I stashed the rest."

"Good luck out there."

Faye chuckled and said, "I don't need luck. All I need is for everybody in Cherryvale to stay the hell outta my way."

"I been trying to get Willie to come around. I mean, I think the Senator in Iowa could really help us, you know? If Willie were get into politics, man..." Tanya's voice trailed off as she thought about how callous Willie was becoming.

"You know my plans for Cherryvale," Faye remarked. "When the time is right, everything will come together."

"That's years from now."

"Maybe, but for the business we're in, it's worth the effort don't you think?"

"It is," Tanya agreed. "You got the number. If you need anything done out there in Kansas don't hesitate to call."

"You'll need me before I need you," Faye joked, never knowing how right she was as she hugged Tanya briefly and stepped into the morning mist and climbed into her Porsche after placing her bag of money in the back of the car. She eased out of the French Quarters and began her journey to Kansas, where she would begin to reestablish herself in her homeland.

****

Tanya, meanwhile, had gone back upstairs and had sat with Helen until the one year-old fell back to sleep. She laid her daughter beside a sleeping Alfredo and went and showered and dressed before leaving her home and climbing into her brown station wagon where she made her way over to the Saint Bernard project.

In spite of her worrying about how Willie was carrying on, Tanya had told everybody she could think of about Willie's plan for Ms. Betty. Bets were being taken this morning and she was on hand to see everything go down. Reaching Gibson Street, where Willie's mother apartment lay, Tanya could see that the place was still and quiet. She exited the car and jumped up the stairs and tapped on the door lightly. A minute or so later, Willie answered wearing a silk robe and matching teddy.

"You ain't dressed! It's almost eight! Betty catches the eight-ten bus!" Tanya complained as she stepped into the apartment.

"I be ready," Willie yawned.

"Well, I'm going over to the lounge. Meet me over there."

"Cool," Willie replied before she closed and locked the door. She was entering the bathroom when she was met in the hall by her mother, Wanda.

"And another thing!" Wanda yelled aloud as she held onto a glass of whiskey. The woman hadn't gone to bed ever since The Night Owl closed down at four thirty in the morning. She'd heard what her daughter was planning and was in full agreement. Betty had no right in interfering in Willie's business in her mind. "When you beat that fat hoe this morning? You get a gut shot in for your mother is what ya' do!" she stated as she downed the remainder of her drink.

"Say what?" Willie asked as she stood in her mother's face.

"Whip—Betty—ass!" Wanda spoke through slurred speech. "I would join ya' out there, but I can't make it because I'm tore up from the floor up. Check the stove before you leave and make sure it's off. My black ass is going to bed!" Wanda ended as she walked into her bedroom and closed the door.

Willie only shook her head as she laughed. She and her mother were two peas in a pod. Rather than school her daughter and diffuse the situation, Wanda Slack only perpetuated the matter. Willie went on and got dressed as she thought about how she was going to take Ms. Betty down this Sunday morning.

Tanya, meanwhile, had just climbed out of her station wagon. She was unlocking the door to the club when a dark blue Nova rounded the corner. "Ohh nooo," she sighed, as Yabba Dabba pulled up in front of the club.

Tanya watched Yabba Dabba's big head moving up and down and the white from his teeth was on clear display as he sat behind the steering wheel. The Sergeant loved to try and make Tanya piss her pants, but he never succeeded. She had urinated outside many a time so as not to let that happen, but after nearly two years of knowing Yabba Dabba, she still couldn't control her laughter whenever she saw the guy.

Yabba Dabba knew that to be true, and he would try to get Tanya to wet herself each and every opportunity presented to him. He climbed out of his car laughing as he removed his sergeant's cap and walked towards Tanya. "Weinyburger, let me ask ya' somethin'!"

"It's Weinberger, you dick. Look here, ya' Fred Flint-stone-looking son-of-a-bitch," Tanya laughed goofily as she snorted and produced a fake yawn while unlocking the barricaded door, "it's early in the mornin' and I ain't laughin' at none of your Bedrock stories today." she remarked, trying to pay Yabba Dabba no attention. Still, she couldn't control her urge to giggle. *This motherfucka is relentless with this shit!"* she thought to herself as she pulled the door open to the club.

Yabba Dabba looked at Tanya's red face and produced another wide smile as the two walked into the club. "No Flint-stone stories this time, Weinerburger, or whatever you calling yourself, ya' long-face flat assed giraffe. I hear, I hear Willie supposed to beat up Betty this morning."

"So you heard, with ya' short dick ass," Tanya stated as she and Yabba Dabba took a seat at the counter.

"Your peppermint stick without the stripes-looking ass was the one put the word out. Look, we can rib all day if ya' want, but word gets around. I bet a hundred on Betty."

"You crazy, Yabba Dabba. Willie gone whip that old lady ass this morning." Tanya retorted.

Just then there was a loud tap on the front door of the club. Tanya peeked out the peep hole and saw Willie and opened the door and she stepped in chomping down on a fried egg sandwich.

"You ready, homegirl?" Tanya asked.

"Beyond ready. Hold up let me get some orange juice first." Willie said as she walked behind the counter.

"I hope I don't lose my fuckin' money this mornin' bettin' on Betty." Yabba Dabba stated.

"She heard you." Tanya remarked as she lit a joint, took a few tokes and passed it to Yabba Dabba.

"Maybe so," Yabba Dabba said in between puffs, "but let this thing play out. A lot of people got money on the line here. Don't taint the participants."

Willie walked over to the bar counter and stood before her friends. She took the joint from Yabba Dabba and sucked down its remnants and finished her juice. With a fortified breakfast and drink under her belt and a quick buzz, she was set to complete her mission. "Let's do this! That bitch Betty got it comin' this mornin'! And as for you Yabba Dabba—don't worry about your money. I got ya' covered!"

"Sorry to hurt your heart, beautiful, but I bet on Betty." Yabba Dabba laughed.

"Fuck wrong with you, Zack?" Willie scoffed as she shoved the huge man's shoulder. "You just lost a grip! You gone regret the day you went against Willameena Slack!"

"Prove me wrong, Willie," Yabba Dabba stated as the three headed towards the exit.

Tanya was going for her station until Willie stopped her. "We takin' the Caprice, girl! I want Betty to see my ass ridin' up on her so she know what to expect this mornin'!" she ended as she threw the keys to Tanya and climbed into the passenger seat.

Yabba Dabba stood before the lounge's entrance and watched as Willie bounced up and down in her seat while pointing her finger at Tanya. She was bucking at this moment, prepared to take down her foe and claim what was rightfully hers in her eyes. "It's war out ta' this bitch!" she exclaimed.

"You tell 'em, Willie!" Tanya chimed in, further fueling Willie's intent as she started the car.

"Say, say what? I say it's a mutherfuckin' war out ta' this bitch!"

"Put Betty ass in check!" Yabba Dabba remarked through laughter from the sidewalk.

"I'm not only gone check Betty—I'm gone, I'm gone *tax* that hoe today, Zack!" Willie yelled aloud as she bounced up and down in the front seat.

Tanya pulled away from the curb, jerking the car forward in the process. Willie could be heard stating her case as she drove off. "Yabba Dabba got money riding on Betty, huh? His ass trippin'! Sally even hoping I whip her momma ass this morning!" she was heard yelling as Tanya turned right onto Senate Street, rode past Jummonville and approached the intersection on St. Bernard Avenue.

When they approached the corners of St. Bernard Avenue and Senate Street, Willie looked to her left and saw Ms. Betty waiting at the bus stop and she immediately began to laugh. Ms. Betty was wearing a white and pink polka dot dress and pink pumps and had on a white straw hat with a pink carnation planted on the right side.

"That bitch over there looking like a fucked up roll of cotton candy! Make the block on her ass!" Willie commanded.

Tanya turned onto the four-lane road and cruised past Ms. Betty. Ms. Betty in turn, eyed the car as it rode by slowly. The forty-five year-old tan-skinned buxom woman could clearly see Willie on side of Tanya in the extremely long vehicle jumping up and down while running off at the mouth.

Tanya made the block and the long, lime green Caprice pulled up slowly in front of the bus stop. Ms. Betty stood by idly as Willie stared her down from the passenger seat as the car cruised to a halt. The older woman threw her pink leather purse to the ground and took two steps back. "Willie, this my last time warning you! You and Tanya take that long, ugly mutherfuckin' car and drive the fuck away from here."

"Nahh, you got it comin' today!" Willie yelled as she flung the door open, leapt from the car and rushed towards Ms. Betty, throwing series of punches in the process.

Tanya stepped onto the sidewalk and watched the scene before her. She grimaced at the punches landed and the screams emanating from the mouths of the females. She then took on a worried look as she feared the ambulance would have to be called because of the pain that was being dished out on this cloudy Sunday morning.

No longer able to stomach the brutality, Tanya screamed aloud, "Willie, that's enough! Let it ride! She done!"

Neither woman stopped fighting, however; Tanya danced around the squabbling females and was finally able to pull Ms. Betty off Willie, who lay on the sidewalk with her arms covering her face, pleading for mercy.

"Ms. Betty, she done! She fuckin' had enough, man, come on!" she pleaded.

Ms. Betty bounced up off Willie and kicked at her legs repeatedly as Tanya pulled her away from Willie's limp and bruised body. She talked major shit as Tanya went and helped an ailing Willie up from the concrete. "You take your punk ass back on Gibson Street and get a set of hands, ya' li'l hoe! And stay away from Sally you nasty bitch!" she yelled as she bowed up at Tanya.

Tanya let go of Willie and she fell back onto the concrete and screamed aloud again as she had bumped her head on the sidewalk. "My fault," she said to Willie as she jumped back and threw up her set to defend herself from the angry mother. Ms. Betty might have knocked Willie senseless, but Tanya was determined not to go out in that manner.

Ms. Betty had no grudges against Tanya, though. "Y'all two got some nerve tryna rush me! With your pale white ass! I oughta fuck you up on general principle, Tanya! Y'all two get the hell from 'round me! Fuckin' up my Sunday and shit before I even get to church!"

Tanya ushered Willie to the car, placed her into the passenger seat and sped off. She turned onto Gibson Street with Willie in the passenger seat holding her forehead and covering her left eye. She couldn't help but to sniggle as she drove Willie home.

"What the fuck funny? Why you ain't jump in when she got the best of me?" Willie asked nearly out of breath.

"You said you had Betty! I lost two hundred dollars over this shit!"

Willie smiled through her half-covered face. "You bet on me?"

"No doubt! I thought you could take her. Brenda was right. Betty got a set of hands on her for her age."

"I knew that, yea?"

"Then why you did that, Willie?"

"Tanya, I ran my mouth and I had ta' at least try and back it up. I got my ass kicked this mornin'. Betty dotted my fuckin' eye, brer—but hey, I went there with that bitch!" Willie stated proudly through light laughter.

"Yea, Willie," Tanya replied in open laughter, "You went there and got your ass kicked."

"Shut up!" Willie snapped as Tanya pulled up to her apartment. She climbed out her Caprice, not even bothering to say goodbye as she was embarrassed over the whole ordeal.

"What you want me to do with your car?"

"Sell the bitch, I don't care!" snapped Willie snapped as she walked into her apartment and slammed the door shut. Tanya merely laughed and drove off and headed back to her family in the French Quarters.

Willie walked through the living room and entered the kitchen in order to place some ice on her eye. She was headed for her bedroom to go back to sleep when Wanda walked out of her room. The woman's eyes grew wide and she tilted her head to the side.

"Momma, don't say shit to me!" Willie barked as she raised her freehand.

"Yo' ass done went up to that bus stop and got beat the fuck down didn't ya'!" Wanda snapped.

"I slipped! I slipped on some M and M's or something and she jumped on me."

"M and M's? You ain't slip on no M and M's! That old woman just put a hurtin' on your ass! You gone learn fuckin' 'round with folks' children! I shoulda known not to bet on your behind ya' no fighting son-of-a-bitch you just cost me five hundred damn dollars this morning!"

"Oh, I'm gone learn not to mess with people children? You was all for me going up there!" Willie snapped as she held the ice to her eye.

"Only because I thought your ass could fight and I could win easy money! Get the fuck outta here!" Wanda dragged as she went in the bathroom and slammed the door shut.

Willie went into her bedroom and laid down on her back. She stared at the ceiling and began thinking real hard about what it was she doing to Sally. She also began to think harder about her future. She was in college and had political ambitions, but she was wasting her talent by running the streets. Giving up the life would be hard. She really wasn't ready to go legit, but cutting Sally off wouldn't be so difficult. She'd told herself if Ms. Betty won, she would honor her request.

On this day, Willie had decided to be true to her word. She would let Sally go and encourage her to do better. But as for her, the show must go on a little while longer. Willie had no clue, however, that her decision to continue on in the life, would eventually place all of her goals nearly out of reach.

CHAPTER TWENTY

HE ASKED FOR TOO MUCH

It was a month after the incident with Miss Betty. April of 1985. Willie, Zelda and Vivian, both were on the stroll on a Saturday night in the heart of the Quarters. They were walking up and down Bourbon Street dressed in thigh-high tight-fitting black silk dresses. The black leather boots they wore cost over a thousand dollars a pair. The white pearl necklaces and gold bracelets coupled with the diamond bezel watches had the girls' wrists and necks sparkling.

Willie and her girls sometimes hung out inside *Big Daddy's,* the world famous gentlemen's club that featured a mannequin in a window swinging to and fro, only its legs visible to the eyeing public. Willie was cool with the DJ, the wait staff, and the owner, who was rarely seen inside the club. Whenever the girls were looking for a client with serious money looking for a good time, *Big Daddy's* was the place they would turn to. This warm April night would be no different.

Willie and her girls strolled slowly down Bourbon Street mingling with the crowd. Holding conversation with a few people along the way and turning down a few offers because the money wasn't good enough. Blame it on the Pat O'Brien's *Hurricane* drinks, or the margaritas that were numbing the revelers, but the hardcore fact was, whenever a person traveled onto to Bourbon Street, it was obvious they were out to have a good time, and Willie and the King Sisters were out to assist the males that wanted to delve into the proud decadence that had earned Bourbon Street its notoriety throughout the seventies and now the eighties. They walked into *Big Daddy's* and took seats in a booth off to the right of the stage where a red-haired slender white woman was dancing in the nude to the Trammps' song *Disco Inferno*.

Willie ordered a glass of beer and sat back and eyed the club while vibing to the music. She had seen the white man with his huge cowboy hat and big blue eyes eyeing her and her girls a few seconds after they entered the place. Under the belief that she had a potential, she went into her mode of seduction. She began making light conversation with Zelda and Vivian to show that they were comfortable with their surroundings while informing the twins of the man, who was sitting at the bar nursing a twelve ounce beer and a mixed drink.

As Willie talked much about nothing, Zelda and Vivian looked towards the man's direction and stared for a few seconds before Zelda pretended to be whispering into Vivian's ear. Vivian then looked back at the man and laughed sexily and turned away. She then looked back again, this time holding her gaze a little longer on the man before she turned back to Willie and Zelda.

Willie and her girls were discussing how much they would charge the man, but to the man who was at the bar, they looked as if they were really interested in him. That was the twins' tactic. It was a seductive lure that Willie had taught Zelda and Vivian to use in order to get a man to approach her and her girls.

The tactic always worked and this night was another success. Willie eyed the man as he grabbed his drinks and approached the booth. He made his way through the crowded bar, brushing up against dancing females and hyper males that were yelling for the dancer on stage to reveal more of her naked flesh. The clean-shaven man now stood before Willie and her girls with a drink in each hand. The three were out their seats dancing to the music, snapping their fingers while rocking in place with their heads to the floor.

"Burn, baby, burn(disco inferno)...burn, baby, burn...burn this muther down y'all...burn, baby, burn(disco inferno)"

The man stood smiling in his tight-fitting light blue Wrangler jeans, light blue, tan and white plaid shirt and ten gallon tan cowboy hat. He soon began rocking next to Willie, leaned over and said, "They call me Dwight! I'm from Amarillo, Texas! What you young ladies doing up in a pace like this?"

"We out for a walk in the park! Only we don't play for free!" Willie yelled over the music as she danced beside the booth.

"I ain't lookin' for no trouble now! I know how this thing works!"

"How does it work?" Willie asked as she patted the man's bulge.

"Shit, honey, it works damn good! You wanna ride my wiener!" Dwight asked in his country-boy twang as he gyrated his hips and laughed aloud before guzzling the remainder of his mixed drink.

Zelda laughed aloud. "What's your name again?" she asked.

"My name Dwight Davis and I'm from Amarillo, Texas!" the happy-go-lucky stranger said aloud.

"Give us your address why don't you?" Vivian laughed aloud at the man. No one had ever given up such information so quickly to the girls.

Willie, believing she had a potential, leaned into the man. "Okay, Dwight! You say you know how this thing work! So tell me how it works!" she stated over the music as she finished her beer and slid the empty glass in Dwight's direction, signaling she wanted another one as she and the King Sisters took a seat back inside the booth. "We drinking vodka, by the way."

Dwight sat his drinks down and slid inside the booth beside Zelda as he flagged down one of the many waitresses working inside of *Big Daddy's* and ordered a bottle of vodka and two can sodas. "Well," Dwight spoke as he rubbed Zelda's leg. "I have a suite not too far from here. We can all retreat to my room and have some fun."

Willie, Zelda and Vivian burst into laughter. "We look like some cheap five or ten dollar tricks to you, Dwight?" Vivian asked as she leaned back in the booth and curled her lips. "He can't afford us, Willie."

"Willie?" Dwight said as his eyes widened. "Your name is Willie? Hey, you not one of those drag queens that be down here are you? 'Cause I ain't with that kinky shit now!"

Willie bowed her head and laughed before she stood up. She began rocking to the music as she slowly raised her dress and put her neatly-trimmed vagina on display. "My name is Willameena. They call me Willie for short, Dwight. Don't worry, I got a fine pussy as you can very well see. She loves to be sucked and fucked. You wanna taste and try it, baby?" she asked as she lowered her dress and sat back down and leaned into Dwight and inhaled his English Leather Cologne.

"You's good! What about them?" Dwight asked in reference to the sisters.

"You askin' too many questions now! We all fuckin' women 'round here! How we know your real name Dwight Davis? You might be a serial killer or somebody! Let, let me see some I.D.!" Zelda snapped over the music as she tapped the table with the finger nail on her index finger.

Dwight went into his wallet to retrieve his identification card. A stack of hundred dollar bills was clearly visible. The girls saw the amount of cash he had on his person, but they didn't let on that they knew they had a live one. "Let me see that picture—Dwight!" Willie snapped as Zelda and Vivian snickered.

As Willie and Zelda looked at Dwight's I.D., Vivian grabbed his hand and placed it on her naked pussy. "That's my sister over there. Nine hundred can get you the both of us. Fifteen hundred dollars, and you can all three of us any way you want." she said as she flicked her tongue across the man's ear.

"And y'all gone do anything I want? Whatever I say?" Dwight asked with a wide smile.

"Whatever you say, cowboy." Vivian whispered into Dwight's ear.

Dwight owned an agricultural machine sales business back in Texas. The man had plenty money. And even though he had a wife and two kids back home in Amarillo, he lived out his wildest dreams whenever he traveled down to New Orleans. To have three sexy black females all to himself was a gift from above if he had to tell it. "Fifteen hundred is chump change! Come on to my room!"

"No, baby," Vivian whispered in Dwight's ear. "We have a deluxe suite at the Marriot on Canal Street. We gone turn you out, cowboy!" she stated seductively as she gripped the man's rock hard shaft.

The waitress returned with the vodka and sodas and the three girls sat at the booth with Dwight and watched a burlesque show that featured three strippers and two male dancers posing in various sex acts with a live Zydeco band as the back drop.

While watching the show, Willie laid down the ground rules. Dwight was feeling Vivian up and tongue kissing Zelda hard and deep inside the dark club and was vaguely listening to Willie. He only said yes to everything she said as he was overjoyed knowing it would only cost him $1500 dollars to spend the night with three females.

On top of that, they would take him to their own suite at the downtown Marriot. Dwight had done this many times before. He often traveled to New Orleans to place some of his oil on the market with Amoco Company; and whenever he did, he was sure to arrive late Friday in order to spend the weekend in the city before he sold his oil inside the city's World Trade Center on Monday mornings. Dwight always took his prostitutes back to his suite to have sex; but Willie and her girls were giving him the royal treatment on this night, which was something he'd never had experienced nor expected.

The four exited the club with Dwight in between Zelda and Vivian hugging either of the two as Willie walked ahead of them. It was nearing one 'o' clock in the morning as the gang walked up Bourbon Street towards Canal Street amid hundreds of people still out enjoying the sights and sounds of the French Quarters.

Willie and the King Sisters had no shame in the game. The French Quarters allowed these three free spirits to do as they pleased. They weren't the only ones turning tricks in the Quarters either. Many women, from strippers to the homeless, sold sex, but Willie and her girls had their game down to a science. The gang stopped at Pat Obrien's and Dwight bought them all *Hurricanes* and they continued on towards the hotel with money on their minds.

****

An hour into their escapade found Willie, Zelda and Vivian on their knees on a king-sized bed inside the suite, which featured a panoramic view of downtown New Orleans along Canal Street with the Mississippi River Bridge in close proximity behind the World Trade Center. Dwight was sliding in and out of Willie, Zelda and Vivian at random as he drank small bottles of J&B Scotch from the girls' mini-bar.

"I ain't never had so much fun in of all my natural born life!" Dwight exclaimed in his country accent as he grabbed Willie's taut ass cheeks and spread them wide and licked the crack of her ass.

Willie moaned as she took tokes of a large marijuana joint she was sharing with Zelda and Vivian. "Yea, slide that hot tongue up and down my fuckin' ass crack you nasty white boy!" she moaned as she rested on her elbows. She laughed to herself as she passed the joint to Vivian, who was on her left waiting her turn.

"Do me! Do me next, Dwight!" Zelda, who was on Willie's right, exclaimed impatiently as she wiggled her thick rear end high in the air and made it jiggle like Jell-O.

Dwight had all three girls spread their cheeks and went down the line licking them from clit to rectum. Lipps Inc's disco hit *Funkytown* was playing loudly as he tongued them from behind, grabbing flesh and squeezing ass as he slid down the line of upturned ass before his face. He then resumed pistoning in and out of the girls at random, his thick cock emanating moans of delight from all three women each time he eased inside an opening. The darkened room was filled with the smell of raw sex and marijuana smoke as Dwight hoot and hollered, steadily getting drunk off the liquor he was consuming. "Okay ladies," he then said as he walked from behind the three and lay flat on the bed on his back. "Time for a pony ride! Who wants to ride daddy's cock?"

"I do! I do!" Vivian answered, imitating a little girl's voice as she scooted up the mattress and straddled Dwight while toking the joint. "Somebody put it in!" she requested while on one knee.

This was whoring at its finest. Dwight was receiving top-notch treatment. Everybody was enjoying themselves right up until the man had made a sudden and forbidden request. "Hey,

Vivian here is gonna raise up a little and I want you two other girls to lick the both of us. Lick us together!"

It seemed as if all the air went out of the room after Dwight's statement. Zelda, although having slept with women before, knew damn well she wasn't going to taste her own sister's pussy, and Willie didn't get down like that with the King Sisters. Their pussies had been everywhere, just like hers, and she wouldn't dare consider. Sally was the only one who'd ever gotten that treatment.

Vivian rose up slightly, leaving just the head of Dwight's dick inside her pussy. She didn't care if Willie licked her, but she was looking back to make sure that her sister didn't put her face near the junction of she and Dwight's genitals as incest was totally out of the question. Hoping the man would let that request slide, she sat back down on Dwight's cock as she handed the joint to Willie. She placed her hands on his chest and rode Dwight for all she was worth. She ground down hard and the man moaned, but it didn't prevent him from making the demand again.

"I don't feel no tongue on my nuts! What's going on?"

"Look, you askin' for too damn much now!" Willie stated angrily as she rose up on her knees. "I gave you the rules inside of Big Daddy's! And rule number one was that we didn't do each other!"

"I didn't hear that part! Anyway, I'm paying fifteen hundred dollars for this shit and what Dwight wants, he gets!"

All three girls immediately jumped from the bed. "You want me to ta' lick my sister pussy? Nigga, you crazy?" Zelda asked angrily as she placed her hands on hips.

"Right now I don't care of Mother Theresa kissed the Virgin Mary! And Willie not kin to you two! I wanna see some lesbian action or else I'm not—"

"We already been paid, sucka!" Willie snapped. "Now, we can do some fucking, but ain't nobody licking nobody in here!"

Dwight jumped from the bed and charged at Willie, but Zelda stepped in the way. He hauled off and punched her in the body and she screamed out in pain before she began swinging back.

Vivian and Willie then jumped in to assist Zelda, who was still going toe-to-toe with the muscular man. The four brawled inside the dark room, the lights from the city creating four silhouettes as they all fought, their naked bodies dancing around in the darkness in a violent frenzy over the sounds of fists landing on naked, bare flesh.

Dwight punched Vivian in the face, and as she stumbled back onto the bed, he jumped on top of her and began choking the breath out of her.

"I can't breathe!" Vivian hissed.

"I'm gone kill your black ass!" Dwight yelled as he tightened his grip around Vivian's neck.

Vivian was kicking her legs furiously and scratching at Dwight's arms when glass was strewn into his face. She screamed again as she felt the glass scratching her cheeks and the weight of Dwight's body collapsing on top of her.

Willie had hit Dwight in the head with one of the heavy ceramic lamps inside the room that was situated on the nightstand. When he went still and silent, she checked on Zelda, who sitting in a chair clutching her side. "You all right, Zel?" she asked anxiously.

"It, it hurt every time I breathe. I think my ribs cracked." Zelda hissed through her pain.

"Just, just take short breaths. Viv, you all right?" Willie asked as she walked towards the bed.

Vivian was pushing Dwight off her body as Willie approached. It was then that Willie noticed the blood that was trickling from the man's head. Vivian was covered in his blood as well. "Shit! We gotta get the fuck outta here! Viv, you all right?" Willie asked again as Vivian sat on the side of the bed.

"I'm okay. I'm just a little shook up. Where Zelda?"

"She okay. We gotta go!" Willie stated in a panicked manner as she moved around in the darkness and clicked on the bathroom light.

Willie had not a scratch, but Zelda and Vivian were hurt and bruised. She knew she and her girls had to disappear quickly. She ran and grabbed Dwight's jeans off the floor and removed his wallet from the back pocket and grabbed every greenback inside. She also took his driver's license and business cards. She flung his pants aside and was moving to assist Zelda when there was a sudden knock on the door.

"Security! We got a report of a disturbance?" a man yelled aloud. Willie, Zelda and Vivian looked at one another for a split second before they all scrambled for their clothes and boots.

"Everything is fine, sir!" Willie called out.

"Hotel policy states that I have come in and do a quick look over, ma'am. Sorry!" the man remarked as his walkie talkie cackled. "Roger, that. We may need NOPD. Can you put them on standby for me?"

"Give me just a minute, sir. I'm grabbing a robe!" Willie called out as she and her girls scrambled to dress. They were so nervous over the security guard being outside that they were putting on one another's panties and blouses, never even bothering to put on their boots.

Zelda had a hard time dressing, but her adrenaline was pumping something fierce. She was still clutching her side and could barely breathe, but what transpired in the room was something she cared not to explain to the security guards, let alone the NOPD, and that gave her more than enough motivation to cover herself.

Willie led the way over to the door, she, Zelda and Vivian tiptoeing towards the entrance with a few clothes, their purses and boots in hand. She eyed the King Sisters and shook her head as she clutched the door handle. "Y'all ready?" she whispered.

Zelda nodded her head through the pain as she clutched her side. Vivian was breathing hard, her nostrils flaring as she nodded to say yes.

"Okay, here I come," Willie yelled aloud as she twisted the handle. As soon as she pulled the door open, the three bum-rushed the security guard. They knocked the short and stout man down onto his back and trampled over him. His walkie talkie slid a ways up the hall and Vivian quickly scooped it up and joined Willie and Zelda. Together, the three made a mad dash for the stairs at the end of the hall, each of them toting a pair of leather boots and wearing too-tight or too-loose fitting blouses and panties with their hair all over their heads and disheveled clothes in their arms. Willie and Vivian were soon well ahead of Zelda, who was now crying out in pain as she descended the stairs.

Two floors down, the women entered the 40th floor and got onto the elevator. The security guard, meanwhile, was surveying the room and using the suite's phone to call the hotel's security to have an ambulance sent for the man he found laying across the bed bleeding from the head.

The girls were now halfway down to the lobby when they decided to switch elevators, moving to the opposite side of the building. They were lucky not to encounter any witnesses, as it was after three in the morning, and nearly everyone inside the hotel was asleep. The security guard had the rest of the staff on the lookout for three black females who were barefooted and wearing disheveled clothes.

The hotel security crew was on alert in the lobby, but Willie stopped the elevator on the third floor and she and her girls took the stairs the remainder of the way. They used the service entrance to exit the building and crept off into the parking garage.

Willie placed Zelda into her Corvette and Vivian got into her and her sister's Camaro and all three headed back to Jummonville. What was normally a routine night had morphed into a possible felony conviction for Willie and her girls. They all knew Dwight would tell the police that he was robbed and beaten by three black women who'd invited him back to their room after he met them on Bourbon Street.

When Willie and the King sisters reached Jummonville, Willie pulled in front of the twins' apartment and she and Vivian helped Zelda into the house and laid her in her bed on the second floor after helping her up the stairs. Willie now needed a doctor to help Zelda, the nineteen year-old was crying in pain, repeatedly telling how her and Vivian much it hurt every time she breathes.

Willie called Yabba Dabba as she knew he knew a doctor that would do him that favor, On top of that, she could get a list of warrants issued within the past hour or so to see if she and her girls were really wanted. It took an hour for Yabba Dabba and his doctor friend to make it over the King Sisters' apartment. The doctor walked into the neatly kept, well-furnished home and Willie guided him upstairs to Zelda's room.

Zelda explained her symptoms as Vivian stood by her side rubbing her forehead. She had never seen her sister in so much pain. She also noticed the doctor looking at her with a look of wonderment on his face as he went into the inside pocket of his silk suit jacket and pulled out a pair of latex gloves. Vivian then remembered she was covered in blood. She excused herself as the doctor raised Zelda's tank top and pressed his latex covered hands to her rib cage until she told him where it hurts.

The doctor told Zelda that her rib was not cracked. "This is a major bruising of the rib. Nothing a couple of week's rest and a few pain pills wouldn't remedy," he remarked as he got up and walked over to the dresser and opened a leather bag. He removed a few items before he sat back down on the king-sized bed and began to bandage Zelda.

Willie, meanwhile, was downstairs in the kitchen talking to Yabba Dabba as the two sipped glasses of Vodka. She paced the kitchen floor back and forth, sipping her drink slowly from time to time as she listened to Yabba Dabba, who was in the middle of giving her some bad news.

"Police have seen this scenario before, Willie," Yabba Dabba remarked. "I'm not saying the guy's tellin' the truth, but many out-of-towners get robbed in the exact same manner in which this guy Dwight Davis had detailed and they believe the man."

"What else they know?" Willie asked as she stopped pacing and set the glass down before she folded her arms and stared at Yabba Dabba.

"Security handed over the name of the renter of the hotel room. They know your full name. An arrest warrant was issued for you, Willie, charging you with assault and battery and simple robbery. Mister Davis also gave detailed descriptions of Zelda and Vivian. They have no warrants, though, since the detectives don't know their last names. But they do have their fingerprints from their juvenile arrest for auto-theft. It's only a matter of time, maybe a day or two at the most before they match those prints. It's bad, Willie."

Willie shook her head in disgust. She knew she was caught up in something that could place her future plans on hold permanently. The women had a good case for self-defense, but Willie knew they would not be believed in court and she wasn't willing to take that gamble. She and the King Sisters would have to lay low until they could figure out how to get out of the predicament they now found themselves in.

CHAPTER TWENTY-ONE

TRANSFORMATIONS

Three days after the incident downtown, Willie was on her way to class over to the University of New Orleans. For the past few nights she'd been sleeping over to Tanya's home in the French Quarters. What'd gone down inside the Marriot had made the local news. The story ran two days in a row on the morning, midday and nightly programs. Willie's name was out there, and pictures of Zelda and Vivian, who'd been identified within twenty-four hours, had been shown multiple times on the broadcasts. New Orleans thrived off of tourism, and to have an out-of-towner assaulted was damaging to the industry.

A manhunt was underway for Willie and the King sisters. Wanda's apartment had been raided and city vice were riding through the Saint Bernard around the clock. The Night Owl was being avoided by the crew as the law knew it was the place where Willie was known to hangout. An uneasiness had overtaken Willie the night before the moment she'd laid down to sleep. Something was in the air today she felt. She went about her routine, polishing her nails and ironing her clothes after showering. Once she'd dressed, she exited Tanya's spare bedroom and walked into the kitchen where Tanya was bottle-feeding Helen.

"Where you going?" Tanya asked as Helen smacked on her Pablum.

"I have a final exam today for Civics. I need this class to move on into Government next semester."

"You going up to UNO?" Tanya asked surprised. "Zack told you to stay away from there, Willie."

"I saw how Faye had to hide out while she was down here and I can't live like that, Tanya." Willie remarked through a sigh. "Something gotta give because I can't keep hiding and ducking. When I let Sally go my ass shoulda quit, too, but no, I had to keep going until this Dwight shit happened."

"What if you're caught?"

"Wouldn't surprise me," Willie answered dejectedly as she looked to the floor. She then laughed and said, "And I was supposed to start working for the mayor's campaign over the summer. If he won, I probably would've got an internship inside City Hall."

"It's still possible, you know?"

"Not after this. I done fucked up big time." Willie remarked dryly.

Tanya didn't reply to what she knew was a true statement. Willie had placed all of her political ambitions in serious jeopardy. Assault and battery and simple robbery would net a three year sentence on a plea bargain for her, and the King Sisters were facing even more time because of prior convictions. Zelda and Vivian was street and could hold their own in a cage. Willie was capable as well, but she was crucial to the crew's future and Tanya knew it all-too-well. She remained silent, looking down at Helen as she contemplated what could be done to get Willie out of her jam.

"I talked to Zack this morning," Willie remarked, shaking Tanya from her thoughts.

"What he say?"

"Not to go to class."

"But you're going anyway, huh?"

"Have to," Willie answered somberly as she looked to the floor. "I'm not tired of hiding. I just don't want what Faye going through to be my life. So I'm just gone act like nothing, like nothing ever happened and accept what's coming."

"Faye wanted for murder and attempted murder, Willie. Yours isn't nearly as serious."

"A conviction will end all of my political goals, Tanya." Willie adamantly stated. "Nobody will vote for a convict. And even if? Whoever I run against will hang that over my head. Imagine the ads on television. I wouldn't be able to get sponsors, no one from the corporate world will donate to my campaigns."

"We your corporation." Tanya declared. "Fuck everybody else out there in the world. Money isn't the issue here because we have that."

"If I get stuck with this charge? It's over, girl," Willie retorted.

Tanya knew what was going to happen if Willie showed up for class this morning. In her heart she felt it was the best thing for the time being, because the longer she stayed on the run, the worse matters would become. She also saw the potential in Willie. They'd never discussed her running for office upon her graduation, but already, Willie was thinking about opponents and campaign donors.

"I'll handle it, Willie. I promise," Tanya said as she bowed her head and contemplated what lay ahead.

Twenty-two-month-year-old old Popeye came walking out the spare bedroom at that moment, rubbing his eyes as he made his way over to his mother and grabbed her legs. "You go bye bye?" he asked softly.

"I have class, son," Willie remarked as she took to one knee before Popeye.

"I want McDonald's, momma."

"After I feed Helen we'll walk and get you McDonald's okay, Popeye? Momma has to get to class now," Tanya stated aloud from her seat inside the library.

Willie hugged her son and rubbed his back gently before standing and reaching out for his hand. Tanya got up with Helen and followed her and Popeye down the stairs. Before opening the door, Willie turned to Tanya. "Tell Zel and Viv to follow my lead," she remarked seriously.

"I don't know how they gone feel about this here, Willie, but I'll let 'em know."

"We have to stand together on this," Willie responded as she pulled the door open. "But I got way more to lose than those two. I would understand if they do something different. Either way, I left fifteen grand on the bed upstairs for a down payment. Get us a lawyer. I'll call after...I'll call later."

"I be here," Tanya replied as she extended her hand and shook Willie's hand. "It's gone be all right, sister."

After kissing her son goodbye, Willie left Tanya's home and walked up Saint Louis Street towards Rampart where she caught the Elysian Fields bus to the University of New Orleans' campus. She stepped off the bus in her olive green knee-length silk dress and matching shoes and purse and walked across campus. Several people spoke along the way, one was a janitor she'd turned tricks with in times past.

"What's up, Willie?" the middle-aged, grey-bearded Caucasian man spoke when Willie passed by him sitting on a bench in front of the Political Science building. "Payday's Friday. Was wondering if ya' could meet me over in my office," he stated through slick laughter while rubbing his neatly-trimmed beard.

Willie's eyes welled up at that moment. Suddenly, all what she'd been doing in the past now brought her shame. Just three days ago she was in the French Quarters with Zelda and Vivian, who weren't even old enough to be inside Big Daddy's, putting her pussy on display before a total stranger in order to make money. She'd been living the life of a whore for years up until this point and the reality of it all was now a burden on her soul. She reflected on the many Fridays she'd followed this particular man up to his 'office', which was no more than a closet on the third floor of the Political Science building, in order to service him orally before allowing him to take her from behind as she leaned over a classroom desk.

Well-known pastors, long-time policemen, high-profile businessmen, and many an average Joe, many of whom had wives and children, had all had their fill of Willie over the years. There wasn't a place she could go in the city without running into someone who recognized her and knew what she looked like naked, and what she felt like on the inside.

Tired. Willie was tired of allowing herself to be abused, because when it got down to it, this is what it was at the core, a form of abuse she willingly accepted, if only to survive as it was how she was taught from her earliest memories back in Davenport, Iowa when her mother was whoring herself out in a lounge much similar to The Night Owl where she whored out not only herself, but Sally and the King sisters as well.

"Is that all you see me as whenever you see me?" Willie asked the janitor curiously. "I'm more than just a sex object, man."

The janitor chuckled as he rested back on the bench. "What? You're a whore with morals now?" he sarcastically questioned while crossing his legs. "You don't want the money, fine. But don't come laying the guilt trip on me about the way you live your life and the shit that you do."

"You're right, mister," Willie admitted while nodding her head. "If I was like many women in my profession I would fuck you up right about now for insulting me, but what you said is the truth. It's not your fault I decided to give up my most precious gift to a greasy ass snake like you. The real losers are me, your wife and your kids, huh? I can deal with my past and face my demons. I can admit my past to everyone who knows me. Can you say the same about yourself?"

"You threatenin' to tell my wife about what we did here on campus, girl?"

"I'm not out to ruin lives, man," Willie professed. "If I can't help you, I damn sure won't hurt you. As far as Friday? My answer to that is no. And don't ever ask me again, or I will report you to the administrators for sexual harassment."

The man stared at Willie stunned as she walked off. For the first time in her life she felt worthy. She felt pride about herself and wanted the feeling to carry on. She left the janitor's presence and made her way over to the Political Science building. Checking her watch, she saw she had a little under two minutes to make it to class. She entered the three story building and ran towards the stairs where she inadvertently bumped into someone just inside the stairwell bursting through the doors.

"Watch where the fuck you going!" a female snapped aloud as she jumped back from the doors Willie had pushed open.

"I'm sorry!" Willie said as she hurried past the female.

"Willie?" the young woman called out as her eyes lit up.

Willie paused halfway up the first flight of stairs. "Sally?" she inquired as she traveled back down to the first floor. "What you doing at UNO, girl?" she asked through a smile.

"I'm enrolled in the G.E.D. program here!" Sally exclaimed. Her voice then lowered and she seemed to be ashamed as she admitted to Willie. "Since you kicked me off the team and loss that fight my momma been going in on me. She said if I didn't go to school she was gone kick me out the house. I had no choice," the eighteen year-old admitted through light laughter.

"You in the right place, Sally."

"I feel I am. I'm majoring in law. I plan on transferring to Loyola after going through remedial classes here at UNO. And you?"

"I plan on running for city counselor someday."

"City Council? Really?" Sally asked through a chuckle of uncertainty as she stared down at Willie.

"I can see why you feel that way, Sally," Willie smiled. "But, things aren't the same now. People change."

"'People change.'" Sally quoted as smiled over to Willie. "That they do. I was so upset at my mother for cock-bloc—" Sally lowered her voice and looked around for any ear hustlers before she went any further. "I was pissed off at Betty for getting in the way of what me, you and the King sisters had going on, but as time went on? I saw she was right. I should be where I am now, Willie—in school."

"Girl, your momma fought hard for your ass!" Willie chuckled.

"I know!" Sally laughed aloud as she tapped Willie's arm lightly. "I bet on you, though, girl!" she admitted as her laughter grew louder.

"I know, bitch!" Willie blurted out as she bent over at the waist and released a belly laugh.

"And my momma fucked you up! I was heartbroken! I said to myself that Sunday morning after I heard you loss? 'Guess I'll be taking my ass back to class!'"

Willie had to walk off she was so tickled over what had gone down the day she fought Miss Betty. There were no hard feelings between the two women and Willie had kept her word. She'd left Sally out of her affairs. And it was a good thing given what she, Zelda and Vivian were now up against. "I, I gotta get to class, girl," Willie joyously spoke through gasps of air as she leaned against the steel railings of the stairwell. "What classes you have left, Sally?"

"I'm on my way to the English building for my final exam. I be free after that."

"Okay. I got a final exam in Civics. Meet me in the commissary around ten. We'll have breakfast and talk about some things."

"I'd like that, Willie. Doesn't this feel right? Like this is where we're supposed to be?"

Just then, Campus Police walked into the building. Willie knew what was about to go down and she turned and tried to run up the stairs. The two officers caught up to her halfway up the staircase and pushed her up against the rails.

"What y'all doing?" Sally asked in dismay. "Willie, what's wrong?"

"Willameena Slack you have a warrant out for your arrest charging you with assault and battery and simple robbery," one of the guards stated while reaching for handcuffs.

"No!" Sally protested. "This isn't right!"

"Stay outta this!" one of the officers admonished.

"She was due to take an exam, man! At least give her that! Give her that much!"

Willie knew she needed to take the Civics exam in order to enroll into the Government program and qualify for aiding in the mayor's upcoming campaign. It wasn't a doubt in her mind that she would ace the test, but if she failed or didn't take the test at all, she would be set back for a semester and would be prevented from having a chance of becoming an intern should the mayor win the election. She was registered for fall classes, five months down the road. The city would have forty-five days to bring her trial, she knew, so taking the test this day, was of the utmost importance.

"We go back, man. Just let me take my exam!" Willie whispered to the officer that was patting her down. Both guards, as a matter of fact, had been clients of Willie in times past and she knew their history. Just like the janitor, these guys had family. "If I go down for this shit, a whole lotta bull gone come to light. I'm gone tell it all."

Sally had an idea what Willie was referring to given their rapport. "That's right!" she chimed in. "She go down, everything gone get exposed on this campus! We gone tell on everybody involved in this shit!"

The two officers eyed one another. "Hey," one of the men spoke, "detectives sent us in here to apprehend you on a warrant for some shit that that happened downtown three days ago. Now, what we did ain't got nothing to do with that."

"I can bring so many men down on this campus it ain't even funny and you know it. Just let me take my exam, man. From there? Fuck it! I'll drive my own ass down to Tulane and Broad!"

The officers relented, allowing Willie to take her Civics exam while they sat in the back of the class. Sally remained at her side the entire time. She sat off to the back of the class watching Willie perform under intense pressure. When the test was completed, Willie turned in her work, walked out of the class and was handcuffed before her astonished classmates. She was escorted out of the building and turned over to detectives thirty minutes later and driven downtown to Orleans Parish Prison for Women.

Willie exercised her right to remain silent while being fingerprinted. After being booked for aggravated battery, strong armed robbery, soliciting for sex and fugitive from the law charges, she was taken to a holding cell.

"Willieeee!" a female called out as Willie strode by one of the cells.

"Zelda!" Willie stated surprised as she eyed Zelda and Vivian sitting on a bench behind a barred cell. "How they caught y'all?" she asked as she walked past the cell that held the twins.

Zelda hopped up and ran to the cell bars. "We was gettin' your 'Vette washed on Chef Highway and them bitches rolled up on us with guns blazin' like we killed the President or some shit! Funky ass bitches!" she shot back as Willie disappeared from sight.

"Don't say nothing! Y'all used the phone yet?" Willie yelled back as correctional officers unlocked her cell, which had a steel door for a barricade.

"Nahh, they actin' a donkey in here! Phone broke and they ain't lettin' us use the desk phones! You gotta get your car out the pound!" Zelda yelled back.

"I got it! I got a phone over here! If it don't work I'm gone pound on the wall!"

"If that phone don't work we fucked! They got a—" Zelda was cut off as the steel door to Willie's cell had slammed shut, preventing her from hearing the rest of her remark.

Zelda and Vivian were in serious trouble, only Zelda hadn't time to relay the full scope of the matter to Willie. They'd had plans on hitting Lake Forest Mall to do some shopping after they'd gotten Willie's car washed. The fraternal twins were decked out in tight-fitting Calvin Klein denim Capri jump sets and white three-inch leather heels with the calf straps and were sporting a ton of jewelry on their neck, wrists, ears and fingers.

Zelda's afro was on point and Vivian had her hair permed and pressed flowing down her back. The sun was blazing and the twins had their stereo pumping George Clinton's song *Atomic Dog* when eight NOPD patrol cars rolled up and hopped out of their rides with shotguns and semi-automatic handguns drawn. Zelda and Vivian were forced to the ground, Willie's car was confiscated and it seems as if the fif-teen-minute drive down to Tulane and Broad had taken all but a couple of seconds.

Zelda and Vivian were stripped of their possessions not even twenty minutes ago and all remained was the perfume they'd adorned themselves with before leaving the motel they were hiding out in. The twins had to keep placing their perfumed hands before their nostrils to ward off the stench from the half dozen women who were down on their luck. They paced the funky cell waiting for Willie's knock, a knock they hope wouldn't come as both twins knew the urgency of the situation at hand.

****

Brenda was home watching *All My Children* and giving her son, RJ, an asthma treatment when her phone rung. With her feet kicked up on the plush velvet sofa and a glass of wine in her hand, she kicked out in frustration over being interrupted during her day time soaps. She snatched the phone up without taking her eyes off her floor model TV. "Yeah?" she asked agi-tated.

"They got all three of us," was all Willie said before quickly ending the call.

Brenda's jaw dropped and her eyes widened. She was expecting this day to arrive, but not so quickly. She jumped up off the sofa and walked to her bedroom and pulled a drawer open and retrieved Dwight Davis' driver's license, sat on the edge of her bed and used a second phone line she had set up to call Yabba Dabba.

"Zack Malone, speaking?" the Sergeant answered from his desk down at the eighth precinct.

"Yab? That thing me and your girl had set up? I need that ASAP."

"Already?" Yabba Dabba asked surprised. "It's gone take me at least week."

"They just got in. Find out what they up against and get that to your other chick." Brenda responded, referencing Tanya, before ending the call.

****

Four hours later, Willameena 'Willie' Slack, Zelda and Vivian King were in district court facing a bail hearing. All three had been relieved of their street gear and were now wearing orange jumpers and black slippers with no socks.

The assistant district attorney eased from behind his desk and presented the charges. "Your Honor," he began as he approached the judge's bench and handed him the preceding docket. "This is the case of the state versus Willameena Slack, Zelda King and Vivian King. Preliminary charges are aggra-

vated battery, strong armed robbery, soliciting for sex and being fugitives from the law. Given Miss Slack's ties to Iowa and
Zelda and Vivian's prior run-ins with the law, the court views
the defendants as a flight risk and is requesting a bond of no
less than two hundred and fifty thousand dollars for Miss Slack
and a bond of no less than five hundred thousand for Zelda and
Vivian King."

"Where the hell we gone run to, man? And how they get a
higher bond than me when we all charged with same shit?"
Willie blurted out.

The judge rapped his gavel several times. "That language
will not be used in this court room, Miss Slack!" he yelled. He
then looked to the prosecutor and asked, "Can the difference in
bond be explained by the prosecution?"

"It should be noted, your Honor, that there was an ounce of
heroin found in the wheel well of the trunk of the Corvette be-
longing to one Willameena Slack, but it is the prosecution's allegation that the drugs confiscated belonged to Zelda and Vivian King."

Willie eyed the red-headed, short in stature public defender
in total dismay as she cut her eyes at Zelda and Vivian. "Y'all
three bitches better straighten this shit out with the quickness,"
she hissed under her breath.

"Give us a minute, your Honor," the public defender responded as he pulled the group into a huddle behind the desk.

Willie glared at the King sisters through clasped jaws and wide eyes, silently asking what the fuck was going on as she hadn't a clue that they'd been busted with drugs inside of her Corvette.

"You got locked up before I could tell you," Zelda professed.

"We gone take the charge, though." Vivian followed. "We can do that, right?" she asked the public defender.

"The prosecution is accusing you and Zelda of being in possession of the drugs so I say yes," the public defender answered. "But," he paused as he thumbed his nose.

"But what?" Zelda asked.

The public defender eyed the King sisters. He knew the full consequences of the two taking the charge, but was reluctant to admit what he knew. "Can you," the man ceased speaking and opened Zelda's jacket. "Zelda? You and Vivian have the same rap sheet," he stated as he rested his hands on the desk. "Both of y'all's juvenile records have been brought to light. The court is aware of the attempted murder charge the two of you faced back in eighty-one and the time y'all spent in juvenile detention. If y'all are found guilty? Both of y'all will be facing a fifteen year sentence over the possession charge."

"Fifteen years?" Vivian questioned as she placed a hand over her heart. "We wasn't even found guilty on that attempted murder charge," she whispered.

"I know," the public defender remarked. "I have to find the loop hole the prosecution used to get those juvenile records admitted into court. In the meantime? I suggest we not contest the bonds and wait for arraignment. I'll ask for an extension, forty-five days max and ask that you all plead not guilty. If either of you girls make bail, I don't want neither of you skip trial. Got me?"

"We, we cool," Willie chimed in as she cut her eyes at Zelda and Vivian.

"It's our charge if we get hit with it." Zelda declared while looking Willie in the eyes.

"The drugs was ours," Vivian followed. "Go on with the bond, man," she told the lawyer.

The public defender nodded towards the judge and the females' bond was set. They were escorted back to the holding cells in order to be transferred to three separate tiers in order to prevent collusion. When the case was closed and the gavel had been rapped, a lone German female eased out of the court room, fully aware of what her friends were up against as she planned for a trip to Cherryvale, Kansas.

CHAPTER TWENTY-TWO

DIE SCHLECHTE ZIMMEER

It'd been nearly two years since Tanya last visited Cherry-vale. During that trip, back in June of '83, she'd met Faye Bender and learned more about the Bender sisters than she'd ever anticipated. Since then, she, Faye and Brenda had colluded and murdered six people from Iowa to Ohio and now had a heroin pipeline that ran from New Orleans to Ohio.

Money was pouring in on an even keel and the crew was prospering. Before Faye had left to return to Kansas, she and Tanya had talked about getting involved in politics by putting Willie in position to run for office. It was a plan whose benefits would be realized in ten years or so if it succeeded at all, but the reward was well worth the risk in both their eyes.

Tanya cruised into town with one year-old Helen riding be-side her in her in car seat. Her brown eyes focused in on the Bender Museum and she noticed a sign highlighting a new display. There was a headshot of Faye with the words *Cherry-*

vale's Living Myth underneath. "What is she doing?" Tanya asked aloud as she sped up towards the center of town.

Downtown Cherryvale was the same as Tanya remembered with its Phillip's 76 gas station, post office and lawyer's office and First National Bank on either of the corners. It was obvious it was political season given the numerous campaign signs that lined the downtown area. One prominent sign that stood out was that of a man by the name of Frederick Cooper. He was running for sheriff of Cherryvale and his signs were everywhere.

Tanya eased through the red-light and made her way west. She traveled down a two-lane road bordered by wheat fields for about four miles and made a left turn onto the Bender family's property. As she cruised onto the land, she could see that a new fence bordering the land had been erected. The dilapidated white house she knew to be the Bender home, which was previously located on her right, had been torn down, and there was a new red barn with large double doors off in the distance to her left. The land's soil had been upturned and several cows milled about on the property. She rode on towards the barn where she saw a white Red Cross van and a shiny black pickup truck parked out front.

While riding across the land, Tanya noticed a Sheriff's patrol car turning onto the property behind her. The car's lights began flaring as she neared the barn. She exited her car with her hands in the open as the Sheriff's car sped up to her and cruised to a halt.

Tanya waited patiently for what seemed like an eternity as she watched the man behind the wheel grab a portable respirator and pump oxygen into his lungs. He then exhaled and pulled a bottle of pills from his top pocket before opening the door and panting his feet on the ground. Tanya, growing tired of waiting, lowered her arms as she watched the slender Caucasian man ease out of the car. He popped a pill into his mouth and washed it down with a diet Pepsi before sighing and closing his door.

"Sheriff Cooper," a female voice called out. "Are you providing escort service to my home again?" the woman asked jovially as she placed her hands on her hips and smiled.

Tanya turned and saw Faye approaching from a side door on the barn. The two nodded towards one another and hugged briefly.

"*Wer ist der Krüppel?*" (Who's the cripple?) Tanya whispered into Faye's ear.

"*Er ist ein Kerl auf unser Team und er weiß nicht einmal. Er versteht nicht, was sagen wir so fortfahren.*" (He's a guy on our team and he doesn't even know. He doesn't understand what we're saying so continue on.) Faye responded through a sly smile while gripping Tanya's shoulder. She then turned her attention to the lawman and said. "Good job, Sheriff Cooper. Have you the tool I requested?"

Sheriff Cooper nodded to say yes and went to the trunk of his 1979 Crown Victoria and unlocked it with his keys. He reached down inside and pulled out a spanking brand new chainsaw. The man seemed to be struggling with the machine, so Tanya went and gave him a hand.

"What are you going to do with this thing?" Tanya asked as she and the Sheriff lowered the chainsaw to the ground.

"*Ich habe einen Körper zu entsorgen, in eine kleine Weile.*" (I have a body to dispose of in a little while.) Faye told Tanya. "You're on your game today, sir," she then stated to Sheriff Cooper.

"I do what I can to help out the woman financing my run for sheriff," Sheriff Cooper responded as he dusted his hands. "How's my election campaign coming along?"

"You're a shoe-in, Mister Cooper. Your last adversary has dropped out of the race."

Sheriff Cooper smiled and nodded. "Your family has made this town a tourist destination. Our economy partly thrives off your name. I've been sheriff since before you were born and have been keeping this town safe for as just as long."

"Right, Mister Cooper," Faye smiled as she eased past Tanya and went and shook the sheriff's hand. "There's nothing to fear with my arrival as you've come to learn. I'm only here to take care of what rightfully belongs to my family."

Sheriff Cooper tipped his hat and nodded. "I have breakfast with the Red Cross this morning. City's giving a blood drive for the tornado victims two towns over."

"I'll be providing the transport for that. I just have to place an oil change on the Red Cross van before dropping it off at the fire station." Faye responded.

"See you there," Sheriff Cooper remarked before climbing back into his patrol car and pulling away from the barn.

Faye kept her friendly smile on her face while waving at the sheriff as he backed away from the barn. When he turned the car around to leave the property, so did her smile. "This thing with Willie and the King sisters has the potential to ruin all of our political ambitions. What was Willie thinking by having a hotel room in her name?" she asked, somewhat agitated as she opened the passenger door on Tanya's station wagon.

"She always did that and never had any problems. The guy wanted them to lick each other pussies and they refused," Tanya replied as she handed Faye Dwight Davis' driver's license and set about removing one year-old Helen from her car seat. "A fight broke out and the trick was cracked across the head with a lamp. Willie stole the man's wallet and got away. She was taken down after completing an exam at her college."

"Zelda and Vivian will have to take the rap for the heroin found in Willie's car," Faye responded as she read over the driver's license. "Seems like our future politician bit of more than she could chew. I can rectify it, but Willie will owe us, and that's a good thing if ever she gets into office."

Tanya placed a babbling Helen inside a large-wheeled buggy and said, "According to the report I got from Yabba Dabba, this guy Dwight Davis is in constant contact with the detectives and the assistant district attorney. He's going to testify if Willie and the King sisters plead not guilty. And if the three of 'em do plead guilty…"

"We run the risk of losing our future political power in Willie." Faye remarked solemnly as she began walking towards her barn with her hands behind her back and her head bowed in deep thought.

Tanya remained silent as she wheeled Helen over the soil and entered the vastness of the barn behind Faye. Right away, she eyed what she knew to be a combine, which was a tractor-like machine with large spinning blades on the front and a device similar to a wood cutter in the back. The contraption was used to harvest and separate wheat, but it seems as if it hadn't been used as its green and yellow John Deere color scheme was still bright and shiny. A lot of what lay on the property seemed new to Tanya, the paint on the equipment and the wood inside the barn still gave off a fresh smell. "What are your plans for this place exactly?" she asked Faye.

"I have three grain silos I have to install near the entrance," Faye responded as she walked along the massive combine. "Wheat has been planted and I have blueprints for a home I'm going to build on the opposite side of the property. It's coming together. I just have this one thing I have to take care of before I move forward."

"What's that?"

"Follow me," was all Faye said as she disappeared behind the combine.

Tanya trailed Faye around while pushing Helen over the hardened dirt inside the barn. The lighting in the place was dim and it gave of a macabre feel to her, as if more than just farming took place. After walking amongst the massive farm equipment, the two rounded the rear of the vehicles and neared a steel door located on a side wall in the middle of the barn.

Faye turned the knob and an enclosed space came into view. A narrow tunnel led to a single steel door on the opposite side, and there was another set of steel double doors just to the left of the single steel door. Faye walked over to the set of double steel doors and pushed one open and a what looked like a modernized cabin came into view for Tanya.

"What's this get up?" Tanya asked while wheeling Helen inside the room.

"My living quarters," Faye answered as she turned and closed the steel double doors and pulled down on a steel barricade, sealing her and Tanya inside the room. "There's no home yet, so I live here for the time being," she added as she stepped off into the domicile.

Tanya looked around amazed at the white marble flooring and charcoal grey granite counters. Porcelain faucets adorned the sink, which lay in the center of the room, and there were steel appliances on the far wall. A grill pit was to her left and a natural wood stove was on her right inside the low-ceiled, cozy structure. She followed Faye on through the kitchen where the two crossed a threshold and entered a small living room that held a plush couch and floor model television with a stereo on top and speakers on either side for the surround system that was playing Crosby, Stills, Nash and Young's song titled *Ohio*.

"Tin soldiers and Nixon's coming...we're finally on our own...this summer I hear the drumming...four dead in O-hi-O...four dead in O-hi-O..."

"This place is awesome," Tanya complimented over the music.

"Thank you," Faye replied as she went and turned the stereo down. "It's a two bedroom with a single garden bath. I myself can't wait until the mansion is built, but you know who loves this place right here, right?"

"Aww, I nearly forgot. Where is she?" Tanya spoke softheartedly as she placed a hand on heart.

Faye walked down a short hall and opened the door on her right. "My room is on the other side," she told Tanya. "But this is little Maggie's room and she just adores it. Look who's here, Maggie!"

Five year-old Maggie was sitting at her desk inside her carpeted room that had a Sesame Street theme, complete with a working Oscar the Grouch trash can and Big Bird statue that worked as a gumball machine. She was reading a picture book based on the life of inventor Benjamin Franklin as Tom and Jerry cartoons ran on a TV screen that sat on a dresser at the foot of her twin bed.

Everything about the place Faye called home was normal to Tanya except for one thing: the place had no windows. It left one feeling as if they were inside a cave or underground bunker, but it was a home nonetheless with all the necessities of life and then some.

Enthralled in her studies, Maggie managed to look over to her doorway. Her eyes widened and she hopped from her desk chair. *"Tante Tanja! Meine Mutter hat mir nicht gesagt, du kamst! Wo ist Helen?"* (Auntie Tanya! My mother did not tell me you were coming here! Where's Helen?) the five year-old exclaimed as she ran over to Tanya and wrapped her arms around her favorite Aunt's slender legs.

"Helen ist hier!" (Helen is here!) Tanya replied happily as she ran her hands through Maggie's thick head of red hair and stepped aside to let the child eye her younger friend.

Maggie knelt before a now sleeping Helen and smiled into the child's face. *"Sie ist meine kleine Schwester."* (She's my baby sister.)

"That's right," Faye approved as she knelt down beside Maggie. *"Während ihre Schwester ist schlafen, ich habe etwas Anderes Ich habe zu zeigen, ihre Tante Tanya."* (While your sister is sleeping, I have something else I have to show your Auntie Tanya.)

Maggie gasped and covered the lower portion of her face. *"Sie zeigen werde, Tantchen Tanya die schlechte Zimmer, Mutter? Sie haben gesagt, es war unser Geheimnis!"* (Are you going to show Auntie Tanya the bad room, mother? You said it was our secret!) the child stated in a near whisper as her eyes constantly shifted back and forth between the faces of Faye and Tanya.

Maggie knew what lay inside the room Faye had showed her. She was on hand the day before to witness her mother, to assist her in fact, by carrying dirty clothes from what she'd been told was the *schlechte Zimmer* or 'bad room', and placing the cloths into a barrel where the two lit a fire inside the wood stove and roasted marshmallows shortly thereafter while watching cartoons in the living room. It was to be their secret was what Maggie was told, but now she was worried that something *schlechte,* (bad) would happen to the woman she'd accepted as being her mother not too long ago by going back into the *schlechte Zimmer.* (bad room)

Faye kissed Maggie's fluffy cheeks, an act she knew to soothe the child. *"Tantchen Tanya wird der einzige neben sie und ich Wissen über die schlechten Zimmer, Maggie."* (Auntie

Tanya will be the only one besides you and I to know about the bad room, Maggie.)

"*Versprechen Sie mir?*" (You promise me?) Maggie asked as she grew anxious. "*Weil, weil ich nicht sie zu sterben wie meine Mutter Gayle, Mutter!*" (Because, because I don't you want you to die like my mother Gayle ever, mother!) the fretted child spoke through tears as she wrapped her arms around Faye's neck and held on tight.

Faye understood Maggie's anxiety, but there was nothing to worry about in her mind as she had the situation at hand under complete control. She wiped her surrogate daughter's tears away with the tips of her thumbs before kissing her forehead and standing to her feet and grabbing one of the child's hands. She then led Maggie back into her bedroom and Tanya followed with a still sleeping Helen.

Maggie climbed onto her plush mattress and grabbed a rubber mallet. At the same time, Helen was laid on the bed beside her surrounded by pillows. Faye knelt beside Maggie and smiled. "I need for you to watch your little sister for me, okay?" she asked while stroking Maggie's thick head of hair. "Me and Auntie Tanya will be right outside. If you need us, just…"

"Hit the wall with the hammer," Maggie responded, cutting Faye's remark short as she pulled down her covers.

"And I'll lock all the doors just like before. Including the one to your bedroom. You have your refrigerator in the corner with sandwiches already made and orange juice, so you'll be fine the little while we're gone."

"If somebody comes or I have to use the bathroom I'll use the hammer."

"Good girl," Faye responded lovingly as she tucked Maggie in and met up with Tanya just outside of the room.

At the young age of five, Maggie McPherson was slowly being taught the life. She'd seen plenty in her short time, but things had taken a turn down a dark path for a child so young. Maggie knew what Tanya didn't know at this moment. She knew what her mother was preparing to do, but the act was not the thing that worried her; Maggie was more worried that Faye would get caught.

Faye on the other hand, knew Maggie's fears. She was rearing the child to be just like herself, and the first thing she knew needed to be done was to rid the child of the fear of being caught doing something wrong, which was the very thing she was up to on this day, the doing of wrong.

Tanya had no qualms about the entire situation. She was more than eager to uncover what Faye was up to exactly, and whatever it was that had Maggie so unnerved. She followed Faye back through the living room and kitchen and out the double steel doors.

Faye walked to her left this time, away from the barn, and headed towards the single steel door at the end of the hall. After removing several padded locks, she pulled the door open and entered a darkened room. Right away, Tanya could see that the area was covered with a low ceiling, one lower than the one inside Faye's living quarters, low enough to have her hunch over a little as she followed Faye through a corridor appearing to be more like a coal miner's tunnel. The walls on either side of the corridor was lined with machetes, bolt cutters, large shears, drills and shovels and it was void of light, save for a single lamp hanging from the ceiling.

Tanya, a little unnerved and wondering where she was headed exactly, tentatively followed Faye down the corridor until it opened up into a small chamber. The room she'd stepped off into was a small, four-walled room with vague lighting. Faye pulled a string and the area became illuminated in a reddish hue. On the back wall inside the cramped structure was a naked, crucified Caucasian man. His hands were above his head and spikes were driven through his palms. His feet rested on two concrete cylinders stacked on top of one another and a plastic tube was running from his neck as blood dripped into a bag wrapped around his waist.

The man whined and whimpered as Faye removed the bag from his waist. Blood spurted out from his neck, but it didn't seem to bother Faye in the least bit as she clamped the bag shut and pulled the lid off a cooler. Smoke from the cooler poured into the air as she placed the plastic bag inside on top of the hot ice and covered it once more.

"Six pints down, three or four more to go," Faye remarked unconcerned as she clamped another plastic bag to the man's waist and reinserted the tube that was slowly draining his blood from his neck.

"Who's that?" Tanya asked, unnerved by the macabre sight.

"A guy who got too close to my business after visiting my exhibit at the museum in town," Faye remarked. "Poor fella trusted that I would actually pay him off to keep quiet after I invited him to my farm to answer questions pertaining to a warrant for my arrest back in Iowa."

"I was meaning to ask you about that, but I see it's no big deal to ya'. This guy tried to bribe you? How'd he find out about the warrants?" Tanya asked.

"I brought a series of new computers and placed them at the library," Faye remarked as she grabbed a roll of duct tape. "You try and do something good for the community and this happens," she laughed as she threw her hands up into the air.

"Faye? Please? I, I'll never speak a word. Just let me go," the man pleaded.

The man was silenced when Faye slapped a strip of duct tape over his mouth. She cared not to hear his pleas of mercy as she wasn't in the business of forgiving those who posed a threat to her freedom, or the survival of her crew. "Excuse me while I put this guy to sleep," she told Tanya as she walked over to prepare the man for another blood drain.

The man's body was drained of his blood completely over a course of an hour. During his time of dying, Faye and Tanya went over their plans for Willie. It was agreed that Faye would handle the job.

"I'll send Maggie back to New Orleans with you while I handle this Dwight, character," Faye told Tanya as she finished draining her latest victim's blood. "Eleven pints. He was a strong one. Most only give up eight or nine," she appreciated.

It was an agonizing death for the man as he slowly drifted off into a peaceful slumber. During the process, both women got to witness his skin constrict and morph into a lovely shade of blue.

"You know how to use a chainsaw?" Faye asked as she donned a leather apron.

"Yeah," Tanya responded.

"Good," Faye responded as she handed Tanya a separate apron and goggles.

Just then, a thud was heard from the wall where Maggie's room lay.

"Really? I mean, really?" Faye sighed while shaking her head. "Maggie either has to use the bathroom or Helen's crying."

"You go on and look after the children. I'll handle this," Tanya stated as she knew Faye had much more to deal with

Maggie given she was somewhat aware of what was going down.

"You do this guy for me and I guarantee Dwight won't make it to court," Faye responded. "Chop him up by cutting off his arms and legs. Place his remains in these plastic bins and I'll handle the rest when I get back from dropping off the Red Cross wagon." she stated as she wheeled the cooler of blood out of the room.

"Done deal," Tanya responded as she followed Faye back out of the chamber to retrieve the chainsaw and finish the job.

CHAPTER TWENTY-THREE

THE DEADLY LIASON

Dwight Davis was sitting in his luxurious downtown Amarillo office located in a small strip mall early Monday morning in late April of 1985 when he heard the door chime. "Eunice?" he called out to his secretary.

A few seconds later, the obese mid-fifties greying blonde walked into Dwight's office with a slender, black-haired, brown-eyed woman dressed in a white, tight-fitting linen outfit with black heels and a matching black purse following her lead as the woman held onto a briefcase.

"This is Miss Valerie Smith and she's interested in purchasing a wheat combine," the secretary smiled as she stepped aside and left the office, closing the door behind her.

"Miss Smith," Dwight remarked as he stood up from his swivel chair and extended his hand.

Valerie walked over and shook Dwight's hand and looked around for a seat.

The woman wore a white straw hat and dark shades and was adorned with jewelry. To Dwight, she emanated money. Always ready to make a sale in his profitable business, the cunning salesman eased from behind his desk and grabbed a chair. "So, you're on the hunt for a combine are ya'?" he asked in his Midwestern accent.

"Yes. I'm from eastern Colorado and need the best of the best equipment to run my business," Valerie responded as she took a seat and placed her purse on her lap while setting the briefcase on the floor.

"Well, we have everything from Caterpillar to John Deere. We also have the latest from New Holland, Minneapolis Moline, and Massey-Ferguson. Any particular brand you're looking for?" Dwight asked as he sat back behind his desk and pulled out an agricultural catalogue.

"I'll go with the most popular. John Deere sounds good."

"Good choice," Dwight remarked as he opened the catalogue. "Base price starts at around sixty-seven thousand dollars. Do you have financing?"

"I prefer to deal in cash." Valerie responded as she leaned down and placed the briefcase atop the desk. "This is fifty thousand dollars in cash. What can that buy me?"

Dwight leaned forward, resting his elbows on his desk. "Fifty thousand can get you three wheels and a seat on a combine, maybe, but we can maybe work something out."

"Something like what, Mister Davis?"

"How long are you in town for?"

"Until I get my combine."

"Well, that means you have time to mingle," Dwight responded as he reached for a note pad and wrote down an address. "Meet me here around seven. We'll discuss sales there."

The woman picked up her briefcase and left Dwight's office and he resumed his duties around the office. He left an hour early and went to his sprawling ranch home and showered. He was in the bedroom dressing when his wife walked in. "What a day out there," the well-toned brunette remarked as she sat on the edge of the bed and removed her cowgirl boots. "I spent half the morning working on the irrigation line and half the evening changing the tires on the water tanker. We're behind on the cattle count, and the oil pump needs new gaskets around the tank truck junction. I spotted a small leak coming from the hose that links up with the pipeline that the truckers use to pull up the crude."

"I got a deal in place to refine the hoses and add new steel to the oil pump to allow better extraction with contacts I made inside Amoco down in New Orleans. We can cut the load time by twenty percent with the refined steel they're selling us. In the meantime, I have to meet a client back over to the office. Got a combine deal to close," Dwight remarked as she dabbed cologne onto his rugged face and broad shoulders.

"Really, Dwight?" the woman sighed. "And it takes cologne and a fresh change of clothes to make a sale? What about what happened when you went to New Orleans to make the deal with Amoco? Will the company still want to business with us after what happened? And now you're off on another sexual tryst!"

"I'm sorry about what happened down in Orleans, okay, baby? The deal is still in place with Amoco and what happened won't come between that. Those women barged into my room the moment I opened the door and robbed me blind. This is a legitimate sale being made tonight so don't go there with me."

"You're still telling the same lie, Dwight! You may have made that deal with Amoco while you were in New Orleans, but at least be man enough to admit you were having a good time down there with three hookers in the process! And now you're on your way to do the same thing tonight with another whore!"

Dwight's wife had read the police report that was mailed to him by detectives working the case. The incident happened over to the Marriott Hotel, but she'd made reservations for her husband at the Sheraton Hotel.

Dwight's story was that the reservation didn't go through so he had to switch hotels. The credit card his wife had used had been charged, however, and there wasn't another bill on any credit card for a room at the Marriott. The woman had no solid proof that her husband was with the women involved, but he was a known philanderer, having slept with his previous secretary. Dwight's wife went and found the most unattractive woman she could find and hired her inside her husband's office. Even then she wasn't sure that he wasn't sleeping with the woman. If it weren't for her two children she would've left years ago.

"Can't you let go of the past?" Dwight asked exasperated. "One time, one time I stepped outside of our marriage. I admitted it, the secretary was fired and you hired Eunice."

"You didn't have to admit a single thing the way I caught you two fucking on the floor in your office, Dwight," the woman mockingly laughed as she stood up from the bed. "Go on and make your deal. Me and the kids will have dinner by ourselves as usual," she ended as she walked into her private bath and slammed the door shut.

Dwight continued dressing and waited in the living room with his daughters until his wife returned. He kissed his kids goodbye and left the home without acknowledging his wife's presence as he was eager to get next to this woman who he believed wanted more than to just cut a deal on a combine. He arrived over to the Rodeo Lounge in downtown Amarillo a little after seven and sought out the woman Valerie Smith. She was spotted sitting at the end of the bar nursing a mixed drink inside the dimly-lit lounge which featured a wooden dance floor, poker slots and a mechanical bull off in the far corner to his right.

"Hey there," Dwight smiled as he pulled up on a stool beside the woman. "Still interested in that combine?"

"Of course, Mister Davis. But you know the circumstances."

"Fifty thousand can get you a good combine. I suggest you put a down payment on it and let me finance the rest for you."

"I don't like lingering bills, Mister Davis."

"Call me Dwight."

"Okay, Dwight. I was hoping we could maybe work out a better deal that would allow me to walk away with a piece of farm equipment with no strings attached." Valerie replied as she leaned in closer to Dwight and rubbed his thigh.

Dwight laughed and raised a finger, calling for the bartender. "What are you drinking?"

"Gin and tonic."

"Two gin and tonics!" Dwight called out. "How long you in town for, baby?"

"Until I get this combine."

"Well, just are what you willing to do for this...combine?"

"Whatever you have in mind that is within reason, Mister Davis."

The drinks were slid before Dwight and he tipped the bartender while smiling over to his client. "I'm a reasonable man," he stated through light laughter while stirring his drink. He took a sip and said, "Now, you know through our prior meeting that I'm married. My place is near here, but we cannot go there."

"I have a place, Mister Davis. Your wife will never have to know about us." Valerie remarked as she, too, sipped her drink.

"Do you smoke weed?" Dwight leaned over and asked over the music.

"I don't use drugs. But if that's your thing that is fine with me." Valerie remarked as she eased up off the bar stool. She then extended her hand towards the door.

"You're ready now?" Dwight smiled.

Valerie responded by nodding her head with hands innocently placed before her body. "This way, sir," she stated as she began making her way towards the exit.

The two left the Rodeo Lounge and climbed into their respective cars, Dwight tailing the woman Valerie back to her motel where they settled into an inconspicuous room located on the second floor of a Red Roof Inn.

"It's not much, but the mattress is soft and the towels are clean," Valerie remarked as she pushed the door open and clicked on a lamp light.

"I think it will serve its purpose." Dwight assured as he trailed his latest sexual conquest inside. He eyed the queen-sized bed off to his right and the sink that lay straight ahead. A television resting atop a dresser was to his left and a table with two chairs was to his left just inside the door.

The two came together and kissed briefly in the center of the room. Dwight was palming ass and groping titties as his body pressed against his client. "Is this what you want for me to get my combine?" the woman asked as she backed away from Dwight.

"You come by my office tomorrow and I'll have the papers drawn up on that combine of yours. John Deere, right?" Dwight asked as he pulled out a small bag of marijuana.

"That's right, Mister Davis," Valerie responded. "Roll us a couple of joints. I'll shower while you do that."

Faye went into the bathroom and closed the door. She turned on the hot water and eased the lid off the toilet and reached for a muzzled .380 she'd duct taped to the bottom of the lid. She was shocked, however, to see that the tape had worn and the pistol was now lying at the bottom of the tank submerged in the water. She grabbed the pistol out of the water and shook it to remove what liquid she could. In the process, the muzzle slipped from the gun's barrel and crashed to the floor.

"Valerie, you all right in there? What's going on?"

Bothering not to respond, Faye twisted the muzzle back onto the gun and eased the door open and crept out of the bathroom with her hands behind her back. She was surprised to see Dwight holding onto a revolver. She backed back into the bathroom just as the man let off three rounds.

The mirror over the sink shattered as she tripped over the toilet and caught her balance amid the steam from the shower.

"I knew this was a deal too good to be true already." Dwight remarked.

Faye could hear Dwight approaching. Cornered, she took a gamble, syncing his footsteps up with the wall that separated the sleeping area from the bathroom, and squeezed the trigger repeatedly on her muzzled semiautomatic. A thud was heard and silence quickly ensued as a gagging sound filled her ears. Faye leaned back against the bathroom wall and looked out towards the shattered mirror. For a brief second she saw Dwight with his hands clutching his neck. Assuming he'd dropped his gun, she eased out of the bathroom just as the man fell face first at her feet with blood spurting from the right side of his neck.

Faye stood over Dwight with the gun aimed at the back of his head. A murdered wealthy businessman would indeed warrant a serious probing, but she knew Dwight Davis was into some shady dealings with his agriculture company. He often stole farming equipment and sold it at a discount. The line of people waiting to get a piece of him was a long one indeed—bankers, environmental lawyers, shipping companies and many others. His wife cared less about him, his own words in past conversation, and she wouldn't be of any consequence in the big scheme of things was Faye's belief. With those thoughts in mind, she pulled the trigger, emptying the remaining rounds from the eight-shot semiautomatic onto the back of his skull and back. She then wiped down everything she'd touched and quietly left the room, returning to Kansas to continue running her farm.

Without Dwight Davis to testify at the trial, Willameena Slack was acquitted of assault and battery and simple robbery in June of 1985 alongside Zelda and Vivian King. She was free to return to her life.

The King Sisters, however, weren't so lucky, Although the charges they were facing alongside Willie had been dropped, both twins were convicted of possession of heroin. Because of their prior charges, they were sentenced to ten years in Saint Gabriel's Prison for Women. A day for three was their sentencing, so they would be out in three and a half years on good behavior—easy time for women of their caliber. Their demise was blow to the crew's ranks, but one expected nonetheless. Tanya and Brenda would pick up the slack and it would be business as usual for the crew for the next several years while the King sisters served their time.

CHAPTER TWENTY-FOUR

UNSOLVED MYSTERIES

"Do you like green eggs and ham? I do not like them, Sam I am. I do not like green eggs and ham," ten year-old Dillon read from his Dr. Suess book as he sat across from his mother inside her mayoral office located in the heart of Patterson, Iowa.

"Sam I am!" eight-year-old Delilah blurted out before leaning back and covering her face as she erupted into laughter.

"Dillon, you are such a fast learner and an excellent reader," Mary Beth proudly complimented. "Continue on. Me and Delilah are loving this, son."

It was now August of 1988, three years and three months after Faye had murdered Dwight Davis and another guy who'd become fertilizer on her land.

Mary Beth Mobley had been Mayor of Patterson for five consecutive years now, having won a second and third term in office. Since her baptism and winning her first political campaign back in November of 1984, Mary Beth had undergone a complete transformation. She was back to her outgoing, spontaneous self. She'd reopened the family store back in Bevington and was in the process of making renovations to the place that had been her and her mother's campaign headquarters for a period of time.

The first thing Mary Beth did was change the store's name from CM's Gas and Grocery to *D & D's Family Oasis*, a way of paying tribute to her daughter Delilah and son Dillon. A café for waiting bus riders was added along with an eight-room motel for travelers.

Back over in the town of Patterson, Mary Beth had expanded postal service to outlying areas and had sought federal dollars from her mother, who was now a lead member of the Republican Senate in D.C., to refurbish the town's grain silos and railroad line in its agricultural district that lay near the Patterson Farm. The project also allowed Mary Beth to hire farmhands to revitalize the Patterson Farm, which had been a prosperous dairy and wheat farm before Franklin was killed by her father.

Good things were happening in Patterson, a town ripe with dark secrets and tragic history. Mary Beth and Mabel were the only ones who knew the truth concerning the reasons why Franklin Patterson was killed along with two other people inside his home, and no one knew of Mary Beth giving birth to children by her youngest brother and father. Some of the townsfolk would mumble, but that was about all, as most people in the town of seven hundred and fifty-four people revered the Mobley family from the youngest to the oldest. They were bringing jobs into the community and putting people to work themselves on their ranch and inside the business they owned back in Bevington. In the eyes of nearly everyone in the town of Patterson, the Mobleys could do no wrong. One person, however, wasn't so moved by the family's good works because something with Mabel and Mary Beth just didn't sit right with him.

The mayor's office was nothing more than a wide-open floor inside a one story white wooden building with two large panes in the front with no back door, and a front door that sat caty-corner in downtown Patterson. The wood was polished to perfection inside the old structure, and there was a small fireplace tucked into the wall on the left when one entered the building.

From behind her desk, Mary Beth could see the Iowa State Trooper patrol car pulling up to her office. She eased up from her seated position and went and stood in the center of her office and waited for Rance Olsen's entrance.

"I see you were expecting me," Rance stated as he entered the building.

"I was beginning to wonder where you were. This is usually about the time of month you arrive. I know because you've synced up with my menstrual cycle." Mary Beth replied nonchalantly. "What questions do you have for me today?"

Rance really didn't like the Mobley women. He resented the power they held in southern Iowa especially. And Mary Beth had become a completely changed woman ever since the night her father had been killed, which was his reason for being in town on this day. "Got some information on the guy found with your father. He was a biker guy from Bentree, West Virginia."

"Okay," Mary Beth replied as she ran one of her hands over her denim all-in-one dress while straightening her shiny, brown hair with the other. "And what does this have to do with my father?"

"It's not pertaining to Corey. Webster Holden was married to Gayle McPherson. The woman found dead in the Patterson home."

"I didn't know that part," Mary Beth replied as she moved to pour herself a cup of coffee.

"What do you mean by part?"

"Mister Olsen, if you must know? My father killed Franklin and those people inside the Patterson home." Mary Beth confessed out loud. "I know it. My mother knows it. Why don't you know it?"

"That is a strong allegation, Mary Beth." Rance calmly retorted. "How is it that I don't know if you and Mabel took Corey down yourselves?"

"Are you investigating the murders over to the Patterson Farm or my father's death? What is it that you want from me?" Mary Beth yelled aloud.

"You're scaring your children." Rance stated. "It's easy to accuse a dead person. They can't defend themselves. And even if Corey was responsible, the man had to have a reason to go and do what he did over to Franklin's home and I believe it has everything to do with the disappearance of Wendell and Jeremy."

"Well, when you find them you can ask them," Mary Beth hissed as she walked off from Rance and knelt down before her children. "Now, if you excuse me, I have business here with my family."

"So, you're content with things being the way they are around here, aren't you? You're just going to go on living life as if this town has no demons to exercise."

"The only demons are the men who you question me about month after month, Mister Olsen. Patterson is far better off without Corey, Wendell and Jeremy around. As far as I'm concerned you're wasting your precious time trying to figure out the reasons why bad things happened to my father and the whereabouts of his no good sons."

"Gayle had a friend named Faye Bender. Ever heard of her?"

"I only know the name Faye Bender because it was her sister, Bonita Bender, who was caught outside of my father's store the night your arm was run over." Mary Beth stated while picking up crayon books and dolls from the floor.

"Corey told me a time or two that he believed Franklin had hidden Faye Bender in his home the night her sister was caught. No way she could've made it out of town so quick after crashing her car that night. It was also the same night Wendell and Jeremy went missing. Why won't you help me Mary Beth?"

"I cannot help you, Mister Olsen," Mary Beth remarked annoyed as she stood and stared the trooper in the eyes. "And even if I could I'm not sure I would given the hell I've been through. I'm happy now, but every time you come around you kick the stitches on my wounds. I can't help you. I'm not going to help you."

Rance swallowed the lump in his throat and nodded his head while looking down at the floor. Inside, he knew he agitated Mary Beth every time he came around with his inquiries, but she knew something. The man could feel it in his heart. There was a huge missing piece of the puzzle in between the time Bonita Bender was apprehended and the death of Corey Mobley five years later. Rance had some clues, but he was far from cracking this case that was causing him to lose sleep, weight and hair in the process. His health was becoming affected by the events. "I'm going to solve this case if it kills me," he told Mary Beth.

"Careful in your speech, Mister Olsen," Mary Beth re-marked.

"Nothing's going to happen to me, mayor."

"Let's hope."

"I won't bother you anymore. It's clear you have no interest in solving this case with me, but if I find out you know more than you're telling me I'll take you down along with everyone else involved." he told Mary Beth before he turned and walked out of the office to continue on with his investigation.

Rance was on to something surrounding the guy Webster Holden and Mary Beth herself, but it would be years before the full scope of the matter would be realized, and once uncovered, Rance Olsen would be forced to make one of the hardest deci-sions of his life.

CHAPTER TWENTY-FIVE

THE WILD SUMMER

"Lord, where are they?" was the first thing Faye said as she sat upright in her bed upon waking from a deep slumber. It was the day after Rance's conversation with Mary Beth, a hot summer's morning down in Cherryvale, Kansas. The night before, Tanya and five-year-old Helen Weinberger had arrived to the Bender Farm for an extended stay.

Tax season, holidays, and especially warm weather, was a drug dealer's wet dream, and being the prolific heroin distributors that they were, the crew would've never let a summer go by without bringing in a fresh load of product to distribute throughout the south and Midwest. The summer of '88 had brought about a change in plans, however; reason being was because the crew had lost a shipment that was loaded up with twenty kilograms of heroin when the massive chains holding over a dozen containers snapped during rough seas stimulated by a tropical depression off the coast of Africa that lay a couple hundred miles to the north.

Twelve containers aboard the crew's vessel named *The Gladiator*, including the one that held their next shipment, had gone overboard, forever lost to the sea, while the remaining two units crashed down onto the ship's topside. Three longshoremen aboard the vessel were crushed to death and The Gladiator's main hull was heavily damaged. The crew's opium now lay 14,000 feet below the surface of the Atlantic Ocean and the ship was now being routed to Mar de Plata, Argentina where Alfredo and Sanjar Darvish were going to oversee repairs to the only vessel the crew owned, and to pay off the families that'd lost loved ones.

Insurance claims by companies such as Pierre Cardin, JVC and Gorton's had to be settled as well. The crew had taken a $1.5 million dollar hit, a fifth of their $7.5 million dollar gross worth, on the loss of life and treasure. To add to their ailing woes, cocaine was becoming the drug of choice for many of the dealers they once sold to, and heroin was now taking a backseat. The streets the crew once controlled with brown, were now spilling blood over white.

Turf wars between rival cocaine networks were erupting throughout New Orleans and Cincinnati. Besides the budding cocaine clicks, the crew's two main hubs in the south and Midwest were now littered with armed bandits out to rob dealers like it was going out of style in a new play known as Cake and Cream where they bum-rushed big time dealers' homes and murdered everyone in sight before making off with the stash.

The crew was up on game, and they had every right to rid the streets of rising drug organizations that did nothing more than heat up the streets with murder and mayhem. Most of the clicks were being run by brash teenagers who reminded them of themselves in their early days, though, and cocaine wasn't their market. Opting to not engage in a battle between clicks pushing the white powder, the main pushers of heroin in the industry, decided to take a backseat to the madness and let the warring cocaine organizations eliminate themselves before they regrouped, so long as no one stepped on their toes. It would take at least six months to have their freighter repaired. From there, the vessel still had to deliver its load of silk, VCRs and frozen seafood before returning to Afghanistan to obtain a new shipment. The crew had basically chalked up the remaining six months or so of the year as a loss and time spent with family had now taken a front seat.

The night before, Faye had lain down with the thoughts of what nine-year-old Maggie had told Helen upon the two's greeting the moment Helen walked into Faye's sprawling two story mansion. *"My backyard is the biggest backyard ever! We gone catch us a cat by the apple trees and play with it tomorrow!"*

"Don't y'all even think about going by them apple trees today, or ever at all, Maggie and Boogie." Faye told Maggie and Helen as she and Tanya greeted one another.

Helen was given the nickname Boogie by her dance instructor after winning a ballet contest at NOCCA, a privately-run school in New Orleans. She was the jewel of the crew. Like her mother and father, she was an eclectic child that went with the flow of things.

Helen wasn't a follower, however; she was the type to observe a scenario and institute her own plan. Whether others went along with her or not was something that had to be dealt with accordingly because when it got down to it, whether she started out as the leader or not, eventually, whenever she was mingling with her peers, Helen Weinberger would eventually become the kid in charge.

Eight-year-old Maggie McPherson attended a private academy in the next town over from Cherryvale where she was a regular studier of Mathematics and World History. Faye made the fifteen mile drive to and fro every day. During those times, she and Maggie would hold some of the most intriguing discussions. Faye didn't pull any punches with Maggie. The child knew her real mother and father along with how they lived and how they died. The eight-year-old, if Faye had to tell it, had both her parents' pedigree. She was fearless, calculating and loving like her father, Webster Holden; and comical, daring and loyal like her mother, Gayle McPherson.

Truth be told, neither Gayle nor Web had much education. Faye knew that to be the truth. Both were more followers than leaders, but strong soldiers nonetheless. Maggie wasn't being raised to be a soldier, however; she and Helen both were being trained to be leaders of crews.

Gayle and Web had given Maggie love, protection and affection. Faye had taken matters a step further by giving Maggie an academic education to go along with those attributes. Maggie and Helen were both on the path to becoming criminals that walked in their parents' footsteps, but much more had to be learned, and sometimes, lessons came about in the oddest ways. The incidents that followed over what would be remembered as The Wild Summer would be a classic case in point.

Faye was so worried about Maggie taking Helen to the apple groves, she'd dreamed of what Maggie and Helen would possibly get into. Reason being was because the apple groves had a story of their own. Over a hundred years earlier, the apple grove was where her great, great grandmother, Kate Bender and the rest of the Bender family had discarded remains of their victims. Faye and Bonita themselves had uncovered human remains of victims of their predecessors' a time or thrice, and Faye herself had buried the remains of the man who'd tried to bribe her into silence four years earlier after she and Tanya had chopped up his remains.

The apple grove was now Faye's personal graveyard. She was every bit her ancestors, and through sheer instinct ingrained in her genes, she had not the capacity to rid herself of a trait where the burying of human remains was the only recourse after committing an act of homicide in Cherryvale, Kansas. When she'd killed Wendell and Jeremy, she had the gumption to dig up the bodies and move them upon learning they could possibly be discovered. Bodies buried on Bender property, however, must remain for all times. It was the Bender way, a tradition amongst the serial killer family. Just as she and Bonita had dug up remains over two decades earlier while playing out in the cornfield behind the home, however, Faye now saw in her mind's eye, Maggie and Helen digging up remains of a man she'd murdered and would then have to explain.

Filled with anxiety over the possibility of having to explain an act gruesome, Faye climbed out of bed in her sleeping shorts and tank top and ran from her room towards Maggie's bedroom where she knew the two girls had slept only to find an empty bed with the covers unturned. She scampered over to the spare room inside her six bedroom home where she knew Tanya had setup and saw her laying atop the covers butt naked with an Uzi at her side. "Not the cornfield!" she complained out loud as she rushed out of the room, stirring Tanya awake in the process.

Faye jumped down her stairs and ran through her living room and crossed her kitchen and eyed the window beside the sink and saw that it was left open. The kitchen window beside the stove was the only window in the home that could be opened from both the inside and the outside. It was rigged to an alarm if ever it was touched from the outside. Maggie knew that to be a fact after Faye had locked the two out of the home a year earlier. She was the one who'd crept inside and unlocked the door before Faye ran in and deactivated the alarm. It was their secret, but Faye realized on this day that Maggie had taken advantage of the circumstances. Now, fifty plus acres was her and Helen's playground and Faye had no clue as to the girls' whereabouts. She deactivated the alarm and ran out the front door.

"*Maggie? Helen? Maggie und Helen, antworten Sie mir!*" (Maggie? Helen? Maggie and Helen, answer me!) she yelled aloud as she ran down her patio stairs, her voice over the land over the rising sun.

Getting no response, Faye grew worried. Her first thought was that the kids had been bitten by rattlesnakes that had taken haven on the land. Knowing she hadn't any antidote for a snake bite, she took off running towards the wheat field, which had stalks maybe two feet high as they were in the early stages of growth. "Maggie! Helen!" she called out as her eyes began to water.

"*Wir kommen, Mutter!*" (We're coming, mother!) Faye heard a tiny voice call out faintly from the apple groves that set about the length of two football fields off to her left.

Looking to her left where she heard the voice, Faye could see the silhouettes of two tiny people making their way back to the home, one whose head was larger than normal with a head full of hair, and the other, a slender, yet shorter figure, skipped alongside her over low cut grass and she immediately took off running in Maggie and Helen's direction.

Tanya had dressed by that time and had made her way downstairs. She emerged onto the patio just as Faye took off running barefoot across the land. "Fuck's going on?" she yelled as she watched Faye run towards two figures she knew to be Helen and Maggie.

Ignoring Tanya's question, Faye kept trotting towards Helen and Maggie. She could see that Maggie was holding onto an object the nearer she approached. Being that the sun was just creeping up over the horizon shortly after six in the morning, everything on the land was coated in an orange and dark brown hue. Only Maggie's large Afro, and the dresses she and Helen wore along with the object Maggie held in her hands could be made out somewhat.

"We caught a cat, momma! We caught a cat with the milk crate I set up by the apple trees last night! I told you it would work!" Maggie stated joyously as she ran towards her mother.

Faye sighed in relief as she eyed the wriggling animal laying in Maggie's clutch. The closer she got, however, she could see the white stripe down the animal's back. *"Das ist nicht eine Katze, die ein Stinktier!"* (That's not a cat that's a skunk!) she exclaimed as she backed away from Maggie.

"Ich erklärte ihnen, dass Katzen sah lustig, Maggie!" (I told you that cat looked funny, Maggie!) Helen declared as she stood beside her friend eyeing the strange creature they'd cap-

tured by using fresh tuna placed underneath a milk crate that was held up by a string.

Maggie held the skunk up near her face and the animal raised its tail. A stream of liquid shot out from its rear end and landed on her bosom and had also coated Faye's legs.

Helen gagged. *"Was zum Teufel ist das für ein Geruch? Mutter, diese hässliche Katze riecht wie Papa, wenn er zu Fuß aus dem Bad!"* (What the fuck is that smell? Mother, this ugly cat smells like daddy when he walk out the bathroom!) the five year-old exclaimed as she took off running towards the house, leaving the skunk, Faye and Maggie in her wake.

Faye and Maggie, meanwhile, were kicking at the skunk after Maggie dropped it on the ground. The animal was hissing and spraying liquid everywhere. Unable to withstand the atrocious odor any longer, mother and daughter took off running towards the home, both removing their clothes in the process.

Tanya ran out and met Helen. The child was crying and laughing at the same time as she hid behind her mother. Tanya looked up just as Faye and Maggie ran past her butt naked. She had to hold her nose over the odor trailing the two. "What happened?"

"Diese beiden jungen Esel ging und hob ein Stinktier denken Es war eine verdammte Katze!" (These two young asses went and picked up a skunk thinking it was a fucking cat!) Faye yelled as she turned on a water house. *"Holen Sie mir einige, Seife, Tanya!"* (Go get me some, soap, Tanya!)

Maggie and Faye stood outside and got hosed down by Tanya as Helen stood beside her, the child now laughing at the naked people as they washed themselves.

During breakfast, which had to be eaten outside because of the lingering stench, Helen was going overboard. The five-year-old kept gagging and coughing over her eggs, oatmeal and bacon. And Tanya was no solace to an embarrassed Faye either. She kept sniffing and complaining that her eyes were watering. "You sure you don't, you don't need me and Helen to hook up the hose for you and Maggie again?" she mockingly asked.

"Mother, can I sleep with you tonight?" Helen asked.

"Why baby?"

"*Da Maggie riecht wie schmutzige Windeln. Und Tante Faye, Tante Faye, riecht wie—*" (Because Maggie smells like dirty diapers. And Auntie Faye, Auntie Faye smells like—"

"We know they're stank, okay? But, they're our friends and sometimes people stink, baby. They can't help it," Tanya smirked.

"They should bathe more. They smell like hot garbage," Helen remarked.

"*So ist es Ich bin auf dem Weg zur Arbeit bin ich nicht dort übernachten, um zu hören, dieser Mist von einem fünf Jahre alten! Komm, Maggie*" (That's it I'm going to work I'm not staying around to listen to this crap from a five-year-old! Come on, Maggie!) Faye snapped as she got up from the table and trotted over to her pickup truck over Tanya's laughter. She climbed inside and immediately climbed right back out and slammed the door and began walking towards the barn on the other side of the property with Maggie trotting behind her to keep up. The day went on, and so did the weeks, but the incident with the skunk was only a prelude to darker things to come for young Helen and Maggie.

****

"You were their leader. And now you are mine to do as I please, little creature," Faye stated through a proud smile as she stroked the spine of feral cat she'd caught in a trap just moments earlier.

It was now two weeks after the incident involving the skunk. During that period of time, Faye had been trying to rid the land of an infestation of feral cats that had set up shop on the Bender Farm; cats in which Maggie and Helen had led to the property from the apple groves. It was bad enough the incident with the skunk for Faye, but this thing with the cats had spun out of control quickly. The felines got into everything and were nothing short of a nuisance in the woman's eyes. They ripped open sacks of seeds in the barn and used them for litter. They'd ripped two leather patio sets Faye had on the patio behind her mansion to shreds and would jump on the screen door and just stare whenever something was being cooked on the stove, and their mating sounds drove her crazy on many a hot summer night.

Faye hated those cats with a passion; having a bunch of felines around every which way she turned aggravated her to the edge of insanity. She often left the home in the early morning hours to tend to the land, but not before having to run off nearly a dozen cats that'd made the Bender Farm their home by posting up on the front porch. The woman would emerge every morning to find cats galore casually licking their paws, meowing and flapping their tails as if they belonged at the joint. She would kick at the animals and try and run them down.

"Fertilizer!" Faye would always scream as the cats scattered in all directions, only to reappear during lunch and dinner.

On this morning, however, the script had been flipped. Faye had laid out a trap the night before which consisted of a can of tuna being placed under a milk crate resting in a stick. Whichever animal stepped under the crate would indirectly brush against the stick while attempting to eat the tuna and entrap itself.

Faye didn't care which cat trapped itself, but on her first night, she had unwittingly captured the prize possession—the perceived leader of the pack in a black, orange, tan and white cat with a short tail. She walked over to her dueler with the cat in tow and placed it gently in the front seat and closed the door. Elated wasn't a strong enough word to describe Faye's emotions as she ran around the front of the luxurious, massive pickup truck and climbed in on the driver's side.

The cat backed up against the passenger side door and hissed as the hair on its back stood up on end. Faye started the truck and reached into her jean jacket pocket, pulled out a can of Devil's Ham and popped the lid and dumped the contents onto the front seat. The feline calmed down and sniffed the food before diving into the meal. Just then, eight-year-old Maggie and five-year-old Helen ran up alongside the truck.

"*Mutter, wo bist du? Ich dachte, ich dachte, sie würden die Frühstück bei uns, im Puppenhaus in meinem Schlafzimmer.*" (Mother, where're you going? I thought, I thought you were going to have breakfast with us at, at the dollhouse inside my bedroom.) young Maggie panted as she was out of breath running towards her mother's truck.

"Hop in," Faye responded as she reached back and pushed the rear door open on the dueler to allow Maggie and Helen entrance to vehicle.

"*Meine Mutter sagt, es gibt keine mehr Speck und Sie haben sollte, um das Speichern und Abrufen wie zwei Packs mehr Speck, so können wir das Essen im Puppenhaus. Und nach, dass Sie sagte es jeder auf mich hören Klavier spielen!*" (My mother says there's no more bacon and you should have to go to the store and get like two packs more of bacon so we can eat at the dollhouse. And after that, she said everybody gets to listen to me play the piano!)

"Wir bekommen, Speck, nachdem ich befruchten die Apple Grove." (We'll get bacon after I fertilize the apple grove.) Faye told Helen.

"Speck! Speck! Speck!" (Bacon! Bacon! Bacon!) Helen sang happily as she bounced up and down in the backseat of the pickup.

The trio rode along a dirt road that led from the back of the home over to a grove of apple trees on the north side of the property. Helen and Maggie were petting the cat, who'd become quite friendly during the ride after eating the entire can of Devil's Ham. The feline had lain on its back to absorb a belly rub while gently nipping at the kids' hands as they tickled its tummy, the pickup bouncing gently across the land.

Faye was all smiles as she watched the little girls gorge themselves on joyful emotions that were being stimulated by being in close proximity to an animal that was to them, had come alive right out the pages of a coloring book. Their feeding leftover catfish to this same cat back in June, the night Helen first arrived, had led to many a morning on the back patio where they were surrounded by a bounty of colorful, furry creatures that rubbed up against their legs while purring softly. It took only two days after Helen's arrival for her and Maggie to begin scratching themselves constantly as bumps appeared on their legs and arms. Tanya and Faye were puzzled over the kids' outbreak of rash. At first, they were convinced that it was because of the bugs that flew around at night while the family enjoyed nights out on the back patio.

The reason behind the rashes were realized when Tanya walked into Maggie's bedroom one early morning, a week into her visit to the Bender Farm, when she eyed a half dozen or so kittens laying around the room. Some of the felines were sleeping atop Helen and Maggie's head, their privates laying across the girls' skulls and closed eyelids while others played a game of tug-o-war with shoestrings on the wooden floor.

Tanya ran and grabbed a plastic garbage bag and placed all of the kittens inside and drove them out to the apple grove and dumped them out amongst the apple trees on the far north side of the property, believing the problem had been rectified. Later that day, she and Faye took Helen and Maggie to the town clinic where they had to endure a barrage of rabies shots. It took nearly a week for the children to recover.

For a while, things had subsided. The cats weren't around, but barely a month later, Faye and Tanya found themselves having to deal with countless cats and kittens running around the outside of the home and tearing into stored seeds inside the barn on the west side of the property and the tearing up patio furniture at the same time.

Unbeknownst to Faye and Tanya, when Helen and Maggie recovered, they went right back to tending to their adopted pets. Many an evening was spent by the women sipping wine as they discussed the cat infestation they were now facing, totally unaware of Helen and Maggie's activities. The two would sneak kittens into the home before bedtime and drop sardines from Maggie's second floor bedroom in the late hours of the night to feed the growing litter.

Remnants of half eaten fish below Maggie's bedroom uncovered by Faye put her up on the girls' activities a month after their rabies shots. She and Tanya had then taken it upon themselves to rid the land of the felines they now knew their daughters had taken a liking to once and for all. The summer of '88 had become a battle of wits between mothers and daughters— the chasing of cats in the morning and killing them off at random by Faye and Tanya, and feeding the felines at night to keep them around on behalf of Helen and Maggie.

For a while, it was a fun game that went unspoken between the two groups, but over time, Helen and Maggie had won out as the cats had multiplied beyond control; but the ring leader had just been captured on this August morning by Faye, who was looking to bring about the beginning of the end to the burgeoning cat haven taking root on the Bender Farm.

The joyous laughter of Maggie and Helen tickled Faye's ears as she rode across the land with a contented smile on her face. She would look over and laugh with Helen and Maggie as they got their kicks out of playing with the animal. She herself managing to reach out and give the furry creature a belly rub or two.

While smiling, Faye pulled up to the apple groves and calmly exited the vehicle. Helen and Maggie watched as she walked over to a large, orange and black machine. It was an odd structure resting on four wheels with what looked like a large megaphone on one end, and a slender pipe on the other.

When Faye reached out and pulled a lever, Helen and Maggie heard a growl and saw puffs of white smoke billow from the top. The girls were in awe over the machine and began smiling when Faye walked back to the passenger side of the truck and pulled the front door open.

"Was für eine Art von Maschine, Mutter?" (What kind of a machine is that, mother?) Maggie asked curiously over the humming machine.

"Das ist ein Terex Deluxe Edition mit Diesel betriebene Holzhacker, Maggie Liebe!" (That is a Terex deluxe edition diesel powered wood chipper, Maggie dear!) Faye responded over the machine's roar as she scooped the cat up into her arms and stroked it gently while smiling down at the purring animal as it happily flapped its stub-of-a-tail to and fro.

Amid the quiet serenity of the truck's interior, Helen and Maggie watched from the backseat of the truck as Faye walked around the front of the ride and neared the megaphone-like opening and held the cat out before her body. The feline began squirming about wildly and trying to bite her hands.

Helen and Maggie tilted their heads in curiosity, wondering what was about to happen. They received their answer when they saw the animal fly through the air and disappear into the opening. Immediately thereafter, a red mist appeared on the opposite end of the machine.

Helen and Maggie looked at one another with blank expressions. *"Die Katze verschwunden!"* (The cat disappeared!) Helen whispered as she looked around, as if someone was watching.

"Sie tötete die Katze!" (She killed the cat!) Maggie smiled.

"Und es machte roter Farbe hinterher?" (And it made red paint afterwards?)

"Nein, Helen. Das war Dünger." (No, Helen. That was fertilizer.) Maggie answered while laughing uncontrollably.

Helen looked back over to the machine and scanned it from end to front. *"Es sah wie Blut."* (It looked like blood.) she told Maggie. *"Ich möchte es wieder zu Tante Faye, also kann ich es wieder sehen."* (I want Aunt Faye to do it again so I can see it again.)

Faye, meanwhile, was using a hose that was hooked up to her irrigation system to rinse out the wood chipper. She was eyeing Helen and Maggie on the sly, watching their behavior, knowing they didn't fully understand what she'd just done. The girls didn't seem shocked over what she'd laid out before them, rather more puzzled over the process. She watched the two go back and forth in their dialogue, studying their behavior as if they were young lionesses on the Serengeti plains. Helen, by her head and hand movements, seemed to be more inquisitive. Maggie, given her constant laughter, appeared to be more inclined to repeat the process for her own amusement.

This was Faye and Tanya's plan all along. Slowly would be the process to bring Helen and Maggie along in the business. The crew dealt in death constantly, and in Faye's mind, the first lesson that needed learning for Helen and Maggie was the understanding of death's process—what actually happens when a living thing is no more.

Faye had shot men and women to death, buried men in swamps, and had a man cut to pieces with a chainsaw. Dwight Davis was her easiest mark to date if one were to lay out her resume`. The various tactics she'd used in times past had made her somewhat of a murder aficionado. She was devoted to the craft and had a deep understanding of the mechanisms involved. She naturally possessed the tutelage needed in order to bring her and Tanya's protégés along casually as they were still young in age, heart, mind and spirit.

Faye went about rinsing the machine. When she was done, she walked over to the truck and pulled the driver's side door open, not knowing what to expect, but when she heard Maggie say,"*Mutter, können mich und Helen drehen Sie eine unserer Katzen in Dünger?*" (Mother, can me and Helen turn one of our cats into fertilizer?) she looked off into the vastness of her sixty-acre farm and smiled proudly.

"Ja. Wenn Sie zwei kann je Catch a Feline, ich will euch beide zurück in die Holzhacker." (Yes. If you two can ever catch a feline, I will take you both back to the wood chipper.) Faye stated lovingly as she climbed back into the truck and backed away from the apple grove.

The summer of '88, for Helen and Maggie, was spent catching and killing cats and kittens at random. The cats were meant to be adults to the children while the kittens represented young life, life although innocent, but deemed worthy of destruction nonetheless.

CHAPTER TWENTY-SIX

THE OLD SCORE

"The gun business belongs to the La Rocca family in this town and there's no room for outsiders," Audi La Rocca told his son, Audi Junior, over the phone inside his suite at Three River Stadium on a mild, late August day in the year 1989, a year after The Wild Summer.

"Dad, all I'm saying is that maybe we should reconsider letting someone else take over. You and uncle Austell are up in age and I'm running the legit business here in Sicily. We've made it. There's no need to continue shipping weapons on our freighters when we're bringing in much more revenue from the legitimate side of the operation."

"I understand, but it's not that easy to back out of the business, son. We have people here that rely on us."

"Let 'em rely on someone else. Look, dad, I have to get back to work. We'll finish this discussion when I come stateside in the next couple of weeks." Audi Junior stated before ending the call.

"Your son may have a point about us getting out of the business, Audi." Austell La Rocca, Audi's older brother remarked as he placed a pair of binoculars to his eyes to get a glimpse of the players running out onto the baseball field.

Audi and Austell La Rocca were still heavily involved in the gun running business in Pittsburgh, Pennsylvania. The men were living a carefree life in the steel city and reaping huge profits. Old timers to organized crime, the men enjoyed their weekly baseball games inside their suite while going over future sells. Their next deal was lined up with Ricky Gross, Brenda's old man, in the upcoming days.

The stadium was packed for the Pittsburgh Pirates' home game against the New York Mets. Audi and Austell had their drinks and were awaiting their sausage dogs and nachos as they enjoyed the soft sounds of George Benson's song *Masquerade*.

As the players ran out onto the field, the bell to their suite rung, Audi got up and answered. A young Asian entered with a tray of hot dogs and nachos and smiled politely. She walked over and set the tray down and began setting up the men's food as Audi returned to his seat.

"You're all set," the young woman remarked a few minutes later after setting up a tray of hot dogs and a large bowl of nachos smothered in cheese. She handed a hot dog to each of the La Rocca brothers, pulled the foil covering off the nachos and then said, "I'll clean the bathroom before I depart. Is there anything else I can help you men with today?'

"No, sweetie," Austell replied before he took a bite of his sausage dog and reached into his pocket and handed the young woman a five dollar bill.

The La Rocca brothers ate while watching the opening inning of the game. Ten minutes in, Austell began to drool. He moved to reach for a napkin, but could not move his arms or his legs.

Audi, meanwhile, was enthralled in the game as a Mets player had hit a two run homer in the first inning. He was rocking in his seat, furious at the Pirates' pitcher. "Why'd you throw a knuckle ball to that guy?" he yelled out. "Austell did you not—"

Audi paused his speech when he saw his brother leaning to one side. "Are you having a heart attack, Austell? Those damn sausage dogs I tell ya'," he remarked in his hoarse voice.

"It wasn't the hot dogs," a woman spoke aloud.

Audi turned around and saw Lisa Vanguard walking in his direction while placing a pair of black leather gloves onto her hands. The young Asian inside the room had closed and locked the door behind her and was moving to pull the side curtains shut inside the suite as the music played on. "...*We tried to talk it over...but the words got in the way...we're lost... inside...this lonely game we play...*"

"Wow," Lisa chuckled as she vibed with the music by nodding her head in appreciation. "That song really sets the mood in this place."

"The fuck are you doing here?" Audi scowled over the music. "What have you done to Austell?"

"He just had a muscle relaxer. I only needed to speak to one of you, didn't matter which one, so I had one of you silenced." Lisa remarked through a smile as she bit her bottom lip while holding her hands behind her back.

Audi looked down at the .9mm he had resting on a small table before him. Lisa followed his eyes and pulled a gun of her own from her back waistband. "The way these people are screaming at this game, no one will notice me pumping slugs into your ass. Make me do it," she demanded as she held onto a silencer-tipped .32 semiautomatic.

Audi leaned back in his seat and placed his hands in his lap. "Speak your peace."

Lisa pulled a chair beside Audi and sat and crossed her legs as she aimed the gun at his side. "Five years ago, an Asian couple down in Cincinnati was killed inside their home. They were good friends of mine."

"Wasn't our doing," Audi remarked as he checked on his brother. He could see that Austell was coherent, the man just couldn't move or speak given the muscle relaxer that he'd ingested. "Why would me and Austell need to kill a couple of Asians in Ohio?"

"I never said you two had them killed, but you were the ones who supplied the guns," Lisa remarked as Tammy walked up behind the La Rocca brothers and showed them the Uzi Lisa had found on the home's second floor six years prior.

Audi stared at the gun and recognized it as the brand and caliber he and his brother were known to sell. "Those guns are everywhere," he stated in a nonchalant manner as he stared out at the ballfield. "Anybody could've killed those people."

"But it starts with you and that guy beside you drooling like a newborn," Lisa retorted. "If you didn't do it, then who did?"

"I wouldn't know," Audi dismissively remarked.

"Wrong answer," Lisa snarled as she placed the gun to Audi's right leg and dumped a slug into his knee cap.

The man groaned and clutched his leg. "I don't know nothing about the Moto deaths!" he yelled aloud.

"I never said their names," Lisa spoke through gritted teeth as she stood and slapped Audi about the head with her pistol. "Who killed Kazuki and Cho Moto? Who killed them?" she asked as she backed away from Audi.

"I sold guns to a guy from New Orleans the month of the hit! We met down in Cincinnati! That's about as good as I can tell you!" Audi cried aloud as blood ran down his face. "A slender black guy!"

"Names!" Lisa commanded. Audi clutched his chest at that moment and began gasping for air as he fell from his seat face down onto the carpet. "Audi," she called out. "Audi?" she then asked anxiously as she kicked the man in his side. Lisa knelt down and checked his pulse only to find a faint one. "Help me get him back into his seat," she asked of Tammy.

During the entire ordeal, Austell could only sit and listen as tears of anger streamed down his sunken cheeks and rolled off the flabby skin underneath his chin. Lisa and Tammy moved around him as if he wasn't present as they went about setting Audi back into his chair. Tammy topped it off by placing the unconscious man's fedora back onto his head.

"I haven't the time to wait for the medication to wear off, Mister La Rocca. Me and Tammy have to be going," Lisa stated as she nodded towards Tammy. "Do them both," she stated nonchalantly as she went about straightening the area before the brothers' chairs.

Tammy pulled a muzzled .32 revolver from her apron and placed the gun just behind Austell's ear and squeezed the trigger. The man's head immediately dropped and he was dead within seconds. The gun was then placed to the back of Audi's head and he received the same dose of lead as his brother, which solidified his death. Tammy then turned to Lisa and asked, "What now?"

"We have to search their homes."

"How will we do that? They have wives."

"The day of the funeral we'll do it," Lisa remarked as she checked the men over, making sure they appeared to be watching the game before she and Tammy left the suite.

****

Two days after the hit on the La Rocca brothers, Ricky 'Mouse' Gross was inside the home he shared with Brenda packing a suitcase in preparation to make a drive up to Pittsburgh from New Orleans. Brenda, meanwhile, was preparing to ride to Saint Gabriel, Louisiana and pick up the King Sisters as today was their release date. Hundreds of thousands of dollars had been banked, and the crew was in the midst of financing Willie's first run at city council.

Things were moving along smoothly for the crew in late August of '88, and with the King sisters' return, the click would be back at full strength. Brenda was all smiles as she moved about the master bedroom dressing herself; it had been nearly a year since she'd seen her girls in a conjugal visit and she'd been looking forward to this day ever since Zelda and Vivian pled guilty back in June of '85.

Ricky was tying a tie around his neck when the phone rang. Brenda answered and handed him the receiver. "It's Audi Junior," she stated as she bobbed to the music coming from the stereo speakers in the corners of the room.

"Yo, Audi J? What it is, my man?" Mouse asked the moment he placed the phone to his ear.

Brenda was vaguely listening when she heard her man say aloud, "What? Who did it? Two days from now? I'm sorry to hear that, brother. I'll be there the day of the funeral."

"What happened?" Brenda asked the moment Mouse hung up the phone.

"Audi and Austell are dead. They was found two days ago shot in they suite over to the ballpark in Pittsburgh," Mouse re-marked stunned.

Brenda bowed her head. "We know who did it?" she asked somberly.

"Audi Junior and the police ain't got a clue. Audi J say he got something to give me so I'm going to funeral in a couple of days."

"You sure that's a good move, baby?"

"Why you ask me that?"

"I mean, the guys were killed, Ricky. This could be some old mafia score or something. You go up there and get caught up in some bullshit, man, and we be facing another setback. Zelda and Viv coming home, the pipeline running from Venezuela. We can do without selling the guns."

"You right about that," Mouse admitted. "But if I don't go it'll be a sign of disrespect to the La Rocca family. If I'm gone cut off ties I'd rather tell Audi J to his face. Anyway, he got some info for me so I have to go."

"You still flying out today?"

"No, baby. I'll just book another flight the morning of the funeral."

"Good," Brenda smiled as she walked over and placed her arms around her man's neck. "You can ride with me and RJ to pick up Zelda and Vivian. But first..."

Ricky scooped Brenda up in his arms and she wrapped her legs around his slender waist. The two kissed passionately as Ricky walked over to the bed and lay Brenda down where the two made passionate love before heading out to pick up the King sisters.

CHAPTER TWENTY-SEVEN

THE PATSY

Mouse was fresh off a flight from New Orleans. It was early Sunday morning in Pittsburgh, a muggy day dominated by low clouds and dense fog in the early hours. He climbed inside a luxurious four door Dynasty and made his way over to a motel about an hour away from the airport and checked in. With a few hours before the funeral, he took the time to make a few calls and then went and had breakfast in the adjoining restaurant.

As time drew nearer for Audi and Austell's funeral, a steady rain burst through the clouds. Mouse donned his rain coat, grabbed an umbrella and had his rental car brought around. He rode over to the funeral, having bypassed the service, and climbed out of the car under the pouring rain.

A large black canopy at the top of the hill inside Allegheny Cemetery let him know where the La Rocca brothers were being placed into the ground. He was actually expecting a large turnout given the men's longtime affiliation with the Italian

Mafia. Instead of a large crowd, however, there were only the women Ricky recognized as the men's wives, a handful of children and a couple of older guys he'd seen around the bar the La Roccas owned over in Bloomfield off Liberty Avenue.

Ricky walked in the rain amid the lush chestnut, maple and dogwood trees that dotted the cemetery that gave off a paradisiac setting. As he neared, Audi J met him at the top of the hill. "It's good to see you, Ricky."

"Sorry for your loss, man. Any word on who's behind this bullshit?"

"Nothing, il mio amico. A couple of ole timers say it might be an old score coming out of Philadelphia, but nobody laying claim to this." Audi J remarked as he and Ricky walked along the hillside.

"It's not like anybody would."

"My father and uncle had very little power, Ricky. Crews back east knew this. So if they were responsible, one of them would've sent flowers with a message attached. My father and uncle were more respected than feared in their old age."

"What about you? What are you gonna do about this?"

"As of now, I'm more of a business man. I run freighters and travel all over the world. No one fears me because they know I was never a part of the business and have no interest in becoming a gun dealer."

"Why did you invite me here?"

"To give you this," Audi J replied as he went into his inside pocket and handed Ricky a cassette player with a tape inside.

"What is this?" Mouse questioned as he inspected the small square box.

"It's a recorder. Listen to it when you get back to your room. My father and uncle kept that as an insurance policy. I don't know if it solves their deaths or not, but he wanted you to have it if he didn't die of natural causes is what he told me."

"You listened to it?"

"No need, Mister Gross. My father and uncle's business is not my business. I'm taking my mother, aunt, nieces and nephews and we're moving to Sicily," Audi J said as his eyes welled up. "I talked to my father the day he was killed and nearly begged him to leave this side of the business alone, but he and Austell was old school, man. They was addicted to crime and it cost them their life. That won't happen to the rest of the family."

"Are there any more copies around?"

"That's the only copy as far as I know. My father kept it in a fireproof safe. It hasn't been touched until now."

Mouse had nothing to say in reply to Audi J's confession. In his mind, the Italian was taking the easy way out. If it had been his father, he would've done all in his power to find out who was behind the death. Audi J wasn't built that way, however, and Ricky knew it given past conversations with Audi and Austell.

"The business yours if you want it, Ricky." Audi J remarked, shaking Ricky from his thoughts.

"It seems as if this gun running racket has run its course, Audi J. I don't want it. Don't even need it. Thought I'd come and tell you in person." Mouse replied.

"You could've told me that over the phone," Audi J chuckled. "I don't care about guns, man. We make millions with our freighters shipping merchandise to the Asian Pacific. I'm so far removed from Pittsburgh," he added through a sigh as he looked back at his father and uncle's grave site.

"My flight leaves in a couple of hours. I'm going pay my respects to the rest of your family before I head back to the motel," Ricky remarked.

"If ever you need me, call me at this number. It's free of charge," Audi J said as he handed Ricky a business card.

******

Lisa Vanguard and Tammy Moto were parked downhill inside the cemetery in Tammy's parents' BMW. Lisa had watched the entire procession until the crowd had dispersed. She had been to the La Rocca family's home earlier, but the place was being packed for moving by two moving crews. She had no way to search the home, so she rode through Allegheny Cemetery to see if she could pick up on anything of use to her endeavors. She'd eyed Audi J and a slender black man talking several yards away from a canopy, and when she witnessed Audi J hand the man what appeared to be a small box, she decided to tail him. With Tammy behind the wheel, the two followed the Dynasty the man was riding in over to a motel near the airport and took note of the room he entered.

With the car parked, Lisa jotted down the license plate. "Stay here," she told Tammy. "If our guy comes out of that room you're to notify me expeditiously."

"Where're you going?"

"To run a check on that tag back at my office in Philadelphia." Lisa answered as she climbed from the car and walked over to a payphone.

Tammy Moto sat behind the wheel of the idling car with a keen eye on the room. For the past four years she'd been under Lisa Vanguard's tutelage. The FBI agent had helped her graduate college and had gotten her enrolled into Temple University where she was majoring in law. She was also a paid intern working for Lisa back in her Philadelphia office.

The death of her parents had warped Tammy's view of the world. For a while, Lisa Vanguard was the only friend she'd had in America. The woman took care of her finances, gave her shelter after moving her to her home in Baltimore, and gave her a proper education. Although she was only ten years older than Tammy, Lisa had become somewhat of a surrogate mother to the troubled youth during her vulnerable teen years.

A deep affection had developed, one in which Lisa was the leader, and Tammy Moto the student and faithful devotee.

The car door's opening once more startled Tammy briefly. Lisa climbed back into the car smiling as she opened the glove box and pulled out a .9mm and a muzzle. "Ricky Gross from New Orleans, Louisiana," she stated in near exuberance as she twisted the muzzle onto the handgun.

Back inside the motel room, Ricky had just pressed play on the cassette player and a conversation began to unfold. *"You want Web dead to save your own ass. Nobody told you to give Sheriff Mobley the lowdown on his sons. You tracked Faye Bender down, figured out that she'd killed the man's sons and gave him the information instead of conducting a proper investigation, knowing Corey, the good ole boy that he was, was going to kill the woman's family to even the score. One thing about us Italians, Miss Lisa Vanguard, we may kill our own made guys, but we never touch a man's, or woman's, for that matter, we never touch a person's family that's not involved."*

"Franklin Patterson hid a secret from his friend the sheriff. He was just as culpable as Faye Bender and Gayle McPherson."

"What about the kid, Lisa?"

"Faye's son had it coming for Faye killing Corey's two sons. Look, I'm not here to talk about ghosts. What I wanna know is if you two will take care of Webster Holden, and do we still have business to conduct here in Pittsburgh?"

Ricky's eyes widened. He realized he now held the proof Faye Bender needed to clear her name once and for all. He went and dialed his home number and Brenda picked up on the second ring. "Baby? You need to get in contact with Faye and tell her—" A knock interrupted Ricky. "Hold on, I think this housekeeping," he stated as he set the receiver down on the nightstand.

When Ricky opened the door, a single, gloved-clad hand holding a black wallet came into view. The wallet unfolded and a silver FBI badge dropped down. A slender, red-haired woman then slowly came into view. "Ricky Gross?" she asked with a sly smile on her face.

"Yeah. That's me." Ricky remarked a little unnerved as he backed into the room. The woman slowly crept inside and stood before Ricky after he'd confirmed his identification. A petite Asian followed, closing the door behind her.

Ricky didn't know how Lisa looked in person, He was under the impression that he was about to be busted for running guns with the La Rocca brothers given Audi and Austell had been murdered. "I want a lawyer," was all he said with his hands slightly raised, putting the cassette recorder on display.

"A lawyer?" Lisa remarked in a cold manner as she eyed the device in Ricky's hand. The calculating agent was willing to bet her life that she'd found what she'd been looking for ever since the day Audi and Austell had her at that ballgame back in

June of '83 where they'd disgraced her by calling her an 'arrogant cunt'.

"There isn't a lawyer on this planet that can help you, Ricky," Lisa let it be known as she raised the gun.

Ricky had suddenly picked up on the woman's voice. "It's you on the tape!" he yelled aloud as he charged at Lisa.

Lisa stepped back and fired a round, hitting Ricky in the neck. The shot was intentional because it prevented the man from screaming any further.

Ricky stumbled into Lisa, grabbing her shoulders as he sunk to the floor with blood spurting from the side of his neck. She reached down and gently eased the recorder from the man's grip before kicking him over onto his back. She then pressed play on the recorder as the man convulsed at her feet.

The conversation where Lisa had admitted to aiding Sheriff Corey Mobley in the killing of Faye Bender's family was heard and she let it play through to the end, if only to assure herself that she'd struck gold. Satisfied she'd obtained the only evidence known that was able to reveal her past crimes, Lisa clicked off the tape. "You're of no longer use to me, Mister Gross," she was happy to confess as she aimed her gun and shot Ricky three times in the face. "Tammy? Hand me your Uzi and go and get the thirty-two you used back at the stadium the other day," she then calmly requested while staring down at her handy work.

When Tammy left, Lisa began a quick search of the motel room as she held onto to the Uzi. She soon discovered the motel's phone receiver laying on the nightstand so she went and picked it up. "Hello?"

"Who's this?" Brenda asked, instantly growing incensed as she believed Ricky had a woman with him inside the motel room. "Where's my man?" she asked agitated.

"Your man is dead," Lisa responded coldly before hanging up the phone and placing the Uzi on the nightstand. Tammy returned at that moment and Lisa had her place the gun she'd used to kill the La Rocca brothers beside Ricky's corpse.

"Okay, everything is all set up," Lisa remarked as she checked over the room to make sure the crime scene was staged to her liking. The phone began to ring as she and Tammy turned to leave. Lisa knew it was the woman she'd talked to seconds prior calling back, but she cared not to engage the woman any further, unlike the time she'd tormented Gayle McPherson before killing her parents. She and Tammy left the room as quietly as they'd entered, leaving the phone to ring repeatedly, knowing no one would answer.

It had taken Lisa Vanguard seven years, nearly to the day, matter of fact, to exact revenge on the La Rocca brothers for cutting ties with her after her previous cohorts, Scully and Ennis, were taken out by Webster Holden, Gayle McPherson and Faye Bender outside of Jonas' back over in Baltimore. Not only did she exact revenge on the La Rocca brothers, she now held in her procession the only evidence that could link her to the Patterson Massacre.

The reward was indeed worth the wait for Lisa Vanguard. She'd killed the La Rocca brothers and had recovered the cassette that had been hanging over her head for some time now. And she was willing to gamble that the La Rocca brothers didn't have a second copy. Either way, this was about as close to a perfect murder as she could get away with was her thinking. And the icing on the cake, should everything go according to plan, would be that the man Ricky Gross would be the one to take all the blame.

Lisa was familiar with the Pittsburgh homicide unit. They would run ballistics on the guns found inside the room. The Uzi would be traced back to the Moto murders, and the .32 revolver would be linked to the La Rocca killings. Ricky would become Lisa's patsy. Killing him had solved all of her problems. She and Tammy would disappear off the scene and turn their attention elsewhere, leaving those affected by the tragedies to put together pieces of a puzzle she'd intentionally distorted for her own personal gain. Years would pass before the two would ever resurface as they both knew, Lisa more than Tammy, that they'd both just gotten away with cold-bloodied murder untraceable.

CHAPTER TWENTY-EIGHT

HONORABLE MENTION

A week after Ricky's murder found Brenda Marshall sitting in a folding chair in the center of the front row with her son sitting beside her crying silently. Before her, set Ricky 'Mouse' Gross's coffin. When the woman on the other end of the phone told her that her man was dead, Brenda took it as a woman trying to mock her because she was kicking it up in Pittsburgh with Mouse. She'd waited, knowing Ricky was schedule to arrive back in New Orleans in the late afternoon. She drove out to New Orleans International and waited at the gate for Ricky, determined to tear into him about the woman in his room.

When Ricky didn't walk off the flight, however, Brenda was hit with an ominous feeling. She went home and called the Pittsburgh airport only to learn that Ricky hadn't made his flight. Tears ran down her cheeks as she called the motel Ricky was staying at and had the staff check the room. It pained her to have to tell the manager that she believed her husband—because that's what Ricky was to her when it got down to it—

was in the room dead. She waited patiently with her son RJ at her side until the manager came back and somberly asked her, "Miss Marshall, how soon can you make it to Pittsburgh?"

Brenda would never forget those words. Her actions haunted her as well. Believing Ricky was cheating on her after all the years they'd spent together left her with a guilty conscious. Her man was in his time of dying while she stood accusing him of infidelity. Living it down would be hard, and to add insult to injury, homicide detectives had linked Ricky to a double murder back in Cincinnati and the death of the La Rocca brothers' double murder. He died an accused murderer and there was nothing that could be done, even though the crew knew Ricky had nothing to with what went down in Pittsburgh. As far as the Cincinnati hit, the crew was left perplexed as to how the gun Ricky had used to kill Kazuki, had turned up inside the hotel room in Pittsburgh where he was killed. Someone was manipulating the crimes, only the crew hadn't a clue as to who was behind it, let alone the why. It was a bullet everybody had to bite in order to move forward for the time being.

Brenda placed a pair of shades over her eyes as Tanya, Alfredo, Zelda and Vivian sat with her on the front row. The reverend had said a few kind words and then looked out over the crowd. "It is my honor," he spoke as he dabbed his face with a silk rag under the hot morning sun that was beaming down on Saint Louis Cemetery Number Three, "it is my honor to introduce future state representative, Willameena Slack. If we want to put an end to the scourge of violence befalling our black men in our community, we do well to help put those running for change into power. With that aside, and not to detract from this tragedy that lay before us, Willameena Slack," the reverend ended as he backed away from the microphone.

Willameena walked onto the small stage before Ricky's casket and thanked the reverend. "I knew Ricky Gross for many years," she began. "He and my sister Brenda Marshall had birthed a child and had built a life for themselves. What the reverend said is true—if we want change, we have to support those who intend on doing right by the citizens. But I'm not here to deliver a campaign speech. I'm here to pay respects to a man that was loved and respected by those who knew and loved him."

While Willie eulogized Ricky, Tanya and Alfredo sat side by side talking amongst themselves. "The Darvish men are getting anxious over the actions of this guy Pablo Escobar back in South America." Alfredo remarked. "Sanjar believes Pablo will try to make his way into Venezuela and establish a new cocaine pipeline."

"Pablo's a loose cannon," Tanya replied in a near whisper. "Mabel gave me some information on him and his organization. The DEA has a program called CENTAC that they're putting into place. They'll be able to track Pablo's every move. It won't be long before he falls."

"I don't underestimate the guy, though. If he escapes his country and makes his way down to Venezuela it will place our own unit in jeopardy." Alfredo stated.

"Don't worry, love," Tanya remarked as she ran her hand over Alfredo's jawline. "I'll keep close contact with the Senator. Pablo stands a good chance of not making it into Venezuela. But if he does cross the border, we'll be there to take him down," she ended as she resumed listening to Willie's commemoration.

When Willie was done, and after Ricky had been lowered into the ground, the crew all convened over to Brenda's home in New Orleans East for the repass. Ricky's death was a blow to the crew's ranks, but business had to go on as the crew entered the world of politics.

Later that night, Willie was scheduled for a televised debate that was to be held inside City Hall. After mingling with the crowd, she went into Brenda's bedroom and sat at her friend's desk and began mentally practicing what she was going to discuss during the debate by having an impromptu conversation with herself. This was new territory for the aspiring politician. She'd graduated from the University of New Orleans a year earlier with a degree in Political Science and a minor in Liberal Arts, degrees and courses that had equipped her professionally for the political scene, but left much to be desired from a personal standpoint. She'd excelled at fact-checking and had an understanding of the issues, but there were areas where she needed work, namely her delivery, as she would quickly come to discover.

Tanya, meanwhile, had been watching Willie the entire day. She knew her friend had a lot on her plate having to deliver a eulogy and then having to debate a capable political opponent who'd been holding onto the district seat encompassing the Saint Bernard project for nearly twenty years in a few hours. Tanya had put up $250,000 dollars on Willie's behalf to run TV ads and to have billboards put up around the city announcing Willie's run for state representative, which was a lot of money for the times. Sally Irving, she, too, having graduated from University of New Orleans and was now enrolled into the Loyola University School of Law, was having her tuition paid by Faye Bender.

Tanya and Faye were placing all of their eggs into Willie's basket. They'd learned from dealing with Mabel that political ties would give the crew a lot of power and they were in great pursuit of that political advantage. They had Mabel and Mary Beth in their pocket, but the Senator was nearing retirement, and Mary Beth was still wet behind the ears being only the mayor of a town with under eight hundred people—her time, was far off. In order to increase their political strength, the crew needed a younger ally who had years left on their resume` and would provide an immediate spark—that person, was Willameena Slack.

As Tanya sat with Helen at her side in Brenda's study, the two of them eating bowls of crawfish etoufee, Sally Irving walked in and pulled up a chair beside her. Sally was Willie's aide and political confidant. The two had bonded the day Willie was arrested back in eighty-five and had formed a tight bond after Willie had beaten the charges she was facing alongside the King Sisters. It was an ironic twist being Willie had once pimped Sally, but it was a perfect alliance as Sally was in tune with many a young person who didn't, but were able to vote. Willie's elderly opponent wasn't reaching out to the younger people in her district, and this was the angle Tanya believed would earn Willie her first political victory.

Sally, dressed in a beige business pant suit and white shoes, pulled her chair closer to the table and laid her briefcase on the table. "Sorry I missed the services," she told Tanya as she flipped the case open.

"It's nothing. We all understand," Tanya remarked as she wiped her mouth with a napkin. "How many voters you got registered today, Sally?"

"I got thirty," Sally replied as she removed a stack of registrations.

Tanya looked over towards Sally with a blank stare. "Thirty?" she asked dryly. "Sally, it's over two thousand people between the ages of eighteen and twenty-one in the Saint Bernard project alone and all you've managed is thirty registrations?"

"Do you know how hard it is to even get people to listen to what it is I'm asking of them?" Sally retorted as she sat upright in the seat and stared Tanya in the eyes. "I know we're going after the young voters, Tanya—but feel me on this—people know Willie—they want to hear from her and not me on her behalf."

Tanya was against Willie returning to the Seventh Ward given her past reputation. She was a known whore and manipulator of men to most and she felt that if Willie tried to establish herself as a political candidate in the place where she was most infamous, it would open her up to ridicule from older residents who knew her background and were aligned with her opponent. "I don't want Willie nowhere near the Saint Bernard now. The election is three months away and we need to keep her image crisp," she said to Sally.

Sally rolled her eyes. Her thinking was of a different nature, but being Tanya was financing Willie's campaign, she felt she had no choice but to fall in line. "I can use some of the budget to hold a weekend lunch at the project office in the Saint Bernard," she stated. "From there, I'm thinking I can get Willie to do an interview with Jammin' Jazzy."

"Jammin' Jazzy?" Tanya asked.

Sally merely shook her head. "You really should let me take the lead on this campaign," she complained. "Jammin' Jazzy is only the hottest urban Dee-Jay in the city and on the gulf coast. If you want to reach young voters, Jazzy is the way to go."

"Set it up, then." Tanya replied. "But I want scripted questions. I want to know what this Dee-Jay is going to ask Willie beforehand."

"It doesn't work like that, Tanya. Jazzy will just ask questions at random and—"

"No script, no Willie." Tanya retorted, cutting Sally off.

Sally threw her hands up and began scraping up the documents. "I'll get these new registrars turned in to the state and get in touch with Jazzy. I'll let you know when the interview is scheduled," she huffed as she pushed the chair away from the table and stormed out of the room.

Willie was still practicing her lines when Sally walked into Brenda's study. She paused midsentence. "Hey, girl," she stated through a smile. "How'd the registration drive go?"

"Willie, you're going to lose this election." Sally stated matter-of-factly.

"Thank you, Sally. I really do appreciate the vote of confidence." Willie sassed.

Sally sighed and ran her hands through her permed, shiny black hair. "It's not that I don't believe in you, Willie," she confessed. "But Tanya is unbelievable in her expectations!" she dreadfully spoke as she walked around in a circle with her arms stretched out before her body. "She's, she's like the Gestapo or something! She doesn't take any of my suggestions and demands that everything goes her way. I know she's concerned about your image, but she gotta let you fly, brer! We're being handcuffed with this campaign."

"My opponent has a sketchy past that she's trying to hide," Willie responded as she looked over a few notes she'd jotted down. "I'm the clean-cut candidate that's above the fray, Sally."

"But by being 'above the fray', aren't you hiding who you are, Willie?" Sally questioned while raising her hands in quotations and stepping closer to Willie.

"I'm with Tanya on this, Sally. Just keep getting as many voters registered as you can up until the election."

Sally bowed her head and shook it somberly. "Fine," she mumbled. "Don't blame me when it's a landslide victory for the other democrat."

"Say what?" Willie asked as she peered over her shoulder.

"Nothing, Willie. I'll see you at City Hall in a few hours," Sally replied as she headed out of the room. At that moment, she'd decided not to schedule the interview with Jammin' Jazzy and had also refused to set up the weekend lunch in the Saint Bernard project.

Although being only twenty-three years of age, Sally had a deep insight into political strategy. She believed to the core that the approach being instituted by Tanya was the wrong avenue. Willie should just be herself and speak to the people candidly instead of trying to pass herself off as a young, up and coming politician looking to change the narrative under false pretenses.

Sally had learned a lot from Willie the short time she'd whored for the woman, and the main thing she'd learned was to be true to oneself. As far as Tanya, Sally had always viewed her as being the reasonable one out of the crew able to compromise. Conviction to one's beliefs was not the asset she was witnessing on the part of the women she held in high esteem, however, and for that, Sally was disappointed in Willie and Tanya both because in her eyes, they weren't understanding the political process and had no real connection to the people that mattered in their campaign. They wanted the people's votes, but were refusing to engage in the interaction needed to drive their rhetoric home.

With those thoughts in mind, Sally had decided to let things play out with the hopes that Willie would prevail, but it was her gut that was telling her that the crew would have to learn a hard lesson in losing before a political victory would ever be recognized. And in her mind, it was deservedly-so given the callous attitudes being put on display by Willie and Tanya alike.

CHAPTER TWENTY-NINE

NEW SHERIFF IN TOWN

It was now November of 1992. Alfredo was down in the tropical city on the Caribbean Sea to meet with the Darvish men to discuss new shipping arrangements on the forty kilograms of heroin the crew was smuggling into America. The previous company they'd been using to smuggle their drugs in with frozen seafood and linens bound for the Port of New Orleans was on the verge of filing for bankruptcy and he and the Darvish men were in town to supply an infusion of cash to their shipping counterparts to become majority owner of the warehouse company.

This was a crucial time for the crew. Although the warehouse company they were transporting freight for was in threat of going bankrupt, the eleven-million-dollar buyout Alfredo was attempting to make would eliminate transportation costs completely.

To add to the crew's prosperity, it was Election Day back in America. Willie was sure to win her second run for state representative as the crew had gone all out in the realm of finance and endorsements after she'd loss her first bid two years earlier in a landslide victory, just as Sally Irving had predicted.

Mabel Sougherbraun had served her purpose. Tanya had reached out and contacted her ace-in-the-hole, saving the favor the crew was owed for the exact and right moment where it would be most beneficial. Mabel's TV ads in support of Willie, which ran throughout the city of New Orleans for over five months, had given Willie a double-digit lead in the polls going into the final weeks of the campaign season. They were powerful ads with cinematic music playing in the background that heralded Willie as being the candidate of the people having grown up in the Saint Bernard project.

Sally Irving, Willie's lead campaign operator, was nothing short of being a beast. After Willie had loss her first bid, just as Sally had predicted, Tanya had relented and given the campaign reins to Sally. The day after Willie had loss, Sally sent her back to the Saint Bernard to begin campaigning once more for the next election two years out. Mabel was on hand to provide guidance being she was an experienced politician. Her advice to Willie and Sally was that the two needed a campaign slogan.

"Think about one of the most profound things you've ever said in your life," Mabel told Willie a year earlier as she sat with her, Sally and Tanya inside of Tanya's loft.

Willie leaned back in the chair she was sitting in and thought about the day she'd gone to jail. Six months later, one of the most powerful ads to ever run in the south was unleashed on the citizens of New Orleans...

..."I can deal with my past and face my demons. I can admit my past to everyone who knows me," the ad began, echoing Willie's voice over sentimental violins and strings as pictures of her shaking hands with constituents faded in and out of the screen. "I grew up on the streets. I know what it's like to face hard times. And unlike my opponent, I'm not out to ruin lives by cutting after school programs and free daycare. It's hard enough trying to survive in this economy. I'm here to help the people in my district. And if I can't help you, I'll surely fight those out to hurt you. My name is Willameena Slack, and I need your vote on first Tuesday,"...

The words Willie had told one lone janitor the day she was arrested had been revamped and used for the positive. Senator Sougherbraun was ingenious with her wording. Willie's opponent was now on the ropes. The crew had rented vans and buses and had fleets of vehicles going from neighborhood to neighborhood to pick up voters and take them to the polls and back. Grills were burning out in front the polling places to offer free ribs and chicken dinners and there was never a shortage of coffee and soda.

Willie may have gotten slaughtered in her first bid for state representative, but this time around, she and her girls had their act together. And it seems as if the stars were lining up in her favor this go around. Willie was riding in on a democrat ticket being led by an opponent running against George H.W. Bush, the nation's current President, by the name of William 'Bill' Clinton. Willie's entire family had first names that began with the letter 'W'. Her son was named William. Her nickname was 'Willie', and 'Bill' was known as 'Slick Willie' by some. No one could tell Willie she was going to lose this campaign, and the way they were pulling people into the polls, victory was now the only outcome.

With the election in full swing back in America, Alfredo and the Darvish men adjoined to a sound proof conference room. After formalities, the three men sat down and began negotiations. "Have you heard about our friend Pablo over in Medellin?" Sanjar Junior asked once the men were all seated.

"I have not," Alfredo replied. "I thought we were here to discuss a buyout."

"We are," Sanjar remarked. "But this news is of importance to us all."

"How so?"

Sanjar leaned forward and said, "Pablo is on the run. Has been for the past year. Two of his top Enforcers in the Gacha brothers were killed by Colombian police not too long ago. The Medelllin Cartel has now broken off into separate factions."

"My woman says the DEA has a program called CENTAC and they're on to Pablo."

"The Central Tactical Program is what is causing the disruption, my friend." Sanjar stated. "It's working too good. That thing about Escobar's men moving into our territory here in Venezuela looks very likely in the near future."

"What can we do to ward them off?" Alfredo asked as he leaned back and crossed his legs.

"The streets aren't talking much. But from what we know, no one from the Medellin Cartel has touched down in Venezuela just yet."

Old Man, his hands resting atop a fourteen karat gold walking stick with a diamond handle, chimed in by saying, "Since no one from the cartel has arrived, we have time to set up our own security force here in Caracas. We've brought a security staff from Israel with us on this trip to survey the city and provide us with the safest location to conduct business in the future."

"Have your men been checked out?" Alfredo asked. "Men from the Middle East have been known to play both sides in this business. Maybe you should let me look into security. I have an Old Italian connect from Italy by way of New Orleans, the Aranello Family. I can contact them and maybe get them to pull some strings and get them to free up some soldiers for our protection as a favor to us."

"Again, you doubt our abilities, Mister Lowes," Old Man stubbornly protested. "The men we have selected for our security detail are Israeli-born citizens. Who better to oversee this new venture than someone from the place of our merchandise's point of origin?"

"Are you not paying attention to what's going on in and around your homeland, Old Man?" Alfredo retorted. "The American military left a mess behind after the Gulf War last year, which is one of the reasons George Bush is going to lose this election today. That war has opened doors for Hamas, which would love to do nothing more than take down some of the most prominent citizens of Israel in yourselves and others like you."

"Not our own kind," Old Man countered. "I'd rather place the life of me and my son in the hands of a natural born Israeli rather than outsiders from Italy."

"The Aranellos specialize in international security. And they have no religious affiliation."

"Meaning they're not Jewish as are all of us."

"I could give a rat fat ass about the Jewish faith!" Alfredo snapped. "This is not a religious war, man! We're drug dealers! Nothing more!"

"The same principle applies," Old Man countered. "This is how we do business."

"The survival of this unit is what's concerning me here and now! You say the Medellin Cartel is on the verge of setting up here in Caracas then we need to be bringing in as many soldiers as possible that are not tied to the Middle East! They can provide us with a different angle to stay ahead of these people while remaining unbiased, dammit!"

"Alfredo, calm down." Sanjar Junior interjected.

"Not this time!" Alfredo refuted as he stood up from his seat. Meetings with the Darvish men, more times than not, always grew heated—mainly because of Old Man and his stubborn ways. "Now, I've been going along with the set up you two have instituted from the start of this thing! When do me and my people get a say so in how things are run within our own organization? We're not just your distributors, we're your partners! But you treat us all like employees!" Alfredo noted.

"We haven't made a deal yet, Alfredo," Old Man replied calmly. "And to be rather frank, this is a deal that can be passed over."

"You pushing me and my family out of this thing?" Alfredo asked in a seething manner as he eyed Old Man from across the table with his hands tucked inside his silk slacks.

"Well, if the shoe fits then by all means feel—"

"I be damned if I back out or get pushed out of something I help build!" Alfredo yelled, cutting Old Man short. "Without us you're nothing! Nothing, old man! And I'm not calling you by your name." he spoke through gritted teeth.

Sanjar Junior, more the voice of reason, chimed in by saying, "Alfredo, you know my father. He can be stubborn, but he means good. We disagree over security for a problem that hasn't yet arrived. Our main objective is to secure the deal with the buying out of the warehouse. From there, we can ship our own freight and rely on ourselves. The deal will give you more power. I assure you that you'll be able to provide your own security—if and when they pass our background checks, of course. Come, now. We meet the warehouse owners tomorrow. In the meantime, there's a Japanese restaurant not too far from here were we can relax and let cooler heads prevail."

"We're beyond handshakes at this moment," Alfredo remarked as he reached for his suit jacket and placed it back onto his body. "I want everything that happens during that meeting put into writing."

"Men of faith need not have a contract, Mister Lowes," Old Man stated as he eased up from his chair and cracked his slender back while smoothening out his silk suit.

"If that were true, God would not have given Moses the ten commandments written in stone," Alfredo responded.

"What does Moses have to do with anything going on here, Alfredo?" Sanjar Junior asked while laughing. "I get your point, though. You tried to go deep with your analogy, but, it didn't work, my friend. You really should take bible lessons."

Alfredo smiled to himself at that moment. "At least you understand my point. Your father doesn't know how lucky he is to have you around, man. He's hard to negotiate with."

"I may be old, but I'm not deaf," Old Man chimed in as he crept towards the sealed double doors with the aid of his walker. "Let's go have dinner before we meet with our sellers tomorrow. The security detail will be instituted in due time—so long as they check out," he reiterated.

Alfredo nodded his approval just before the door to the conference room was opened by Sanjar. The three men exited the room and walked through the crowded lobby that was filled with arriving and departing tourists from different parts of the world. Kids ran around, chasing one another as their joyous laughter bounced off the walls of the pristine interior. Spanish was being spoken aloud and vendors selling souvenirs paraded around the lobby making deals as they made their way to a waiting limousine that sat under the city lights.

****

Back in America, polls were closing. The entire crew, Tanya, Brenda, the King Sisters, Yabba Dabba, Sally Irving and Willie herself, were all posted up inside the conference room inside the project office located in heart of the Saint Bernard project with scores of constituents waiting for the outcome. Many wore birthday hats and were blowing small plastic trumpets while throwing confetti in the air. Televisions were on every table inside the medium-sized room along with un-corked bottles of champagne.

While everyone around her chit and chattered in their happy state, Willie sat at the front of the conference room off in a cor-ner beside the stage by her lonesome. She'd chosen to remain hidden from sight and was preparing her concession speech should she lose. She had no victory speech as that was going to come from the heart.

Despite her knowingly being in the pocket of German drug dealers, Willie had every intention of doing right by the people she would possibly represent. She had goals of providing free daycare and after school care for working parents. She also wanted to improve bus transportation to the area and to re-model the two parks in the Saint Bernard project. City Park and a historical cemetery were also in Willie's district. Her aim there was to hire full time Park and Grave Attendees and re-open the amusement park.

Willie had run for state representative her second time around on the promise of helping struggling parents while bringing jobs back into the community. She wanted to make things easy on the people she'd grown up with; if she were to lose, she saw herself giving up and going back to what she knew how to do best, which was whoring and running a night club as she wasn't sure if she had what it took to enter another brutal campaign, especially after baring her soul for all to de-construct this time around. The hopeful politician didn't want that life for herself, though, so a lot hinged on the outcome of this political campaign.

"First predictions! First predictions are in! We're watching ABC! Everybody turn to ABC if your screen isn't already set to that channel!" Willie heard Sally scream aloud.

The festive atmosphere quieted down and televisions were tuned in and turned up. "We wanna welcome everybody that's been following the ninety-two-campaign season," a reporter was heard throughout the room. "Nationwide, with polls closing on the east coast, we have predictions from Massachusetts and New York coming in and this, I think I speak for the majority when I say this was totally unexpected," the reporter remarked astonished. "Opponent Bill Clinton has taken what seems like the entire New England area. Not only is he predicted to win New York and Massachusetts, but Maine, Vermont, New Jersey, Maryland and Rhode Island are projecting him as the winner, and yes, Louisiana will go to Bill Clinton."

Upon hearing that Bill Clinton had taken Louisiana, the crowd inside the conference room erupted into cheers. When a map of the district in which Willie was campaigning for came across screen, however, the revelry subsided and all ears tuned in as a political analyst was brought in from the streets. "I'm outside of City Hall where democrat Mayor Sidney Barthelemy is awaiting election results. Everyone inside this building," the reporter spoke as she turned and faced the multi-story steel and glass building in downtown New Orleans. "Everyone inside

City Hall is hoping, just as it seems as if we'll have a democrat in the White House for the first time in over twelve years, that the state's legislative branch will have a democratic majority going forth. There're a lot of programs that have been proposed by several candidates and every victory is crucial, one being a second run for state representative by hopeful Willameena Slack from the city's seventh district."

More cheers erupted until Sally, having to grab a microphone from the stage, silenced everybody by tapping the device's top. "Listen!" she schooled.

"I have no results being on the ground, but what can we learn from y'all in the studio?" the reporter asked.

"And we were just about to say that with fifteen percent of the polls closing in the city's seventh district the incumbent is ahead by several percentage points."

The air seemed to leave the room upon hearing the first results. Sally, knowing how the polls operated, grabbed the microphone once again and took to the stage. "We've come too far to get discouraged!" she yelled. "Come on now!" she fretted.

Willie sat beside the stage with a cold stare. She also knew how the polling ran, and unlike the first time, when Sally had been her mouthpiece, she was compelled to speak up for herself this time around. She jumped up from her seat and jumped up onto the stage, nearly tripping in her three-inch heels as she stormed to the center of the platform and took control of the microphone. "Now wait a minute!" she barked as a loud screeching sound shot through the speakers.

The crowd silenced and everybody faced the stage. Willie removed some of her black hair from tan-skinned face and eyed the crowd in disappointment and said, "This has been our plight for so damn long! And I'm including myself in the—excuse my language—the bullshit! We give up too easy as black people! I been sitting over there by myself the entire time watching y'all celebrate and the first sign of bad news y'all ready to give up? My people don't quit! My voters don't quit! We've done our part! You all have done y'all's part! They can count us down, but they can't count us out! Now, we gone win this election! So now ain't the time to start to stop believing! Who with me?"

"I'm withca, 'Slick Willie'!" Wanda Slack yelled way from the back room as she poured herself another glass of champagne. "Shit, you all we the fuck got right about now so the rest of these moochers better fall in line or fall the fuck out!"

Many of the people laughed over Wanda's remarks. She was a legend in her own right in the Saint Bernard and everybody knew she meant no harm. "Thank God there're no cameras," Willie chuckled. "I, I appreciate your support, momma but you could've said it—"

"That's the only way I know how ta' say it, got dammit! Nah, who gone check me on that?"

"Nobody!" several dozen constituents remarked in unison as they chuckled over Wanda's remarks.

Just then, a second wave of poll results came across the televisions. This time around, Willie had a single digit lead. The celebration kicked up again as Sally ran over to Willie and hugged her. "You know what this means?" she asked.

"I'm leading for now," Willie laughed.

"No, Willie. You've won! You're going to win!" Sally said as she covered her lower face with tears pouring over her fingers. "All we've worked for! It's here!" she cried joyously.

Sally knew what Willie didn't know. The polling places in and around the Saint Bernard project were going to be the last ballots totaled as they were deemed a low priority. It'd been a long-standing tradition that belittled the poorest citizens in the district. The money pumped into the neighborhood, however, had paid off. Never before had so many turned out to vote, and being Willie was popular on name alone, whether people wanted to or not, they went out and supported one of their own, someone they knew, someone they believed in.

Whereas no more than a quarter of registered voters showed up to the voting booth in times past, through Sally's political-savvy and shrewdness coupled with Mabel's insight and Tanya and Faye's money, Willie's campaign had managed to turn out over eighty percent of their targeted market. She also won over a third of the vote from wealthier citizens in her district. It was money well-spent and by evening's end,

Willameena Slack got to sit before her fan base and watch the concession speech of her opponent congratulating her on a resounding victory before the real celebration began.

****

While Willie and company were celebrating her victory, back down in Caracas, amid the warm night weather, Alfredo and the Darvish men had just enjoyed a glorious seafood dinner inside a Japanese restaurant consisting of spicy Saba (mackeral) with sautéed olives and cherry tomatoes. The Mai Tai drinks were on point and the Mochi (sticky rice) strawberry ice cream left the men joking over how the dessert reminded them of women they'd tasted over the years.

With a five-man security team tailing them, the top men inside the organization walked out of the restaurant and stepped out into the bustling streets of Caracas with all its bright lights, heavy pedestrian traffic and passing vehicles. They climbed into the backseat of their waiting limousine parked in front of the restaurant to make the short drive back to the hotel where they were staying in order to wind down for the night and prepare for their meeting with the owners of the warehouse the following afternoon. The door was shut and the partition was lowered at soon after.

"Man, what a meal," Alfredo sighed as he tilted his head back on headrest of the backseat.

"One like no other, my man. Raise the partition will you driver?" Sanjar asked politely as the men made idle chat about the meal they'd experienced.

There was no response from the driver, however; Old Man leaned forward in his side seat and was preparing to ask the driver to raise the partition once more. He suddenly noticed the driver eyeing him through the rearview mirror as he held up a remote control. "Sanjar! Alfredo! Get out! Get out now!" he yelled as he moved towards the rear door.

Alfredo and Sanjar grabbed the handles on each side of the limousine and tried to open the door, but it wouldn't budge. "Son of a bitch!" Alfredo screamed as he went for his semiautomatic tucked in his back waistband.

Just then, the limo driver turned around and yelled aloud, "Allah Ackbar!" (God is great!)

Alfredo was able to get off several rounds. He struck the driver in the face one time, but the detonator had already been activated. The device fell from the suicide bomber's hands, landing on the back floorboard of the limousine as he slumped over in the front seat. A red light started flashing on the detonator as it counted down with short beeps. "Ten...nine... eight..."

Alfredo, Sanjar and Old Man were frantically pounding on the windows of the limousine trying to escape. They'd gotten their security team's attention the moment Alfredo pulled the trigger. Three men ran over and pried the door open.

Just as the door was pulled open, however, the bomb planted in the champagne cabinet of the limousine detonated. The rear of the limousine lifted off the ground, disintegrating half the vehicle and engulfing the rest of the car in flames. The three security guards surrounding the vehicle had their bodies torn to pieces.

Alfredo, Sanjar and Old Man never even had a chance of surviving. They were blown to pieces as well, and windows two stories up on the hotel shattered over the detonated bomb blast that sent tourists and locals alike scattering for cover.

A block away from the unfolding chaos, as patrons of a coffee shop ran out into the night streets bawling in horror, a lone woman wearing a white pant suit and heels sat sipping her coffee unabatedly. She waited until the coffee shop cleared out and calmly eased her chair back as she grabbed her purse and walked off in the opposite direction. She rounded the block, walking away from the masses of people that were running towards the bomb scene and climbed into the back seat of a black 1988 Rolls Royce with tinted windows and the car slowly peeled away.

"I felt the ground shake, Madame," the Colombian driver chuckled. The woman didn't reply. She merely sat back and crossed legs and remained silent as the driver began making his way to their preordained location.

After a two hour ride through steep mountain terrain where she listened to Spanish guitar and sipped wine, the young woman rode onto an orange grove located in San Joaquin, Carabobo. San Joaquin was a fertile valley located on the eastern shore of Venezuela near the Caribbean Sea, just north of Lake Valencia in an area that produced the famed Valencia orange. Riding along the dirt road bordered by rows and rows of orange trees, the Rolls Royce pulled up to a small, white stone, two-story villa that was trimmed in dark brown wood.

The woman exited the car and walked amongst the colorful roses and fountains and entered a courtyard where three men were seated under a lighted patio. They were talking amongst themselves amid the surrounding darkness of the mountainous terrain until one of the men, a muscular, tatted up man with curly black hair wearing a pair of linen shorts and sandals, spotted her walking through the entrance.

"Ah," the man smiled as he extended his hand. "I take it all went well back in Caracas, Bridgette?" he inquired.

"There was no trouble about it," Bridgette remarked in her heavy Jamaican accent as she leaned down and kissed the cheeks of a man by name of Rafael Gacha.

Rafael Gacha was a former underboss inside the Medellin Cartel. Two and a half years earlier, back in the summer of 1990, six months after Pablo Escobar had blown up Colombian Flight 203, he and Bridgette had purchased a villa in San Joaquin to hide out and let things blow over. Both had plans on returning to Colombia to handle unfinished business, but Rafael had seen the writing on the wall with Pablo and his recklessness over the bombing of an airplane filled with inno-cent travelers.

Escobar had signed his own death certificate with the bomb-ing of Flight 203. Not only were the Colombian citizens out-raged and calling for his head over the deaths of innocent citi-zens, but there were also two American citizens aboard the plane where one hundred and ten people perished.

The deaths of two American citizens gave the Bush adminis-tration the right to prosecute Escobar on federal acts of terror-ism. He was now a wanted man and on the run from the Colombian and American governments alike.

With Pablo's demise all but a certainty, Rafael began map-ping out plans to set up his own organization in the country of Venezuela once his boss was disposed of. Learning from some of the best cartel bosses in the business, he sought land to grow his own product. Cocaine was his specialty.

The ties Rafael had made had placed him in position to be the *Los Jefes de Jefes* (Boss of Bosses) in the state of Venezuela. And he had a couple of men of distinguished power on his team to aide him in his endeavor. One was a man by the name of Iiyahd Sheinheimer, who sat on the board of Tropi-cana Produce.

Iiayad was VP of Marketing for the Valencia groves and had a measure of influence back in America. He was key to Rafael gaining a foothold in the United States' cocaine drug market as they were planning to ship his product via rail hidden amongst frozen produce Tropicana exported from South America.

The other man sitting with Rafael was named Hugo Chavez. Chavez was a recently retired Lieutenant Colonel from Caracas with high political ambitions. Rafael was in the opening phases of financing Chavez' run for President in the upcoming years after Chavez served a two year sentence for staging a coup de` tat against Venezuela's current political regime.

Assured that he would be protected by Gacha behind bars, Hugo Chavez agreed to allow the man to transport cocaine should his run for President be successful. Time would be the deciding factor, but as of present, Gacha and Chavez were destined for power unmitigated. And with all enemies eliminated, the Darvish men and Alfredo Lowes being the last to fall in a bloody Venezuelan street coup, and with Iiayahd Sheinheimer, his American contact on board assuring the shipment of refined cocaine into America via railroad, a formidable organization was now on the horizon—one that had the potential to bring the Germans down to their knees.

CHAPTER THIRTY

AT THE RIVER'S EDGE

The double doors on the first floor of Tanya's home were wide open on this cool autumn morning in early November of 1992, ten days after Alfredo Lowes and the Darvish men had been killed. Black sackcloth was draped over the second and third story balconies of the loft and a horse carriage attached to a pair of white mustang horses was before the home. The area before Tanya's home on Saint Louis Street was coated with a sea of people, all wearing black, and facing the home's front door.

Tanya was sitting up in her loft with her daughter, Helen. Brenda and Willie were at her side offering comfort as best they could. She wore a black silk dress and matching shoes and had a light coating of makeup on her face. The mascara lining her eyes was blemished as her eyes kept watering over and over again. For a long time, Tanya just sat quietly with her daughter and friends. Alfredo's death came as a shock to everyone. And the aching thing was that no one had a clue as to who was behind the killings, although everybody involved was under the assumption that the hit came from a foreign source given the tactic used.

Suicide bombers were nonexistent within American organizations, so it couldn't have been anything connected to the Philadelphia mob, which was the crew's next anticipated rival given what Faye and Alfredo had done to the Moto family in Cincinnati. On top of that, the Moto family had been taken down eight years prior. It was suspected by all that retaliation from the Asians would not have taken such a long time, but they just weren't sure because the Asians may just be crazy enough to use a suicide bomber to accomplish their goals. Another possibility, the one being pushed by the Federal Bureau of Investigations, was that the Darvish men were the intended targets all along and Alfredo and the security guards were simply collateral damage.

The Darvish men had made many an enemy back in Israel by attempting to aid the Reagan administration in the negotiating of a peace treaty between the nations of Israel and Iran. Many from their homeland viewed them as traitors, but for the Darvish men, it was simply business. The freighter company they had intentions on buying with Alfredo had the capacity to transport crude oil from Iran to refineries in Great Britain. It was to be the crew's way out of the heroin market if the Darvish men could've brokered the deal, but their untimely deaths had set the crew back for time undetermined.

If the Iranians were involved, Tanya knew she and the crew had no way to retaliate, especially with Alfredo being dead. He was the only one out of the crew who could fly in and out of Israel without having a background check. And through the Darvish men, he was able to enter into Iran. No one from the crew had the ability to navigate such a foreign territory, and the risks were astronomical for someone with no ties to the country as they weren't sure who they could trust in a land halfway around the world.

Revenge was wanted for Alfredo, but the hard truth was that the crew's hands were tied. It would be years, if ever at all, before the full scope of the events surrounding Alfredo's death would come to light. Just like Mouse's murder, the death of Alfredo Lowes would be a mystery no one inside the crew would be able to solve on their own.

"Willie wins her first election and this is the reward we get," Tanya stated through a painful laugh as she dabbed her tears with a paper napkin.

"I'm not on any committees yet," Willie somberly remarked. "It's too early for me. And they not too keen on Louisiana politics up there. But I'm gone look into this once the new congress convenes. It won't be until January, though," she ended somberly.

Tanya was totally caught off guard by Alfredo's death. She had learned of her man's demise the day of via the World News. The Darvish men were identified first, and an unknown accomplice and the suicide bomber himself was also killed along with three members of the security team; although neither had been identified.

Tanya knew from the names mentioned, and the bombing having taken place in Caracas, that Alfredo was one of the unidentified men. For two days she and Helen walked the French Quarters where Tanya explained to her daughter that her father would not be returning home from his trip to Venezuela.

Sitting inside her library, Tanya spread out a map and showed her daughter the city in which her father was killed. Helen was due for a piano recital at NOCCA the day after her father's return flight. When she learned of his death, the eight year-old changed her rendition from Billy Joel's song *Piano Man*, to that of a rendition more befitting the occasion in her young, but educated mind.

Helen Weinberger was a go-with-flow-type of child. She easily accepted what came her way while trying to understand the whys behind the matter. In an odd way, maybe because of her ability to fully comprehend the concept of death, it all made sense to this eight year-old that'd grown up around people in which death often befell them. Helen had sat in on several conversations with her mother and father and had listened to them discuss heroin dealers who'd been murdered on the streets of New Orleans. It was always, "You know that guy got killed last week," or, "Since so and so is dead, we gone have to fill the gap on the next shipment."

Death was very familiar to Helen. It was nothing to see a person come into her parents' home and do strange things, the passing of items. The only thing recognizable to her being the piles of money her mother and father would take from people before handing them one, two, or more brown paper bags, bags she understood to be concealing a product known as 'boy'.

Those same people that received that 'boy', some in which eight year-old Helen Weinberger knew by name, often turned up in conversations concerning their death and the child would soon find herself in what she knew to be a funeral procession, because the people her mother and father once talked to happily were now sleeping for what she'd learned to be an eternity. This was nothing new to Helen. Two times before she'd played her ebony and ivory-keyed baby grand piano before a crowd of what her mother told her were mourners.

On this day, however, young Helen understood the meaning of the word 'mourner'. She'd felt nothing for the people who'd mourned before her because she didn't know them personally; but now, having gone through the loss of her father, the impact of death was fully understood and the word 'mourning' had taken on new meaning, much different from the cats she and Maggie had killed years ago, and it wasn't a good feeling for Helen Weinberger. Now she understood the concept of death completely in her young age and the pain that went alone with it.

Tanya knelt before her daughter and placed the back of her hand to her cheek. "We've been here before, Helen. You don't have to do this, you know?"

"I've played for people that have died that weren't my daddy. I can do this, momma," Helen stated.

Meek was Helen's demeanor, but Tanya knew her daughter was nothing short of a lioness in-the-making. She had stood with her throughout the entire ordeal. Mother and daughter had cried together at night the days following Alfredo's death. The day after her father had been killed, it was Helen who'd awaken Tanya for her piano lessons, lessons Tanya had no intentions on attending as she was giving her daughter time to grieve. All Helen said was that, "I want to have my lessons so I won't be too sad."

Tanya wanted to tell herself that it was because of the fact that Helen couldn't comprehend the magnitude of the loss, but as time wore on, she came to realize that her daughter was able to deal with death in a manner far better than she was able to deal at this point in time. And in Tanya's eyes, that ingrained quality was an asset to the psyche needed in a business where tomorrow was never certain and the ones in which you love dearly could be taken away in an instant. She checked the clock on her wall and noticed that it was drawing nearer the procession. "Anybody heard from Zelda and Vivian?" she asked while straightening Helen's black tuxedo.

****

"I'm saying, though? When you and twin gone let me and my nigga tap that ass again? And why you and Vivian dressed like y'all going to a funeral or something" eighteen-year-old Manuel 'Manny' Lawson asked thirty-year-old Zelda King as he and his best friend, Dirty Red, stood inside their dope house located in a courtyard on Benefit Street inside the Desire Housing project.

"We sayin', though? You niggas want this next lick or not?" Zelda asked Manny in return as she shifted her weight while standing on the other side of a small table inside the apartment's kitchen that was laced with two and half kilograms of powder cocaine and a money counter.

Eighteen-year-olds Dirty Red and Manny's names were ringing out on the streets of New Orleans in 1992. The King Sisters had run into them at a club in the Ninth Ward called *Detours*. While hanging out in the parking lot of *Detours* before they all went inside, the four ran down eps while toking blunts and drinking liquor.

Zelda and Vivian bragged on crimes they'd committed, telling Dirty Red and Manny about their first kill, a woman by the name of Penelope, whose body they'd left under the Almonaster Bridge back in 1982. Manny and Dirty Red didn't divulge much, but they quickly realized they had some gangster bitches in their midst. The conversation soon turned to Cake and Cream for pay.

Although, Zelda and Vivian had over ten years on Dirty Red and Manny, they were on the twins' level when it came to the game. Not to mention the twins loved young gangsters that knew how to handle their business and lay their murder down. Through word on the street, the King Sisters had already known that Manny and Dirty Red were heavy into Cake and Cream, street lingo for robbing dope houses.

As old as they were, Zelda and Vivian were still young-minded when it came to certain aspects of the business, which is why they never held any leadership positions with the crew besides that of running dope houses. They were left out of politics because of their lack of understanding and quickness to become offended when they couldn't comprehend what they were being told in a professional manner. The fraternal twins were the top street earners, however; so their position was solidified and never doubted. And whenever they brought a racket to the table, it always paid off. Manny and Dirty Red was their latest hustle in 1992.

For a quarter of the take, the King Sisters would turn Manny, who was in Vivian's words, her 'young dick', and Dirty Red, who was Zelda's 'dick on call', onto licks all around the city. Some of the licks were on rival competition, others were for the sheer fuck of it all. Either way, with Zelda and Vivian, Manny and Dirty Red always hit pay dirt whenever they linked up with the King sisters.

On this November morning in 1992, the day of Alfredo's funeral, Zelda and Vivian were on hand to offer another lick to their young lovers.

"We got a funeral to attend. If we didn't? Believe you can get it." Vivian told Manny as she stood across from him in a knee-length, black silk dress with her hair permed and pressed. "But never mind all that, young dick," she stated through a smile as her eyes scanned Manny in his baggy black Girbaud jeans and long-sleeved black, red and white striped Polo shirt with a fresh pair of red Bally's on his feet, his hair neatly braided to the back.

"Let's make this short and sweet," Zelda stated as she rested her hands on the table and looked over to Dirty Red. "We need a lick done as soon as possible, brer."

"A lick done on who, Zel?" eighteen year-old Dirty Red asked nonchalantly as he placed a stack of twenties into the money counter sitting atop the table, never bothering to look up at Zelda as he stood in a black short-sleeved Polo, navy blue Polo Jeans and black Bally's tennis with his jet-black hair in a single ponytail.

Zelda knew she was being taken lightly, but she was enthralled over Dirty Red's aptitude in his young age. Whereas Manny was more into sexing down Vivian whenever the four met, Dirty Red was about his money. Sex came after the job for him, and she was just as sprung on Dirty Red as Vivian was on Manny.

"A click off Techwood up in Atlanta." Zelda replied as she felt her temperature rise slightly.

"I heard about that set," Manny remarked as he rubbed his chin. "Gone be hard to get at 'em, yeh?"

"Nahh," Vivian chimed in. "We used to deal with 'em. Since we lost our connect? We ain't got nothing coming in right now. Word is, they got plans on moving in on our territory down here."

"If them Atlanta boys set up shop, it's gone get real difficult for the players down here to push weight," Zelda followed. "Me and my girls not in power as far as heroin, but we can prevent a takeover from some out-of-town-niggas—if we have help."

"What the lick be like?" Dirty Red asked as he removed the bills from the money counter and banded five thousand dollars.

"We sold 'em seven kilograms last month—the last of our product. We scheduled for a re-up on six hundred thousand dollars next week." Zelda answered.

"What you think, dog?" Manny asked as he looked over to Dirty Red while palming a giggling Vivian's ass.

"We gone have to get a team together, Manny brer. I know O down. We still got Haywood, too."

"Nahh," Zelda interjected. "Fuck a O, fuck a Haywood. We do this, this gone be our deal. Us four gone go and do the job and we split whatever we hit up there two ways. And really? This ain't even about no drugs, this about preventing some out-of-town dealers from setting up shop down here."

"You ran down they sitting on at least six hundred thousand," Dirty Red stated as he placed another stack of twenties into the money counter. "Split two ways, that's three hundred thousand dollars. We gone need that regardless of what happen in the ATL, ya' dig?"

Zelda was about to reply until her pager went off with the numbers 911 displayed over the screen. At the same time, Vivian's pager began buzzing with the same numbers on display. "They calling for us," the fraternal twins stated in unison as they eyed one another.

"We gone discuss numbers later," Zelda remarked as she and Vivian turned and walked out of the kitchen. Little did the party of four know, that it would be years before two of them would ever see one another face-to-face again.

****

Back over to Tanya's loft, Faye had just come down the stairs with Maggie in tow. The child had fractured her elbow when she'd fallen from an apple tree back in Cherryvale and Faye was in Tanya's bathroom giving her bath as the two had just arrived into town not even an hour ago.

Tanya had told Faye that it wasn't necessary for her to travel back to New Orleans for Alfredo's funeral given her situation, but the woman insisted on being in town to not just to see a man she revered sent home, but to be there for one of the women in her life who'd become her sister.

"*Zelda und Vivian fand ein paar Kerle, anfassen kann, Crew aus Atlanta für uns.*" (Zelda and Vivian found a couple of guys that can handle that crew from Atlanta for us.) Tanya told Faye the time she walked into the library, she herself having talked to Zelda over a payphone.

"*Füllen mich nach der Prozession. Das ist nicht, was wichtig ist. Sie tun, okay?*" (Fill me in after the procession. That's not what's important. You're doing okay?) Faye responded in a comforting manner as she placed a hand on Tanya's shoulder.

"*So gut, wie ich es jemals sein unter den gegebenen Umständen. Ich wünschte nur, sie würden schon entfernt.*" (As good as I'll ever be under the circumstances. I wish you would've stayed away.) Tanya snapped at Faye through her tears. "*Aber, aber ich bin froh, dass du hier bist. Wenn das keinen Sinn macht.*" (But, but I'm glad you're here. If that makes any sense) she added as she laid her head on Faye's hand and wept openly. "*Ich habe die Liebe meines Lebens. Mein Freund, meine Tochter Vater, mein Alles.*" (I lost the love of my life. My friend, my daughter's father, my everything.)

Thirty-five year-old Faye looked towards the ceiling and closed her eyes as tears ran from their corners and ran down her cheeks. She knew all-too-well what Tanya was going through and more having not only lost her everything in Franklin Patterson, but that of her best friend, and ultimately, the only child she'd ever given life to.

Regardless of what anybody said, she had to be there for Tanya, even if it meant leaving the safety of her home back in Kansas where she was sheltered. Nothing more needed to be said on this day because the pain was understood and felt by all. While remaining silent, Faye took a seat beside Tanya as Maggie went and sat beside Helen. Together, they all waited for the beginning of Alfredo's final farewell.

****

An hour later, funeral attendees, all dressed in black were all out in front of Tanya's home in the middle of the street. Resting on a trailer being pulled by two white mustangs, sat Helen's grand piano. The eight year-old was perched on a bench looking down at the ebony and ivory keys while mentally going over her rendition.

A jazz band, whose members were dressed in all black and wearing white gloves, slowly walked past the carriage while swaying side to side. The lead member held onto a black umbrella as his thick frame swayed to and fro. "Gonna send a good man home today, y'all," he spoke in a deep-pitched voice. "Alfredo Lowes. Good man in the eyes of many!"

The tuba player began playing, woofing out the sounds to Chopin's song *Funeral March*. On cue, Helen began strumming the keys on her piano in complete harmony. The reins on the horses were pulled and they moved forward, following the jazz band as funeral attendees followed Helen.

Tanya, Brenda, Willie and the King Sisters followed the trailer pulling Helen with Tanya out front, her face covered by a black veil as she held onto a bunch of white carnations. The procession continued onto Bourbon Street where they made a left turn and began a slow march through the French Quarters.

Tourists on hand began snapping pictures, happy they were getting a chance to witness an authentic jazz funeral in it truest form. People cleared the streets as scores of mourners followed the band and a little girl playing a piano in the heart of the French Quarters on this sunny, cool morning in November of 1992.

****

At the same time, a thousand miles to the north, back in Mitchellville, Iowa, Bonita Bender was pacing the floor as she dialed Faye's number repeatedly. Although she'd been known her sister was back on the family land in Cherryvale, it was understood that she could never call home for fear the call would be traced. Faye was hiding in plain sight, and it was a gamble that was paying off, so no one, not even Bonita, wanted to risk blowing her sister's cover. On this day, in November of 1992, however, all bets were off.

"Dammit! She's not answering!" Bonita screamed as she slammed the phone down after calling Faye for the tenth time in a row. "What now?" she asked Sascha Merkendorf, the woman who'd brought her the bad news after she herself had uncovered the betrayal.

"We prepare for the fight of our lives," Sascha remarked somberly. "I will have people watching over you while I'm away in New Orleans. I am the one you must trust now lest you and Cikala die in here."

"Don't forget about us," Bonita, now in her weakest moment ever, remarked as she balled her fists and bowed head. "It can't end like this," she cried.

"I couldn't forget you and Cikala if I tried. Let's just hope Faye Bender is brought in alive, and you and Cikala are alive as well when I get back." Sascha replied as she turned and walked out of the prisoner's phone room.

"I can't believe she did that," Bonita growled.

"It is the business we have chosen for ourselves," Sascha stated as she turned around to face Bonita. "And the people in this business? They come with the business, along with all of their treachery. Some people are more loyal than others as you now know. And it is a lesson I myself shall never forget." Sascha remarked. "I come from a family of snakes, but I have no venom within me that I can pour into the veins of those I know who are loyal. You, Bonita Bender, and your clan are loyal. Thank me, for without me, your sister would be grieving more than what she already is."

"I know. I know," Bonita spoke in disbelief as she leaned against the wall beside the phones.

Sascha tilted her head as she clasped her hands before her midsection while towering over Bonita.

Bonita, in turn, knew what Sascha was awaiting as it was a phrase she'd never uttered to the woman. "Thank you," she stated humbly.

"That is all I ask," Sascha remarked seriously while staring down at Bonita. "To be thanked for my loyalty to you is all I ever wanted, Bonita Bender. Just as World War Two brought about a change in power, so are we in the midst of a change in power. I am not the leader, you are, and your family is, in the beginning stages of a power shift, but for now, it is I who hold the reins of power for your family. And your family's power is in good hands with me. Let me work the power I've been afforded before it is given back to you."

"What choice do I have," Bonita stated as she stood face-to-face with Sascha, readying herself for an attack as she knew not who to trust given all that was going down on this day.

Sascha raised her hands and backed away from Bonita. "I do my own killing of leaders," she confessed. "I understand your lack of trust, but I have done one thing to prove to you that I… am…the loyal one."

"What's that?"

"I will bring your sister in alive—which is the best I can do since there's no way to contact them. Should Faye die? You would have justification to take my life. And I know you would spend the rest of your years here if only to kill me should something happen to Faye, which I am trying to prevent."

****

Back down in New Orleans, a large celebration was underway on Bourbon Street. Faye was mingling in with the crowd as she held onto Maggie's hand. She could see Boogie atop the horse carriage towering over the crowd as she strummed Chopin's song on her cherished piano. The slow procession continued on, Faye never noticing four men in brown and yellow uniforms being trailed by two men in black suits.

The men removed their guns from their holsters as they approached Faye from the opposite direction on the opposite side of the street, going against the mourning crowd.

Faye was ever alert. Through scores of people, she recognized the brown shirts and tan trousers. Her eyes widened and she let go of Maggie's hand and backed away in total shock over what was about to go down.

"Mutter, was ist falsch? Bist Du traurig?" (Mother what's wrong? Are you sad again?) Maggie asked concerned over Helen's rendition as she walked back towards her mother.

Faye had a gun on her. She was opting to pull it and open fire, but she looked around at all the innocent bystanders and decided against it. She let the gun slide from her hand as she turned and began walking backwards. "Faye Bender!" she heard one of the Iowa State Troopers call out. "Rance Olsen from the Iowa State Patrol!"

"Rance!" Faye whispered as she turned and began walking away from the procession.

"Mother! Mother don't leave me!" Maggie called out over the music as she fought through the crowd, trying to make her way to Faye.

Tanya, by sheer fate, happened to look over her right shoulder in Faye's direction. She, too, could recognize the uniforms of the Iowa State Patrol as she followed Boogie, who was still perched atop the horse carriage and enthralled in her rendition. She changed directions, stepping away from the carriage as she began hurrying towards the area she'd last seen Faye. She came up on Maggie, who was standing in the doorway of a closed restaurant crying her heart out.

"*Ich möchte meine Mutter! Tante Tanja, wo ist meine Mutter?*" (I want my mother! Auntie Tanya, where's my mother?)

Tanya had no reply. All she could do was kneel down and hug Maggie as she watched her friend take off running through the crowd with six lawmen on her heels.

Knocking several people aside, Faye entered into a swift sprint up Bourbon Street and made a left turn onto Saint Louis Street, running away from Tanya's loft and headed towards Jackson Square. Rance Olsen and his entourage picked up the pace, the officers running full speed through the French Quarters under the bright morning sun. "Surrender!" "Faye, make it easy on yourself and surrender!" the men yelled at random.

Ignoring the officer's pleas, Faye kept running in her knee length boots and silk dress. Restaurant workers hosing down the sidewalk she sprinted up backed into their businesses and slammed the doors shut. They'd seen foot chases more times than they could count and knew the possible outcome.

****

Back over to the procession, Tanya held onto Maggie as she looked around and found the revolver Faye had discarded before she took off running. She passed the gun off to Brenda, who took it and walked ahead of the crowd.

Brenda ran onto an empty block and discarded the pistol down a drain before making her way back over to Tanya. "How the fuck did they get on to her?" she asked anxiously upon her return.

"I don't know. I...I don't know," Tanya whispered through her stunned, watery eyes as the reality of the day took over her psyche.

****

Faye, meanwhile, was in the midst of a freedom run. She knew why the Iowa law was out to apprehend her, and it wasn't her running over a trooper's arm fourteen years earlier. Her greatest fear, which was being accused of murdering her own family, had instantaneously become a living nightmare. Never had she known fear of this magnitude. The men and women she had killed, the deceitful games she'd played with her victims' hearts and the deplorable tactics she'd used to eliminate those who stood in her way, none of that mattered. Her past demons was something she could live with, but not that of her being indicted for killing the group of people who mattered to her more than her own life.

She continued running alongside the Saint Louis Cathedral, making her way towards Jackson Square, which sat across from Café Du Monde, a place she and Tanya often perused with Maggie the time she'd spent in the city. Flashes of the life she'd grown so comfortable living forced tears to fall from eyes she ran at a furious pace down the middle of the street with over a dozen officers now giving chase. Running out into the traffic, she had to brace herself and roll over the hood of a slow-moving car before righting herself and running past Café Du Monde.

The horn from an approaching freight train began blaring as crossing gates lowered. Pedestrians ceased their movements and began looking up and down the tracks. People pointing off to their right alerted Faye to the direction from which the train was approaching. Floodgates on either side narrowed her path as she neared the tracks and she could see the lead engine approaching the crossover as dark smoke billowed from its top vents from behind the floodgates. The ground vibrated and the train's massive horns roared once more, the engineer this time laying down on the horn as he watched a woman who he believed was on the verge of committing suicide run towards his engine.

The man's arm could be seen waving by Faye as the engine neared. Witnesses looked on in horror as a wild woman ran past them and jumped to her left. They all screamed upon witnessing the woman disappear from sight as the freight train thundered by.

Faye, having dodged the train, rolled several times and slowly pulled herself up from the ground. She looked around and could see the lawmen that were chasing her slamming their hats to the ground and moving to and fro trying to pinpoint her location.

Now in the clear, she ran along the Riverwalk as the sounds of the local ferry off to her left filled her ears. She watched as the last car rode onto the ferry before the gate was lowered. The gate allowing passengers to board the ferry was closed, but Faye could clearly see that pedestrians were still walking onto the ship via the passenger bridge.

Believing she still had time to catch the ferry, which would take her across the Mississippi River into the town of Algiers,

Faye ran on. The law on her tail was relentless, however. Off in the distance she could hear sirens. As she ran along the river on her left, she could see lawmen, those ambitious enough to earn her capture, hopping the fast-moving train on her right.

The train was moving in the opposite direction of Faye. She didn't know how long the unit was, but she was hoping it was long enough to allow her the time needed to make it to the ferry, which was about five hundred feet ahead of her.

Just as she neared the ferry, the train that had been shielding her from the lawmen out to take her down had cleared the tracks. Unable to make it to the passenger gate, as its entrance sat at the edge of the railroad tracks where police units and officers on foot were approaching, Faye turned and ran down the last leg of Canal Street. Here, the famed street that cut through the heart of downtown New Orleans and ran all the way north to City Park, came to an end on the banks of the Mississippi River at the ferry crossing. There was a long line of cars and trucks facing the river awaiting the ferry's return, and as the cops neared, Faye began ducking in and out of the idling vehicles, trying her best to hide.

The ferry's horn woofed into the air as it began pulling away from the river's edge. The walls were closing in on Faye. She'd backed herself into a corner like a trapped cockroach about to be stomped out of existence. With no other place to go, she took off running towards the river and the departing ferry while trying to hide. She crouched beside a dump truck as the lawmen's footsteps grew nearer. Trying to avoid being spotted, she hid in a gap between the truck's cab and bed as she peeked out and saw two Iowa troopers and at least six NOPD officers welding twelve gauges as they crept alongside the waiting cars.

Doors were pulled open at random and people were being pulled from their cars in order to have their vehicles searched.

Kneeling down, Faye could see an insurmountable number of legs moving about. "Faye Bender, show yourself!" "We will kill you on sight if you don't surrender!" "It's over!" "You have nowhere to run!" officers yelled out at random.

Refusing to surrender, Faye jumped out from behind the dump truck and began running towards the departing ferry. From her position on ground level, it looked as if the ferry was still close enough to the shore to where she could jump onto its sides. The closer she got to the barge, however, Faye realized that the ferry was at least fifteen feet away. It was neither a jump she knew she could make nor a chance she was willing to take.

The water's wake would pull her down beneath the surface to a certain death, she knew. Defeated, Faye paused and stood staring at the deserting ferry in utter disbelief over the way things had played out as anger and regret coursed through her veins. Her last chance at freedom was slowly moving over the murky waters of Ole Man River while woofing its horn. Along with the fading ship went her future, which was now uncertain, and she was powerless to do anything about it.

Metal clinging against metal and the racking of guns was heard behind Faye. "Hands up!" "Get on the ground" "Hands in the air!" "Raise your hands up before I fire!" "Don't you fuckin' move or I'll blow your ass into the next century!" "Let her move! I want her to move!" "Let's shoot the bitch anyway it'll be her dead word against ours!"

Faye inhaled, taking her last breath of life as she stood with her back to the officers with her hands raised just above her shoulders. Flashes of her falling face-first into the muddy Mississippi ran through her mind as she stood in a surrendering posture.

"Are you all fuckin' crazy in this town?" Rance Olsen asked loudly as he ran and stood before the dozen or more officers who were aiming their guns at Faye as they prepared to shoot the woman down in cold blood. "This is still my collar, dammit! Iowa's collar," the man screamed over the violently-mounting frenzy of killer cops. The Iowa trooper was now the only thing that stood in between Faye and his fellow lawmen's' line of fire. "We're taking her in alive!" Rance yelled as he pointed back towards Faye. "Alive, dammit! She has a right to a trial before the court of law so lower your guns now!"

The officers groaned as they lowered their guns. "Really?" "I'm not doing the paperwork on this bitch!" "We could've made it an open and shut case, but this Iowa guy!" several officers complained.

Rance turned and faced Faye's backside. He trotted over and patted her down as officers behind him slowly approached the scene. Seeing she was free of a weapon, he grabbed her wrists and placed them behind her back. "Sascha Merkendorf sent me. Just go with me," was all he said, whispering into Faye's ear. "Do you even know how much time and money you've cost my unit having to hunt your ass down?" he then screamed as he handcuffed her, pretending to be seething over having to track her down out-of-state as she shoved her around at the river's edge.

They say when your past sins come home to roost, they come back ten times harder than what you've dished out. On this day in November of 1992, Faye Bender had come to that understanding. Her past, her violent lifestyle, was just too hard to escape and she was now forced to face the music, whatever tune would be played, as she'd run out of notes to continue on beating her own drum.

Her long run had come to an abrupt end on the banks of the Mighty Mississippi River down in New Orleans, Louisiana. But as Iowa State Trooper Rance Olsen walked her up the sloping street towards an awaiting patrol car, the German outlaw couldn't help but to think that her apprehension was only a segue onto a road that was paved with nothing but that of more violence and bloodshed.

Author's note:

For all intents and purposes, this will be the last installment of Outlaw Chics as we all know it. The remainder of their story will now be incorporated into The Holland Family Saga going forward as the two stories have now become one.

Questions still remain as pertaining to how Faye was captured and how she beat the charges, what actually went down with Dirty Red, Manny and the King Sisters, and the damage Lisa Vanguard and Rafael Gacha have done to the crew. This is by no means the end to this story, only an expansion of The Holland Family Saga as I've chosen to combine both stories into an already epic saga.

Next up, is The Holland Family Saga Part Ten. Hopefully, with this writing, I was able to whet the appetites of all who've taken the time to follow Outlaw Chics, as now a bigger picture has been laid bare. You've seen the current enemies and how they came about and have learned a little bit about their history. Now, let us move forward with this ongoing, drama-filled tale. Weaving plots of this nature isn't easy, all I ask is time, but I stay working, even when I'm not writing because I'm constantly thinking.

For those interested, the Germans first appeared in The Holland Family Saga at the end of book eight titled Definition of A Boss. There story, as it ends here, picks up inside that installment of the series and they are now completely woven into the saga. At the end of this installment, I was on book ten of The

Holland Family Saga. I implore you to pick up their story in book eight titled Definition of a Boss, but for the full impact, one should start at the beginning of The Holland Family Saga with part one titled They Don't Mind Dying. This now concludes the Outlaw Chics series. Than yous all around and I hope it was worth the time invested.

Clever Black.

Made in the USA
Monee, IL
14 June 2022

98017946R00246